FIRST
LIGHT

Also by Charles Baxter

Harmony of the World (stories)
Through the Safety Net (stories)

FIRST LIGHT

Charles Baxter

Viking

VIKING
Viking Penguin Inc., 40 West 23rd Street,
New York, New York 10010, U.S.A.
Penguin Books Ltd, 27 Wrights Lane, London W8 5TZ
(Publishing & Editorial), and Harmondsworth, Middlesex,
England (Distribution & Warehouse)
Penguin Books Australia Ltd, Ringwood,
Victoria, Australia
Penguin Books Canada Limited, 2801 John Street,
Markham, Ontario, Canada L3R 1B4
Penguin Books (N.Z.) Ltd, 182–190 Wairau Road,
Auckland 10, New Zealand

First published in 1987 by Viking Penguin Inc.
Published simultaneously in Canada

Grateful acknowledgment is made for permission to reprint excerpts
from the following works:
"All Alone," by Irving Berlin. © Copyright 1924 Irving Berlin.
© Copyright renewed 1951 Irving Berlin.
Reprinted by permission of Irving Berlin Music Corporation.
"Crossing," by J. Robert Oppenheimer. First published in
Hound and Horn, September 1927. Reprinted by permission.

The author gratefully acknowledges the generous support of the
Guggenheim Foundation and the Wayne State Fund.

LIBRARY OF CONGRESS CATALOGING IN PUBLICATION DATA
Baxter, Charles.
First light.
I. Title.
PS3552.A854F5   1987   813'.54   86-40615
ISBN 0-670-81701-5

Printed in the United States of America by
Arcata Graphics, Fairfield, Pennsylvania
Set in Bembo
Designed by Jeff Ward

For
Mary Eaton
and
John Baxter

Life can only be understood backwards;
but it must be lived forwards.

—Kierkegaard

I

1

On the Fourth of July, Hugh agrees to drive out to Mrs. LaMonte's house to get "the explosives," as he likes to call them. Halfway there, coming out of a long silence, his sister corrects him: they aren't explosives, she says. They're just fireworks. Toys. Hugh keeps both hands near the top of the steering wheel the way cautious men often do, and he does not turn to argue with her, not at first. He watches the panorama of drought colors go by for a full minute before he says, very quietly, "Yes. I know that."

"What? What do you know?" Dorsey sits slouched on the passenger side, her bare feet raised and crossed at the ankles on the leatherette dashboard, her arms wrapped around her knees, a compact circular mass.

"I know they're not explosives," he says. "Although they *do* explode. I was being ironic."

"Oh," she says. This time she is the one who lets the minute go by. Then she says, "That's unusual," and they both smile to themselves, gazing in different directions at the highway and the broad landscape of dried roadside grass and wilting crops.

June, a hot and rainless month, had paled the natural greens in the fields outside Five Oaks to a faded pastel in which the yellow is now, at the beginning of July, beginning to be visible. The corn stalks are stunted, and each tree leaf has its own coating of dust. In the heat the sky is an ashy stagnant blue. Dorsey's son, Noah, a deaf child, sits in the back and is sweating so much that his sportshirt is darkened with blotches. He is spinning a soccer ball on his index finger and rhythmically kicking the back of his mother's bucket seat. Without turning around, Dorsey makes the sign for *stop it* in the air above her head: right hand chopping into the palm of the left. The second time she does it, her hand motions rise in volume to a pantomime shout.

The car smells of hot leather and the lotion Hugh has spread that morning over his sunburned legs. A showroom salesman, he seldom encounters the sun directly, and when he does, especially on holidays and weekends, he sits in it as blank-faced as a lizard. Dorsey points down at her brother's legs, taking her gaze off the fields. "Why don't you ever remember about sunburn?" she asks.

"Pain makes no impression on me."

"That's a prideful lie," Dorsey says. "And why haven't you had the air conditioner in this car fixed? You sell these cars. You ought to be able to—"

"—Yesterday," he says. "The condenser went out yesterday. I haven't had time. I'm all right. You don't have to waste your time worrying about me *or* this car. We can take care of ourselves."

"I'm not worrying," she says quietly, "and if I were, I wouldn't be wasting my time." Noah begins to kick the back of the seat again, and Dorsey turns around to glower for a moment at her son. She forms a quick sentence with her hands.

"What're you telling him?" Hugh asks.

"To behave himself, or we won't get any fireworks."

"Now *that's* a prideful lie," Hugh says. "We have to get them for *my* daughters, and *your* husband, and—"

"Leave Simon out of this. Look out for that car," Dorsey tells him, pointing at a red Dodge convertible snugly in its own lane, approaching them, passing by, disappearing. Hugh makes a disapproving, interiorized snickering sound. Dorsey shrugs. "You never know," she says. She puts her head down on her knees, bunching

herself again. Hugh remembers this posture from other trips she and
he once took as children and adolescents—not only the posture, but
also her habit of taking her shoes and socks off when she was in the
car for any summer trip, no matter how short. In her rare, happy
moods, she liked to put her feet up on the dashboard and leave toe
prints on the window. She's still beautiful, Hugh thinks: a beauty
without innocence, though, because of her eyes. Insomniac atten-
tiveness has darkened them. In her T-shirt and jeans, and her light
hair cut short into a modified pageboy, she almost looks girlish. But
with those eyes, grandmother eyes without the wrinkles, she shows
a history, its inflictions.

"You *did* call Mrs. LaMonte?" Dorsey asks.

"I told you. I called. She says she still has 'some inventory,' as
she calls it. She squealed when I told her you were coming along.
'I can't wait!' she said. She asked me if you looked like a famous
professor and astronomer."

"What'd you say?"

"I said you still looked pretty much like yourself. Was that a lie?
Should I have said something else?"

"Yes."

The county road takes a sidearm turn to the left around a farm
with a blue-and-white plaster Virgin Mary standing under a cedar
shelter in the front yard. Behind the farm is a small hill, a sun-
smelted pond at its bottom and a stony knob of basswoods at the
top. "We're almost there," Hugh says. "I can always remember
where Mrs. LaMonte's place is by the sight of those creepy-looking
basswoods."

He accelerates, passing a Jeep with a bumper sticker that says
I ♥ MY PARACHUTE, and is pleased to see the dust flying up in a
golden brown cloud behind his Buick.

He turns into Mrs. LaMonte's driveway and parks in the shade of
a walnut tree. Mrs. LaMonte's house is peach-colored—it has been
this hue for as long as he has been coming out to buy fireworks—
and Hugh wonders vaguely what company would be so immoral
as to sell a house paint in that color. The house looks like something
in a fairy tale, a huge piece of poisonous candy. Mrs. LaMonte, her
gray hair spewing up from her head, drops her rake as soon as she

sees the car, and comes running toward them, peering into the passenger-side window to get a look before Dorsey even has a chance to get out. With surprising strength, she pulls the door open, reaches in, and yanks Dorsey to her feet. As soon as Dorsey is standing, Mrs. LaMonte puts her huge old arms around her.

She releases her and stares into Dorsey's face. "You're looking a wonder," she says. "Beautiful and still smart, I can see that. Such eyes! We don't have eyes like this very much around Five Oaks, do we, Hugh?"

Hugh, on the other side of the car, shakes his head.

"Your parents would have been so proud of you!" Mrs. LaMonte says. "I read about you in the paper. How long are you here in town?"

"Only another day," Dorsey says. "We're on our way to Minneapolis."

"What's in Minneapolis?" the old woman asks.

"An acting job for Simon." As soon as Dorsey has mentioned her husband's name, Mrs. LaMonte turns her head and squints at her. "Simon . . . my husband," Dorsey explains.

"Oh, you don't have to tell me," Mrs. LaMonte says. "I keep up. You're one of the best things that ever happened to this town, and it behooves an old woman to keep your name up there on the slate." She taps her head. "But of course you haven't introduced him to me," Mrs. LaMonte says, carefully expressing just enough irritation to show that she means well. She gazes into Dorsey's eyes and then readjusts her weight so that she is looking away. "Smell the skunk?"

Dorsey, Hugh, and Mrs. LaMonte sniff the air in unison, and Hugh sees Dorsey smile with the lost pleasure of country odors. "They've been all over my farm," she says. "Lucky thing they didn't get into the shed."

"Is that where you keep the fireworks?" Hugh asks.

"Your brother is all business," Mrs. LaMonte says to Dorsey, holding on to the younger woman's arm to steady herself. "Like your father. Hugh knows they're in the shed because they *always* have been and he's the one who comes out here year after year to buy them, so he ought to know. Now who's this?" Noah has been examining something underneath the car and has just stood up.

"Noah. My son. He's deaf." Dorsey makes a sign to Noah, and

the boy steps forward to shake Mrs. LaMonte's hand. The old woman holds on to the boy's arm after he has finished pumping, and she then slowly places both of her palms on top of his shoulders, and while Noah fidgets, she sighs. "More family," she says. "Thank goodness." She looks at the three of them. "Well, come on back. Let's get you some of this year's illegals, and then we'll have some lemonade."

"Hope you still have some good ones," Dorsey says.

"Business has been dribbly this year." The old woman shakes her head. "People are getting too lawful and timid. It's the priests and the government. Everybody's enforcing everything. So we still have a good selection for sale. You'll see." She glances down at Dorsey's feet. "You might want shoes."

The shed stands in the shadow of a broad, untrimmed apple tree, and Hugh can see some of last year's leaves moldering in the gutters. Apples are dryrotting in the hot dust of the driveway. As she always does at this time of year, Mrs. LaMonte has removed the antiques she usually keeps on display and replaced them with the fireworks that her son Roy, a trucker, has smuggled in on Inter-Mountain Express. Her hurricane lamps, coach-and-four weathervanes, and blue glass cloisonné jars are crowded together in the two south corners. Inside the shed, Noah is breathing the gunpowdered air appreciatively. He holds up a Roman Candle and makes a sign to his mother.

"Yes," Mrs. LaMonte says, "that's a good one, made in Hunan, China." She nods quickly, standing in a wedge of sunlight, so that the sun reflects off her glasses onto the wall. "The Orientals like to name their fireworks with poetry names. That one's called 'Plum Blossoms Report Spring.' Somewhere around here is one called 'Purple Lilac Petals in Three Streams.'" She points at the far table. "I have chasers over there. These are Catharines. Standard rockets over there, near where your boy is standing. That group, on the low side of the table, those are Battles in the Clouds. I've got some Frightened Birds over here, and the usual Giant Howlers. The Battles in the Clouds are very good this year. Roy tried them out. They're manufactured in the world capital of fireworks—Macao, of all places. Don't buy those." Hugh has picked up an arrangement of six barrels on a platform. "They're called Dynamites. They're duds, most of them. Don't know why."

Hugh has never seen so many fireworks at Mrs. LaMonte's before, and now Noah is sweating with excitement. Dorsey's sandals are leaving light prints in the reddish dust of the garage floor. "What about cherry bombs?" she asks.

"They're illegal," Mrs. LaMonte says, straightening up.

"So is everything else here."

"Not quite everything else."

"Most of it."

"All right. I won't quarrel." She sweeps her hand over the display. "With all this, why do you want cherry bombs? They aren't beautiful. They have no poetry. They're just loud."

"For Noah," Dorsey says.

Mrs. LaMonte stands perplexed. "But your boy is deaf," she says.

"Not to cherry bombs," Dorsey says. "He can feel their shock waves with his skin. It's as close as he ever gets to hearing."

"In that case," Mrs. LaMonte says. She rushes over to a dark corner and picks up a white thin-mesh reticule. She reaches in and pulls out a half-dozen, which she holds up for display as she smiles benignly. "Royal bought these from a bald man with a tattoo and a string tie who works out of the back of a station wagon near Fargo. They wake up the skunks, these ones." She drops them into Dorsey's outstretched hands. "More bang for the buck," she says.

Hugh and Dorsey buy an assortment, which they load up in three grocery bags and put in the Buick's trunk. Then they sit on the front porch while Mrs. LaMonte serves them all lemonade, and Noah practices his soccer kicks, aiming the ball at the trunk of a sugar maple in the front yard. Across the seared grass he runs back and forth, not even panting. Mrs. LaMonte settles herself down in a cane chair beside Hugh and Dorsey, and she watches Noah, making an old woman's approving mutter. "Your father would've been proud of that boy," she says. "Good-looking. Doesn't mind the heat. I admired that man. He was always honest with me. Your mother, too."

Dorsey and Hugh let the silence go by.

"Where's Laurie?" Mrs. LaMonte asks. "You never bring her out here."

"She's back at the house, minding the girls," Hugh tells her. "She said it was too hot for her to come out here. Droughts like this get her depressed."

"Droughts," Mrs. LaMonte says, clinking the ice cubes in her glass. "You know, preachers used to come through here, during droughts, when I was little. In this part of Michigan people always used to crowd into the tents by the lake to hear the preachers, who visited all through the summer. The one everybody liked best was this shouter with silver hair, James Biggs Hope. He could heal. He said he would put the doctors out of business with the medicine he carried in his hands. *I* didn't like him. He didn't make anybody well, that I ever saw. The one *I* liked was somebody who came through once, I forget his name, who called himself the Good Shepherd of Love. A short man with a limp, with an assistant who looked like Bess Truman. He set his tent up south side of town, within sight of the lake."

She takes a sip of her lemonade and swallows noisily, checking Dorsey and Hugh's faces to see if they are listening attentively. Satisfied, she begins to flutter her right hand near her cheek.

"Anyway, this one, this Reverend Whatever-his-name-was, had quite a get-up: green silk scarf, black coat, black shirt, black pants. And a gold chain with a gold heart, a Valentine's Day heart, hanging around his neck so it was over his real heart, where a cross would usually be. So all you had to look at was the scarf, that head of hair that looked like sheared cardboard, and the heart, the gold one. He started low and quiet, like one of those late-night radio announcers. Everybody was expecting hellfire and the catalogue of sins and the falling-away from the true faith. Everybody was hoping for, you know, threats of punishment. He gave us a little of that but it was just a prelude to what he really wanted to do, which was to praise what he called the abounding power of love. From him, this ugly man. No one expected it. People are always happy to hear that they've been sinning, which is why it won't rain, but they don't expect it when you tell them they've come up short on love."

Mrs. LaMonte looks over at Dorsey as if the story is for her benefit. Then she leans back, the cane chair creaks, and she continues.

"What he did was, he quoted Matthew and the Epistles, he quoted Jeremiah and Micah and the Song of Solomon. He made them think it hadn't rained because people didn't kiss one another, didn't like one another enough to give what he called 'a little human shade.' He called it the Gospel of Tongues. He said the Bible said to put your arms around your fellow man. He said Jesus kissed. I thought he'd be a big hit. After all, I was a girl, thirteen. Tongues. Well, my goodness. But no. They didn't run him out of town, but they left that tent morose and grumpy. He didn't collect more than a few dollars. The people of Five Oaks were not about to listen to a man preaching about kissing. My mother said it was wicked filth. She made my father agree with her on the way home. But as I remember, it rained the next day. And the day after that. Maybe people took his advice. You never know what people do at home." She turns to glance at Hugh. "Or anywhere else."

On the way back, Dorsey's feet are propped up on the dashboard again, but she is thrumming her fingers on her leg and squirming. Hugh would like to see the expression in her eyes, but she has put on her dark glasses. Noah is sitting quietly now, with the soccer ball in his lap and his head turned so that he can look up at the sky through the back window.

"So how long are you planning to stay in Minneapolis?" Hugh asks.

"Long enough to get Simon settled in."

"Then you're going back to Buffalo?"

She nods.

"With Noah?"

She nods again.

"This isn't a separation?"

"No, this isn't a separation. We'll just be separate for a few months." She plays with her hair by swirling it around her index finger.

"Does Simon have someone in Minneapolis?" Hugh asks.

"Simon has someone everywhere, and, love, it's none of your business." Hugh is conscious that she continues to lecture him and justify herself, but she does it silently, staring straight ahead. Although he concentrates on the road, Hugh also sees, in his mind's eye, as if projected there by his sister, an image of Simon. In it, Simon is lying on the floor. His eyes are closed, and his posture does not suggest sleep so much as a lazy and narcissistic form of martyr-dom. The image is that of a successful martyr, realizing obscure profits. His arms are raised far above his head and are crossed at the wrists. Then someone is lying down on top of Simon.

Hugh puts his left hand to his eyes, rubs them violently, and looks out the front window. Bastien's U-pick Apple Orchard is still there, passing by on the right-hand side of the road, five miles south of town. He'd once sold a Buick Century—blue, stripped down, only an AM radio—to Harry Bastien, but the car was repossessed by the bank, and Harry hasn't spoken to him since.

Landscape in the plain style passes by them at sixty miles an hour. Hugh is a moody driver, and the thought of his brother-in-law, the actor, depresses him: he accelerates to sixty-five.

"What're you working on these days?" Hugh asks.

"My work?" Dorsey looks at Hugh, her mouth dropping open in surprise.

"Yeah, your work. What're you doing?"

Dorsey waits a long time. Then she says, "I'm working with someone else on what's called missing mass. If you take the usual calculations related to the Big Bang, you discover that there's just enough density in the Universe to make it closed, to stop the expansion of space. That's called flatness. Anyway, the problem is, if you estimate density with the galaxies that are currently observed, you're missing about eighty percent of the mass that's supposed to be there. If you count the leptons and the baryonic matter, there's still eighty percent missing. It may be nonbaryonic matter, gauge particles, but no one is sure. That's what missing mass is. People are even talking about shadow matter now, invisible planets, stars, and galaxies that have a gravitational pull. That's what I'm working on."

"Missing mass."

"That's right."

"I don't get it," he says.

"You don't have to."

Hugh notices a ruffling black crow profiled on the roof of Tom Rangan's Auto Parts. Behind the front building is a long field seeded with rusting Buicks and Ramblers and smashed and broken Cougars and Lynxes. The cars are halved and amputated and chopped in thirds and have bites taken out of them at acute angles, pure metal geometry. Hugh has always loved automobile junkyards, this one especially. The brown, oxydized metals give him peace of mind. Against the image of Simon sprawled on the floor, or the problem of missing mass, Hugh consoles himself with car parts and dented chrome.

"You always had the brains," he says to her.

"It's no fun," she says. After a pause, she holds out her hands, making arcs. "Imagine going back to the first second of the Big Bang. To the first fraction of a fraction of a second. Imagine getting on a time machine and seeing space contract. Imagine time reversed. If you—"

"—No," he says.

"What?"

"No. You think about it. I don't have to—I live here."

Where the amusement park once stood on the shore of the lake is a cluster of condominiums. The farm store, just outside of town, has turned into Kathy's Tack Shop. The five-and-dime has been renovated and now sells antiques. "What's happened to this place?" Dorsey asks. "It's turned frilly."

"Gentry," Hugh tells her. "Rich people moved in. I'll be damned if I know where they came from. They're everywhere. Small towns with lake frontage are chic, I guess. Even out here. Some of these stores still sell what a person needs. Otherwise it's luxuries."

Five stoplights, six blocks, one statue of a veteran of the First World War, two right-hand turns, and one bridge over the torn-up railroad track, and they are parked in Hugh's driveway. Hugh's daughters, Tina and Amy, come running from the porch, their hair flying, and begin to pound on the back windows and the trunk with small fists. "Where is it?" they shout. "Where's the stuff?"

Hugh tells them. He takes out the three bags of fireworks and places them in a corner of the porch, near the sand bucket. He tells the girls to leave them there, to touch nothing. He asks them what they did while he was gone.

"We played with Uncle Simon," Tina says.

"What'd you do with him?"

"We built embassies," Amy says, giggling.

"And airplane terminals. And cars and apartment buildings."

"Why did you do that? What did you use to make them?"

"Daddy, it's a secret," Amy says. "We're not supposed to tell."

"Cardboard," Tina blurts out.

Finished with their father, the girls run around the corner of the house with Noah. Dorsey has already disappeared into the house in that quiet and almost motionless way of hers. Hugh fingers a seashell, an alphabet cone, in his right pocket, then goes up to the front door. He stands in the front hallway, listening. He'd like to play with Noah, but Noah is elsewhere. The house is hot and quiet. In summer, he can always smell the house's age in the dusty pine and old carpeting. He calls upstairs; no one answers. He thinks he hears a radio playing. That would be Simon, either listening to or imitating a radio. Hugh looks through the long front hallway, past the living room and into the kitchen and thinks he sees Laurie in the backyard, bent over something in the garden. He knows he hasn't actually seen her, but he imagines her back there among the flowers, down on her knees among the baby's breath.

It's not baby's breath. It's pansies. She is pulling dried blossoms off the flowers and leaving them in piles of shriveled colors in the grass on either side of her knees. Hugh creeps up behind her and gives her a kiss on the back of her neck.

"Such large mosquitoes," she says, looking him up and down. As sweat inches down the sides of her face, she frowns at him. "How was Mrs. LaMonte? Was Roy there?"

"She was all right. Sales are bad this year, so she had a big inventory. I didn't see Roy. She talked about hot weather and drought and preachers. She talked about kissing." Hugh allows himself a look at his wife, but she doesn't bother to react. "Where's your hat?" he asks.

Laurie touches the top of her head. "I lost it. I'm letting my brains cook. How much did you spend on the fireworks?"

"You shouldn't be out without a hat."

"I'm all right. It can get as hot as it likes. I'll just burn. And then I'll peel. You must've spent a lot."

She isn't standing, so Hugh squats down so he'll be at her eye level. He doesn't know why she hasn't stood up. Priorities. "Where's Simon?" he asks.

"Upstairs. Inside. He hasn't been out all day. He's been doing something with the girls. You know how he hates sunlight."

"They were building embassies, Amy said."

"Well, I wouldn't know. I've been out here." She pulls at another pansy. "Embassies. Maybe it's a joke."

"Maybe," he says, looking up at the roof of the house. The lightning rod, he now notices, is crooked, at a slant.

"Look at the roses," she says, pointing. "We should do something. You name it, they've got it: blackspot, powdery mildew, rust. Poor things."

Hugh counts to ten, then walks inside for a glass of water.

At three o'clock, Dorsey and Simon are still nowhere in sight, and Laurie has gone inside to take a nap, and Noah, Tina, and Amy are lighting sparklers and then playing a wrong way, clockwise-around-the-bases softball game whose rules they have communicated to each other by means of an improvised sign language. Hugh is sitting on the backyard hammock, staring intently at the house. His shirt sticks to his back. Bees drone in the hollow of an elm above him and to his left. He can't doze and is afraid to lie backwards on the hammock. All around, distantly, are reports of gunfire, explosions, and bombs. His sunburned legs are throbbing painfully.

With smoke from his cigarette descending into his lungs like spirit-fingers, Hugh looks toward the second floor and sees the window of the guest room, where Dorsey and Simon are doing whatever they do together. Thinking of Dorsey up there in her old room, Hugh imagines time moving backward. It's an unpleasant thought, and he shivers in the heat. He watches Tina write Noah a note before she rushes into the house. Hugh winks at Noah, and Noah winks back, a co-conspirator. Tina likes it that Noah is deaf. She can write him notes, as if they were in love. She can scream at him, and he'll go on smiling. She can pretend that she knows sign language, and Noah can pretend that he understands. They're both good athletes and enjoy playing soccer together. In this group of two girls and a deaf boy, the outsider is Amy, with her dark watchful eyes and her faultless memory for slights. Her cousin, the deaf boy, and her sister gang up on her. From his hammock, Hugh can see Amy's face, shadowed with anger, as she follows Noah into the house, trying to get the boy's attention by throwing grass at his back.

Hugh looks up at the bent lightning rod. His moodiness takes itself out of his mind and rests against the exterior painted wood, puttied glass, and bent gutters he has failed to repair. He takes one last puff from the cigarette, stubs it out on the lawn, and stands up. A cloud covers the sun, and from the distance he hears the cooing of a dove. No one is watching him. Hugh feels this as a great, rare freedom.

From the rafters of the garage, Hugh takes down his aluminum extension ladder, and, grunting and swaying, carries it to the house's south side, where the roof can be approached, and the ladder's anti-slip swivel feet can be planted in the lawn instead of in Laurie's roses or baby's breath. On the ground he extends the ladder to its full length and then tests the hook to make sure that the rear sections are locked into place. Then he pulls the ladder up, losing control of it for a moment so that it perks and dips. He holds his leg out, bracing himself, and pulls the ladder back so that it is settled against the gutter. Its top is two feet above the lowest edge of shingles. So far he has made almost no noise, just a vague metallic rattle.

As he climbs, he feels the flimsy aluminum shake with an oscillating, palsied tremble. He stops, waiting for the trembling to subside, then continues up.

He lifts himself onto the roof's green shingles and slowly creeps up the high-angled roof toward the apex, the soles of his running shoes giving him traction. The shingles are as hot as the sidewalks and handrails in Hell. (His father's phrase, which he remembers now, smiling, his face heat-bathed.) He inches his way toward the edge of the roof, reaches out, grabs the ten-inch lightning rod, and bends the metal so that it points straight up. This is important, he thinks. Lightning doesn't come down sideways.

He feels in his pants pocket the bulge of the seashell that Noah gave him. He moves himself backwards and allows himself one moment of recreation, one gaze outward.

The hill on which his house had been built eighty-five years ago descends in a series of passive angles toward the river, which broadens at the town's edge to become what is called Five Oaks Lake, its shore blocked to his view by willows along its bank. But he can see the various roofs of the houses and businesses of Five Oaks and quietly names them: the Quimbys, the Russells, the hardware store, the flat roof with the smoking incinerator in back which must be the IGA, and the municipal park with its baseball diamond on the hill itself. He counts up other houses, knowing all the names. Underneath him is his own house, old and solid. From it he feels through his skin a low sub-audible murmuring.

The keys in his left pocket are irritating him, pressing inside his trouser against his leg. He reaches in, pulls out his keychain, and throws the keys high into the air. They disappear into the sun, then fly out in a long curve and land on the lawn, sounding out like small bells.

That night, Simon does not come to the table for dinner. Dorsey sits next to Noah, who has already seated himself next to Tina, and she announces that Simon is still learning his lines and will skip eating. The hot dogs are piled in a pyramid on the serving plate in front of Hugh and are surrounded by bottles of ketchup and mustard, bowls of potato chips, pickles, salad, and Jell-O.

Hugh looks at the food, at his two daughters and his nephew, his wife and his sister. He looks at them and then stands up. "I'm going to get Simon," he says.

"What?" Dorsey says. "No."

The three children watch Hugh. Noah tugs at his mother, and Dorsey makes an explanatory sign.

"Hugh," Laurie says, pronouncing his name with an unusual emphasis. "I already talked to him. He doesn't want to come down for dinner."

"I'll go see," Hugh says.

He takes long steps out of the room and hurries up the stairs two at a time. He hears the women talking, and his sister calling his name to retrieve him. They won't chase me, he thinks; my hairline is receding. After rushing down the long upstairs hallway, he stops outside the guest room, Simon and Dorsey's room. He waits for a moment, then knocks. Just above a whisper, Simon tells him to come in.

Simon is sitting by the window, the late-afternoon light coming in over his shoulder, throwing his face into shadow. A bound script lies in his lap, and his right index finger points at a line. The room is stifling, but Simon seems cool and relaxed, not a sign of sweat on him.

"Oh, Hugh," he says. "What a surprise."

"I just came to see if you wanted some dinner. We're all having hot dogs." Hugh glances at the clothes all over the floor, the rumpled unmade bed, the maple tree in the yard outside the window. *My* maple tree, he thinks. The room smells of somebody's lovemaking.

"I know," his brother-in-law sighs. "Dorsey told me the menu. Hot dogs and potato chips and pickles with ice cream and Jell-O salad and cookies with surprises inside. Not in that order, of course. Very appetizing. Very Fourth-of-July. Sorry I can't come down." He smiles. "I have to learn my lines."

Hugh nods. He tries not to peer at Simon's back-lighted face, which has transformed itself slightly in the service of the role he is learning. Hugh never knows from one moment to the next what Simon's face will look like; it has an unpleasant plasticity.

"You'll come down to help me with the fireworks?" Hugh asks.

"Oh, I have that all planned."

"Good." He holds on to the door. "What's the play?"

"A farce. By an Englishman, Joe Orton."

"A big part?"

Simon shrugs. "A good part."

Hugh nods. He looks uncomfortable and he knows it. "Well," he says, "see you later." He turns and is about to go downstairs when Simon says, "Hugh."

"What?" He glances in again. Simon's face has changed: now he looks older, paternal. A judge. It's a father's expression, and Hugh is horrified to see this look on Simon's face when that face is gazing back at him. He doesn't want to be anyone's child anymore, especially Simon's.

"I saw you going up that ladder earlier this afternoon. I was just curious. What in the world were you doing that for?"

"You and Dorsey saw me?"

"I saw you. Dorsey was dozing." Simon continues to give Hugh his father-gaze, the blank look of surveillance.

"Actually, Simon," Hugh says, "I went up there to straighten a lightning rod and to check the condition of the shingles. Besides, I was a little bored. Everyone had gone inside."

"Yes." Simon's face edges toward amusement without exactly expressing it. "I understand that. Every man wants to climb onto the roof of his house. It makes him feel like a homeowner and a desperado, a perfect and impossible combination."

"I didn't know you were watching."

"I know you didn't." He smiles. "Most people don't."

"Don't what?"

"Don't know when I'm watching." He taps his fingers. "I would have been a great spy."

"I was feeling . . ." Hugh doesn't finish the sentence.

"You were feeling old," Simon tells him.

The two men look away from each other, and at last Hugh says, "Sure you don't want any dinner?"

"Oh, I've already eaten," Simon tells him.

"What? What did you have?"

"Whatever it was," Simon says, "I ate it."

At sunset, Hugh turns on the porchlight and carries all the fireworks and the bucket of sand to the backyard, which he had mowed, raked, and trimmed two days before. It occurs to him that it doesn't make any sense to keep the porchlight on when they'd all be in back, but he leaves it on anyway: there are always intruders and thieves, specialists in holiday crimes. Tina, Amy, and Noah are grouped together near one of the clothesline poles, their heads down as if they're talking, and when Noah sees his uncle he runs toward him and holds his arms up. Hugh gives the boy one of the bags, and they both walk to the far end of the lawn. As soon as they've lowered the bags to the grass, Hugh feels his nephew taking his hand and quickly pressing it to his lips. Hugh has never understood why his nephew loves him so much, but he has seen so many gestures like this by now that he must accept this love as a gift, and so he stands there immobilized, feeling, even after Noah has rejoined the girls, the imprint of the boy's lips on his hand.

"Tina," Hugh says at last, "where're your Aunt Dorsey and Uncle Simon?" She points and at once starts to giggle. Simon has appeared, walking around the north corner of the house, a carton the size of a chair held between his arms. When he reaches the lawn, he lowers the carton and takes out of it little cardboard buildings with crayoned labels, which he sets up along parallel lines, as if they were part of a small city.

"Let the fun commence," he says.

"Everybody's here but Laurie," Hugh says. "Where is she?"

"Right here, silly," she says, just behind Hugh. He turns quickly and sees her standing with her hand on her hip and her smile fixed on him. People are always seeing me, Hugh thinks, before I see them. Laurie smiles at his visible shock. "You're the only man I know," she says in a half-whisper, "who is startled when he sees his wife. What a faraway man you are. Well. I've been putting out the citronella candles. See?" She points to the four red-glass candle holders on the four points of the lawn. The flames flicker inside them, and belatedly Hugh smells their acid fruit scent. He doesn't like the look of these candles. They're funereal. Hugh shakes his head, hoping to clear it. "All right," he says, "let's do this."

"Me first," Simon says. He has a cherry bomb in his hand and is inserting it through the door of one of the buildings he has made. "This," he says, "is the Beirut Hilton, which rises, many gleaming stories high, into the air above the Paris of the Middle East." He looks over to Tina and Amy and gives them a cue with his finger.

"Yankee go home, Yankee go home," the girls chant.

Simon lights the fuse and runs back toward the house. Hugh waits, looking at the windows painstakingly drawn on the walls of the Beirut Hilton. It's a dud, he thinks, and then the Beirut Hilton blows up. The explosion is concussive, and Hugh feels it against his body as a force wave. The sound hits both his eardrums and his head; a person doesn't need ears to hear such a thing. The cardboard rips, splinters, flies up in thumbnail-sized pieces in irregularly circular arcs, leaving a halo of cardboard pieces of different sizes on the ground and a small ball of pale blue smoke rising into the air. Hugh thinks of his neighbors' windows but then instinctively looks toward the children. He hears Simon clapping in the aftermath. In the diminishing echo, the shocked crickets have fallen silent.

On Noah's face is an expression of the purest radiance, an angel look. His eyes are closed, and he is swinging his head slowly back and forth. When he opens his eyes, he looks toward his mother, then Simon, and then his uncle. His eyes are wet.

"Filthy Americans," Simon says. "Imperialist lackeys. Death to the nest of spies and traitors." He cues the girls.

"Death to the nest of spies," Tina says. Amy can't remember the phrase, and blows her line.

Simon is putting a second cherry bomb into a building labeled AMERICAN EMBASSY. In a guttural voice, he says, "Down with Yankee imperialist aggression. Down with American meddling."

"Death to the Shah," Tina says.

"Wait a minute," Hugh interrupts.

Seeing the expression on Hugh's face, Simon switches back to his own voice. "Just kidding, Hugh. Just a joke. They aren't American embassies at all. Just little cardboard boxes. Or maybe Cuban enclaves in Grenada or Nicaragua. How's that? Is that better?"

"Hmmm."

Simon lights the fuse to the bomb in the American embassy. When the embassy blows up, Hugh is watching his nephew. The expression of pleasure on the boy's face is so naked and pure that Hugh feels something like embarrassment in seeing it. The explosion is a blessing, a rupture of the air that somehow makes its way into the boy's interior silence.

Hugh looks over at his two daughters, who are holding their ears and shrieking happily. He feels the weight of the day lifting, buoyed up by the children's happiness.

"How about a rocket?" Hugh asks.

"There's too much daylight for rockets," Laurie tells him. "What else have you got?"

"Well," Hugh says, "there are the fountains." He puts his arm into one of the bags and pulls out a long cylinder called the Tiger Roaring Fountain. He sets the fountain down on the burned whitened grass where the Beirut Hilton had been, and he lights the fuse. The fuse burns down to the tube, and then the device begins to spurt upward a thick shower of brilliant red sparks.

Over the noise of gunpowder igniting, Simon's voice rises, accented. "This is the blood of the blessed martyrs fountain! This is blood shed for the holy cause of Islam! All hail the great Islamic Revolution!"

"Cut it out, would you?" Hugh shouts, interrupting him. After fifteen more seconds of sparks, the Tiger Roaring Fountain expires with a few final broken bursts.

"No more blood," Simon announces sadly after the mild applause dies away. "No more martyrs."

"You boys." Laurie is bending down to the lawn and picking up a glass of iced tea. "How you like things that go off."

"Uncle Simon," Tina shouts, "what can we blow up next? Maybe the airport?"

"Definitely the airport. The Athens airport, over here. I think we've got that nice car bomb you made this afternoon. We'll just put this small explosive device here, in the trunk . . ."

"It's not an explosive," Hugh says. "It's just a toy."

"Tell that to the people in the airport. Imperialist running dogs."

"No," Hugh says.

"No, what?" Simon is about to light the car bomb.

"No car bombs."

"Why not?"

"It's the Fourth of July!"

"So?"

"We're supposed to be celebrating liberty, not terrorism!"

"A revolution is a revolution!" Simon shouts, lighting the cherry bomb in the car. "Bombs bursting in air!" Hugh raises his head, closes his eyes as the bomb explodes, tearing apart both the car and the Athens airport next to it, and blowing out several cardboard people inside the airport onto the grass. Hugh looks up and sees a flock of sparrows. He wants to see them form into a pattern, an arrow or a letter, but flocks of sparrows never make formations, he reminds himself; they go where they want to. Let them stay up there, he thinks; never let them come down.

"Almost time for the rockets," Dorsey says. "Any last explosives?"

"One," Simon tells her. "This one is for the American consulate and apartment building. See the windows?"

"Just light it," Dorsey tells him.

"See the balcony I added on?"

"Just light it."

He puts the cherry bomb into a cardboard revolving door. "American hands off Central America," he says.

It explodes, and Dorsey says in the jarring silence that follows, "All right, damn it, you boys have had your fun. I've always said you can't trust men with fireworks. It gets them excited and crazy. See what a mess you've made of things? Damn it all, stand back." She walks out on the grass and pushes both Hugh and Simon toward the house. "Go sit down. Both of you. I will be the pyrotechnician from now on."

"Aunt Dorsey," Tina shouts, "what are you doing?"

"I'm taking over, honey. It's time for the women."

"Spoilsport," Simon mutters. "We still had the Marine barracks and the BOQ, and the USIA transmitting tower, and the busload of nuns, and the missionary flotilla. You agreed, honey," he whines. "It's realism. It's so contemporary."

"We didn't agree," Dorsey says. "You just want to see me squirm. And you want to terrify the children."

"They love it," he tells her.

"Shut up," Dorsey says. "Don't be a creep. Sit down and eat something. I saw some candy around here a minute ago. Just because this is an American holiday doesn't mean you have to be ironic. Now where are those goddamn rockets?"

"Over there," Laurie points. "In the box."

"Come on, Laurie," Dorsey says, pulling her sister-in-law along with her. "We can't trust the men to do this. We'd only have a war on our hands. Come on."

Hugh looks over at Simon, who is now sitting with Noah on the grass just under the linden. Together, they make such a composed traditional picture, a Fourth-of-July father and son, that Hugh wants to leave them there forever.

Dorsey has taken Laurie out to the back of the lawn and is making hand gestures like a blackjack dealer; Laurie makes several return gestures, then runs into the house and comes back with an empty Coke bottle in her left hand and several nails in her right. Dorsey has hung a Happy Lamp on the clothesline and has lit a Buzz Bomb, which leaves a spark trail of indigo and concludes with a report that shakes the bathroom window directly behind where Hugh is sitting.

"All right, everybody," Dorsey says. "Here's a Chrysanthemum we're setting off."

"What's a chrysanthemum?" Tina asks her father.

Before Hugh can reply, the Happy Lantern hanging from the clothesline starts to spin, radiating snow, and seed, and fire sparks; then the lantern itself drops down, and inside the folded paper white insect sparks jump in anxious fading paths.

"That's no chrysanthemum," Hugh says.

"No, but *this* is," Dorsey announces, and the shell ignites with the sound of a giant cough, throwing the charge into the air, which bursts open into trailed circles of red, white, and blue. Hugh hears his daughter *ooh*ing, and for the first time he notices that Amy is clutching her stuffed monkey.

"And this," Dorsey says, lighting a multi-cylindered platform arrangement, "is called the shell of shells. Like—" The sound of the shell erases her voice. The shell fragments into a cluster of stars accompanied by volley shots, followed by a screaming descending cry. Simon and Noah begin to clap together.

"Pa-boom," Tina says.

"Pa-boom." Amy repeats it, her voice higher than her sister's, and thinned by excited child fright. Hugh sees Amy trembling intermittently with late-night shock.

"This," Laurie says, hardly visible behind a cloud of bluish smoke, "is the Hen Laying Eggs."

It lifts up; in the air the eggs, white spherical fires, drop down in smooth quiet arcs, blink, go out, and are gone.

"There's Mr. and Mrs. MacDiarmid," Tina says, pointing to Hugh's neighbors, who stand together, their hands clasped, behind where Simon is sitting with Noah. In the evening light Hugh can see almost no distinct features of their faces or the rest of their bodies, and with his vision of them obscured by smoke and darkness, the generalized outline of the man's shoulders and the curve of the woman's hair, and even the shy way they hold hands summon before him the presence of his parents. Almost invisible, withdrawn, for a moment they *are* his parents, and when Mrs. MacDiarmid waves, using all the fingers of her right hand, Hugh lets out an abrupt, involuntary, "Oh."

In the next thirty minutes the two women set off everything else they have: the bottle rockets, chasers, dancing butterflies, a Chinese fountain called a Screaming Meemie, Roman Candles, a whistling cicada, and for the grand finale a ten-shot "aerial surprise." Off in his corner with Noah, Simon is muttering about "no surprises in the aerial surprise," but from where Hugh is standing Simon's voice is hardly audible, soaked into the smoke that rests unmoving in the breezeless yard.

   Then they are all looking up at the sky as a plane passes over, its lights blinking yellow and white and red, and beyond the plane the stars seem immobilized in their usual darkness. In the middle of the cloud of gunpowder and the exploded rubble of the fireworks at their feet, Dorsey is explaining to Tina and Amy about the constellations: there, she says, pointing a bit toward the east, that's Cygnus, the Swan. It's sometimes called the Northern Cross. At the head of the swan is Albireo, a double star. And over there, close by it, that little box of stars, that's Lyra, the Lyre. A lyre's a harp you can carry around and play by yourself. And over there, north, there's Cassiopeia. It looks like a chair. See? See? It's named after the woman, Cassiopeia, who's sitting in the chair. But you can't see her unless you imagine her and then she's still not there.

   The two girls nod, rubbing their eyes. Hugh takes their hands and leads them up the back steps. He pulls them through the storage room to the kitchen stairs up to the second floor. Amy says, "Daddy, carry me." Slowly he picks her up, astonished by how weightless she seems to be, and holds his other arm out so that Tina can clasp his hand as they go up.

   In the bedroom, they undress vaguely and absentmindedly. Hugh gives Tina instructions while helping Amy into her Wonder Woman pajamas. Tina insists on the air conditioner, which starts up with a rhythmic rattle. The two girls get into their beds with their eyes closed but their heads held up, like small queens. Hugh sits on the side of Amy's bed, smoothing her hair and kissing her good night. Then he wishes Tina a happy Fourth of July, and she reaches

up and squeezes his hand. Hugh is halfway out of the room when
Tina says, "Daddy?"

"What?"

"Was Aunt Dorsey making that up?"

"What?"

"About the constellations. The swan and harp stuff."

"No. That's real. It's called Cygnus and the other one's called the
Lyre. I've heard her say that before. I've seen pictures of them in
books."

"I was wondering."

"She knows. That's her life. She knows everything about the stars
that there is to know."

"Did she name them herself?"

"No. Someone else did."

"Who?"

"I don't know. Go to sleep."

She turns her head softly on the pillow away from him.
Smoke from the backyard has made its way into the room, so
that the thin line of light from the hallway seems smeared and
haloed, like the light in a barroom around midnight. It bothers
Hugh that his daughters' bedroom has pool hall air in it. The old
machine, if it still works, will wheeze the air clear in a few minutes. He hears Tina say a two-syllable word to him after the
door is closed, but he can't make out what it is and he won't
open the door to ask her. On the stairs, he passes Laurie, who is
headed up. They raise their eyebrows to each other as they pass
and smile businesslike complicit smiles, but they do not stop—
Hugh has already decided that he won't say anything to anyone
until he has cleared up the back lawn—and it isn't until he is
already outside again that he even registers that there is a smudge
or a bruise on the side of his wife's face.

He wakes at three. The night air has cooled but not enough to keep
him asleep. He hears a faint rumbling of thunder or fireworks, he
can't be sure which. He rises from the bed wearing his boxer shorts
and feels the warm smooth texture of the oak floor under his feet
as he makes his slow night way toward the hall, then past his

daughters' bedroom and the solidly closed door of the guest bed-room, to the stairway down to the kitchen.

Hugh likes to eat in the dark. He pours himself a glass of low-fat milk, claws a fistful of cookies from the jar, and walks into the back den. He stands in front of the picture window and gazes out at the night. Heat lightning breaks behind the clouds. Clouds! He hasn't seen any clouds for a month; we're saved, he thinks. He dips a cookie into his glass of milk long enough to soak it but not so long that it disintegrates, then pops it into his mouth. The heat lightning behind one cloud flickers three times: a code, a private telegraph.

"Nice, isn't it?"

He spins around, almost losing his grip on the glass of milk. Dorsey sits in the room's dark, curled on the edge of the sofa, her legs drawn up close to her chest underneath her summer nightshirt.

"What are you doing here?" he asks.

"What are *you* doing here?" she answers.

"Want a cookie?" He holds one out.

"I don't like them. What's that you're drinking?"

"Milk."

"That's showing 'em. Yeah, I'll have a sip."

He walks over to where she is sitting. Instead of handing the glass to her, he positions it at her mouth and tilts it. When she lowers her head, he takes the glass away.

"Always the frustrated priest," she says. When he turns his back to her, she says, "Your life is such a secret. Sometimes I think I don't know you at all. I don't know how you go on living this way. Oh: how's Laurie?"

"That bruise on her face? I asked her. She said she just slipped on the lawn. She's all right." The lightning behind one cloud makes the cloud look like an advertisement. "It didn't hurt."

She inhales audibly, as if she were smoking a cigarette. "Being in this house, I keep thinking of Mom and Dad. All day today I've been seeing Mom standing in front of the stove with a mixing bowl in one hand and one of those wire egg-whips she always carried around in the other, and I've been hearing that Statue-of-Liberty voice of hers, telling me how much I—"

"—She didn't have a Statue-of-Liberty voice."

"Time has magnified it. She believed in me, you know, and in all the wonders I would do with my life." She shifts position on the sofa. "She always spoke softly, but now, in my memory, she's loud. She's *quite* loud. Like a statue."

"Statues don't speak."

"Oh, yes, they do," she says, and the lightning flashes closer and brighter behind her. "Hugh, we haven't talked this time. How are you, really?"

He faces her in the dark. "I'm all right." She doesn't believe this, he realizes, and gives him a silence to prove it. "What's wrong between you and Laurie?"

"Nothing."

"Why doesn't she enjoy touching you? I get the feeling she doesn't like it at all anymore."

"Stop it. Don't you say another word. There are some questions you can't ask me."

"You're too damn decent, Hugh. How'd you get to be so decent? You didn't use to be. You were randy and lowdown and foul. You've become a slave to your decency, sugar pie."

"It's a marriage, like any other," he says. He tries to see her more clearly. "What else did you dig out of my life today?"

"Everything," she says, "which was there." She smiles at him, her imp's smile, only the right-hand side of her mouth raised up. She lifts herself and walks over to where he is standing by the window. For a few seconds she stares at the heat lightning, but she seems bored by it. She begins to hum. Hugh doesn't recognize the tune. The volume of her humming increases, and Dorsey does a step in time to her own music. "Fox trot," she says quickly, careful not to break the rhythm. She raises her arms and curls her fingers at her waist as if to make small fists. Her bare feet whisper and brush the wood floor. A triple burst of lightning miles away illuminates her in three distinct positions. "Simon likes to dance," she says, "but I taught myself this step." She stops. "You don't dance anymore, do you?" He shakes his head. "You're so serious," she says, starting up again. "Such an *adult* adult." Now she is humming "The Blue Danube" and doing a small box waltz by herself near an endtable. She interrupts herself again. "Want to try it?"

"No."

"It's easy," she says. Standing at a dancing-class distance from him, she takes his hand. "Watch. One-two-three, one-two-three, turn-two-three, turn-two-three." He tries to follow but cannot. "It's so simple," she says, "there's nothing to it. Time and space. Move your left foot out like this. One-two-three. See? Come on, Hughie." She counts out the beat twice more, then gives up. She takes her hands away from him, and her humming fades out. "A person has to dance sometimes," she says. "Alone or with strangers, it doesn't matter, it has to be done. Even when there's no music. Especially then." She breathes softly. "You think this is very Dorsey-like, don't you?"

He shrugs.

"Trust me on this one. A person has to be grateful to Simon sometimes for the pastimes Simon suggests."

"A person *has* to be grateful?"

She stands in front of the window, looking out. "It's Simon's business who he loves," Dorsey says, aiming her words at her brother. "Sorry: *whom* he loves. *I* know who it is because he tells me. I don't mind anymore that Simon loves so many different people. I know you didn't ask this time, but you asked before and so I'm telling you now. Simon gets infatuated. That's how he got me. The world's a garden for him. He goes around like this, pick, pick, pick." Her hands pluck imaginary blossoms. "I say to him, 'Simon, don't get any diseases.' He says he's careful. I believe him. That's all I'm telling you."

"If everything is so wonderful," he asks, "what are you doing up in the middle of the night?"

"I'm not sleeping because I never sleep."

Hugh nods. "I see."

"And I'm not used to being in this house," she tells him. "Too many ghosts. I don't care how kind and loving they are."

He stares out through the window. All over the county, he thinks, farmers are standing at their bedroom windows, breathing lightly, watching the sky in hopes of the sudden downpour, the odd cloudburst. "All I ever wanted," he says, suddenly afraid of his own generalization, "was to make sure . . . that you were all right. You know: safe."

"That's sweet," she says. "But it won't ever work. Not for me. It hasn't ever worked. Besides, there's no safety in safety. So I might as well live with Simon. You and I, Hugh—we've been divorced, haven't we? Can brothers and sisters get divorces from each other? I think they can, and I think we got one." She gives her brother a kiss on the cheek, then goes upstairs.

He puts down the glass of milk. Why is it, he thinks, every time I talk to her, I get blindsided? It's happened so often that no one's even keeping count. All the scores are settled.

He looks out onto the grass and thinks he sees some silver forks lying on the lawn, lit by the high-altitude cloud lightning, which makes the backyard appear to be black and white, a landscape of tarnished metal. The keys. Hugh's keys are still out there somewhere on the grass, at the end of an arc that began at the roof. He gazes at the ceiling with impatience at himself—*I love my parachute*—then opens the back door quietly and stands on the lawn. The hot summer night air presses against his skin like a heavy paw. Up above him, at the second-floor window, his sister gazes down at him, and he sees her there, a small familiar figure in white, standing in the room where she once, long ago, grew up. He waves, but she moves back as if she hasn't seen him. When he hears thunder, Hugh bends down and begins to search in the burned grass for his keys, the ones to the car and the house and the garage and his office door, and the one that opens a lock he's forgotten about, and the one that he forgot to give back at the motel's check-out desk twenty miles out of town, and in the next flash of lightning, he sees a frog, and what he thinks may be a garter snake, but when the first drop of rain falls on his back, he hasn't found what he's looking for, but he knows he will, in a moment or two.

2

"Ordinary white wine," Dorsey says, when Simon asks her to name her favorite alcoholic drink. They drive for another half mile before Simon asks her for the brand of her favorite candy bar. She looks at a silo, and at the rotting wooden frame of a billboard, vacant, framing only the scrub pine trees behind it, before she says, "Almond Joy."

Driving the back roads of Ohio, on their way to Hugh and Laurie's for the Fourth of July, Dorsey and Simon play Simon's preference game for as long as Simon can think of categories. After an hour of this, Simon sinks into a traveler's stupor, and his hands hang limply on the steering wheel. He and Dorsey both look out in silence at what there is of Ohio to see. They have been wandering on county highways, service drives, and township line roads, heading in a northwesterly direction. Simon does not, on principle, drive on freeways or use road maps. Maps, he says, take all the creativity out of getting somewhere. Why travel if you already know how to get where you're going? For direction they use the angle of the sun and a water-ball compass stuck to the front windshield with a black suction cup.

Noah sleeps in the back, the visor of his Boston Red Sox cap down over his eyes.

"Hugh," Simon says, suddenly alert again, pronouncing his brother-in-law's name as if the name itself were in doubtful taste. He peers at the highway, then says Hugh's name three times, trying out different intonations, projecting the sounds as a groan, a sigh, a quiet bird call.

"Come on. We're only staying with them for a day or two," Dorsey says. "You can tolerate my brother for that long."

"It's not your brother I mind," Simon tells her, gripping the steering wheel tightly again. "It's his behavior I don't like. And his looks. That furrowed brow of his. He's so earnest. And then there's his decency. You know I can't handle decency. It gives me the shivers."

They are cruising past someone's farm, where the corn is waist high, pale green, and dried out. A DEKALB sign, with the brand name blazoned over a winged corn cob, stands at the edge of the field. Dorsey looks at her fingernails and says, "Sweetie, you don't like it when people are predictable. You have a fetish for surprise."

"It's not a fetish. It's a craving. That's different. It's not that he's dull, I don't mind dull, I even like dull sometimes. Dull can be pretty. Remember Sandra?"

"Sandra in Sausalito?" Dorsey asks.

Simon nods. "She was soulfully dull," he sighs.

"No, she wasn't," Dorsey tells him. "She was languid. There's a difference. Don't you remember? I met her. I caught you with her once. She had herself draped over the sofa and she was drinking that alcoholic Kool-Aid you had made and were calling sangria, and she was wearing a purple silk skirt and a blouse with no bra. Yeah, I remember her. But listen: you don't have to make a social effort. You can stay in your room and study your script. We'll occupy ourselves. You don't have to mingle, honey. You can stay in your room."

Simon nods, pleased by the idea, and begins to hum the Beach Boys' "In My Room." His face has cleared. It's an unusually broad face, suited for the stage, with a high forehead curtained by a mop of nondescript hair. Everyone who sees him says that Simon looks

like . . . *someone* they're sure they've seen before. Some say Alan
Arkin. Others say Anthony Perkins or Glenda Jackson. Always they
recognize him but then are unsure by what means they have done
so. Simon has this characteristic: he usually looks like someone else.
Like a plastic manufactured doll, he has no face of his own. He
leaves nothing in the visual memory.

"All the dull, decent people should have a convention," Simon
says, turning the steering wheel for a slow S-curve around a greenish
muddy lake, only two boat docks visible in a tiny bay of lily pads.
"They could elect your brother the supreme King of Dullness. No,"
he says, suddenly looking animated, "not the supreme king. The
Pope. The terrible Pope of Torpor."

Dorsey looks over at him. "I hate it when you struggle for bitchy
adjectives," she says. "It's not a winning characteristic."

Simon laughs with his mouth gripped shut, silently. He pretends
to hunch over the wheel like a little troll pleased by his own
vileness. Suddenly both he and Dorsey are being hit on the shoulders
by back-seat hands. Dorsey turns around, where Noah is excitedly
pointing to a roadside billboard, three lines of copy on three red
slats.

SEASHELL CITY

WONDERS OF THE DEEP

TWO MILES

Noah holds his hands in the air. Stop there! his hands say. Tell
Daddy to stop there.

Dorsey turns around to face him. Do you have to go to the
bathroom? she asks.

No. I want to stop. I want to see the shells.

"What's he want?" Simon asks. "I can't read his hands in the
rearview mirror."

"He wants to stop at the seashell place up here."

"Oh." Simon's face moves out of its troll mode and takes on an
air of pleased parental concern. He puts his left hand on the wheel
and lifts his right hand.

We'll stop, the hand spells out.

TREASURES OF THE DEEP
GIANT MAN EATING CLAM
SEASHELL CITY——ONE MILE

"Sounds like my kind of place," Simon tells Dorsey. "I can't wait to see that man eating that clam. You don't see giant men——"

"——We need a rest anyway," Dorsey says, interrupting Simon, shutting him off. "Maybe we can find out where we are."

"That's cheating," Simon tells her, running his hand through his hair in a petulant gesture. "That would be telling. Honey, you know the rules. We don't ever ask strangers for directions. I mean, we know we're in Ohio, so who cares where we are? Don't you dare ask them how to get where we're going. They wouldn't know anyway."

40,000 SHELLS!
FREE ICE WATER
SEASHELL CITY——½ MILE

They pull off into a dusty parking lot enclosed on two sides by a flaking picket fence. There is one other car in the lot, a battered and rusting peach-colored Hornet, its back bumper attached to the frame with wire and twine. Seashell City has an open front entryway, like a fruit stand, with a glass case filled with smooth polished stones, next to a circular postcard rack, a carousel of scenes of rural and urban Ohio. Behind the register is a large, balding man smoking the stump of a cigar. The man's red face is mottled and blotched so that it looks like an enlarged, angry apple. Leaning on the counter, he fabricates a smile when Simon, Dorsey, and Noah come in. His huge meaty forearms are splayed over his newspaper. Above him, on a shelf, a radio is playing country-western: Hank Williams, Jr.

Seashell City is all one large room with long divided tables on both sides of the aisles; the large shells are arranged in parallel rows, and the small shells and the polished stones are separated on the tables so that the least expensive are closest to the door. Tourist ashtrays in the shape of upturned hands, novelty clocks that run backwards, placemats, and cedar outhouse salt-and-pepper shakers are grouped together along the north wall.

Dorsey solemnly thumbs through a stack of plastic-covered scenic placemats in Kodachrome colors: western Colorado, San Francisco Bay, Mount Rainier. She puts them back, then glances at the cast-iron dog thermometer hanging on the wall near the front—eighty-two degrees here inside Seashell City—and walks over to where Noah stands with his fingers in a small bin of seashells. The air smells of fertilized farm soil and varnished wood souvenirs. The country-western station, now playing Tammy Wynette, seems much louder than before, much louder than a radio in a public place has any right to be. Feeling a shiver of displacement, Dorsey begins to hear all the objects in Seashell City. What she hears is not a sound but instead an inaudible sensation of the ocean's and the earth's artifacts. Gastropods from the Atlantic, oyster shells from the Pacific, polished agates from Lake Superior, flea-sized pieces of gold from Nevada, glittering iron pyrite from California, yellow quartz crystals from closed subterranean caves all begin in Dorsey's ears a silent inanimate chorus of inorganic longing to be anywhere but here, this place, where they are arranged in groups, for sale. A violation of the elements.

She is about to call over to Simon when Noah, who is still standing beside her, holds up a smooth brown-spotted shell.

Mom, what's this?

She looks down at the label. The vibrations of longing fade. It's called a Juno's Volute, she tells him, spelling it out.

What's a volute?

A spiral. Anything that turns, she says. Like this. She holds her index finger in the air, turning it and raising it at the same time, a party gesture.

And this? He points to a brown shell with knobby shoulders.

A fighting conch, she says.

It fights? How does it fight? I don't understand.

I don't know, she tells him. Probably the males fight.

And this?

It's an alphabet cone.

Where are the letters?

They're not real letters. They only look like letters, she says.

I want it.

Why?

Because I want to give it to Uncle Hugh.

Why do you want to do that?

Because I love him, Noah says with his hands: thumb at heart, index finger across forehead, arms crossed, then index finger pointed out.

Dorsey looks down at her son's face. Noah is an ordinary, wild-haired kid with scabs on his elbows and gaps in his mouth where his big teeth have been emerging in irregular juts. The left side of his shirt isn't tucked in. Like a horse, he needs a groom. And of course he is deaf, a fact that Dorsey never forgets but on which she has managed not to fixate. She insists on thinking of Noah as a normal kid of above-average intelligence and is astonished only at times like this, when he is pointlessly affectionate and generous.

She picks up the shell. It has an almost industrial smoothness. She holds it to her nose, hoping for a whiff of the ocean, a barnacle-and-oyster saltiness, but the shell's odor has been boiled or soaped off somewhere on its long way from the ocean to Ohio. She bends down into the bin of freckled brown scallop shells, and then into the bin of wentletraps. Where's the damn ocean? she mutters to herself. Still holding Noah's alphabet cone, she steps to the bin of limpets, umbrella-shaped shells heaped together like toy plastic cars in a dime store, and she tries again to smell something oceanic, fathoms deep, itchy and primal. She moves down to the moon shells, the venus clams, the brown pygmy whelks. Then she finds the rocks. She passes her hand tenderly over the malachite, the rose quartz, the bloodstones and jasper and onyx, the banded agates from Mexico and the eye agates from Brazil. She touches the polished hematite, the arrowheads and pieces of chert. She puts her hand deep into a pile of smoothed mica and lifts the stones to her nose. She smells nothing—the stones and shells have no scent at all.

At the front counter she pays the furious-looking owner seventy-five cents for the alphabet cone. As he is putting the money into the cash register till, she says, "Your shells don't have any odor."

The man shakes his head, not looking at her. "They've been cleaned," he says. "We buy them after the supplier's cleaned them all up." He puts the shell into a small brown paper bag, staples it shut, then hands it to her.

"You should leave some of them dirty," Dorsey says, trying to be heard over the blare of the radio. "Your customers would like it better."

He looks at her, the thick bulk of his neck reddening. His dark eyes check her out, top to bottom, and, just as quickly, dismiss her. "It's unsanitary," he says, putting the cigar back into his mouth and lighting up.

He is arrogant—she can see this—with all the undirected aggression of a physically powerful man who is running a failing business. She decides to speak up. "Tell me," she asks, "what in the hell is a seashell without the fucking ocean?"

"Dorsey. Mind your language." It is Simon, standing behind her. He is holding a souvenir coffee cup with a picture of the Ohio state bird, the cardinal, printed on its side.

"We don't take to that kind of talk here," the owner says, standing up, aiming the protuberant bulk of his stomach in her direction. "You can all just be on your way now." His right hand, a reflex, makes a fist. He glares at them. Blue cigar smoke issues from his mouth, uncoiling.

"Let's go," Simon says. He bangs the souvenir cup down on the counter and leads Dorsey, followed by Noah, into the eye-burning light of Seashell City's parking lot. Before Dorsey can say a word, Simon puts his arms around her and says, "And that's why they call it a tourist trap, sweetie pie. It's supposed to break your heart."

"Simon," she says, "all those stones and shells, they're relics, they look like relics, they don't have any business being here, they don't *want* to be here, they should go right back to the earth, into the sea. No price tags, no polishing, no cleaning. Selling shells in Ohio . . . it's so . . . Jesus, it's so American."

Simon scratches his neck. "And you say *I* struggle for bitchy adjectives." He gives her a practiced gaze, sees that she is angry but not miserable, kisses her, and then lets her go. "I saw you sniffing those shells like a pig rooting for truffles, and I said to myself, 'Simon, let's get the little woman and Baby Leroy into the car and get this dumbshow on the road.'"

Once they're in the car, Simon starts the engine and pulls out onto the highway. Dorsey removes the shell from the bag and places it up on the dashboard over the defroster vents, where it rolls pleasingly back and forth whenever they make a sudden turn in their wanderings across northern Ohio, gradually, through trial and error, nearing Hugh's house in Five Oaks, Michigan, for the Fourth of July.

3

Hugh sits with his feet up on his desk in his glassy cubicle at Bruckner Buick on July first, very quietly testing out sentences he may use tomorrow or Thursday when Dorsey and her husband arrive. He is measuring these sentences for the specific gravity of their stupidity. "Dorsey . . . great to see you . . . how was the trip . . . Simon . . . you're looking well . . . you're . . . you." Every word he can think of, every sentence of good will and greeting, sounds dull and duncelike. Though Dorsey and Simon are scheduled to arrive soon, Hugh has no clear idea when they'll appear, because those two refuse to take freeways, ask for directions, or use maps. "Simon . . . what a pleasant . . ." Mouthing sentences in this way makes Hugh think of his brother-in-law, the actor, the man of plastic, the connoisseur of witty, cutting remarks. With Simon, you don't notice you're bleeding until two or three minutes later. You're on the stairs or in the bathroom and suddenly you realize how carefully you've been put down, and there you are, hemorrhaging pride and self-confidence, schooled one more time.

"Dorsey? How've you been? How was . . ."

"Dorsey. Welcome back."

"Well, well."

The sentences shrink word by word to nothing. Hugh dreads Dorsey and Simon's arrival. It's an irrational dread: he feels himself stronger and bigger and more of a man than his brother-in-law. If he could hit Simon, punch him out in a straightforward way, he'd be all right. But here he is, practicing his lines, an actor himself. "Dorsey." He looks out the front window at the highway. "Dorsey," he says again, watching the waves of heat rising from the asphalt. "Let's go buy some fireworks."

Outside the seven front plate-glass windows of Bruckner Buick the summer lunchtime sun is sending everybody, distracted and sweaty, into the shade. It's not a day to buy a car, or to sell one, either. For one thing, the demos have heated up in the sun, and their steering wheels are irritatingly sticky, and the cars can't be cooled just by idling them with the AC on for a few moments before the customer gets inside. In this kind of heat the engines may perform erratically, and the AC blowers have to be set so high the customer can't hear the salesman. Though the showroom is cool, and the sales manager's beautiful-music tape is coating the air with string-orchestra syrup, Hugh and his fellow salesman, Larry Hammerman, have no customers. There's nothing to look at or to listen to except the saltless music, or Larry's methodically calm voice as he makes a follow-up call to a prospect, a high school biology teacher, a Mr. Peterfreund, who has set his sights on an Electra he probably can't afford.

Thinking about Dorsey and her actor husband, Hugh looks around his semi-office—his imitation brass nameplate on the desk, his sales awards framed and hung with glued hooks on the wall behind him, his Rolodex and his inventory book set to the right of the decorative Bruckner Buick blotter, the pictures of Laurie, Tina, and Amy at the side of the desk, where both he and his distrustful customers can see them—and he stares at the highway shimmering in the windless heat, not even the used-car lot's colored banners flapping. He tries out a sentence: "Dorsey, it's been so long since I've seen you." He waits. "What are you working on? Are you happy? Is it all right?"

The questions come dropping out of his mind like stones. These

stones fall into a pond where they make no waves. Simon has all
the good lines. He memorizes them. That's his job. The person in
the family Hugh has felt closest to lately has been his nephew, Noah,
who never says anything, except with his hands. Sitting in his
cubicle, sipping his cold coffee, Hugh has a sudden impulse to learn
American Sign Language, or signed English, some way or other. I
would be more articulate with my hands, he thinks, than I ever have
been with my voice. He opens his desk drawer and pulls out a letter,
with paper gone soft from much handling. The letter is addressed
to Hugh and is written in a child's hand. Noah sent it, by himself:
Hugh knows this because the envelope's stamp is upside down, a
mistake Dorsey has never been capable of making. Although he has
memorized the letter, Hugh reads it anyway.

> Dear Uncle Hugh,
>   We will be seeing you soon. We are driving up and will
> stay with you. I am looking forward to seeing my cousins but
> I also can't wait to see you. I miss you. I am going to bring
> you a present.
>
>   Love,
>   Noah

Hugh puts the letter into his pocket and walks out to the showroom. As usual, the cars give him a huge sense of their own appro-
priateness. They are antidotes to life as it is. Hugh loves Buicks. He
loves them almost as much as he loves his own family, almost as
much as he loves women. A person can't stay with women all day,
however. Hugh thinks of his attraction to women, his love for them,
as a character flaw. Resolute men do not obsess themselves about
women. They get on with things. Absentmindedly, he pats the dark
gray Skylark on the fender above the left front wheel. The steel and
wax do not feel like skin but an approximation of it, a powerfully
erotic metallic sheath.

Unlike some salesmen, Hugh does not think of the customer as
his victim. Any man or woman who strolls into Bruckner Buick
is, in Hugh's eyes, looking for a partner; his role as a salesman is
therefore that of a matchmaker. Specials and Skylarks for the young,
Skyhawks for married couples, Electras and Somersets and Regals

and LeSabres for the demonstrably successful. The customer is the bride; the car is the bridegroom. An unhappy customer has only the matchmaker to blame.

On the other side of Highway 63 Hugh can see the flapless banners and cars hot as frypans lined up in the Pentel Ford lot. The Ford dealership gives him a low-level physical discomfort. He has an anthropological interest in other cars; they are the pointless and absurd competition. With downcast fascination he watches the competition's commercials and studies their fact sheets. He loathes Lee Iacocca and had his heart set on the bankruptcy of Chrysler. Other cars are error, the result of a society dedicated to free choice.

With his salesman's radar Hugh knows that Larry Hammerman has finished his call to Mr. Peterfreund and that the biology teacher has chickened out. (The wrong car for him, Hugh knows; the Electra was too much car for the man, clearly a Skyhawk type.) Larry is cramped over his desk in his cubicle, ruffling through a list of names for follow-up calls. In a town like Five Oaks there are never that many new names to call, and now Larry sighs, curses under his breath, and pulls his right hand, missing half its index finger (summer, lawn mower) through his thick expressive hair. Larry's skin is pink; his hair is rusty brown, and when he's frustrated the fires in his chest rage upwards past his neck and become visible in his forehead. His face turns a bright, desolate rouge.

Larry is, just now, under financial duress. His wife, Stella Hammerman, is wildly beautiful but spends money passionately on home furnishings and clothes, and has recently purchased with Larry's approval a twenty-foot fiberglass boat with a thirty-five-horse-power outboard motor. To hear Larry tell it, all weekend long Stella and Larry speed around Saginaw Bay, occasionally throwing overboard a fishing line, sometimes baited. Stella is a good-time woman—Larry has told Hugh, in private, what Stella also likes to do in the open air on this boat as it drifts through the choppy excited waters—and Hugh respects Larry's efforts to keep the bills paid. A man will do many things for a long-legged woman with cravings like Stella's. And they have a daughter, too, fifteen years old, who has lately been seen perched on the backs of motorcycles, hugging the black-leather-jacketed greaseball drivers as they roar down the main street of Five Oaks toward the bowling alley and the video arcade. Her mother's daughter, eager to please and to be pleased. Larry's demons are starting to chitter; lately they've been keeping him awake, so that he sometimes staggers into the dealership in the morning with a wooden zombie gait and full-moon eyes.

He straightens up, seems to recognize where he is, and comes over to where Hugh is standing, and together they stare out the window.

"Nothing?"

"Punked out," Larry says, shaking his head.

"How come?"

"The little woman saw the literature."

"And?"

" 'Too much car.' "

"That's what she said?"

"Those were Mrs. Peterfreund's exact words. 'Too much car.' I'd like to give her too much car."

"I saw her husband," Hugh says. "She's right."

"Even a high school biology teacher can escape his condition, is what I say."

"Don't be so sure," Hugh says. "He needs more than that Electra."

"Such as?"

"A whole new life, for starters."

Larry laughs quietly, a close-mouthed rhythmic wheeze. "I had faith in the guy," he says. "He was already talking about options. Power windows and the visibility group. It got that far."

Hugh nods. He is still looking out the window. "Hot," he says.

"I've never sold a car," Larry says, "when the temperature was over eighty-seven degrees Fahrenheit. Can't be done. Except to accident victims."

"Accident victims?"

"Yeah." Larry worries the change in his pocket. "You know what I mean. People who've just totaled the beloved family auto. They never shop. They just come roaring in here and they buy the first thing they see. Remember the Klingerman family?"

"The LeSabre Estate wagon."

"That's the one. You weren't in the showroom when this happened. You came in the day they took possession. The elder Klingerman came in here, no, excuse me, he *wobbled* in here sporting a neck brace and clutching a hospital-issue aluminum cane, and he pointed at the wagon, which was out on the floor, with that cane of his, and he said, 'I'll take that.' The car had a noisy speedometer cable but I wasn't about to dampen his enthusiasm. It was ninety degrees out. I didn't even have a chance to remark on the heat or to ask him for his blood type." This is a reference to Hugh's matchmaker theory of selling cars. "He sat down and pulled out his fountain pen and his checkbook. You've got to respect a man in a neck brace who can write a check for over ten thousand dollars, especially in this town. Well, maybe you don't. Hot weather sales are unpredictable. I don't know." He smiles. "Pray for accidents. Don't pray for fatalities. With fatalities you lose the customer."

"How's Stella?" Hugh asks. It strikes him immediately as the wrong question, in this context.

"Fine," Larry says. "She just bought a VCR with capacity for stereo sound. She's been renting films faster than we can see them. Romance, horror, adventure, musicals, porn—I can't keep up. How's Laurie?"

"Laurie's fine."

"The girls?"

"Same as always."

"Your sister's coming to town, right?"

"Right."

"With that husband of hers, the faggot."

"Simon. He's not a fag, not exactly. It's more complicated."

"Sure it is. When're they getting here?"

"In time for the Fourth. I don't know exactly. They don't believe in maps."

Larry nods, as if this makes perfect sense. "Where are they headed?"

"Minneapolis," Hugh says. "Simon's got an acting job there."

"What about your sister?"

"I don't know. She has a job in Buffalo, and maybe she'll go back there because they've got their boy in a private school for the deaf that doesn't force oralism and lip-reading on them. They do American Sign Language and signed English, and Dorsey wants to keep him there. She says he's thriving. I don't know if it's so good for her to stay there, but . . . it's her life."

"Buffalo," Larry says, a judgment.

"Yeah." Hugh feels a moment of faintness, a sensation of helium filling up his head, so that, if he had no anchors, he would float to the showroom ceiling. Too much coffee, he thinks, trying to shake himself back to ground level. Where he is standing, the air conditioning hums with white noise, and the music and the thought of his sister together are giving him the willies. The showroom at Bruckner Buick, as he looks at it, is advancing toward him, then receding, accordion-fashion.

"What's the matter with you?" Larry asks. "You just turned white."

"Don't know," Hugh says. "Suddenly I feel terrible."

"Take a breather," Larry says. "My advice to you is, take the afternoon off. I can handle all this heavy showroom traffic. If I can't, Leachman is around here somewhere." Leachman is the sales manager. "You look like dogshit."

"I feel like it," Hugh says. "I think maybe I'll take your advice." He looks over to his cubicle, gazes for a moment at the sales awards, then heads out to his car, thinking of Dorsey and his own flawed, inherited circulatory system.

Behind the wheel, the air conditioner blowing uncooled air toward him—something's wrong with it—the radio tuned to WFOM's community billboard program, he feels a little better, but still hot. Because he has nowhere special to go, he is heading in the general direction of home, on the north side of Five Oaks. This daily drive takes him past Mason Motors (Chrysler-Plymouth), the Red Owl supermarket, Lampert Lumber, across the two Grand Trunk Railway tracks (the main tracks and the siding for the lumber yard), Knapp radio and TV, and then into what is called downtown Five Oaks. The few people out on the sidewalk in the business district, most of whom he recognizes, are pathetically wrinkled and wilted. He sees Mrs. Castlehoff, the pharmacist's wife, red hair like a peat fire above a potato-famine face, carrying a large lumpy brown paper bag. Her hair is matted flat, and her birdlike face wears an expression of suppressed alarm—that she has been seen in public carrying a large bag full of lumpy suspicious personal articles? Or alarm at the heat? Or just alarm? Hugh smiles, waves to her, and though she sees him and acknowledges the nod with an irritated flick of her sun-drenched head, she doesn't wave back. She clutches the bag to her chest and hurries on to her car, an Escort with two good years left on it.

He brakes hard at the intersection of Lake Street and Cross, the site of one of Five Oaks' hanging stoplights. As he waits, he closes his eyes and imagines this whole scene, Bacon Drug to his right, the Quik-'n'-Ezy to his left, buried under the water left behind by the melting glaciers. He thinks of huge Pleistocene fish swimming down the main street, and of clam shells washed up onto the stoop of the shoe store.

On the other side of town, near the park, he hears a loud resonant ringing and at first believes that this clamor originates inside his own head, the vibrating ring of tinnitus. He puts his hand to his neck to check his pulse. But no: as he moves up the street, he can tell that the bells are ringing, if that's what they're doing, in St. Luke's Catholic Church. They're louder and in some ways more distinct than he has ever heard them. Hugh, a non-Catholic, has set foot in this church only for baptisms, weddings, and funerals, so the place has for him an aura of crisis, of squalling, kissing, and sobbing. A small church, it smells on the inside of white pine and varnish. No one is parked outside and the bells continue to chime for no reason. His forehead is damp with sweat, and he has nowhere to go; he parks the car and hurries up the front stairs of the church.

The idea of no one being inside the church is pleasing to him. He wants to smell the inside of St. Luke's, especially the old, thick resinous wood. As soon as he steps inside the heavy front doors and stands in the foyer, he takes a breath and gazes toward the altar draped with white linen. The circular stained-glass window overhead throws down thickened beams of colored sunlight, tinting the dust in the air. It seems pure. Standing there, he thinks: *virginity*.

From a door Hugh hadn't noticed at the back, a priest appears, a young man he doesn't recognize. Though Hugh doesn't attend any church, he knows the regular priest here is Father Yaeger, and this person isn't Father Yaeger. The priest is in a hurry but slows down as soon as he sees Hugh. He smiles, startled, and Hugh notices the priest's large hands with thick fingers, a physical contrast to the young man's tame, delicate face. Father a farmer, mother a waitress, Hugh thinks. "Hi," the priest says. "Welcome. You must have heard the bells."

"Hard to miss them," Hugh says.

"I just turned them on," the priest informs him, punctuating the sentence with a pantomime flicking-on of a switch. "Are they too loud, do you think?" He looks superficially pensive. "Because they aren't really bells. They're, well, I mean they're *bells* all right, but they're recorded. It's a tape, a cassette. We have a new two-stage amplifier and a speaker system, Mackintosh and Micro-Acoustic." He points to the ceiling for a moment. "It sounds pretty good, don't you think?"

"Very nice." Hugh notes scars on the young man's face.

"We took up a collection for them last year. Our old bells weren't solid, they were flaking and chipping . . . well, you don't want to hear all this church talk, I'm sure. I'm Father Albert Duquesne." He holds out his hand, and Hugh shakes it.

"I'm . . . " Hugh plays with the idea of giving the priest an alias, but he can't think of one fast enough. "Hugh Welch," he says.

"What can I do for you?" the priest asks.

"Not really anything," Hugh says. "I was feeling light-headed in the car from the heat, and then I heard some bells. So I came in to cool off for a moment."

"Can I get you some water?" The priest doesn't wait for Hugh to answer. He reappears a minute later holding a small Dixie cup. "Here." The water is not cold, but Hugh drinks it anyway. A bad well: it tastes of iron.

"It's not cold, is it?" the priest says, trying to laugh. "It came from the tap downstairs. But at least it's clean."

"Thanks," Hugh says, handing the cup back. The young man crumples it up, looks around for a place to throw it, glances at Hugh, and keeps it in his fist.

"Have we . . . have we seen you here before?"

"No," Hugh says. "I'm not a Catholic. I live near here, and I've been in this church a few times. But I'm not a churchgoer."

The priest nods and wipes his other hand on his cassock. "But here you are anyway. An accident of, I guess you would call it, fate." The priest smiles publicly to himself. "Excuse me for a moment. I should go turn off those bells." He hurries out, and suddenly the sound of the bells goes instantly dead, without reverberations or echo. The air holds its pocket of silence, and then the priest comes bustling back. "People probably thought it was for a wedding, I suppose. Except it's too early in the day. People don't like to get married before lunch. They *could,* but they don't. More likely, everyone driving by here thought we were having a funeral. Those you can have in the morning. You can have a funeral anytime. Why is that? I should think about it." Hugh notices that he has gotten rid of the Dixie cup somehow.

"My wife and I were married in the morning," Hugh says. "Around ten o'clock or so. I can't remember why."

"That's unusual," the priest says. "I almost don't believe you. In a church? Oh, no. You said you weren't a churchgoer." The priest is scratching hard at his scalp. He sees Hugh watching him and says, "Chigger fly bite. I was fishing two days ago and forgot to wear a hat."

"Bites like that can be pretty bad," Hugh says, feigning sympathy. "No, we weren't married in a church. My wife's cousin Harold did it. He's a Presbyterian minister, but he had to be somewhere else that afternoon. A football game, I think. It was a Saturday. He came to our house, married us, drank a glass of champagne, and that was that. It was either Harold or city hall, and I didn't want to be married by a clerk."

"The clerk doesn't do it. The judge does."

"The city clerk can marry you. They have the power."

"No, they don't," the priest insists. "I'm *quite* sure. After all, they're just clerks." He looks at Hugh with an uncertain expression. "Well," he says. "Can I show you around? Do you have a few minutes for that?"

He shows Hugh the font for holy water, then takes him forward past the rows of pews to the altar. He genuflects, then points out details of the window glass and gives a brief history of the church, which goes back, he says, to 1936, when the previous church, which was also called St. Luke's and stood on this site, was destroyed by a fire whose origin to this day has remained mysterious. "I was told," the priest says, "that a Lutheran did it." He laughs mechanically. "You say you live here, in Five Oaks?"

"Nearly all my life," Hugh tells him. He gazes toward the back, the southwest side of the church.

"I'm new to this town," the priest says. "I'm the assistant here. Do you fish?"

"Some," Hugh says. As a favor, he decides to give the priest a tip to a good spot, but not his best tip. "Try the south side of Silver Lake, in the afternoon especially, when the shade of those poplar trees gets out over the water. Near the Bill Martin summer place, this is, just beyond his boat dock. You've got to keep your lure from getting caught in the lily pads. If you can do that, you can probably catch yourself some bass. Big ones." He holds his hands out, measuring.

The priest nods. "I'll remember that. Thanks."

Hugh nods in return.

After another silence, the priest also gazes toward the back of the church, as if something were there, and in a quiet voice says, "Now what can I do for you?"

Hugh points. "What are those?"

"The confessional boxes."

"Do you listen to confessions?"

"Yes." The priest begins to walk back toward the rear doors. "Of course I do." He makes quick, distressed movements of his fingers over his cassock.

"You're very young."

"Yes. People say that. I know I look like a kid. But a man's age makes no real difference. He's merely an instrument. The priest is an intermediary."

"Do people feel better after confessions?" Hugh asks, speaking to the priest's back.

"They feel better because they *are* better," he says.

"I've never confessed anything to anybody in my life," Hugh says. "Not since sixth grade. I don't think I could. It doesn't seem very . . ." He stops in the center of the aisle, trying to find the word, while perspiration drips down the sides of his chest. The priest turns around and looks at him carefully. It is an adult look, Hugh notices: a shrewd look.

"Very dignified?"

"No," Hugh says. "That's not what I was thinking. It's not very grown-up."

"Oh." The priest leans against the side of a pew, whose wood lets out a groan from the weight, and in a gesture of great youthful fatigue Father Duquesne puts his hands to his face and brings them slowly downward, as if trying to wake himself. "Well, I suppose I could say that in the church, in *this* church, we are all children before God. That's important: becoming a child again. It can happen. I could say that. But I think you know that already, and besides, that's not what you came inside this church to hear. Or to do."

Hugh smiles. "What did I come in here to do?"

The priest makes a throat-clearing sound. He glances at Hugh, then looks away. "Let me guess."

"Okay."

The priest suddenly turns the full force of his attention on Hugh, and Hugh sees in his eyes a cold intelligent glint that tells him why this young man is here, dressed up in these black institutional clothes, tethered by his love for the Blessed Virgin and for God. "It's your life," the priest says, "that brought you in here this morning."

"Okay. But what about my life?"

"A weight in it."

"What kind of weight?"

"You can't talk," the priest says. "You can't ever talk." Instantly Hugh's hand dives down to his left pocket, where Noah's letter is. Noah: *but with my hands,* Hugh thinks. "It's not despair, but you feel dispirited. You feel mute."

Hugh smiles.

"Do you have a house?" the priest asks.

"Yes."

"You're like me," the priest says. "You wander around the house late at night."

"Sometimes I do that."

"Everybody says, I bet that all your friends say, about you, I mean, that you're doing just fine." Father Duquesne smiles, enjoying this despite the heat, and Hugh thinks: *this kid is acting as if he's a fortune teller.* "Of course, I'm overstepping the bounds here."

"That's all right."

"You must, well, you must imagine that there's some way to the spirit besides God, and you probably say to yourself that this whole structure"—he waves his right arm in a large, room-inclusive gesture—"is a sizable fraud. But," he adds, "here you are anyway."

The two men smile at each other and wait.

"I wanted to talk about my sister," Hugh says suddenly.

"What about her?" They are still standing in the aisle. Outside a horn honks twice. *Honk if you love . . . something.*

"She's coming here, for a visit. With her husband and son. She's real brilliant, my sister, a physicist. I don't even know what it is she works on. I can't understand it. But she's had a hard life, in some ways, and I've tried to help her when things have happened. I've tried to be a brother to her. No one knows how to do that in this country, how to be a brother. But now I don't know that she ever needed my help. I thought she did. Maybe not. I've lived my life thinking she needed me to help her. Now I'm not sure."

"You must love her very much," Father Duquesne says.

"I did." Hugh corrects himself. "I do."

"What does she mean to you?"

"My sister? What does she *mean?* Do people *mean?* My father once told me to watch after her, to take care of her. So I tried. Maybe that's not something you're supposed to do, but those were the instructions I had. I think about her a lot. It's not like being married. It's this other kind of love. There's no name for it. Sometimes I think I've spent my life watching her, watching over her."

"Oh," Father Duquesne says. "What," he asks quietly, "did you ever do that was so terrible?"

"What?"

"In your life," the priest says, a strained expression on his boyish face. "That would make you take care of someone who didn't need it?" He shakes his head. "Well, listen, Hugh. I should . . . there are some things here I should be doing. But we can talk some more, if you'd like. We could set up an appointment."

"Maybe."

"You want to go fishing some day this summer?"

Hugh looks at the priest. *Smart ass.* "Thanks, but probably not."

"Well, if you do, give me a call."

"I will." Hugh smiles. "Now let *me* guess."

"Guess? Guess what?"

"Let me guess about your life. You guessed about mine. No reason why I can't do the same."

Father Duquesne raises his hand to his scalp, pats his head on a bald spot over which he has combed hair from the side, and glances out one of the leaded windows at the traffic, passing in distorted waves through the thick irregular glass.

He shrugs. "All right."

"What about this? Your father worked as a farmer, probably, and your mother was a waitress when they met. Or he was a farm boy, and she lived in town and read books, and they met in one of their high school classes. One of your parents was rough and the other wasn't." He has steam on it, power, and he knows he can go as far as he wants to, and he'll still be right. "Your father was the one who taught you to fish, and it was your mother who usually went to church. She was the one you really loved."

The priest's mouth is opening in surprise or anger or even amusement, but Hugh can't be sure which one it is, and he is determined to continue in any case.

"You were the smart one in the family," Hugh says, "the one with all the brains, the kid they put their small hopes on. Older, younger, it doesn't matter in a Catholic family. Your mother stood at the sink doing dishes, and whenever you were in the house, she'd say, without turning around, *Where's my best boy?* and you'd answer, *Here I am. Best boy right here.* Your brothers and sister got you to help them with their homework. You kept to your books." Hugh is hearing all this, taking dictation. "You didn't go out much. Everyone was worse than you were. They always got into trouble, but not you. You weren't on any teams, and you—"

"—No," Father Duquesne interrupts. "That's not true. I played basketball."

"Okay." Hugh nods. "There was a hoop and a backboard set up on the garage roof. Anyway, you were the first one in the family to go to college. You took courses in everything but mostly in psychology, so you could understand why you had turned out the way you had, so unusual. You liked girls, but not so much that you couldn't do without them. You didn't lie awake at night thinking about them, the way your friends did. After graduation, you signed up. You signed your name on the line. Your whole huge family, all your cousins, came out for your . . . what's the word?"

"Ordination."

"That's it. Ordination."

Hugh stops. It has gone far enough. The priest's face has reddened —facial alchemy going on underneath—but now Hugh sees that the color, which appears in mottled, speckled dots where the acne has left its scars that make him think of a star map, is one of humor and laughter. The priest is laughing. He is exploding charges deep within his stomach. He puts his hand down on a windowsill for a moment's support. He coughs twice. Fumbling, he reaches into a pocket for a piece of Kleenex. He wipes his mouth.

"That's some tune you can play," he says.

"Was I right?"

"Some," the priest says. "Some right. I won't say what. But there is one last thing I'd like to know. Wherever did you learn to do that?"

"From my mother," Hugh says. "My family is full of failed psychics. And I'm a salesman." He puts his hand out. "Thanks for your time, Father." They shake.

He turns and is heading out the door, getting one last whiff of the pine wood, when the priest calls after him, "Sure you don't want to go fishing later this summer?"

"I'll give you a call," Hugh says, not turning around. Then the impulse takes him, and he does turn around to get a last glimpse of the priest. "Don't you go blessing me," he says loudly. "Don't you pray for me."

Hugh thinks he hears the priest say, "I won't," but it may only be his imagination speaking to him, because he is already halfway down to his car, radiating heat waves in the summer sunlight. As he unlocks the car, he glances toward the church and sees Father Duquesne at the back window, looking out at him, his face partitioned and colored by the leaded-glass segments. The priest is smiling. He is waving. His hand is segmented by the glass frames so that the wave is broken and jerky, as if seen in a repeatedly spliced film that has been run through a projector too often.

. . .

He drives twenty miles away from Five Oaks, southbound down the interstate freeway until he reaches an exit for a Holiday Inn. It is early afternoon. He takes a single room, drives his car around to the entry door, and goes inside. He turns on the air conditioner. He takes off his shoes and lies on the bed for almost thirty minutes. He loves motel rooms and always has. He stares at the wallpaper, which depicts a Venetian canal, complete with gondola and gondolier, in a broad and crude Impressionist style. He dials a number, receives no answer, then dials another. In one hour there is a knock on the door. He rises from the bed, opens the door and lets a tall, quiet-looking woman of great dignity into the room. Once inside, they kiss. She is carrying a small brown paper bag; from this bag she removes a bottle of New York State rosé wine. After toasting each other with glasses from the motel's bathroom, they take off each other's clothes and get into bed.

The two of them stay in the room for a few hours. They talk, make love, talk some more, then doze off. When Hugh wakes from one of these brief episodes of sleep, he looks over at his lover, the brown-haired, brown-eyed woman next to him. She is watching the television, a black-and-white movie about gangsters. She has kept the sound low for his benefit. Watching the film, she gives off charged particles of female contentment; Hugh can feel them in his shoulders. As he puts his hand over her thin, delicate waist, he sees in his mind's eye the young priest, Father Duquesne, waving at him from behind the leaded-glass window. A wave, he thinks; not a blessing.

He feels light-headed, a bit unhinged. The sensation is similar to the texture of faintness he felt in the showroom earlier this morning.

All his life, he has wanted to be a good man, a soldier in the army of tenderness; yet here he is in this brutally plush motel. The authorities on how to be a good man disapprove of what he is doing. These authorities are all self-proclaimed; like the black-and-white movie gangsters, they, too, are on television. To get through the long hours of the day, Hugh needs help; love, from any source, makes the time pass. He believes in love, in giving away as much of it as he has, as he can find. But there must be something wrong with his forms of affection. Looking at his lover's frizzy hair, he thinks of how people keep walking away from what he offers them. They don't need it. But Noah: his nephew, Noah, doesn't do that. Hugh reminds himself to buy Noah a present for his arrival, maybe a soccer ball. This woman, in bed with him now, has very little time for him. She complains about his calls, but sometimes she'll see him. It's something. It fills the afternoon. He bends down, and, against everything the world believes he should be doing, kisses her on the arm, just below the wrist. Her skin, damp minutes ago from love but now dry, gives off a slightly acidic taste to his tongue of salt and brine, and it makes Hugh think of the sea.

II

4

She would like to begin by saying to her class: imagine the universe, its colossal size. Imagine the energies in the interaction of particles as they combine and recombine. Imagine the features of naked singularities and wave fluctuation and the shape of de Sitter spacetime. She'd like to stand there in front of them and give them, these hard-headed kids, a good dose of awe. Not using chalk for once, she would just speak about the possibility of a universe, perhaps this one, trapped in a false vacuum of the Higgs field. What would happen? she'd ask, and no one would answer. Well, there might be a process of tunneling through the energy barrier until the universe came to the state of the true vacuum. Imagine *that*.

She'd like to say something about the metaphors of space. She won't, but she'd like to. In many religions, the sun is viewed as an analogue to God, and in some Near Eastern cults, the fire cults that interested Nietzsche, the sun is a deity, the origin of all energy, heat, light, and life. A masculine force, this sun, countered by the feminine lucent moon, mutable, pale pink at the horizon, grayish white overhead, and silver in daytime. The moon is a friend to women.

Its attraction, its capacity to pull objects toward itself, is traditionally a metaphor for womanly force. Lovers know and understand the moon as a sign for love: a cliché, certainly, but one that does not wear out. "The moon," they whisper, infinitely.

If the sun is God, what, then, is a black hole? What is this—call it an object even though it has no objecthood—what is this object that can draw matter within its event horizon and obliterate it? Is it primitive, and naïve, to say that physics has at last discovered the physics of nothingness? Yes, it *is* naïve to say so, but if Stephen Hawking is correct, and black holes do eventually evaporate and explode, what would a mind that has made a god of the sun make of this? Steven Weinberg, who has won the Nobel Prize, says that the more the universe seems comprehensible, the more it also seems pointless. What would such a mind do with the idea that the universe is closed and finite and will collapse again, come to a point, and then re-expand? What if the universe is in an infinite process of expansion and contraction, like the bellows of an accordion being played through the creation of time, its obliteration, and its recreation? Oh, children, she'd like to say, staring out starkly at their faces, for whose enjoyment is this cosmic tune being played?

She doesn't say such things. She is a professional and knows what she is supposed to be doing. Besides, this class is filled, not with children, but with careerists, young go-getters with minds like calculators, calculators that are unmoved by metaphors but can easily quantify salaries and perks and benefits.

She stands in a university classroom in Buffalo, writing out

$$ E \; = \; mR^2(t) \left[\frac{1}{2}H^2(t) \; - \; \frac{4}{3}\pi\rho(t)G \right] $$

where $H(t)$ and $\rho(t)$ are the values of the Hubble "constant"—they know, because she has explained, that it's not a constant at all—and the cosmic mass density at time t. She's getting white chalk dust all over the sleeves of her blouse. There she is, her blondish hair cut short, her eyes ringed with insomniac circles, explaining the function of these formulas to her students, an international ragbag of brilliant, scruffy, brooding-faced men and three women, all of whom have probably never had physics taught to them by a woman before. The course is Physics 501, Astrophysics, which includes atomic spectroscopy, quantum mechanics, stellar evolution, the general theory of relativity, and an introduction to recent theories of cosmology. Dorsey's wedding ring and her slightly bored explanations of the materials give her an offhand and disconcerting authority in front of this class. Only the bravest ask questions, trying to employ the same bored intonations that she uses.

After class, she wants to get home—it's a day with no committee meetings—but she's met at her office door by Bobby Chin, who is working out for himself a problem in cosmological parameters for a restricted class of closed Big-Bang universes. She agrees to talk to him and look at his calculations for five minutes. Bobby's face falls. He doesn't really care about cosmological parameters, Dorsey thinks; what he wants is more than five minutes, with her. His face struggles to suppress its yearning. He's a slender, good-looking boy, with raven hair and eyes she might fall into, if she were a different sort of person and let herself do such things. She examines his calculations, which are excellent though flawed, and closes her eyes for a moment against the force of what she knows to be his feelings. Eros and mathematics: in one possible universe, though not this one, the two can meet.

At last Dorsey is driving down Main Street in Buffalo to get Noah at his school, the Pendrick School for the Deaf, where students are not forced day in and day out to verbalize or to lip-read. Its emphasis is on dual-language signing, and as much lip-reading and speaking as the child can take. A miracle of a school. It's late March, and Noah comes rushing out of the stony, functional brown building with his jacket unzipped and his arms making happy arcs in the ugly damp air. He waves good-bye to a small cluster of his friends, gets into the car, and kisses his mother on the cheek.

Soon they are back home in their large old rented house that faces the Delaware Park Zoo. Noah stays downstairs, in the back playroom, building with his Lego Masterbuilder set, while Dorsey goes upstairs to her study to slit open the mail. Simon is out. Simon is very often out, no explanations given and none asked, though he does leave phone numbers on pieces of paper stuck with magnets to the refrigerator. These numbers tell Dorsey where he may be reached: theaters, studios, apartments, places where he plays. The point of these letters is, he will be back.

The mail is mostly bills, but here is a letter addressed to Dorsey Welch, not Dorsey O'Rourke, with a California return address. The envelope is tissue-thin, European stationery paper, the handwriting both formal and ornate in its tiny methodical hand with no traces of the Palmer Method. It's not ballpoint ink, either; the ink is sea-blue, straight from the gold fountain pen Dorsey knows is kept in an engraved silver case at the front of her correspondent's desk.

The tone of the letter is both fierce and autumnal. It begins with the writer's assertion that he will say nothing about their last phone call. A cruel misunderstanding, he says, and repeats that he will not speak of it. Without any transition he announces that he is learning Danish, the better to read Kierkegaard, whose thoughts on faith and psychic cataclysm he is eager to examine in the original. In the same paragraph (he is a man without transitions), he says that he will soon apply himself (again) to the learning of Sanskrit so that he may once more read the Upanishads as they are meant to be read. He would like to read the Panchatantra, Sanskrit fairy tales, but he does not believe that he will be able to achieve this goal for another three or four years.

The Oppenheimer project, he says, is coming along, always coming along. About his work on Yang-Mills gauge theories he says nothing.

He asks Dorsey how she is. The wording of the question is kindly but also gruff: "I am deeply interested, as you know, in your condition. What is it?" He says, as he has said before, that a woman of her promise and potential should not be in an urban caricature like Buffalo. He asks about Noah. Please, he says, send me a picture. He does not ask about Simon, nor does he mention Simon's name.

I have some displeasing equations here that I've been working on, he says. I may be getting too old to stalk and discover the elusive banality of truth.

Is this the twilight of the Age of Science? he suddenly asks. The generation of data has become a tiresome joke. Even educated persons are becoming weary of the information glut that science has produced, and of its Kali-like thirst for destructive energies. This is a clear cultural sign. It is a mistake, of course, to think of physics as a destructive art, and yet that *is* how people tend to think of it. Not all these people under contract to the Defense Department are engineers. Some call themselves physicists, after all. Even worse, they think of themselves as Americans, with that dangerous innocence. All right: if it isn't new data, what is it?

Dorsey, reading, says aloud, "How should I know?"

What we will get from now on, he says, is the organization of data, not new data, but old data leashed and whipped by the computer boys. Power is moving from science, the discovery of new information, to data processing, old information used in new ways. This means that the human spirit is reaching the end of its tolerance for discoveries. Human beings want to forget, he says. Humankind has gone forward; now it will go back. They have learned all they want to know about the universe. In any case, advances in cosmology may soon bring about the end of physics as we know it. The end, the end, he writes.

New paragraph, a short one. I think, he writes, of the arch of your foot. I think of the metatarsal bone structure and the pale sheath of skin. With you, the darkness stays at its own distance. This paragraph concludes with a reference to the late poetry of William Butler Yeats.

There is one page left to the letter, and the handwriting is getting tinier, the letters looking more algebraic.

The writer complains of aches, of arthritic stiffness in the knees, and pain in the lower back. Physics, he says, is no field for old men obsessed with their own anatomic breakdown. He says he has gotten rid of his dogs; he is incapable of walking them.

In the last paragraph he says that he knows he has rambled but that the point is this: what about Dorsey's professional advances? Where are they? Should she, he asks, make her life unnecessarily miserable by staying in this field that is bringing about its own end? Should she not give herself up to the pleasures and vicissitudes of common life? Life is infinite, he says, and there's no disgrace in setting aside science for an untormented life, particularly in a diminished epoch like ours. Take care of Noah, he says. Don't forget the child and don't let him feed on the imbecilities of the age. Ah, he writes, catching himself, I am beginning to sound like a patriarch, which I have no right to do. What I am, he says in the final sentence, is your *loving* (he underlines the word) . . . Carlo Pavorese.

Dorsey lets the letter drop on her desk and she closes her eyes, counting to twenty. She raises her hand to her forehead and is relieved that no perspiration, hot or cold, has been squeezed out of the glands onto her skin. Outside her study window a nuthatch flickers from branch to branch of the oak tree. Watching it, Dorsey tests her mouth and finds it dry. She picks up the letter again, puts the thin sheets of paper into the envelope, and holds it in both hands. A car honks as it passes on Parkside, startling her. With her fingertips she worries the fine paper of the envelope back and forth, so that the paper rustles rhythmically, sounding like a small machine. This noise grows louder as Dorsey tugs harder at the paper, ripping it slightly at the top. She stands up.

She goes downstairs, the letter still in her left hand, letting the cool bannister pass under the fingers of her right. Breathing quietly, she walks back to the rear study where Noah is playing with his Lego set, sent to him by his Uncle Hugh. Already he has built what seems to be the lower half of a motorized oil derrick.

Noah, she says, I'm going out for a quick walk. I'll be right back. You want to come?

No, Mom. I'll stay here.

Do you want a snack?

I got one already.

Daddy should be home anytime.

I know.

He has already started to turn away from her. It's a safe neighborhood, and he doesn't mind being alone for a few minutes. Dorsey puts on her coat and stands in the hallway, the letter still in her left hand. What to do with it? She swears heavily to herself, then drops the envelope into the ceramic bowl on top of the steam radiator. The bowl is the place for messages, for mail, for change and money for babysitters. She opens the front door, breathes in a gulp of Lake Erie air, and locks the door behind her.

She begins her walk by heading north on Parkside toward the zoo. She looks down at her hands, sees that they are clenched into fists, and relaxes them, putting them into her coat pockets. To her left is the fenced area for lawn bowling, the grass still brown and muddy from the spring thaws.

She crosses Parkside and enters the Delaware Park Zoo. From every corner wafts the smell of popcorn and animal dung and peanuts. It's a small zoo, the old-fashioned kind with animals—except for the lions—tightly caged; they either sleep or gaze glumly at the onlookers. Since it's a Wednesday afternoon in March, there aren't many people here, though Dorsey does see one couple, teenagers, soul kissing in front of the gorilla cage, as if to provoke the animal to some kind of violence. But the sidewalk is gray, the sky is gray, and most of the people are dressed in Great Lakes Industrial grays and browns, and the gorilla doesn't budge.

Where are the lions? Dorsey wants to stand in front of a lion, though she's not sure what she'll do once she finds one. She knows the zoo well enough to make her way to the seal pool, but she has to check the directions posted on the side of a peanut stand to find out where the big cats are located. A bag lady in a long, oversized parka glances at Dorsey and then goes on surveying the ground for peanuts still in their shells. She finds one near a sidewalk puddle underneath an overflowing drinking fountain; she breaks the nut open, eats it, and looks directly at Dorsey: *I'm eating. What are you doing?*

The lion cage is one of the larger displays, half indoors and half out, built with an incline to suggest an African slope, on whose lumps are positioned some rocks and some upright branching sticks to suggest trees. A deep uncrossable man-made gorge separates the lions from the spectators, of whom there are three: Dorsey, and two police officers who are strolling in the general direction of the giraffe. With her hands down on the barrier, Dorsey gazes across the gulf toward the one lion she can see, a female. The animal is awake but apparently immobilized, gazing at something just to Dorsey's right. Dorsey turns, sees nothing there, and turns back toward the lion. The animal is resting, down on its stomach like the Sphinx, its front paws out in front of it, its head held up, the eyes alert. The yellow-gold fur, for all the animal's captivity, is textured with ridged muscle underneath. Now the animal turns its head to the right, as if it heard something from that direction. No. Nothing there. It turns its head back, again looking at some object, visible or invisible, just beyond Dorsey. It has not glanced at Dorsey; it does not seem to see her. All its head movements are slow.

"*Arrgh,*" Dorsey says softly.

The lion has perhaps not heard. Dorsey repeats the sound, more loudly, not yet a shout. It's not conversational level, this cry, and is not meant for other people. It is meant for the lion. But the lion still has not heard, or if it has, it shows no sign. Dorsey spins around to see how many people will hear her. There is the sound of traffic, of an elephant halfheartedly trumpeting. No one is nearby except for the bag lady, muttering to herself.

Dorsey opens her mouth involuntarily. This time she shouts without knowing. She discovers herself making noises, loud quavering vowels, which echo off the back of the pseudo-African scene, and this time the lion notices. Unhurried, it turns its head so that its gaze is fixed on Dorsey. With the lion looking at her, Dorsey is jammed into her own quiet. The animal's gaze, now that Dorsey can see it directly, is not empty and blank; it is watchful and intelligent, but pitiless: the face of a well-traveled old woman. The lion does not seem surprised that Dorsey would shout, but it is not that interested, either. After a few seconds, it turns its massive head and powerful thoughtless eyes so that it is once again gazing at whatever is just above the horizon to Dorsey's right. Dorsey turns to look. She follows the lion's eyes to a poplar tree planted in the middle of the zoo's walkway. A squirrel perches in the bare branches. It chitters, climbing down one branch and then up another, all its motions rushed and jerky, squirrel-manic. Dorsey looks one last time at the lion, who in turn still watches the squirrel with a calm predatory gaze. And now the lion yawns, exposing its huge instrumental teeth and pink cavernous mouth. Dorsey turns away and heads home.

After Dorsey lets herself in through the side door, she sees across the width of the house Simon sitting on the floor near Noah. They are working together on the oil derrick. Simon is stringing the threads over the hanging pulley. Pulleys? Threads? Perhaps the oil derrick has turned into a crane. She walks into the room and watches them working quietly together, Simon pointing and signing, Noah signing in response. Simon's great talent for physical expression helps him in these situations. He and Noah can work together on a project faster and more efficiently than Dorsey and Noah can. Dorsey is always trying to explain things in detail, while Simon finds the quick, expressive, inclusive gesture.

"You're back," Simon says, not glancing up. Noah looks briefly at his mother, to smile.

"So are you."

"Ten minutes ago." He attaches a square red piece to a triangular blue piece underneath a small crank near the crane's pivot point. "I saw Carlo's letter. That is, I *read* Carlo's letter. I snooped. It was a very disagreeable experience. I wish that man would trade up to a better class of clichés. Where did you go?"

"I walked over to the zoo," Dorsey says. "I spent a minute or two shouting at the lion."

Simon turns, a great smile on his face. "Shouting at the lion! Well, God bless you and keep you, sweetheart. What a great idea. Next week I'll do that. I wouldn't mind if the lion shouted back. By the way, I've started dinner."

"You have? What is it?"

"It's sort of a spaghetti sauce, with subtle ambitions. It's bubbling away there on the burner. I'll start the pasta in a minute."

"All right. Fine."

"Your friend Carlo," Simon says, still assembling parts for the crane, "is becoming avuncular in a new and, I think, deeply unattractive manner. Is there anything more tiresome than a man who is faking the wisdom thing? What wisdom? I hate wisdom anyway. Wisdom is always a drag. Of course, he's a genius, we all know he's a genius, we've been told that often enough: *Carlo is a genius.* Lucky for him, but not for you."

Dorsey sits on the floor. "I wish I knew why he was doing it. Why can't he just leave me alone?"

"He's old and crabby and arthritic and it gives him pleasure to make you miserable. And of course he still loves you, in his crabby and miserable way. And you . . . you still listen, when he talks."

Noah stops, looks at Dorsey, and asks, What are you two talking about?

Someone. A teacher I once had.

"I got an offer last week," Simon announces. "I forgot to tell you.

That director in Minneapolis has offered me a part in a Joe Orton play that this group near the university is putting on. They'll actually pay me Equity and they also want some help in the direction. This is for four weeks. We could load the car and spend July and August up there, and he says there are other jobs . . . who knows, even the Guthrie . . ."

"We could visit Hugh on the way," Dorsey says.

"Yes," Simon says, and the moment passes. "But back to Carlo. You aren't going to let his affection get you down, are you? Fuck Mr. Wizard. He's just a notorious old man with brains enough for three normal people, and you don't have to pay attention to his attentions."

"I don't," Dorsey says. Simon smiles at her denial. "All right. I pay attention. He's still on my scorecard, and I admit it."

"Listen," Simon tells her. "These generalissimos of intellect have shriveled hearts, I'm here to tell you. Love confuses them. He's envious. He'll eat his words with a fork and spoon. You'll see." Simon puts his hand gently on Dorsey's back. "How do you feel, kiddo?"

"Like a piece of chewed string."

"I have the cure," Simon tells her. "But you have to wait."

"How was your afternoon?" she asks him.

Simon sighs, eyes raised in mock-exasperation. "Rehearsals, naturally. I keep telling them, quietly of course, my best *sotto voce,* that if you're going to do Tennessee Williams the point is to do the bad taste with delicate exuberance, just the right frequency of leering, of creeping things coming out of closets. I mean, I've played *Cat on a Hot Tin Roof* before, but never with a director who thinks it's drawing-room comedy and who instructs us in enunciation and elocution. This stuff *ain't* genteel. So I've been overplaying a bit. You know, to compensate. A touch of show biz."

"Good."

"For the rehearsal breaks, they serve herb tea." Simon attaches a crane claw to the end of Noah's pulley string. "Herb tea, my God. Talk about narcissistic gentility. I've been asking everyone what herb it is but no one will tell me. It's probably deadly nightshade. I'm worried about my hair falling out in tangled clumps. This tea

smells like mosquito repellent. Soon I'll only be able to play but-
lers."

Dorsey smiles, in spite of herself. Simon leans back, triumphant.

Am I your fool? he signs.

Dorsey grabs Simon behind the neck and pulls his head over to
her. Then she lets him go. You're just shanty Irish, she tells him.

Am I your chattering magpie? Simon asks.

Yes.

Do you love me?

You're such a sentimentalist.

Do you?

I won't tell.

Come on. Cleanse your soul. Don't hold it all in.

No. I don't love you.

You lie.

All right. It's true. I lied.

I knew it, he signs.

Noah, ignoring them, switches on the crane, and as the three of
them watch, the toy machine lowers its hopper, picks up a ballpoint
pen from the floor, swivels over, and drops it into Dorsey's lap.

At the dinner table the conversation is all in sign. Between forkfuls
of Simon's fettucini, Noah tells his parents about this girl who sits
in front of him in class, and how when she blows her nose, she wipes
her nose, and the gunk, on her sleeve. Noah pantomimes this action,
which pleases Simon so much that he shows his teeth. She doesn't
think I see her do it, Noah tells them, but I do. He makes another
face. What's her name? Dorsey asks. Patty. Patty what? Patty Yzem-
berg, he spells out. Both Simon and Dorsey watch his fingers,
thinking that he's misspelled it, but unsure.

She's so . . . and he makes a vulgar, tasteless gesture in American
Sign Language.

Noah! Dorsey signs. You should be ashamed of yourself. But
Simon, of course, is laughing and applauding.

There is an evening rehearsal, and when Simon comes back from
it after midnight, smelling of sweat and herb tea, Dorsey is curled

in bed. Simon walks into Noah's room to check on him and then returns to the bedroom, where he undresses in the dark, humming "Stop in the Name of Love," as he takes off his maroon nylon bikini briefs and his white socks and running shoes. He snuggles in next to Dorsey and sees that her eyes are wide open, fixed on the ceiling. He puts his hand on her cheek and says, "Playing night watchman again?" and she nods. He reaches under her nightgown and places his hand on her hip. She shakes her head no, she does not want to make the slow theatrical love that Simon favors, not tonight. All the same, she puts one arm around him, and they lie there quietly, with only the sound of cars going by every few seconds. She kisses him, a kiss without desire but full of affection, a kiss he returns.

She pulls back and returns her head to the pillow. "Simon," she whispers, "I can't sleep."

"Of course you can't," he whispers. "That's your métier."

"No, I mean I can't sleep *tonight.*"

"You've been thinking about Mr. Wizard."

"Yes. Simon, damn it, can't you be serious?"

"No. I'm much too weird."

"I know it." She waits. There is a faint, odd sound in the distance, which may be an elephant trumpeting in the zoo. "Yes, I have been thinking about him. *You* know what it means when you can't stop thinking about somebody."

"Think about something else."

"Like what?"

"We'll do a category game. Down the alphabet, as usual."

"What's the category?"

Simon is quiet, thinking. "Railroads," he says at last.

"I don't know any railroads."

"Of course you do. Everyone knows railroads. Search your mind. It'll put you to sleep. A."

"Amtrak."

"Amtrak is *not* a railroad. It is a wholly-owned government-operated passenger service. Give me a company that owns *track.*"

"Atlantic Coast Line."

"That's better. See? You do know a few things. B."

"Boston and Maine," Dorsey says.

"C."

"Chesapeake and Ohio."

"Pretty good. D."

"I don't know any D railroads."

"Think. Think of a city."

"Denver and Something," she says, after a minute.

"Denver and Western," Simon tells her. "E."

"Erie Lackawanna. That's easy."

"F."

"Frisco Line," she says sleepily.

"G." He waits for two minutes. "G," he whispers. She is breathing lightly, her eyes closed at last.

5

In her upstairs desk drawer she
keeps four photographs and a collection of postcards whose messages
she reads when she is stuck in her own work and needs a distraction.
The postcards are all from Simon and were mailed one or two
blocks away from where she is sitting now. They are expressions of
his fantasies of being somewhere else. The Empire State Building:
"Dear Dorsey, I thought of you as the wind roughed up my hair
here on the observation deck, 102 floors above sea level. Love,
Simon." The Eiffel Tower: "Darling Dorsey, I am sipping an unpre-
tentious burgundy as I write to you here where I am sitting on the
Left Bank. Love, Simon." The Grand Canyon: "Dear Dorsey, Sitting on my burro, I think of you. Kisses."

Throughout the winter, when she isn't teaching at the university
or taking Noah to school or watching Simon come and go, Dorsey
sits up here, tapping the computer's keyboard or scribbling out
equations on her yellow pad. On the wall is a picture of Maria
Mitchell, an astronomer who worked on sun spots in the nineteenth
century and who was the first woman admitted into the American
Academy of Arts and Sciences. Next to this photograph are three

lines of Whitman's poetry, written out in calligraphic ink and framed by Simon.

Darest thou now O soul
Walk out with me toward the unknown region
Where neither ground is for the feet nor any path to follow?

She doesn't really like the lines, but a gift is a gift.

Copies of *Nature*, *The Astrophysical Journal*, *Scientific American*, *Astrophysical Letters*, and other journals are scattered on her desk and the floor and the empty chair on the other side of the desk. She scans the table of contents of a current issue: steady hydromagnetic flows in open magnetic fields . . . relativistic beaming and quasar emission lines . . . gravitational collapse and the cosmic antineutrino background. . . .

She has been collaborating on a theory of missing mass with her colleague, Leo Henderson, a brilliant man and something of a sociopath in his private life. She likes to collaborate with him at a distance, over the phone or through the mails, even though he lives only two miles away. A pudgy man who reads science fiction and watches "Star Trek," and whose face has an odd warped geometry to it, Leo has only one true avocation: making up stories about the private lives of his professional colleagues. He is a fictionalist, a hobbyist of lies. Dorsey thinks she can get a year's worth of useful collaboration with Leo before he insists on betrayal and begins to make up stories about her. She looks down at her pad of paper and starts to work.

The equations she has been writing are complicated, inefficient, and discordant. Aesthetically, they are unattractive and therefore incorrect. And yet she sees in these equations something latent and beautiful that desires to be expressed more simply than she has found a means to express it. The truth wants to emerge in all its beautiful simplicity, without these complications cluttering everything up. As she works, covering page after page with speculations in mathematical form (with occasional notes in the margin, such as "No!" or "Can't be right"), she feels as if she has an itch that she can't quite scratch. At such times she leans back and stares at the picture of Maria Mitchell. Problems in physics always have, for her, a specific mood, a psychological feel. This one feels like a wall she can't climb over or burrow under or go through.

She looks over at the old black-and-white television set in the room's northeast corner. Whenever she is working upstairs, she keeps it switched on but tuned to the vacant channel, with the sound muted. The screen shows a line of static, the random visuals of the atmosphere and of the cosmic radiation background.

She breathes in and closes her eyes. She runs the expansion of space backwards, crunching it, so that space heats up and approaches the point at which it once began—or began again. She runs through the theories like a pack of flash cards: broken symmetry, the Higgs field, inflation, gauge particles, supersymmetric grand unified theories, magnetic monopoles, folded dimensions, string theories. She'd like to make a movie of it, though there are few visual representations for any of it; even so, some of the theories have a singular kind of beauty, those that she can understand. She tries to keep up, but she doesn't understand all the developments in her field; she keeps this fact to herself. She looks down again at her own work, and as she stares at the symbols and numbers and brackets and signs, the lines themselves, shadow figures for the forces loose in the universe, begin to waver and dance like puppets suddenly pulled upright on strings. She shakes her head and rubs her eyes, and the lines settle down once more. But whenever she is tired, the same process occurs: the equations she has written out, stared at for too long, begin to move and to shudder.

She even has a name for it: differential nausea.

Why is the universe isotropic? If the universe ends its expansion and collapses back into a final spacetime singularity, what happens to the laws of physics? In a singularity, these laws are obliterated. The idea of naked singularity, of all matter and spacetime compressed to a point, nauseates her. At least with dust and ashes you have dust and ashes, blown somewhere to reactivate the soil. With singularities there is not anything, anywhere, left to note that a universe once existed.

She shouldn't think about these things. She should work on more practical problems. Leo Henderson calls it "Your unfortunate tendency to speculate." He should talk. She will never be invited to conferences where Minkowski space and cosmological constants are discussed; she will never be able to get up and say what she thinks about these theories: that they are vertiginous, wondrous, terrible.

$$d\,s^2 = x^2(d\tilde{\iota}/4M)^2 + (r/2M)^4\,d\,x^2 + r^2\,d\Omega^2$$

What's being discovered in cosmology is in equal parts exhilarating and disturbing: at last the physicists, too, are staring into theoretical abysses of their own making, cosmic vacuum cleaners obliterating time and history.

She's asked some of her colleagues whether they've ever stared at equations for so long that they started to move, right there on the paper; and of course they've said, "No, never." That's what Leo says. Though he's a sociopath, he's practical, often sensible, and goal-oriented. A good cook. Professor Planetarium. The man can repair anything mechanical and makes the best *osso buco* she's ever tasted. Like many physicists he projects a sense of well-being, of generosity and happiness. After the likes of Carlo Pavorese, Dorsey would like to have men around her with the souls of garage mechanics.

It is now early December. Heavy snow is piled on the branches outside her window. But in Dorsey's mind—she is leaning back, her eyes are closed—the universe has returned to the first tenth of a nanosecond. The weak interaction force and the electromagnetic force are still in a state of symmetry. She opens her eyes, looks at the calculations she has made on her own set of problems, and goes to work. But in the midst of this problem, she is also a mind of subatomic particles loose among what there is of space, curved, and expanding or contracting, it doesn't matter. At such times Dorsey does not feel like herself: she is an electromagnetic conglomerate of atoms that have combined to figure out where they have been and what has happened in the universe to bring them to this point. I am, Dorsey thinks, formed from the ashes of long dead stars, and I want to know what I was.

She looks up. The television is on, as usual, to Channel 10, a blank station, a field of static, cosmic background. Outside the snow is falling in heavy fat flakes, a thickening texture like a snow dome paperweight that someone has shaken hard or dropped. The snow gives her the unpleasant sensation of being here and not being here simultaneously. She has been working for over two hours. To calm herself, she opens the drawer and pulls out her four favorite photographs.

One, two, three, four: she sets them on the desk. They are tender from much handling, from being packed in purses and wallets and suitcases.

One: this is a picture of William and Katharine Welch, her parents, now both dead. It's in black and white, a snapshot, but taken in over-the-shoulder sunlight so that the definitions are jagged and sharp, and in it her mother and father stand outside the house in Five Oaks in worn-out late summer, her mother leaning toward her father. She smiles, generating light rather than reflecting it, and he smiles too, less brilliantly. She wears a light cotton dress, and her dark hair is parted in the middle. Her right hand touches her husband's elbow in affection or support. William Welch holds a glass of something—Dorsey has always thought it was a gin and tonic—and on his face is a worldly, calm smile. Though the mouth smiles, the eyes hold something back, some final commitment to happiness. Her father's face in this picture reminds Dorsey of faces in nineteenth-century paintings. Her father's eyes have a quality of intelligent melancholy that seems to have vanished from American faces.

Two: a snapshot of Dorsey's mother, sitting on a cane chair at the front of the porch. She is glancing up from her book to the camera lens. The season is summer. Her dress is dark, not quite appropriate for the season. On her face is not so much a smile as the visible evidence of happiness: the thought of a smile, not meant for others, just there. Her expression blesses life. It forgives everything. Dorsey would give her life's savings to know the title of the book in her mother's lap, but no one she has asked has ever known what it was.

Three: her brother, Hugh. Dorsey has many pictures of Hugh and Laurie and their two girls, but this is the photograph of her brother she likes to return to. In it, Hugh is eighteen and has just graduated from high school. Captain of the hockey team that year, he was at his moment of greatest physical grace. In this picture Hugh stands in the driveway next to his car, which he has been sponging with

Ivory flakes dissolved in warm water. He looks like a minor deity who rules over drive-ins, beaches, and lovers' lanes. The car is a red Chevrolet Nova and is called "Hugh's Bad News," with the vowel in "bad" stretched to last a second. He is wearing cut-offs and a sleeveless jock-in-his-glory T-shirt. Though the photograph ends at Hugh's knees, Dorsey knows that her brother was barefoot, because she took the picture and remembers how he tried to stomp on her tennis shoes. Hugh's hair, blond from lifeguarding, flies every which way across his head. He's grinning at the lens with his happy-animal smile. Dorsey remembers exactly what she thought the day she took this picture: she thought her brother that summer was the most beautiful man she'd ever seen.

Four: Simon and Noah, taken last fall. They're squatting outside next to each other near the Delaware Park playground swings. Simon has stuck two fingers for devil's horns above Noah's head, and Noah has done the same for Simon. This juvenile trick is one that Simon had taught Noah just a moment before the shutter snapped. The boy's face is giggly; behind the camera, Dorsey was getting cross and sternly telling them not to do that. But Simon likes to spoil moments of solemnity with gestural pranks, razzing insults to the serious world, and so here they are: Simon, with his merry prankster look, and Noah, almost dizzy with the high, light mood, his mouth open in a soundless laugh. Of the four pictures this one may be Dorsey's favorite. Simon is teaching Noah how to resist seriousness. He is teaching the boy to fool around. With Simon in the vicinity, a kid doesn't mind being deaf. All he thinks he's missing is the sound of grown-ups yelling at him. What luck.

Dorsey handles the photographs gently, looking at them one after the other, before putting them back into the drawer. She stares out the window, her mind clamped on nothing. She returns to the paper in front of her and works intently, gradually losing track of the time. When she looks up again, snow is cascading down from the skies into the poplar outside her window. She sees a sparrow whiffling the snow off its wings. Every few moments the snow seems to stop. Then it gathers energy again and cuts the visibility down to nothing. She puts her pencil down. Mathematically she has been running into the wall, but today the wall is tender. Today the wall loves her. It says, "It's your job to solve this problem. Okay. Well, it's my job to make sure you don't. That's how it is."

When the phone rings, Dorsey remembers that she never bothered to unplug it. It demands to be answered. It may be the school calling, telling her to bring Noah home. No, it's not that: the school is only a few blocks away, and Noah can walk home, even through snow, perfectly well by himself. Maybe it's Simon, stuck somewhere.

"Hello," the voice says. "Dorsey O'Rourke?"

"Oh, my God," she says. "Carlo. Are you in town?"

"Downtown, at a hotel," Carlo Pavorese says, his voice calm and authoritative. "My plane from New York to Chicago was forced down here. The weather."

"No, it wasn't," Dorsey says. "No one's plane was forced down. You planned this."

"Ha ha. I could never fool you, could I?" When Dorsey does not answer this question, he continues. "It seemed a good opportunity to call you. I'll be here all evening."

Damn his pauses, she thinks, his implications. "It's snowing, Carlo. The roads are slippery. They've issued traveler's advisories. And besides, I'm working on something here."

"All right. I'm sure I could get a cab to your place. How about a casual visit?"

"That's unthinkable," she says. "You can't come here. Don't even *think* about coming here. We can't make casual visits to each other —you aren't casual, and neither am I."

Now there is another chess-game pause, and Dorsey can hear the television set in his hotel room, the fitful cries of a studio audience. "Dorsey," Carlo says, "I'm an old man in a hotel. Come get me."

"No. I can't do that."

"You don't have to shout."

"I'm not shouting."

"I'm holding the telephone away from my ear. Maybe you have a volume control." He waits. "Considering the past," he says, "*our* past, I would think the least you could do is drive down here to this hotel and say hello to me. Step into the lobby and shake my aging hand. It's not much."

"Carlo, any meeting is too much."

"Why?"

"You don't know?"

"No. How should I know?" She can imagine him tenderly cradling the phone on his shoulder and holding his two arms out in a classic Old World shrug.

"It's not love anymore," she says. "It's explanations. And I don't feel like explaining."

"Don't be silly. You don't have to explain anything to me."

"I always had to explain," she says. "We were a couple of explainers. You explained physics to me and I explained people to you. You don't notice people. You live in a post-people universe."

"I notice. Oh, yes, I notice. I noticed *you,* didn't I?"

"Yes," she says. "You noticed me." She is rubbing her left cheek with the palm of her hand. "And I noticed you."

"Please come here," he says. "I'm asking for the last time. I will not beg. I may be old, but by God I am not pathetic."

"No, for the last time, I can't."

They wait.

"Isn't the snow remarkable as it falls?" he says at last. "What I love most about it are the patterns of swirls, the visible vectors." His breathing is audible. "I'm not oblivious to beauty, you know. Not at all oblivious."

"Yes, it is beautiful."

"They have big windows here, in this hotel. It's all windows, this place. It's a glass palace. A transparent box. Windows and visible heating ducts. Just like the Pompidou Center. In Paris," he adds.

"I know where it is."

"Do you know," he asks, "what Dante writes about people who will not come to help? Do you know where he puts them in the *Commedia?*"

"No, but I'm sure *you* do. Carlo, listen to me. We can't talk. We can't talk any more. From now on, if you want to have . . . contact with me, write. Write in that lovely tiny handwriting of yours. Just don't call me again. Please please please. I can't see you and I don't want you asking about my work. All right?"

"Là giù trovammo una genta dipinta," Carlo says, *"che giva—"*

"Oh, no. Carlo, stop it."

"—che giva intorno assai con lenti passi, piangendo—"

"Carlo, stop that! Stop it!"

"*—piangendo e nel sembiante stanca e vinta. Elli—*"

She puts the telephone receiver down gently into the cradle, hearing the voice recede.

The shredded seconds tick for one endless flattened minute. Dorsey feels her concentration drain away, Pavorized, its place taken by the dry breath of Carlo's voice in her ear, quoting from Dante, talking about power, sin and equations, appointments, the minds of women, guilt, the origins and intentions of the universe. It's an uncle's voice but it speaks with the harrying persistence of a lover equipped with desire's inexhaustible nag. There he sits, the great man, downtown in a hotel.

Dorsey tries the window, where outside the snow is accumulating in a little mound on the sill; but the window frame seems to be stuck, frozen shut. The strength has left her arms. So she stands there, looking out, and curses Carlo Pavorese with creativity and fervor: a woman's curse, against his mindless overbearing power, his childish demands, his wooden inflexible selfishness, his inhuman isolation, his exalted interior life, his dogged and selfish affections.

Downstairs at the kitchen table she eats a Granny Smith apple, and as she leans over the table, propping herself on her elbows, she looks out the window and watches the snow tap against the glass and pile up in a thin and perfectly smooth sine curve on the wood frame. The sine curve makes her think of audiology tests, the flattened line on the screen of the oscilloscope. Noah's line. After throwing the apple core in the trash, she stands up and crosses her arms on her chest and massages her own shoulders. Winter is the quietest season, she thinks, with its silent winds and muffled storms.

She stands alone in the dark kitchen until it is time to get Noah.

Poles held in her gloved hands, boots clamped to her skis, Dorsey makes her way up the sidewalk toward the Pendrick School for the Deaf on Main Street. She passes a businessman in a Burberry overcoat, carrying a briefcase and heading the other way. He is gloveless, bootless. He sinks into snow up to his knees, his polished and now very snowy black wingtips already ruined. The man is balding, and the snow makes a church-pageant halo in his thinning hair. He glances at Dorsey, grunts, then continues on, stumbling, off-balance, toward the park. For Dorsey this man, in the wake of her call from Carlo, is an image for all serious men, throwing their willfulness against nature, their little-boy egomania disguised as dignity. Oliver Hardys, all of them. She looks back at him. He has just recovered from a near-fall. He makes her think of Robert Falcon Scott, the explorer, staggering toward the South Pole, only his Victorian sensibility shielding him from his reckless bad planning until the bad planning and bad luck finally caught up with him. She has read, with awe, Scott's journals. He wrote fine prose in his tent as he was freezing to death. These serious men, with their world-historical airs, want love, but they do not wish to be understood. But Simon: Simon she understands.

She reaches the corner and stops to take a breath. To her left is a greasy spoon, the Main Street Café. She looks inside the thickly misted windows at the smoky grease-blackened grill where a black chef dressed all in white is flipping hamburgers. He pulls a wire fryer out of the boiling fat and flips it over, dumping a pile of French fries into an aluminum mesh drainer. Out on the sidewalk, Dorsey sniffs the grease and the bread. Men in checkered flannel shirts and women in unzipped parkas are sitting at the booths near the window, where they sip coffee and pour ketchup over their food. They talk, gesturing with stubby fingers. This café is Dorsey's favorite restaurant in the world. It's warm and loud, and everyone here knows her as "the professor," and buys her coffee and doughnuts, pleased to have her here. One man, who has been dipping a cookie into his coffee, sees Dorsey standing there, and waves to her. She holds up her pole and waves back.

She skis toward the intersection and is about to cross Main Street when she looks north and sees a funeral procession making its way toward her, a beaded string of headlights approaching through the falling snow. From where she stands she can even see the little snow-weighted flags set with magnets onto the fenders of the cars. A miniature parade.

In front, the hearse—heavy with laminated wood and special coil and leaf springs—rolls past her silently and sure-treaded over the six or seven inches of accumulated snow on the pavement. Behind it, chaos. The cars of the mourners are sliding, fishtailing, bumping each other, fender-bending, their headlights pointing this way and now that. The second car in the cortège, a Ford Pinto, skids in front of her, inches away from the sidewalk, just missing another pedestrian, its rear wheels spinning over the glaze. Inside, two middle-aged passengers dressed up in colorless formality look straight ahead, sweaty with panic and grief. Behind the Pinto is an Oldsmobile with a bad muffler. It too is fishtailing, and inside two heavy men and one woman wearing a fur hat that looks like a sleeping muskrat are shouting instructions at the driver. And behind the Oldsmobile is a young man driving a sports car. The interior of the car is blue from cigarette or marijuana smoke; despite the car's performance capacities, it too is out of control, going down the street sideways. There are five more cars behind this one, a chain-link pageant of spoiled dignity. It's a clown parade, Dorsey thinks, just like the circus, except here the living are doing their best to follow in make-believe seriousness the imperturbable dead, and all of it—the dignity and, yes, the death—somehow makes her think of Carlo Pavorese, sitting in the glass hotel.

She skis back and forth across the long front yard of the school until a few of the children begin racing out, after a bell has rung. A bell! Appearances must be kept up. Meeting the air, the children hold their mouths open to catch the snow on their tongues. After a minute Noah bursts through the front doors with his friend Eddie Sachs. They're pounding each other, then making quick signs. When they see the snow, they hold their faces up to the sky, stilled for three seconds. Then they bend down, grab fistfuls of snow, and throw the powder into each other's faces. Noah is more accurate, and soon Eddie's face has a thin white outer layer, snow skin.

After Noah has found Dorsey, and Eddie has gotten on his bus, Dorsey and Noah cross Main Street together and head down to the house. Noah tugs at Dorsey's sleeve to complain.

You didn't bring my skis. It's not fair.

I didn't think I could carry them. Too big.

You have those—he points at her skis—but all I have are these old boots.

Dorsey pantomimes a crying fit for his benefit, then continues on ahead of him. One block down he catches up to her and stops her.

How about if I stood on your skis? he asks.

What? I don't get it.

Easy, he says, brushing the back of his left open hand with the fingers of his other hand with long strokes. I just get on here.

He steps in front of her so that he's facing her, and he puts his boots on top of the skis just forward of the bindings. He leans toward her and holds his mother by grabbing the pockets on both sides of her jacket. The top of his head comes up to her waist.

He looks up at her and nods.

You'll be too heavy, she says.

No, I won't.

She begins to walk with her son on her skis. He's right: it's not too hard. The skis are strong, the snow is powdery, and they're going down a slight incline. When they reach the house, Noah leans back to free his hands.

Let's do this some more.

Only for a few minutes, she says.

They head down the street toward the park, Dorsey looking forward, her son still hanging on. In someone's yard there are four snowmen sitting at a card table, playing poker. Each snowman is holding a hand; the one with his back to the street has a pair of jacks, the one to the right side has a full house. Dorsey and Noah cross into the park and for a moment Dorsey looks behind her, and she thinks she sees a yellow cab. The visibility is poor; it might be a yellow anything. But if it is a yellow cab, it may contain Carlo Pavorese smouldering inside it, wound up tightly in his black cashmere coat and his cocoon of prideful importance. She looks at the pine trees, at the snow, and her son clinging to her, and all at once she knows that the past is over. Gravity lifts, releasing her. How has this happened? She looks around. No idea, no accusation, and no love—not even that—has the power to hurt her.

There is a blessing in this snowstorm and she is standing in the middle of it. She stops, bends down, and kisses Noah on the forehead. He crinkles his eyebrows together, meaning: what's going on?

She shrugs.

She skis away from the pines. Even with her son weighing down her skis, she cannot escape the sensation of freedom, though the contents of this freedom are unknown to her. Then all at once, she looks down at her son.

She sees an image of one figure moving forward while, in close proximity to it, a second figure, facing the first, moves backwards in directly parallel movement, though both figures, because they share the same base, are moving in the same direction. She shouts. The shout is muffled by the snow. There is something in this image that applies to her work, though she doesn't know yet how to make the calculations, or when they might ever apply. She stops, leans her head back, and feels the snowflakes dropping on her eyelids.

Noah gets off her skis and lies down on the snow, moving his arms and legs back and forth in wide angel arcs. All over the city, Dorsey thinks, children are making snow angels, and tomorrow, or the next day, when the sun is bound to come out, there will still be this visual evidence of wings and of the gravity that brought them down.

6

Upstairs, at night, Simon never repeats himself. His techniques are imperative and unpredictable, a mixture of eros and theater. He dislikes the enforcements of married lovemaking and says you can't play that script the same way every night unless you're bound to the bush leagues, to the call-and-answer of tedium. So for the several years she has known him he has insisted on music, cologne, costumes, role playing, and words. Dorsey plays along. Simon doesn't expect her to be as inventive as he is. She's an amateur, devoted to the reality principle. His devotions are to illusion and frailty, the armatures, he says, of sex.

In a bad mood, he has criticized her in a loud relentless voice for wearing stockings with a hole in one of the heels. Once when her hair was cut and layered in a way he didn't like—he called it an Eleanor Roosevelt perm—he wouldn't speak to her for three days. He believes being a woman is a job of acting, that it is an act, and in drugstores he examines glamour magazines and suggests some tricks Dorsey might try to brighten her eyes. He is an expert in all matters of makeup and disguise. Careful about lighting, he believes in candles for intimacy. He believes that every mood should be enhanced.

He has carried her in his arms into the bedroom many times. He has undressed her, button by button and hook by hook, and then served her champagne in a fluted glass. He has brought her caviar on crackers. Late at night, after Noah is asleep, he has taught her to dance: his favorite is a slow waltz, his nakedness against hers, as he hums Johann Strauss the younger. He has been teaching her other steps, slow and quiet erotic tangos and two-steps. He likes endearments. His favorite is "Darling." "Oh, darling Dorsey," he says, cutting the romanticism with slyness as he undresses her, peeling off her clothes with cool implacable delicacy. He has kept her up many times through the night with kisses and coupling and champagne and dancing. He seems incapable of tiring of it, preferring the permutations of lovemaking to the banality of sleep. Sleep, he says, is a drag. Her work has occasionally suffered from his insatiability. Papers have gone uncorrected.

He likes love in showers and bathtubs, on rugs in front of electric heaters, on tables, in settees and chairs, and standing up. They have made love in a loveseat. He has taught her how to make love while dancing, the feet hardly moving, his hips swaying against hers. They have made love in front of windows, looking out at the unnatural black of the Buffalo night, and on the dining room table, which creaked and groaned. He has initiated these scenes with his hey-guess-what look and his eager hands. He has whispered the names of constellations to her while her head swung back in her orgasm and she pushed her pelvic bone forward.

"Arcturus," he says. "Orion."

He has asked her to let her fingernails grow, so that she can touch him on the backs of his thighs and his ribcage. "I can't," she says. "I work at a blackboard." He says it doesn't matter. He watches her hands in their gestures and brings them to his lips and teeth.

In these encounters he has played Brick and the Gentleman Caller and Stanley Kowalski and Superman and Estragon and Lord Byron and Prince Hal and Casanova and Jay Gatsby and Don Giovanni and Tarzan and Peg Leg Pete and Peer Gynt and Pinocchio. He has invented accents and gestures for the various international styles. He admits playing these characters in the bedrooms of his other lovers. Of love, he says, there's no getting enough.

Dorsey, worn down at times by these charades, has asked him for something straight, unimaginative, with the clothes off and the bodies meeting each other simply, between the sheets. Something quick and sweaty and all-American. He would like to, but he cannot. That is, he is incapable. Without the pretending, he is bored and impotent, prudishly offended by the predictabilities. "We're going into training here," he says. "I'm teaching you how to act." Look, he says: desire is a spell. You rouse it. You wake it. Watch this.

Desire brings itself to bed with talk. Unless he is kissing Dorsey, he keeps up a ceaseless whispering murmur, a concoction of praise for her body and mind and spirit. He makes offers and demands. She is free to gratify or refuse. Refusals, if they are delivered in a certain tone, are as much fun as agreements. They inspire erotic pleading, poetry, deals, and bribes. At times she initiates the play, though she has no talent for roles and usually cannot think them up. Simon can be tiring; he keeps her guessing. In his determination to play variations on the simple one-fingered tune of sex, he dreads repetition, enacting the same role twice. Simon dreads boredom. Desire dies in boredom, in the fateful repetitions of himself in her.

"What's more exciting than my tongue on the loose?" he has asked. And the proof is that there is not a part of her exposed skin that he has not touched with his tongue. He has brought her dinner on a tray in bed and challenged her to eat it while he stroked and kissed her available skin. She made it as far as the crab martiniquais and the steamed rice but could not progress to the broccoli in béarnaise sauce or the poached plums. She daintily removed the tray from the bed, putting it on the floor. Then she gave herself to Simon, wrapping her legs around him hard, urging him in.

There will be no children from this. Because of what happened with Noah, she has had her tubes tied, and that is that.

She goes along with Simon because he takes care and does not insist on anything if she says "No" twice. Sometimes she will not and cannot play the other part in the duet. But she believes in Simon's tenderness, and believes, as he has claimed, that bored love leads to casual cruelty, to lengthening shadows on the soul. She believes that love can make the spirit rise and walk. She believes that it is a fact, violating no laws of physics, that her soul has risen and intertwined with his at the moment that they have come together.

For all his failings, he has become her other half, their improbably twined selves as solidly linked as two knotted ropes, or Plato's first unitary soul. Interested in love, she has reread Plato's *Symposium,* where love is described as finding an abode in the softest things there are, settled in the tempers and souls of gods and men. Wherever he meets a soul hard in temper, Plato says, the god of love departs, but where it is soft, he abides.

"If I were always true and faithful," Simon says, sitting behind her on the bed, his legs over hers, one hand rubbing her back and the other cupping one of her breasts, "I'd be someone else."

Simon's infidelities have been Simon's life. Because of them, she has shouted and delivered ultimatums and threats. She could not once stand to imagine his body—a beautiful one, she thinks, from all the grooming and tending he gives it—encircled by someone else's flesh, sucked by another mouth. One time, and one time only, she picked up a urinary infection from him, which led to more hard words, absences, and promises of precautionary measures. Simon has openly claimed his obvious inability to accept the terms of ordinary life. "I subvert," he says. "I burn all the contracts." To have Simon means having most of Simon; the rest he gives away.

"It's my only gift," he says, running his fingers through her hair, caressing her scalp with the tips. "The bedroom and the stage. The only two places where I thrive. That's it. You know I love you. But I need to prowl around sometimes."

Simon's erotic adventures, she has finally decided, are spontaneous and undeceitful. They are occasioned by his promiscuous tenderness, and he can't help himself any more than Santa Claus can. Because she has no doubts about his love for her and for Noah, and because she cannot imagine any man being better with Noah than Simon is, she gets up in the morning, looks in the mirror, sees herself, and nods. The light of her self-respect has stayed on; she is not ashamed of herself for remaining in Simon's company.

·   ·   ·

In other ways he is a child, an adult-impersonator. He is at his worst with home repair. Their landlord, an octogenarian housepainter, lives in Brockport and is slow to fix anything himself. Get it done and I'll pay for it, he says. As a result, ever since they moved to Buffalo, Simon has had the idea that he could become a handyman. Dorsey, who knows how things work and can, in fact, fix most things in the house, has come home to find Simon in the bathroom, trying to repair a faucet, washers and seals and stems and O-rings scattered around in a gritty wet mess on the tile floor, Noah building with his Legos in the hallway outside, keeping Simon company while Simon plays plumber.

Simon has done worse. He has pretended to be an electrician. With Dorsey out of the house, he has turned off the basement circuits and tried to replace a faulty overhead light fixture. When Dorsey came home and found him on his ladder, the *Reader's Digest Do-It-Yourself Manual* open to the section on wiring, she also saw that he had misconnected the leads and that he would blow a fuse as soon as he turned the power back on. She pushed and kicked him off the ladder and in five minutes rewired the fixture herself. He has promised not to fix anything else but she knows the handyman instinct in him is overpowering.

He has threatened to change the oil filter in the car; he has even offered to tune the engine. The last time he interfered with the car's motor, it had to be towed to a certified mechanic, who smiled shrewdly and wiped his hands in a predatory manner when the hapless car was pulled into his garage. Dorsey has warned Simon that if he ever lays his hands—those hands expert in love and nothing else—on the car's engine again, she will take a hammer to his fingers and reduce the bones to pebbles. This threat of violence amused him, but he has, nevertheless, raised no more hoods.

He has made a mess of the screens, hanging them backwards, and has built for Dorsey a bookcase that will not stand on its own. It must be supported on one side with a strong table and on the other side with a desk. The bookcase is decorative and holds only light-weight knicknacks, no books. Now, down in the basement, Simon is building a chair. Dorsey worries about the chair and wonders what will happen if Simon finishes this thing and anyone sits in it.

She especially worries about a lawsuit, the result of flying wood splinters and breakaway doweled joints. She has confidence, however, that the chair will not be completed. Simon's drawings for it make it look like an uncomfortable American primitive, but so far all he's been able to do is assemble a few parts of the frame. Pieces of hardboard, nails, tubes of resin glue, and plastic wood are arranged in no pattern in the basement.

The last time she went down there to check on his progress, she found him trying to teach Noah how to juggle three tangerines. The pieces of the proto-chair had been pushed off into the corner, and Simon was tossing the tangerines up rhythmically in small circles. Noah's mouth was open in wonder as he sat on the basement floor. Dorsey watched Simon, unobserved herself. The tangerines, which she had bought the previous day at the A&P and had planned to eat, went up, down, up, down, in Simon's smooth hands, and as she watched him she felt heat behind her eyes. Her heart skipped. She went back upstairs and sat down, wiping her face with her sleeves. By the time Simon and Noah came upstairs, she was reading the paper, a pleasant look on her face.

To whom can she talk about Simon? Most of the time she doesn't want to talk about him at all, and when she has the impulse to say anything, it is not to her brother, Hugh, who telephones every other week. She reports to him on her health and good fortune and good feelings; she thinks of him as her parole officer and has said so. These calls, and the letters that cross between them, have from her side one message: "I'm okay. Don't worry." She can't talk to her colleagues or her girlfriends about Simon. That leaves her neighbor, Mrs. Dlugoszewski.

Mrs. Dlugoszewski is only eight years older than Dorsey but looks fully committed to middle-age. Her skin is grayish-white from a lifetime of eating candy bars, and her head nods intermittently, a tic, which gives the impression that she agrees with herself and everyone else she talks to. Her husband, Ben, died of a prematurely bad heart the year before Simon and Dorsey came to Buffalo. No children, though there had been plans. Now Mrs. Dlugoszewski works part-time in the women's-wear department of Kleinhans', and when she sits in her living room, decorated with faded red wallpaper and pictures of Mary, Jesus, and Ben Dlugoszewski, she eyes Dorsey greedily. She cannot believe Dorsey's life. It is beyond imagination.

It is a Saturday morning. Simon has gone out, so Dorsey has decided to take a walk down the street with Noah. They have ended up at Mrs. Dlugoszewski's. Noah sits at Mrs. Dlugoszewski's player piano, watching the keys hammer themselves down, to no effect. The roll, with its bug-sized rectangular holes, unwinds before his smiling-puzzled face. Meanwhile, Mrs. Dlugoszewski and Dorsey sit in the kitchen, coffee and cookies out in front of them.

"Honey," Mrs. Dlugoszewski says, "what's that Simon of yours been up to?" She bites into a cookie, raises her eyebrows, and nods. "Don't tell me anything you don't want to tell me." She waits. "But of course it's good to get things off your chest. Don't forget that."

Dorsey nods. She looks at Mrs. Dlugoszewski's hair, fenced down this morning with a yellow scarf. She's been cleaning the oven. Below the scarf are the cold, blue eyes of a woman who has not been fooled by men, by their casual fictions and incessant self-promotion. Her face, with its high Slavic cheekbones, has a permanently skeptical expression, a secret-police look.

Dorsey shrugs, nibbling a cookie. The player piano continues its Chopin. "He's been getting home late. He rehearses."

"What play is this?" She has seen Simon once on stage in a Sam Shepard play; she left at the intermission.

"Something called *American Buffalo*. He's doing a Tennessee Williams play later this spring."

"*American Buffalo?* Not about this city, I hope."

"No. Not about Buffalo."

"Good." Mrs. Dlugoszewski waits, examining the ceiling. "I never liked it when Ben went out at night. No. Even when I knew where he was going, I didn't like it. A man on the loose is trouble."

"Simon's an actor," Dorsey reminds her.

"Sometimes I don't know how you stand it," Mrs. Dlugoszewski says, referring to the late hours and Simon's habit of sleeping around, which Mrs. Dlugoszewski has picked up on, a shivery, exciting scandal. "You have a tough heart. Me? I'm more . . . I don't know"—she waves her hand in the air—"more sensitive." She opens her eyes, apparently realizing that her choice of words is unhappy. "I'd get more upset than you do, Dorsey. Around men

I have a bad temper. There was this boy in high school I hit in the face. With my fingers closed, like this." She holds up her fist for Dorsey's inspection. "He didn't hit back. He didn't dare. I was stronger than I am now, believe me." She gazes at the stove, dreamily. "I was the captain of the girls' field hockey team." She nods and looks at her nails.

"I couldn't do that," Dorsey says. "I wouldn't want to."

"You could take care of Simon when he gets out of line," Mrs. Dlugoszewski says. "He's not so big."

The piano roll comes to its end. Mrs. Dlugoszewski gets to her feet with a double pump of her arms on the table and puts on another roll, a Jerome Kern medley. She comes back to the kitchen and picks up another cookie, gesturing with it. "He had it coming," she says.

"The boy you hit?"

She nods. "He said something about me. He was spreading it around. A woman has to protect her reputation."

"What? What did he say?"

"I don't remember. The kind of trash boys say to other boys. It doesn't matter. You can't allow men to do that. Once they get started, they won't stop. They just keep grinding and grinding away, making you cheap, so you have to give yourself away." Mrs. Dlugoszewski smiles. "I didn't *want* to hit him. He had the face of an angel. One of those angels you see painted on the ceilings in Europe. With eyes like this!" Mrs. Dlugoszewski does an angel-gaze, smiling raptly, tilting her head back and gazing toward the spice shelf.

"I see your point," Dorsey says.

"Have another cookie," Mrs. Dlugoszewski says, pushing the plate in Dorsey's direction. "You're looking great, though a little thin. You work too hard, honey. You need more exercise."

"I don't sleep too well," Dorsey says. "I never have."

"Does Simon keep you up?" Mrs. Dlugoszewski has lowered her voice.

"Yeah." Dorsey smiles and looks in toward the living room. "He's very inventive. And then, when I can't sleep, he does category games with me. He doesn't mind not sleeping."

"Category games?" She looks puzzled but does not ask for an

explanation. "He's not my sort of man," Mrs. Dlugoszewski says, shaking her head. "I like them with more sense, less make-believe."

"He loves love," Dorsey says. "He does love me."

The angel expression momentarily returns to Mrs. Dlugoszewski's face. "You're sure this is true?"

Dorsey nods. "We dance in the bedroom," she says. Selfishly she waits for this sentence to have its effect on Mrs. Dlugoszewski's face, and it does. "He calls me 'darling.' " She smiles and bites her lower lip.

Mrs. Dlugoszewski leans back and puts her hand on the flesh over her heart. "Not many men like that in Buffalo," she says. "In this city, they don't . . ." She searches for the word, then finds it. "They don't linger. Not with a woman."

"Simon lingers. He takes his time."

Mrs. Dlugoszewski's hand drops onto the kitchen table, a gesture that is like a judge's mallet falling on wood: *case closed.* "I'll say this," Mrs. Dlugoszewski tells Dorsey in a half-whisper, leaning toward her, as the player piano does a lugubrious version of "Ol' Man River." "You look a hundred times better than you did when you arrived in the neighborhood. I remember when you got here, pulling that trailer of furniture, just you and Simon and Noah, a baby then, I remember."

Dorsey nods.

"I remember you two unloading your furniture, with almost no help. You both looked so young. You still do. There was another man here, I remember, carrying things. A solid-looking man, more my type. Yes."

"Hugh," Dorsey says. "My brother."

"Yes. Hugh. You didn't talk much, the three of you, unless the little one wanted something. I thought you all looked so miserable. As if you'd all just gotten out of jail. Such faces!" Mrs. Dlugoszewski shakes her head, flapping the skin between the chin and her throat. "Like faces you used to see in the newsreels."

Dorsey sits quietly, remembering.

"I thought you'd come from some terrible place."

"We had."

"Things are better now, aren't they?"

"They certainly are."

"Well, if it's Simon you have to thank, with all of his faults even, then take care of him." Mrs. Dlugoszewski spreads her arms wide.

The Jerome Kern medley ends with two low repeated chords, and Mrs. Dlugoszewski looks in toward the living room, where Noah sits, pressing one of the piano keys repeatedly, louder and louder. As it increases in volume, he hits the key faster, until the note is almost like a siren, and Mrs. Dlugoszewski squirms, smiles, and covers her ears.

7

To record the passage of time through his life, Hugh alters his house room by room. He surrounds himself with the work of his hands. Weekend visitors, such as Laurie's many cousins, are often escorted to the back porch, enclosed and winterized by Hugh himself. Without prompting, Hugh explains how he put in fiberglass batting insulation just above the knotty-pine ceiling and inside the wallboard. He points and gestures like a contractor. He describes how he reduced the window space by replacing the screens with double-paned casement windows. Below the windows he installed glass radiant heaters. "Look at this," he says, touching the floor with the toe of his shoe. "Wool carpet, and high-density urethane foam underneath. For warmth," he adds, unnecessarily.

If anyone is still listening, he points out how he attached floodlights to the outside wall so that the whole family could sit on the porch in winter, warmed by the radiant heaters, and watch the snow fall in the backyard, covering the grass and the swings.

"Though we haven't *actually* done that yet," Laurie says from the doorway. "But maybe we will. Maybe we'll all sit together and watch the snow fall. It would be nice."

Unsure of her tone, he glares at her and takes the visitors downstairs, where he has built a playroom for the girls. With a twelve-inch spacer he nailed up furring strips at right angles to the rafters and then installed ceiling tile with a staple gun. From this job he had neck pains for two weeks. For the recessed fixtures he loaded the junction boxes on the adapter plates and connected the socket to the power line himself. He covered the cement walls with fake wood paneling, so that the girls would feel comfortable down there, playing with their dollhouses.

He remembers which year he built the dollhouses; he can even remember the month. For Tina he bought an unfinished cabinet and cut away windows and doors in the back and the sides. He made furniture from lumber scraps and bits of hardboard. For Amy he built the dollhouse wall by wall, adding on a textured gable and crafting the interior with slotted joints and movable partitions, a stairway with a handrail, and completely appointed kitchen and bathroom. He used staples as toy cabinet handles and white tacks as doorknobs. With a band saw in his workroom he made domestic and farm animals—horses, dogs, and sheep—to stand outside the dollhouses in imaginary fields. He stood all the animals on dowel legs and drilled holes in hardboard for platforms, then put the platforms on wheels that he had made by slicing up a snapped broom handle. He attached the wheels to the platforms with toothpicks and glue. He thought animals looked friendlier when they were standing on platforms and wheels.

He can remember how, the year Laurie gave up smoking, he made a walking tricycle for Amy and a small HO train layout for Tina. He put the trains on a four-by-eight sheet of plywood, a basic oval layout with two spur lines for storing extra freight cars. He built a small wire-and-plaster-of-Paris tunnel that served no freight-yard function but which looked handsome on the board. He had never asked Tina if she wanted any model trains, and when he unveiled it, her face looked surprised rather than pleased. Laurie insisted that she play with her father's gift, and she did, for two dutiful weeks. Then the train set was hoisted onto its side and stored against the wall in the furnace room, its wires dangling down onto the floor.

Hugh needs projects; unless he has something to do, he frets and dozes off and stares at the clock. Without a project, he must sit with Laurie in the living room in front of the TV set and watch entertainment. He doesn't understand most television. Dramatic shows make him squirm and pull his hand back and forth across his scalp. Instead of seeing characters and conflicts, he sees actors reciting unusual lines in unreal settings. Nothing on television ever looks familiar to him. He can't identify with anyone, either the heroes or the villains. The commercials come on as a great, generous relief from the agonies of narrative.

He works on his projects in the basement, near a wall where his hockey skates are hung on a peg. In the four months before Amy's birth, he built a pine bed for Tina; then, upstairs, he built a partition in the room so that Tina would have some privacy after her baby sister was born. He built for her three toy boxes on movable bases, and a set of outdoor tables and chairs for her doll-and-stuffed-animal tea parties.

In the months when Tina was still toddling around the house, he laid down extra fiberglass insulation in the attic to reduce the draftiness in her room, and he wallpapered the room with a pattern showing circus clowns and red balloons. He didn't like the pattern —he always hated clowns and feared their smiles—but Laurie had picked the pattern out, and he felt that he had no rights as a father to argue with her over wallpaper. He took out the old wall switchplate and put in a new one with Winnie-the-Pooh on it, the bear's paw in a jar of honey.

That summer, as a favor to Laurie, he Rototilled a strip along the south backyard fence and helped her start a garden. It marked the season and the year. He sees the garden now and knows how far he has traveled in time away from its beginning. He knows exactly when he built the trapdoor stairs to the attic; he measures Tina's age by his reckoning of how old she was when he put in the last bolt. When he can think of nothing to do, he sits in the living room, dazed, trying to imagine something he can construct by hand. He looks down at his large scooplike palms, as the laugh track roars from the TV's loudspeaker. He opens and closes his fingers and feels the tightening of his forearm muscles.

He draws mental blueprints for something to destroy or build, even if no one will notice; not the cousins or his daughters or even Laurie herself. He comes back home from work and sits in the kitchen chair near the south window, and Laurie asks him how his day has been, expecting no news. After that, she offers a few sentences about her day at the library: an irritable borrower, a virus going around and depleting the staff. Then she smiles at him, a smile not without its measure of sweetness. She sets out the forks and spoons for dinner, and asks Hugh to reach for a pitcher on an upper shelf, and as he stretches up to grasp it, Hugh imagines himself tearing down the entire kitchen, the whole wing of the house, leaving nothing but scrap lumber and nails scattered in the yard.

At night they make love to each other in silence, joylessly and without variations, Laurie's closed eyes turned away from Hugh, her face as far away from his as she can manage. They are obligated by their bodies to pay this obscure debt to each other, some invisible mortgage held until, in old age, each one owns the other, outright.

Adulthood is a puzzle. Its logic is unknown. For logic Hugh sits at his workbench in the basement, where the old buzztone Motorola serenades him, and he can look at the nails in their glass jars, at his variable-speed grinder, his radial saw, his hammers and wrenches and drill bits. He looks at these tools, and thinks of how he worked on the porch with them, and how, the year before, he constructed the playroom, and how, the year before that, he built the dollhouses. He remembers how he made the trains and the partition and the desk and the kitchen counter. He looks at a jar of nails and thinks of the year he reshingled the roof and put in a new lightning rod on the corner peak of the house. Years ago. He was nailing down shingles when Dorsey called him from California, where she had earned her Ph.D.

"Hugh." Dorsey's voice is long distanced, blank and static-shot.

"Hi, Dorsey! How are you? How's the baby?"

"Hugh. I'll tell you about him later. I'm not sure. We think he may have some hearing problems. But the thing is, I've been offered a job in Buffalo, and we have to leave here."

"Buffalo?"

"Buffalo, New York."

"I know where it is," he says. "Why Buffalo?"

"Because they called me up and offered me a job. It's a matter of connections. Let's not talk about this now. The point is, I need some help moving. And I need help driving. Simon will do some of it, but—"

"—Dorsey . . ."

"—I think we could do it in four days, don't you? Five days? The car's in pretty good shape."

"I can't leave my job that long. Clarence Findley will have my hide if I'm gone for five days. Who's this Simon?"

"I'll tell you when you get here. Why can't you explain to your boss that this is a family emergency? It *is* a family emergency. I have to get out of here."

"Why?"

"I have to get out of here now! Look, I'll explain everything when you get here."

"With you, everything is an emergency."

"Don't you say that to me," she tells him. "Don't you say that."

"All right. I'm sorry."

"Hugh. Please come out. We've got to have some help."

"What is this 'we'?"

"Noah and I. And Simon."

"Simon who?"

"Simon O'Rourke. He's an actor. He can't drive all the way, and I have to take care of Noah. You know how I am about driving."

"Where'd you meet him?"

"Simon? In the grocery. I was down there to get some bananas when I was pregnant and we struck up a conversation."

"I thought you said he was an actor."

"I didn't say he was working in produce, I said I met him there. Don't be a prig."

"I *am* a prig."

"Well, don't be more of one than you already are."

"If this guy is working, how come he's coming east with you?"

"Because he can. I'll explain."

"He sounds pretty suspi—"

"Don't do that," she says. "You don't have the right."

"To do what?"

"To criticize a man, sight unseen. He's helping me. I don't get that many offers of help, you know. Disinterested offers, anyway."

Hugh imagines a calendar, and sees six days blacked out by a child's pencil. "Dorsey, I just don't think—"

"Don't think at all. Just buy the ticket and come out here and help me. Please."

Hugh thinks of his father, himself, Dorsey: time lifts up around him, and his father says, "Take care of her." The pause in the line opens up, and after ten seconds she says, "Are you still there?"

"All right," he says.

"Thank you. Oh, God, thank you. I don't know how we would have done this on our own."

"You're saying 'we' a lot."

"I am, aren't I? Oh, thank you, kiddo. How's my little niece?"

"Nice of you to ask. She's fine."

"Bring a picture. When can you be here?"

"Day after tomorrow," he tells her. They mutter good-byes, and Hugh hangs up. Laurie is looking at him as she stands near the door, her left arm crossed onto her right, and her free hand raised, two fingers framing the side of her cheek. Hugh nods at her, without speaking. She often listens in to his calls on the extension; he doesn't care about it enough to embarrass her and himself by telling her to stop it.

Just outside the San Francisco airport, driving to Dorsey's house in a rented Chevrolet, Hugh smells the ocean. He sees hills that might be mountains. The soft nameless foliage along the freeway, and the stimulating salt charge in the air, draw him into the city. He hasn't planned to stop here—Dorsey's place is close to the university, forty minutes away—but it's only an hour's lost time and he's seen the ocean only twice before in his life. He puzzles out the traffic, stops to ask directions from a blond woman cop in a patrol car in Golden Gate Park, and at last the light in front of him breaks open into a clear view of the Pacific, at Ocean Beach. The colors are those of precious metals, gold and silver, and they stretch out unbroken to the horizon. He breathes in and feels his blood pressure dropping.

After parking his car, he remembers to lock it—in this city you can't trust strangers—and he walks to the Cliff House, where he buys some touristy color postcards for Laurie. Beyond the plate-glass windows are the seal rocks; yes, there are seals there, barking as advertised. Gulls volplane along the cliffs. Dazed, holding his bag of postcards, Hugh walks south along the wall down to the beach, until he finds a spot of his own, where he stops.

Behind him, next to him, men and women of all ages and various exotic national origins are sunning themselves, or gazing, or jogging. The air is soft, smoothed by thousands of miles of salt water. Around him, the others on the beach observe the horizon to the west or the seal rocks to the north, or they gaze happily in no particular direction at all. How much more beautiful the people are here! he thinks. Relaxation or the ocean has improved their looks significantly. Also, their faces—watchful, calmed—seem more attentive than the ones he is familiar with in Five Oaks, but this might be a side effect of the coastal relaxation. Above all—he can feel the waves taking him over, lulling him—the waves are reliable and infinite. The waves don't give a damn. He feels the tranquil sun on his face and groans with pleasure as a breeze that might have come all the way from China touches his forehead. He feels unable to control the dangerous contentment he suddenly feels. Slowly he unbuttons his shirt, letting the sun and sea air touch him impersonally.

To shade his eyes, he weaves his fingers together at his forehead, thumbs at temples, and he remembers his home improvements, the shingles and gutters he has just hammered onto his house, and they impress him as luckless empty things. The waves come in. Time politely stops. Why has he ever set himself up in Five Oaks, Michigan, when he could live for the rest of his life in a tent on this beautiful beach? He realizes that he is feeling drugged, but he does not move. After a few minutes, he turns around to glance at the city behind him, built according to a plan and on a scale unimaginable to the practical midwesterners who buy cars from him. There it is, the cable-car city, America's Naples: you could indeed come here and die. Many had. He would like to strip down to his Jockey shorts and dive into the water, into the undertow. The waves pound in his ears.

What time is it? He looks at his watch; it has stopped, the stem
still out from the moment the plane landed and he reset it for Pacific
Time. He asks a woman in a red outfit sitting on a blanket, but, no,
she doesn't know the time either. Maybe no one does. Hugh stands
in the sun and cannot imagine anyone out here winding a clock.
Except maybe Dorsey. He can imagine Dorsey waking up in the
morning and winding her noisy Big Ben with the black face and
the luminous numbers. He remembers that clock and its spine-
shocking alarm. In the center of this place, she will have remained
as pale as typing paper. She will be alert. Hugh buttons his shirt,
thinking of Dorsey and her baby.

It takes him an hour and a half to find her house, near the famous
university where she has earned her doctorate and become pregnant.
When he does find it, he can't understand why she moved from her
nice apartment to this place, with its flaking green paint and broken
porch swing. The house is untended. The front patch of lawn is
gouged and pitted as if a dinosaur had grazed on it, and there is a
torn screen on one of the upstairs windows. But that's the address.
He finds a place to park two blocks away. Walking to the house,
he passes a woman so unnaturally beautiful that the hair on the back
of his neck stands up.

From the porch steps he looks in through the screen door and sees
his sister at the back of the house, leaning forward in a kitchen chair,
her hands clasped around a cup of coffee. He knocks. "Dorsey," he
says.

She screams and at once rushes out of the kitchen through the
living room and out onto the porch. "You came," she says, and gives
him a long hug. In this embrace he feels, guiltily, her breasts,
enlarged from their production of milk, pressing against him. She
gives off a mother smell of bread and oatmeal and baby fluids. She
pulls away from him, takes his hand, and says, "Come inside.
Where's your suitcase?"

"In the car."

"Shouldn't leave it there. Better get it soon. We're in kind of a
mess here." She walks through the living room, side-stepping boxes
of newspaper-wrapped household items on one side, and grocery
bags loaded with books on the other. The boxes and bags take up

most of the available space. There is a mean smell, acidic and tense, in the air, different from his sister's fragrance, but Hugh can't tell where it comes from. It might be book dust, or the residue of generations of students hemmed and penned up, their fires raging, in this house.

In the kitchen he studies his sister's face, luminous with its sweet intelligence. Her eyes are wounded, circled with a kind of shadow-flesh, but still inhabited with light. On the kitchen table are her yellow legal pads scribbled over with equations. Hugh has seen these before. Everywhere his sister goes, she is accompanied by these ciphers. And on the kitchen floor is Noah, now a year old, sitting up, his hair wild, staring at his uncle.

"There he is," she says proudly. "Isn't he beautiful?"

"He sure is. Can I pick him up?"

"Of course."

Hugh bends down and puts his hands around Noah. The boy looks alarmed and opens his mouth, and his eyes widen in toddler fear. As Hugh brings him up to eye level, Noah's face calms, though his arms reach toward his mother. Hugh bounces and jiggles him, and Noah's mouth closes. His hands begin to make intense motions in front of him.

"There's no explanation," Dorsey says. "We've had him checked by a number of specialists. I didn't have German measles during my pregnancy, so that's not it. No one knows. He has a very, very low level of hearing, and with some powerful hearing aids he may hear slightly, but not very much, not ever. We're learning sign."

"You and this Simon person."

Dorsey nods.

"How come you called me so suddenly? Why're you leaving so fast?"

"I just have to get away from Carlo." Hugh is careful not to interrupt. "I think he's trying to take me over, haunt me in some way. He's very upsetting." She crosses her arms and raises her knee to the kitchen chair. "He tried to get power over me and wreck my life. He wouldn't call it that. He'd call it . . . I don't know what he'd call it, actually. He might call it love. He'd invent a name for it. He'd find a name in Dante and use that."

"How did you ever meet him?" Hugh asks.

Dorsey doesn't answer. She is through talking about Carlo Pavorese. "I made phone calls all around the country and found this one-year lectureship in Buffalo," she says. "They may make it tenure-track, I don't know. They need women in the physics department there worse than most places. And Simon thinks he can get acting work there. We decided not to wait any longer."

"It's so beautiful here," Hugh says. "The ocean—"

"—Don't tell me about the fucking ocean," Dorsey whispers. "God! All the people out here mesmerized by that goddamn bay and that bridge and that fucking expanse of water! And don't tell me about fog, either. I sucked my share of fog. Fuck all that."

Hugh is so shocked by his sister's language that he can't think of anything to say for a moment. At last he says, "Where's your friend Simon?" He takes Noah from his knee and puts him back into his playpen.

"He's out getting a big U-Haul trailer attached to our car. He should be back any minute now. So. How's Laurie? And Tina?"

"They're fine. And the house is fine. I was working on it when you called."

Dorsey gazes at him. He feels the full intelligent force of her attention sweeping over him. "You'll never leave Five Oaks, will you? You'll always stay in that house. Always and forever."

"I will never leave Five Oaks," Hugh says, reciting it like a pledge of allegiance. "I will always stay in that house. Always and forever."

Dorsey nods.

"You always go," Hugh tells her. "I always stay. That's my job. Then, every once or so often, I come to patch things up." He reaches down for an unclaimed cookie on the kitchen table. As he bites into it, he feels the presence of someone else in the room.

At that moment Dorsey says, "Well, look who's here!"

Simon stands in the doorway, smiling like a poster of a man standing in a hallway. He is wearing sunglasses; a Venice, California, T-shirt; cut-off denim shorts; and sandals. The sunglasses are ultradark, and Hugh can't see the man's eyes. Simon's hair seems to have streaks of some blonding agent in it, and it curls, Hugh thinks, for effect, as if it had been interfered with in some way. The hair isn't artificial, but something about it is fussy and photographic. He looks two–dimensional, all flat surfaces. He smiles in Hugh's direction, but the smile is ironic, refrigerated. Seeing it, Hugh feels himself mocked. He's never seen a smile like that in Five Oaks and hopes he won't. He looks again at Simon's sunglasses and can only see himself—unsure, tentative—reflected there.

"Hugh, this is Simon. Simon, meet my brother."

Simon walks forward, his arm extended dramatically, and Hugh knows instantly that this is a parody of a handshake, this British-style pump. "How do you do?" Hugh says, and then realizes that his mouth is still full of the cookie he has been eating and that some of the crumbs have sprayed out onto Simon's T-shirt, and he knows that of course Simon has seen it happen, he's that kind of person.

"How do *you* do?" Simon asks, as if it were a real question, his voice overripe with sincerity. "Welcome," he says, in a bus-tour voice, "to California, home of avocado pears and passion fruit."

Hugh cannot remember disliking anyone—man, woman, or child—as much on first sight as he dislikes this man. "Yes," he says, before realizing that his agreement is attached to no question. His fears of looking stupid flare up again. "Dorsey said you were out getting a trailer. Did you find one?"

"Did I!" Hugh sees Simon's eyebrows lifting up behind the dark glasses. "They were everywhere. No matter where I stopped, *there they were!* I had to fight them off. They're very aggressive, those U-Hauls. Did you know," and here his voice slithers down to a whisper, "that they follow you around?"

Hugh stares at him. The face in the glasses stares back. Dorsey is watching both men carefully.

"I got the biggest one they had, the behemoth model. Of course, it may pull off the trailer hitch, but then we'll have an adventure, won't we? Stuck in Death Valley with nothing to eat but cactus. Oh, no, we don't go through Death Valley. We go through Sacramento and then Reno. I mean, that's almost Death Valley, isn't it? Do we go through the Donner Pass? I hope you have a good appetite. We're so lucky"—he claps his hands together once—"that you came here to help us drive across the country." He looks down at Hugh's legs. "*Where* did you get those pants?"

"In Five Oaks."

"Is that virgin polyester?"

"Simon!" Dorsey says. "Cut it out."

"I'm just nervous," he says. "You know how I chatter when I get nervous." He approaches the playpen and looks down at Noah. "How's Baby Leroy?"

"He's been okay."

Simon takes off his dark glasses, fastidiously placing them on the kitchen table. Then he reaches down to pick up Noah, making a finger signal to him first. Vaguely astonished, Hugh sees Simon lift up Noah with ease and confidence, and he also sees Noah's happiness in Simon's company. Simon puts his index finger into Noah's hand, and the boy closes his fingers around it.

"My God," Hugh says.

Simon smiles quickly. Pride and something equally severe are in his face. "Imagine me," he says. "A daddy."

"What?"

"Oh, I don't mean . . . ," Simon says, looking at Dorsey. "Didn't you . . . ?" he asks.

"No," she says. "He didn't notice. Maybe I covered it up." She holds out her left hand toward her brother. Her wedding ring, with its small diamond, glitters at him; Simon holds his own hand out: another ring. "We waited," she says, "until you came out here. We wanted to tell you in person."

Hugh sits in the kitchen chair, the room at once in a state of evaporation. Outside on the street a car honks twice, and to Hugh the two sounds make a celebratory blaring scrawl in the air. He lifts his head, finds a window, and gazes out. Here in California the leaves on the trees have altered shapes, he thinks: more tropical, the inflated geometries of jungle flowers. He wonders how much change he has in his pants pocket: is it fifty cents, or much less?

Dorsey's voice swims to him through the thickening air. "Well, areyougoing tocongratulateus?"

He catches himself breathing through his mouth, small shallow breaths. Less than fifty cents, he thinks; much less. More like thirty cents, not even enough for a bus token. "Of course," he says, remembering to smile. "Congratulations. To you both."

"I think he's shocked," Dorsey says to Simon.

"I do take a bit of getting used to," Simon's voice says, rising out of the floor of the kitchen.

"It's . . . I wasn't expecting."

"No, of course not." Dorsey takes her brother by the elbow, brings him to a standing state, and pilots him through the boxes of packed pots and pans out the back door, into the yard. Hugh looks up: the birds are singing unusual songs, with twisting funneled notes. The backyard itself is a miniature, with a tiny two-row vegetable garden, bordered by a fence on one side of an alley. On the branches of a small eucalyptus someone has attached several tiny bells that tinkle absently every few seconds. In front of Dorsey and Hugh a rusting chair lies on its side, and Dorsey stands it up and puts her brother in front of it.

"There," she says. "Sit down."

He does. She stands behind him and puts her hands on his shoulders and says that Simon is a good man—he'll see that soon—a man of real tenderness. She repeats the word so he'll be sure to register it: "tenderness." Hugh can't remember when he's ever heard that word spoken before at home. It's the sort of word you hear in old, sentimental songs. No one uses it in conversation, not in Five Oaks.

Dorsey's hands rub Hugh's shoulders. She's picked up this trick from Simon; Hugh knows without asking. Instantly his mind holds onto an image of Simon standing behind Dorsey, massaging her shoulders. His mind's eye sees the calm on his sister's face. There it is.

"He's a little strange," she says, her hands keeping up their work. "You'll find that he—"

Hugh brings his palm up into the air, a flag, holding it steadily until she stops talking; at the same time he shakes his head back and forth. "You don't have to explain anything." Then, to prove that he understands and to put an end to her justifications, he says, "You sit in the kitchen. Simon rubs your shoulders. You learned this from him. He rubs your shoulders and there's this thing he does with his fingers just behind your ears. I can see him doing it. I can imagine it." Instantly she stops her hand motions, and Hugh knows he's right. She is listening now. "No one ever did this for you until you met him." He turns in the chair to look at her. "So you see? I do understand."

"Yes."

"Congratulations," he says, gazing toward a wisteria, wondering what it's called. He won't ask. He won't play that game.

"Thank you."

That evening Dorsey, Simon, and Hugh load the trailer with the baby furniture, the books, the kitchen articles, and Dorsey's file cabinets and computer materials. Dorsey explains that they've had a real estate agent in Buffalo find them a rental house near a school for the deaf, in case . . . Well. They have a photograph. Would Hugh like to see the house they're moving to? No. He's been a fool often enough, long enough, not to fall for this trick. "No," he says, "I want to see it in person." Carrying a load of Dorsey's clothes down the stairs, Hugh passes Simon going up, and he says, "Where's your stuff, Simon? All this is Dorsey's."

"I don't have any stuff," Simon shouts back. "A suitcase of clothes. That's it."

At the bottom of the stairs, Hugh turns around, his heart pounding from the weight he carries, and he stares at the slender man with the television face gazing down at him from the landing with that mocking smile and the dark glasses that seem permanently attached to his head. "No books? No anything?" Hugh asks.

"I have Dorsey," Simon tells him, in a voice which is not his own but a mimicry of some Hollywood actor, whom Hugh can recognize but not identify. Hugh knows he's meant to laugh, but he won't. He does his job; he carries the clothes to the trailer.

The next day, after they return Hugh's car to the rental agency, they begin the trip with Hugh and Simon in front, Dorsey with Noah in back. Soon after they pull out, Simon takes off his shoes and puts his feet up on the dashboard, and the action makes Hugh think of his sister displaced somehow inside this stranger's skin. Every time Simon leans his head back, his eyes close, like a doll with weighted lids. Hugh tries to keep his own eyes on the road, and he listens to the Pontiac's tappet noises as they climb up the hills around the bay. Approaching Sacramento, Hugh insists that they stay on Route 80, after Simon has suggested some back roads.

"No back roads," Hugh says, gripping the steering wheel near the top.

"No roadside attractions?" Simon whines. "No stops at Mom's Chow House? No small towns with lumpy beds and lonesome strangers?"

"No," Hugh says. "Not any of it. I have a job to get back to."

"Gee," Simon says, boyishly disappointed. "Well, maybe next time we'll stay on the back roads. No maps."

"Fine."

"No superhighways."

"Suit yourself."

Simon wants to stop for the evening in a place called Cant Read, but Hugh insists that they continue until they reach Reno. Simon's complaining makes Dorsey laugh, and when Dorsey laughs, Noah sees his mother's face and begins laughing himself, a sound like a flute. Just inside the Reno city limits, they stop at a yellow motel called the Cactus Court. When Hugh comes out of the office with their room keys, Simon is sitting on the Pontiac's hood and complaining to Dorsey that the motel looks like a haven for subhumans and that self-respecting people would not register at a yellow motel that has a loudspeaker bolted to the electric sign on the office roof. The sign shows a pink-neon cactus blinking on and off every two seconds. The loudspeaker is playing Andy Williams tunes. Dorsey hands Noah over to Simon and tells him to stuff it.

Two hours later, after Noah has been bathed and Dorsey has showered, and they are sitting in Heap Big Hamburger, Simon is still complaining. There are slot machines near the restaurant's door, bordered on both sides by cigar-store Indians holding huge plastic hamburgers. Hugh has ordered the Apache burger, and Dorsey and Simon have both ordered the Sitting Bull Special. With his mouth full, Simon tells Dorsey that they'd be having a better time, right now, if they had stopped for the night in Cant Read.

"Simon," Dorsey says, "please stop whining." Her eyes are heavy and she lifts her hands for the flatware and the napkin as if her fingers were weighted. "You've done enough. Don't embarrass me." She reaches out and takes his hand. "We're in the desert, right? You can be quiet here. That's the custom. You can play the slot machines." She gestures toward the door. "No one ever says much in Nevada. Look." She points at the landscape outside the window. "There's nothing to say about that, is there?"

"It's the home of bomb tests. You can say that," Simon tells her.

"No no no no no no no," Dorsey says, through her teeth. "By God, I thought you'd leave me alone on that one."

"On what?" Hugh asks. "What're you talking about?"

"She means . . . ," Simon begins to say.

"Don't tell him what I mean."

"I was only going to explain about—"

"—No!" she says, dropping her fork. "As if he doesn't follow me around enough. I don't mean you," she says to her brother. "You know who I mean. Carlo—I'm trying to get away from him. I'm trying to . . . withdraw from his obsessions. All that conscience," she says disconnectedly, and without further explanation. She takes out two jars of baby food—sweet potatoes and mashed beans—and feeds Noah his dinner before eating her own. Noah eats in his usual silence, and Hugh watches his sister making rudimentary signs toward her son. *Eat:* fingers together moving toward the mouth. *Good:* right-hand fingertips at the mouth, moving out and down. Hugh can't take his eyes off them—his sister, her son. How, he wonders, has she ever survived her own life?

Hugh finishes his hamburger and gets up to play the slot machines. He limits himself to a five-dollar loss; when he has lost it, as he knows he will, his sister is ready to go.

It's a ten-hour drive to Salt Lake City, through a vulcanized, sun-blanched landscape of sallow gold rock. Simon, now driving, is behaving better, Hugh thinks, but he notices that his brother-in-law is incorporating into his conversations a slight stutter over *th* sounds that Hugh has never been able to get out of his own speech in moments of stress. He has never heard himself being mimicked before, never heard his own voice coming back at him. He thinks it may not be deliberate; maybe it's an actor's habit. If Dorsey notices what Simon is doing, she doesn't mention it. She is playing with Noah in back, bouncing him on her lap, having taken him out of the baby Safe-T-Seat.

"T-t-t-tell me about your parents," Simon says, sounding like Hugh. "Tell me a story. Talk us straight through to the Utah line."

Hugh thinks. Doors open to other doors. In these distances, everything looks so small. What's the difference? It's just another story. As he begins to talk, he looks out the window and sees a freight train, tiny in the distance, moving along in a direction parallel to theirs. The train's size, its movement through the flattening ranchland, gives him a pleasurable shiver of time and its losses.

"Dorsey's probably told you some things about them." Simon nods. Hugh fears that Simon's eyes will close when he nods, but they do not. "They died young. Dorsey had just started college and I was already selling cars. My father had three heart attacks, the first one on his fifty-third birthday, as he was eating his birthday cake. The third one killed him. He was reading the Sunday paper at breakfast. My mother was at the other end of the table and saw the newspaper —it was the travel section—begin to crumple and fold in on itself, and when it dropped below his face, she saw his expression. His eyes were squinting shut and his teeth were clenched."

Simon listens, his eyes fixed on the highway. The train, miles away on Hugh's right, seems to keep pace with the car, shimmering in the rock heat, a mirage train.

"Then my mother started to go. It was that kind of marriage, where they get so . . ."

"Symbiotic," Simon suggests.

"Yeah. She couldn't live without him. For the next two years she did things to herself, eating badly and smoking and drinking, to make sure she'd follow him soon, and she did. The house was left to me in the will. That's where I live now."

"Why is it," Simon asks, "when you ask people about somebody's life, they tell you how the person died?"

"You start with the last things first, ass-backwards, if you're me," Hugh says, sure of that. "You start with the period instead of the capital letter. That way you're always sure how everything ends." He waits for Simon to cut into this statement, but he doesn't.

"My father," Hugh says, "sold insurance, but he loved the outdoors and said he'd prefer to live there if he could. When he was young, he wrote poetry to my mother. I still have his letters. They did that in those days, you know." He expects Simon to nod in agreement, but it doesn't happen. "My father was an expert woodworker and made tables and chairs and even made a violin once, a beautiful thing, which actually played. He was a fair athlete. He skated. He showed me how to skate and taught me how to play hockey, some of the tricks a boy needs in stick-handling and passing. He was complicated. Gawky and conscientious. So was my mother. They'd gone to college. Don't believe what they tell you about small towns. They were good people. Smart. They'd traveled and talked at dinner about places they'd seen. All the great sights, Paris and London. Each night, when my father came in the house, he gave me a tap on the head with his newspaper. It was a good luck tap . . . a blessing. 'Good evening, Tiger,' he'd say to me. Then he'd tap Dorsey. 'Evening, Cass.' "

" 'Cass'?" Simon asks.

"Short for Cassiopeia," Dorsey says, from the backseat.

"Yes." Hugh waits, then continues. "I don't know how to say this. I think his talent wasn't for woodworking or selling insurance exactly, though he loved doing that. He loved to arrive after a disaster and give people some money. He called himself 'God's apologist.' But what he really lived for was loving my mother. It sounds strange. They talked to each other in the evening, and they never ran out of things to say. That's what the long hours came to: conversation. It was what the day was for. Their talk is what I remember best about them. I remember how much they liked to eat and talk together. You don't see that much anymore. People can't do it. They don't know how. They wrap up their little monologues and throw them at you, and you have to catch them, and throw them back."

He keeps his eyes on the train, a bit closer now: a Denver and Rio Grande freight: boxcars, coal cars, flatcars loaded with some kind of green-and-orange machinery. It is getting toward evening, and the gold light gives the cars a shimmering toy distinctness.

"Tell me about your mother," Simon asks.

"People said my mother looked a little like Eve Arden, the actress." Simon flicks his head, annoyed that the name has been explained for him. "She was sharp. Ironic, people said. An ironic woman. She wasn't that popular in town, except with my father. She made people laugh, but that made them uncomfortable instead of happy. 'A funny woman.' That's what people said about her. Men were supposed to be funny, not women, especially women who laughed at men. And she had this habit of guessing about people when she'd just met them. 'You came from a farm,' she'd say, 'and you had a pet cow named Nell, and you joined 4-H when you were ten years old, and the cow won a blue ribbon at the county fair.' She did that all the time, and she was usually right. I can do it sometimes. So can Dorsey. It scared people, that she could make them laugh any time she wanted to and guess what their lives were like. She wasn't psychic, just intuitive. It was sort of beyond a talent. It was like a gift. There was no real way to use it, except with my father. Back and forth. He was her straight man. He gave her lines."

"Daddy drove a Nash, but my mother drove a Mercury," Dorsey says from the backseat. "Do you know why?"

"No," Simon shakes his head. "Why?"

"Because," Dorsey and Hugh say together, *"it's the only car with the name of a god."* Hugh smiles. "That's what she always said."

"Oh."

"She saw how smart Dorsey was," Hugh says, "for things, for the way they worked. She bought her a microscope and a telescope later, and all sorts of mechanical devices that Dorsey could take apart. Clocks and switches and valves. They were all over the place. My parents weren't afraid that this was ungirlish."

"How do you know?" Dorsey interrupts.

"I just do. They believed in you. They thought you were capable of great things."

This sentence brings the car to a whistling desert quiet. Hugh looks in the backseat and sees Dorsey, her face softened into the past, time parting in a wave in front of her. The trailer jerks and weaves behind them. To the side, Hugh sees the Denver and Rio Grande ebbing away into the distance, disappearing into a coupled link of traveling points.

"They raised us, and then they left us alone by ourselves to manage any way we could," Dorsey says. "The way parents do. They died, and there we were, out in the world. Hell, everyone's an orphan sooner or later."

There is in her unsentimentality, her toughness, something that strikes Hugh as oversimplified, so he says, "It's not that simple," but he doesn't construct an argument to go with it. He thinks: *orphan.*

They have reached Utah, the edge of the Great Salt Desert, white flats ahead of them to the horizon.

· · ·

At a rest stop just outside Cheyenne, Wyoming, one hundred thirty miles east of the Continental Divide and on this side of another bad night's sleep, Hugh is sitting in the Pontiac, waiting for Simon and Dorsey to return from the public restrooms. The passenger door is open; a damp early June breeze, a springtime greenhouse smell, passes through the car, and Hugh inhales it, trying to make himself remember it. Noah sits in Hugh's lap, pulling urgently at one of the buttons on his uncle's shirt. To the west the sky blurs, loses its focus over the Rockies, whose inclines and fallen rocks and majesties they have just escaped. Hugh puts his index finger on the back of Noah's neck and gives it a tickling rub. The boy closes his eyes in a happy squint. Pleased with his success, Hugh inserts his finger inside Noah's shirt and tickles the boy again.

"I've been robbed."

It's Simon: standing, amused. His hands in his pockets, he rocks back and forth, watching Hugh, surveying the rest stop's parking lot, the trucks on the interstate.

"What?"

"I was robbed."

"When?"

"Just now."

Hugh stands up, holding Noah, and stares at Simon. "Good God. How?"

"I was pissing," Simon tells him. "Into the urinal. And this gentleman wearing a fishing cap with a very low visor saunters along and snitches my wallet out of my back pocket. Zip zip, just like that. I had to admire his speed. And I couldn't chase him, could I? After all, I *was* pissing. I can't stop once I've started. Some can. I can't. And there wasn't anyone else in the bathroom to shout to. I'm sure he's gone by now, spending all my money on trinkets in Cheyenne."

"Simon," Hugh says, outraged, "that's terrible. You've got to call the police."

"What?" Dorsey has appeared. Taking the baby in her arms, she is told the story, looks surprised, but does not appear to be frightened or demoralized. "Oh," is all she says.

"What about the money?" Hugh asks, catching Noah's eye, and smiling.

"I've got that." Dorsey pats her purse. "All the traveler's checks are right here. You can't trust Simon with money. We don't let him have more than forty dollars at a time."

"Well," Hugh says, trying to maintain the heat of outrage, "what about your driver's licence?"

"I don't have one," Simon says.

"What?"

"I don't have one," Simon repeats. "Never have. I couldn't pass the test."

"Goddamn it, Simon," Hugh shouts, "you've been driving hour after hour, all of us, including this child, half the way from San Francisco, and you're telling me you don't have a fucking licence?"

Simon's voice is placid. "I've been driving fifteen years without a licence. Never needed it. Never been ticketed. I'm *very* careful. Some might even say I'm a meticulous driver. If you're careful, you don't need a licence." He smiles, showing his brilliant teeth.

"What about your credit cards?"

Simon squinches his nose. "Don't like them. Dorsey's got a few, don't you, darling?"

"That's right," she says.

Hugh looks at his brother-in-law, then the sky, then the ground. "Simon," he asks, "just what *do* you keep in your wallet?"

"A few dollars," Simon smiles, putting his hand around his wife's shoulders, "condoms, and pictures of your sister, this woman, my wife. Nine pictures of Dorsey, and five pictures of Dorsey and Noah. That's about all. And what I say is, if a criminal wants to steal a wallet like that, let him. Let him feast his eyes. I think it'd do wonders for his criminal character to gaze on this woman's face, don't you? Let him fall in love at a distance, is what I say. He's got the money; I've got her."

Holding Noah, Dorsey kisses Simon on the cheek, then turns to stare at her brother, her eyes full of pride: *this is the man I married. He owns nothing a stranger can steal.*

They have a flat tire outside of Ogallala, Nebraska, and by the time Hugh has fixed it—Simon can't figure out how to get the hubcap off—it's late afternoon, and they decide to stay for the night. They take two rooms in the Royalty Inn, eat an early dinner, then retire.

Hugh tries to watch television, a police show. He struggles to believe the story, to understand it, but cannot. The actors are acting, the commercials interrupt the drift of things, then the actors act some more, but it's not a story about people: it's a spectacle in which actors speak lines and shoot blanks from guns and other actors, in response, clutch their stomachs and pretend to fall dead, while the music swells before the credits come on.

He glances around the room for something to read. There is a standing card on the bedside table that explains the existence of Ogallala, pop. 5,700, el. 3,216 ft. The town's heyday was the decade between 1874 and 1884. It was a railroad town and cattle-shipping point. The Oregon Trail passed nearby. So much for Ogallala. Putting his fingers in the bedside drawer, he feels the imitation leather of the Gideon Bible and pulls it out. He opens it to the Book of Nahum. Who is Nahum? He's never heard of Nahum.

> The chariots rage in the streets,
> they rush to and fro through the squares;
> they gleam like torches,
> they dart like lightning.

He reads until the violence of the events and the language disturbs him, and he puts the book back in the drawer. There is a bump against the wall, then another. After a third bump he hears a woman's throaty laughter. He thinks of motels, their thin walls, and gets to his feet. He slips on his shoes, takes his room key, and goes outside.

He walks until he's out of town—ten minutes—and stands on a straight paved road that cuts through a field until it is absorbed by the horizon. It's almost Five Oaks: it has the same forlorn unloveliness. The noise of the insects is louder here, like ratchets. Crickets and grasshoppers and other exoskeletal life—he remembers the illustrations in his high school biology book—live here under the blades of the long grass. He looks along a line of dead trees, their branches shaped as if with arthritis, toward a field whose soil has recently been turned up for spring planting. At the other, far end of the field, the downstairs lights of a farmhouse are shining, and he thinks of the family sitting around the table in the kitchen, the children and the parents eating their dinner rapidly, without thought. There would be a dog lying underneath the table, watching for spills. He remembers to call home as soon as he has walked back into Ogallala. A car drives by on the road and the driver waves to Hugh as if he knows him, his whole left bare arm raised and in motion outside the car's window. The red tail lights recede into the distance. Another light, much farther out, miles away on the horizon, blinks on.

Hugh breathes in the weighted and dense odor of farmland, the rich heaviness of the soil, and thinks of his sister lying naked, covered by Simon, in the motel's wide bed. He shuts his eyes and when he opens them again he sees the first star of the evening, which he knows must be Venus. The planet's light, its bright point, is just above the light on the horizon. They match perfectly, vertically linked. Twin points of light, earth and air, Gemini. Hugh feels a pleasurable chill of dislocation, abandonment, a traveler's feeling. Another car drives by, a Dodge, and its driver also waves at him, a generous wide-arcing wave. Why are they waving at me? he wonders. They must think I live here. As the car recedes, Hugh waves back. Hello, I don't live here.

As he walks back, he sees the motel, the Royalty Inn, its large VACANCY sign shining in orange letters over the plowed fields. Yes —much vacancy here. Several blocks from the motel he calls Laurie from a phone booth. Very soon after she answers she begins to tell him about a small cold Tina has caught somehow, the sore-throat, hacking kind. And there's been a storm, she says, which has frightened Tina and awakened her, so that she coughed part of the night. Laurie's mother has telephoned and will be visiting soon, but just for a few days. Last night, Laurie says, she had cooked up some chicken breasts for dinner. What recipe? Hugh asks, and waits without hope after her answer for Laurie to ask him a question, any kind of question, about his trip. She doesn't ask. She doesn't like to ask him questions over the telephone; her mother had once told her that asking questions over the telephone was unmannerly and rude and bad form for a woman. Whatever Laurie hears, she waits to be told. So Hugh explains what he can, and when he says that his sister is now married, Laurie's voice alters: it rises in interest. "I can't believe that," she says, sounding as if she believes it quite readily.

"Dorsey is married? Who's the guy?" And Hugh, standing in the phone booth in Ogallala, staring at the sign that says VACANCY over the fields of Nebraska, tells his wife, "I don't know. His name is Simon O'Rourke. He's an actor. I don't know who he is."

In western Iowa, past Council Bluffs, Dorsey in front, Hugh driving, and Simon in back with Noah, they see a thunderhead to the east, the back of it, lit from within by paneled lightning, and underneath it, rain falling in a solid mass. Hugh turns on the headlights—the air is a pastel green—and they drive over a hill and into the teeming water. Hugh grips the steering wheel so hard his knuckles turn white; ahead of him, cars are vanishing into separate waterfalls. "Well, folks," Simon says loudly in a New England accent, "there're some people lost on the freeway, and a few cars sideswiped and demolished, but up there in the skies the stars are moving in those old-fashioned zodiacs, and I guess there's not much we can do about it one way or the other. There's been some travelers who've spun off the pavement into the ditch, and one old lady in a brown Chrysler havin' chest pains, but that's the way it goes out here. It's a hard life on the interstate, but folks've been drivin' it now for decades—families, bachelors, single girls lookin' for a husband —sort of like a river of—"

"—Please shut up, would you?" Hugh asks.

"Simon," Dorsey says. "Not now. Please. No *Our Town* on this trip."

"Yup," Simon says, as if he hasn't heard them, "cars pitchin' forward, and cars lost, and cars goin' to Illinois and not meanin' to and never comin' back, but it's all out of our hands. Pretty soon it'll be nightfall and folks'll be checkin' into motels, married folks, and folks that'll never be married no matter what kind of plastic surgery they get, and they'll be sleepin' soon, and the old stars'll just keep turnin', rain or no rain."

"A character," Hugh says, his teeth clenched. "No more characters, Simon."

"It's what I do," Simon says from the back, his voice altering to an explanatory monotone.

"I'm sorry," Hugh says. "I am so sorry about this." He is creeping at twenty miles an hour. The trailer is pulled and jerked in the tailwinds. "I can't believe this guy," Hugh says, in his calmest rage.

"Hugh," Dorsey says, touching his knee.

"Simon, are you gay?" Hugh asks, his voice thick.

"Define your terms."

"Because you certainly sound like it to me."

"Has it come to this?" Simon's voice has altered and sounds like a network sports announcer. "Accusations?" And then Hugh hears a perfect imitation of his own voice coming from the back seat. He hears, in his own voice, Simon's voice saying, "I th-th-thought you wanted to hear about the stars. And if I were . . . what you called me, I wouldn't ever tell you."

"Dorsey," Hugh says, as the rain starts to let up. "I'm sorry I lost my temper. It's been—"

"He's my husband," Dorsey says. "And you don't know him." She looks at her brother. "He can be anyone he wants to be. Isn't that amazing? That's his gift. He can be you. Or anyone he wants to be. Leave him alone."

"I thought he wanted to hear about the stars," Simon says, his voice sounding like Hugh's. "I guess he didn't want to hear."

In Illinois, Dorsey wakes up and looks at the cornfields. "You know why I became a physicist?" she asks. She rubs her eyes and reaches into her purse for a pair of dark glasses. "I became a physicist so that I'd be free of this." Hugh looks out across a field and sees an old broken windmill and a grain elevator far in the distance. Free? Free of what? He's afraid to ask. Then Dorsey says, "I thought it would take me away from the earth, and for a while, it did."

At the James Whitcomb Riley rest stop in Indiana just past South Bend, Dorsey is changing Noah's diapers—she and Simon have been trading off this task—while Simon does wind sprints in a grassy area signposted as a dog walk south of the parking lot. Hugh is checking the Pontiac's engine; though it's taken three quarts of oil, it hasn't overheated or broken down, and he can't understand why. Cars like this, pulling trailers, are supposed to experience systems-failure on cross-country trips. But everything, the fluid levels and the spark plugs and the belts and the hoses, everything is in order.

He slams down the hood of the car and turns to see his brother-in-law running back and forth in sprints of less than a hundred yards each. Each one of these sprints begins with Simon lowering himself into a crouch, right foot behind the left, fingertips down on the grass, before he snaps forward. He is barefoot, and his T-shirt is soaked through in a funnel pattern with sweat. It makes Hugh remember how, years ago, before hockey practice would begin on the ice, he and his teammates would sprint back and forth in the Five Oaks gym to get their wind strong after a summer of smoking and parties. He remembers big guys heaving and passing out, nausea-white, underneath the water fountains.

He walks toward Simon. He smiles. On his right is a family eating cold chicken for lunch at a picnic table. "Simon," he says, "cool it out. We're going to have to sit with you in the car for the next hour and you're going to stink. You'll be rank."

Simon doesn't look at him. He watches the ground. He puts his feet into position and begins to lower himself to a crouch. "I don't smell," he says. He is breathing quickly, regularly. "My sweat does *not* smell. You won't smell me. No one ever has."

"But everyone sm—" Hugh says before Simon takes off. He waits until Simon runs back, past him. "Everyone smells when they sweat. You take me. When I—"

"No," Simon says. "I sweat pure salt water."

Hugh is standing just above Simon and to the side. Against his better judgment, he sniffs the air. It smells like air.

"Wanna race?" Simon asks, turning his head and looking up at Hugh. "Wanna race to that trash receptacle down there?"

Hugh laughs. "You look like you did some running in high school or something." He waits. "I don't know."

"You played hockey," Simon says, staring at the ground. "Your sister told me. She said you were *real good.*"

"I've lost my speed." Hugh looks quickly toward the car, trying to see Dorsey motioning him back. But she is leaning against a poplar with Noah, in the shade, her hands moving in front of her child.

"Yeah," Simon says, "and I've been running for the last ten minutes. Come on, man. Where's your pride? You can beat me. You can whip my pansy ass. Think of the pleasure in that."

"I don't know. I'm sort of old for this." All four members of the family eating chicken are watching him.

"So am I," Simon tells him. "Take off your shoes, man, and let's do this thing. Now." He points to Hugh's Adidas. "My mistake, you're all set to run. You don't have to take your shoes off, you can get down right now, and in ten seconds we can start. See that trash can?" Simon points; Hugh doesn't have to look. "First one past that. Do you want a stake in this?"

"What kind of stake?"

"If I win," Simon breathes out, "we get off this terrible tollway and we take the back roads to Buffalo. All right?"

"I don't know."

"Come on, man. Look at me. I'm beat. I'm winded. And I'm a pussy. You can beat a pussy. You've wanted to ever since you first met me, right? Come on, bro. Let's do this thing now!"

"All right, goddamn it." Hugh bends down next to Simon and puts his fist in the grass. He feels the blades work between his fingers as his heart accelerates and he hears Simon whisper, "On your mark." Hugh inhales quickly, trying for a fix of oxygen. "Get set." He looks up at the trash receptacle and sees a woman walking toward it with a German shepherd on a leash. He opens his mouth to say something, and just at that moment, Simon shouts, "Go."

He flings himself up and out, the park area instantly becoming a blur, whitened. As he runs, thinking only of himself, he sees the trash receptacle gaining in size and the woman with her dog now in back of it, safely away: she has seen him and, alarmed, is watching him sprint toward her. He can't see or hear Simon. He feels the air sucked down into his lungs and blown out again, and the ground hitting his feet with hammerlike thumps. Then he runs past the can, and he looks back and sees Simon crossing it, inches behind him.

Hugh slows down, stops, puts his hands on his knees and tries to breathe in and out. In what he feels now, he perceives a small shadow of something disturbed and sick, and as it moves away from his chest and out into the air, Hugh knows that it is his own death, a small pinprick shadow of what will darken him later from his head to his feet. Simon puts his sweaty arm over Hugh's back and lowers his head next to his. "By God, you saved your honor today," Simon pants, "and that of the whole civilized world." He is smiling.

"Yeah."

"I said you could beat me."

"Then why'd you want to race?"

"It's the difference between us," Simon half-whispers. "I'm not afraid of losing." He straightens up. "Let's go find Dorsey."

They walk together toward the car, past the family at their picnic table, and Simon raises a hand in greeting. "Looks good," he says, glancing at the chicken and the paper plates and the Jell-O. The father nods, and one of the two children says, "I saw you running over there."

Simon stops and says something about getting his old blood circulating, but Hugh keeps walking, leaving him there. He crosses the service drive and reaches the shaded area where Dorsey is humming as she watches Noah crawling around on a blanket she has set out on the grass. Hugh sits next to her. "I had a race with Simon," he tells her. "I beat him."

"Congratulations," Dorsey says, tapping him on the forearm.

"We had a bet. If I won, we'd stay on the tollway. If I lost, we'd take the back roads."

"You'd do that?"

"No," Hugh says. "Very perceptive of you. I wouldn't." He scratches his arm. "Simon should be back in a minute. He's talking to those people."

"I can see." Dorsey smiles, watching Simon talk. "Simon loves to pick up people."

"Huh?"

"You know. You're a grown-up." She smiles and ruffles her hair. "Talk to people and pick them up and bring them home. That's how he met me."

"But then he stopped doing it."

"No." Dorsey shakes her head, looking unconcerned. "No, he went on doing it." She laughs and pulls at the grass. In a moment Simon's feet are next to her hands. She throws some grass at his ankles.

"Hi." He sits down and puts his head on her shoulder. "I'm bushed."

"You must be. And feel this." She runs her palm along Simon's back. "You're soaking wet."

"Your brother was afraid I would stink up the car."

"Oh, no." Dorsey gives Hugh her hard, prideful look. "Simon's sweat doesn't smell. Not a bit. It tastes just like salt water." And before Hugh can remember to turn away, she raises her lips to Simon's forehead and breathes in through her mouth.

On the eastern side of Ohio, just past Cleveland, both Simon and Noah asleep in the back seat, Hugh driving and Dorsey sighing with boredom, Hugh asks about Simon's family.

"He says he doesn't have any. I haven't pressed him about it."

Hugh can't wait any longer; he's waited this long. The road is going on forever. "Then tell me about Carlo Pavorese," he says.

His sister turns and looks at him. "No," she says. "I won't."

Just outside Buffalo, Dorsey says, "I'm sick. I have *Autobahnschmerz*. It's not the distance. It's the freeways and tolls and the speed and the time, and the fact that there aren't any decisions a human being can make. It's like being . . ." She thinks for a moment. "It's like being a photon. You can't decide where you're going."

Hugh shrugs and keeps his eyes on the road.

They are lost outside Buffalo and circle the freeway loop of the city twice before they find the proper exit on something called the Scajaquada Expressway, whose name Simon cannot stop saying aloud. Once they find the house, they call their agent at his office, and thirty minutes later he pulls up behind their trailer, waving the keys and smiling a Welcome-Wagon smile, festive with insincerity. As if he were the King of Buffalo, the agent—whose name is Vic Schroeder—praises the land and the people, making an all-purpose gesture toward the park as he describes "the good people of my town." Reluctantly, he tells Dorsey and Simon that the electricity is on in their house, but not the gas; they'll have to wait for a day before they can cook. "I don't want to cook," Dorsey tells him, as she stands near the front door, holding Noah, who is crying hysterically. "I don't know how." The agent gives her the keys, has her sign several papers,

and then waddles back to his Cadillac, shouting praise of the city
as he fits himself behind the wheel.

"It's not as though we haven't *seen* Buffalo," Simon grouses,
sitting on the front steps, pulling a drumstick out of a Kentucky
Fried Chicken bucket that Dorsey walked up the street to get them.
Chicken sauce speckles his shirt and his pants; he looks tired and
happy, a man who has finally arrived in a city that suits him
perfectly. "We were lost. We saw *all* of it. Where are the good
parts?"

"Of Buffalo? There aren't any," Dorsey says. Sitting on the lawn,
she watches the sky darken. "That's what everyone told me."

Hugh is keeping his thoughts to himself. The fact is that he's
never seen a city like this before, an industrial antique, gone to gray,
with narrow lumpish lawns and a brooding Slavic resignation, the
whole thing running on spare parts. Maybe it's what Dorsey needs,
after California; there'd be no happiness hysteria here, no therapeu-
tic guerrilla theater. Nobody in Buffalo could possibly think that
life was supposed to be fun. He hears an odd sound and thinks that
it might be—he wonders if he's hallucinating—the trumpeting of
an elephant.

Through the afternoon, Simon and Hugh carry in the contents
of the trailer; by six o'clock they have started to unpack the
boxes. Because he has to leave tomorrow, Hugh is trying to get
as much of this work done as he can, before he falls asleep on the
job, as he knows he will. At nine-twenty a knock sounds at the
front door. Simon is temporarily upstairs. Dorsey has been ar-
ranging the two chairs and the three lamps in the living room,
and Noah, who has slept for most of the day, is now playing on
the living room floor, watching *Bowling for Dollars.* He loves
bowling shows; he stops crying if he sees pins falling. By the
time that Hugh has gone to the door, he knows that it must be
a neighbor and this will mean that they will have to explain
themselves, the who what and where of their existences. He's not
in the mood. When he opens the door, his fears are instantly
realized: a large woman with a face as white as meringue is nodding at him and holding a plate of chocolate chip cookies, each
cookie almost the size of a 45-rpm record.

"Welcome to the neighborhood," she says. "I am Mrs. Dlugos-zewski, two doors down. I brought you some cookies." When Hugh does not invite her in, and instead tactlessly examines the cookie plate—he's never seen such large cookies or so many chocolate chips crammed into them—she says, rather angrily, "I baked them myself!"

"Well," he says, "I'm sure you did." He reaches for the plate, gives it a tug, but Mrs. Dlugoszewski does not release it. Belatedly he realizes that he's not supposed to take it; he's supposed to take a cookie and leave the plate alone. So he does. "Thank you," he says. "I'm Hugh Welch. And this is my sister, Dorsey."

"Ah ha!" Mrs. Dlugoszewski marches past him, clutching the plate, heading straight for Dorsey, her quick glances taking in Noah in front of the television set, the two chairs, the three lamps, the boxes of books and kitchenware scattered on the floor of the dining room. She puts the plate down on a chair and stands in front of Dorsey, giving her a gaze of womanly concern, before nodding to herself. "Welcome to Buffalo," she says, putting her hands on Dorsey's shoulders. "The Queen City."

Dorsey seems surprised by the woman's warmth; she flinches, jerking backwards. "The Queen City? Why's it called that?"

"No one knows," Mrs. Dlugoszewski says. "Some people say Toronto is the king, and Buffalo is the queen. But it's a continuing mystery."

"Oh. Well, thank you for coming over," Dorsey says. "Thank you very much."

"All these books." Mrs. Dlugoszewski flutters a thick, capable hand in their direction. "You're a student?"

"A teacher," Dorsey says. "Physics."

"Physics!" Mrs. Dlugoszewski laughs and wipes her brow. "My goodness. I was never much for science. You all look so tired. You must have had a long drive. And this must be your husband."

Having come down silently, Simon now stands at the bottom of the stairs, watching. "Hello hello," Mrs. Dlugoszewski says. "I'm your neighbor, Krystyna Dlugoszewski."

"I can see that," Simon tells her. "I'm Simon O'Rourke."

"I brought you some cookies. I'll leave the plate here. You can bring it back tomorrow. Take your time with them, though. You are . . . ?"

"Simon. Thank you very much." He bows his head.

"And this little one." She glances toward Noah. "Watching the television." She looks at Noah, then at Simon, then back at Noah, and at last at Dorsey. "He certainly looks like his father!" Mrs. Dlugoszewski says, meaning to be kind.

8

After she calls him from the hospital, he knows he has no choice but to fly out to the West Coast and see her and the new baby. He thinks, putting the telephone down, that he'll have to help her get back on her feet. After all this time, he says to himself. She didn't even tell me she was pregnant. She didn't tell me she was seeing anyone. After all this time, he says to himself, finally able to complete the sentence, after all the prizes and scholarships, after all the praise and glory and report cards with solid As, after all that, my sister has gone and done something crazy. My sister has finally messed up.

At the San Francisco Airport Hugh gives the address of the hospital to the cabbie, who tells him it'll be a thirty-dollar fare, seeing as how it's kind of out of town. "That's fine," Hugh says. "Just take me there."

In the hospital he stands in the doorway, unobserved, and watches his sister as she holds the baby in her arms. The pillow frames her head and it makes Hugh think of a square cotton halo. He's trying not to inhale deeply; hospitals, and particularly their soapy antiseptic smells, frighten him. Sunlight streams into the room across the foot of the hospital bed. The baby's eyes are closed; he yawns, as Hugh watches, and one of his arms stretches out, the little fingers flexing.

After Hugh steps into the room, carrying the cut flowers he bought in the hospital gift shop, Dorsey sees him and smiles wearily. He's never seen her like this: and the word that comes into his mind is *adulterated*. She's been adulterated. Her hair is stringy and her eyes seem permanently darkened. She's been wounded and interfered with but for the first time she looks completely happy, despite all the punishment she seems to have taken. Because he doesn't know what to say, for a minute he just smiles and tilts his head to get a better look at the baby. But he also wants to look at his sister and to understand how a woman can have been hurt in that way and still, or therefore, be so quietly ecstatic.

Dorsey says, "I suppose this needs some explanation."

Hugh shakes his head. "I'm not clever," he says. "You know I'm not. You don't have to explain things to me." He lays the flowers on the windowsill and bends down to kiss Dorsey on the forehead. Her skin is warm and milky against his lips. "Your baby is beautiful," he says. "He looks a lot like Daddy."

"I know." She waits. "You like the name?"

"Noah." He nods. "Yes, I do. It's a beautiful name."

"Oh, love," she says, "thank you for coming." With her free hand, she squeezes him on the wrist. "I mean, with no grandparents, or parents, or cousins, you're the only . . . the only . . ."

"The word is 'family.' "

"Is it? Well, thank you anyway."

"You're welcome." She slips her hand into his, her thin fingers giving him a tiny sensual charge. "I can't stay for more than a couple of days, just long enough to get you back to your place and set up."

"That's fine. The baby's healthy. We'll be going home today."

"There's something I want to ask you," Hugh says, examining his sister's face for evasiveness or guile. Not a trace. "I'll just ask you once, and you don't have to tell me, but I want to do this, and then I won't bother you again." He touches the baby's forehead with the thumb of his left hand. "Will you tell me who the father is?"

Dorsey gazes at the sunlight cutting across the foot of the bed. "Do you remember calling me and asking me who I was seeing? You said I was *seeing* this person, somehow."

Hugh shakes his head. He can't remember. Sometimes, in the deep end of the night, drunk, he has called his sister, and he doesn't remember what he's said.

"You said," Dorsey tells him, "that I was seeing somebody who had bad teeth and was maybe tall. I swear I don't know how you knew."

"I don't remember any of this."

"You don't have to. You won't ever meet him. I won't let you. He's a strange, wonderful, terrible man. I'll say his name and then I won't ever say it again. All right?"

He nods.

She speaks the name, Carlo Pavorese, then closes her eyes. When she opens them again, she is blinking rapidly. Having stepped backwards, Hugh can feel the heat of the sun across his shoulders and arms, and he can tell from her expression that she still might love the man whose name she has just spoken.

III

9

"Light," Carlo Pavorese says, glittering himself at his students. He chalks an equation on the board, balancing first on one foot, then the other. Back and forth, in rhythmical shifts from one foot to the other, he sways in front of them, a human pendulum articulating the mathematics of photons. As he speaks, the sun reflects off his glasses. Dorsey looks up from her notes to examine his face. The frames of his glasses hold the lenses in grooves of burning gold wire. The lenses themselves are set so close together that they almost form the sideways figure eight of infinity.

He interrupts himself, the interruptions signaled by a change in his facial tone, as if he were about to blush. Like a horse suddenly startled by a wolf, he will jerk backwards, pause, and without looking at anyone's eyes, he will say, "This discipline is a nightmare from which . . . no one will ever awaken." Ignoring himself and what he has just said, he then continues his lecture. His students ignore his other outbursts as well, as they ignore his quotations from William Blake. He says poetry is physics, and they smile.

His voice is often soft and the students must lean forward to hear.

Between sentences, while he is thinking, he makes a sound: *huhum, uhmmm, uhumum.* It is rhythmic and persistent; his mouth opens and shuts like a baby after a feeding. These rhythmic vocal pulsations are the rippling sound of thought, the sound of the infernal machine of his mind, the sound, one student has whispered, of one hand clapping.

"Why do you do that?" Dorsey asks him, months later.

"It's a tic I picked up from Oppenheimer," he says. "Where *he* got it is anyone's guess. He infected me with it. Can't you see the value in it?"

"No," Dorsey says.

"It prevents interruptions. Robert hated to be interrupted."

This enormous building, the Hall of Physics, constructed in 1960s rectangles of glass and brick and cement, with its long corridors of offices and seminar rooms receding to pinpoints at their far ends, is filled with students rushing all day long from one place to another. Some wave their arms, spilling papers, while others walk near the windows, brooding. Dorsey has waved her arms herself, happily gripped by the power of these various puzzles, by the power of the discipline. Her teachers are practical and straightforward. It is a profession that thrives on joking and playfulness, on the perpetual "Why?" addressed to the drip of a faucet or the rotations of a spinning plate. The enigmas of matter and energy are slowly decoded by persistence and ingenuity, by neat men and women who line up their papers and pencils carefully on their desks.

In the fellowship, and sanity, and good sense, and liberality of his profession, Carlo Pavorese takes no part. Dorsey has been warned away from him. "Pavorese? He's temperamental and impossible to his students. His productive period is over. He's gloomy. He *broods.* Stay away from him." This is the conventional wisdom, articulated by her teachers and friends.

And yet here she is, in his seminar room. And here she is in his office, cluttered with papers and books. And here she is in his home, allowing herself to be directed, in her dissertation, by Carlo Pavorese, the eccentric, a man past his prime. There is this curious promise of darkened light he holds out to her. "Miss Welch," he says to her, "I'm odd. I'm not like the others, I'm warning you. If you stick with me, you will not only learn how to solve these problems that your mind conceives, you will also begin to experience the history of modern physics, all its mixed blessings. You seem like a well-balanced woman. Do you really want what I can give you?"

"Why not?" she says, her cheerfulness breaking through. "Maybe you don't always have an effect on people."

"Oh, yes," he says. "In every life there are cracks into which wedges can be driven."

He claims to be the tallest physicist on the West Coast. Professor Pavorese's face is narrow and angular, punctuated by the generous overbite of his upper incisors—reminders, he says, of a childhood without braces, without dental repairs, without money. It might have been a purely Italian childhood but in fact it was spent in the Bronx, in a crowded squalling apartment where his two brothers and three sisters came and went and crooned and screamed, while quiet Carlo sat in his corner, surrounded by books, his face turned away from his family. He was so quiet, they didn't notice him. They forgot about him: the idiot of the family, the runt, "the little librarian," his sister Mirella called him. A big head of curly black hair, and at thirteen a dark heavy beard coming in, and grades skipped, and full scholarships and early admission to Princeton. In school no one teased him. You can't tease someone who doesn't live in the world.

Later, when they are almost through with each other, Dorsey says, "Sometimes you look like a gargoyle. There's something eerie about you. Indolent and harsh." She runs her hand along the side of his face. "But it's beautiful, in its way."

"No," he says. "I *am* a gargoyle. I look out at the world and I frighten it."

"You're not so frightening."

"Wait and see."

He lives in a large house that is walking distance from the university, and all day his two black Labradors, Trayf and Tummler, sit in the fenced backyard, snapping at flies, and wait for him to come home. "They are the only ones who understand me, these fellows," he says. Morning finds him being pulled by the two dogs around the block, Carlo Pavorese leaning backwards as he walks to prevent himself from pitching forward onto the pavement, yanked off his feet by their energy.

How long ago did his wife leave him? How long ago did his children go away? He says he doesn't remember. "Of course I was married once," he says, pointing to a photograph that is no longer on the wall. "My wife was beautiful. Her name was Margaret. She left. They all leave. I had two handsome children, two boys. They left too. Well, of course children should leave. After a while, no one can stand it. And you," he says to Dorsey, "you will be like the others. One day you will hurry out of the door, and that will be that. You won't turn back to look." His bony fingers grip her hand. It almost hurts, and then it does hurt. "Don't bother saying you won't," he tells her, squeezing even harder. "I know what I do to people."

His house is wired shut. The windows are never opened. Electrical foil tape frames the edges of the glass panes, and if anyone breaks in, opening the circuit, an alarm will sound in police headquarters. The front door is protected by an electrical burglar alarm system that can be shut off only with a special circular key. The entire house is air-conditioned, but Dorsey thinks that something is wrong with the exterior air intake: the air in the house seems old, and each month it gets older.

She has tried to leave the front door open, but he has noticed immediately and rushed to slam it shut. "Don't ever do that," he says. "Don't ever leave the door open."

"Why?"

He turns his glasses toward her, glittering himself at her for a moment—the beautiful eyes, the infinity of his glasses—and, having communicated what he knows about extended open spaces with that look, he turns away.

At the beginning, all she discusses with him are purely technical issues in physics. He keeps his distance, is courtly and polite. She considers him a first-rate mathematician, who can spot flaws in her calculations in an instant through a kind of Gestalt scanning. "Here," he says, "and here," pointing to inexactitude and theoretical messiness. Even in this superficial guidance he projects a quality that is rarer than brilliance, more interesting, more curious. All the other physicists she has known have not had it. She is forced to think of it as darkness. Some shadow is eating away at Carlo Pavorese. Dorsey thinks she can eventually get close enough to him to find out what it is; perhaps she can even stop its progress, open up the house, bring in some fresh air. She thinks she can ventilate the mind of Carlo Pavorese.

As she nears the end of her time at the great university and comes close to the end of her dissertation ("Relativistic Gravity in the Solar System: The Brans-Dicke Scalar-Tensor Theory and Gravitational Anisotropy"), Carlo Pavorese appears to be noticing her with considerably more interest, as if she is interesting as a person, rather than a generator of problems. He looks in her eyes. He says, "Miss Welch, you shouldn't take a job right away. Take a year off. Give yourself time to think. And I don't mean problems *in* physics. I mean problems *about* physics."

He leans back in his office chair, almost spilling a pile of yellow lined papers on top of the typewriter. "Damn these things," he says. Dorsey glances down at his thin, bony ankles: the socks *do* match. She wonders how he manages to be so intense without ever becoming absentminded or funny.

"Are you listening to me?" he asks. "Why are you staring at my socks?"

"I don't know."

"Listen," he says. "I have to be away for a week, next week. I want to ask a favor of you. Would you house-sit during the time I'm gone? It'd save me some worries, and some money, too, since I wouldn't have to take Trayf and Tummler to the vet. The only thing you'd have to do is give them heartworm pills. Would you do that?"

"Sure," she says, not thinking.

Much later, she thinks, It often begins so simply: watch my house, feed my dogs. There's nothing to it. Here, come on, just try. There. There. That's my girl.

· · ·

Dorsey has been living in her own apartment, which she shares with a casual lover, a musician named Brant Wachtel. For his own reasons, which Dorsey has no inkling of, Brant has been sleeping with Dorsey for two years now. He comes and goes and is friendly, though he has periods of depression when he sits in the living room, wearing three or four layers of clothes in the eighty-degree heat, mumbling to himself.

He teaches music to children in a neighboring elementary school and he plays rhythm guitar in a local bar band. His face is as smooth as a boy's, the skin so flawless it seems to have been processed out of a high-speed machine. Brant Wachtel says whatever he thinks, at the moment he has those thoughts. He has no disguises and, except for his depressions, no undisplayed interiors. He loves to take off his clothes, make love, and then go out for pizza. "Smile, honey," he likes to say. "Let me see that pretty smile." Her smile has a certain lack of enthusiasm, but she does not feel this as a deficiency in herself. She cannot stay totally interested—she never *has* been interested—in the intermittent broad sunlight of Brant Wachtel after having been exposed to the chiaroscuro of Carlo Pavorese. She gives Brant her best imitation of a grin, then leaves her apartment, carrying her backpack with a week's worth of clothes.

"Welcome to Pavor Manor," he says, as he greets Dorsey at the flaking burglar-proof door.

The furniture in this house defies style: the chairs are wood and leather with high, straight backs, and the tables have been refinished so often that they seem to glow with the abuse they have taken. On the walls he has hung an odd and confusing array of posters and reproductions: Dürer, Nicolas Poussin, Tiepolo, Max Ernst, and several pictures by an American whose work he admires and whom Dorsey has never heard of before, Ralston Crawford. Upstairs he has hung pictures by Georgia O'Keeffe, sky and flowers and bones. In them, light approaches the absolute. It strips objects, then obliterates them.

There is one other picture upstairs, an old illustration showing Phaëthon driving the chariot of the sun across the heavens. "Do you know the story of Phaëthon?" he asks her. When she shakes her head, he says, "You should. If you're a physicist, it's the only story."

Upstairs the two rooms once inhabited by his sons have been cleared of banners and high school letters and photos of girlfriends; the rooms have been converted into studies. One room is the Pavorese room. Here he keeps his professional journals. In this room, where the shades always are drawn, he came upon—he says he didn't discover it, it was just there—what is now called the Pavorese effect, which, he proudly says, cannot be explained in words, only in its mathematical formulation. It has to do with large-body gravitational interaction in certain theoretical dimensions of spacetime. "I did it here," Carlo Pavorese says, pointing at the desk. "I was sitting down."

The other room upstairs, the second study, is the Oppenheimer room; its windows face north and east, and if the curtains were ever drawn, it would be sunny for a few hours in the morning. The walls are painted sky blue. A signed photograph of Oppenheimer hangs on the wall. On the shelves of this room are many books written by Oppenheimer or about him, along with histories of Los Alamos, Livermore, and nuclear strategy. On a separate shelf are the books Oppenheimer claimed had helped to form his character: Baudelaire's *Les Fleurs du Mal,* the notebooks of Michael Faraday, *L'Éducation Sentimentale, Hamlet, The Divine Comedy, The Waste Land, The Bhagavad Gita,* and Plato's *Theaetetus.*

In this room Carlo Pavorese claims to be writing the spiritual biography of J. Robert Oppenheimer. He insists that it will never be published, that it is for his own benefit.

"Oppenheimer," he says, "was the only American scientist of the twentieth century whose life was worth telling. And I know why. It is because, in Oppenheimer's life, science and poetry and history came face to face with one another. First science defeated poetry. Then science defeated history. Then history defeated Oppenheimer. The symmetry is perfect, even down to Oppenheimer's late rehabilitation. It's an American life: a farce that has the appearance of a tragedy, but with a happy ending."

The look on Carlo Pavorese's face does not suggest that he actually thinks it was a farce.

. . .

During the week when Carlo Pavorese is gone, Dorsey prowls through the house every day before taking the dogs out for their walk. Trayf, she discovers, has an interest in birds and watches nothing else during the walk, while Tummler is concerned only with cars and watches each one go by with a suspicious gaze. Dorsey keeps both dogs—spayed females—on leashes, and even with one leash in each hand, the dogs control her completely, leading her, following the route Carlo always takes them on, as if there were no other possible places they might go.

She hides their heartworm pills in their dogfood, but Tummler carefully eats around hers. Against her own instincts and conscious wishes, Dorsey is forced to open the dog's mouth and place the pill on the back of her pink tongue, and as soon as she has removed her hand from the dog's mouth, she rushes to the bathroom to wash the saliva from her fingers.

She settles down in one of Carlo Pavorese's ancient creaking chairs with her notepad in her lap, intending to work on physics, the dogs panting at her feet. Instead she begins to doze off, and she sees in front of her a set of distorted coordinates, curved from the effect of gravity, and numbers whose function she does not know passing in front of her mind's screen. One of the dogs licks her on the soles of her bare feet. She sees her father, and then Hugh, waving their arms at her, and she tries to read the message that they're giving her with this vigorous pantomime. Hello. Stand up. Get out.

Opening her eyes, she feels for a moment a sense that this house and everything in it has a purpose, which she does not know, directed toward her; she shakes her head, and now, the dark furniture and faded curtains and echoing wood floors seem to be expressing sadness and oppression. Desolation of spirit rises from the soiled rugs and ashtrays and floats out from the cluttered and crammed bookshelves. She gets up from her chair, puts on her shoes, and walks back to her apartment.

That night, she goes out with Brant Wachtel for burgers and beer. They end up at a dance club filled with cleverly dressed young people. Brant knows the musicians in the band, a local group called Peoria ("We *will* play in Peoria") that performs Top Forty and oldies that are easy to dance to. Brant is an absentmindedly good dancer and can steer his way physically into almost any rhythm: his dancing resembles rhythmic sleepwalking, a bodily expression of a dream state that is both deeply remote and sensual. His specialty is a relaxed, easy sweatiness, a set of California moves: invitations offered, invitations withdrawn.

But Dorsey dances awkwardly. She's never danced well, and now she knows that she looks like someone released from a cloister. The bar smells of cigarettes, beer, and musky physical meetings, and in this brackish air and doped-out light Dorsey would like to recover the rhythms of Brant's unconscious pleasure in things, but she can't, and Brant Wachtel won't teach her. It's her problem, not his. He's doing fine. She's the one who's house-sitting at Carlo's. Carlo Pavorese has done this to her. Four years of graduate study have done this to her. A life of study has done this to her. But until now, she hasn't felt herself becoming self-detached.

Finally even Brant Wachtel notices. "Hey," he says, "you're a real nervous dancer tonight. I've never seen you do that." He does a quick imitation of her splay beat stomp. It's painful for her to see this decent man, this teacher of children, doing a version of her rhythmic spasms; it's like hearing a child imitating, for laughs, the cries of an adult in pain. Seeing him, she walks off the dance floor, rattling her bracelets with nervous flicks. When he catches up to her, she grabs his arms and says, "I want to go home."

The car is her car; she drives back. At home Brant Wachtel makes her a sandwich; he pours her a glass of water; he tries, in his quiet furry way, to soothe her.

They bed down, and he touches her in the way she likes. In the techniques of skin touching skin, he acknowledges the common sexual decencies. As soon as they're finished, he falls asleep and snores, not an unpleasant sound. Dorsey finds it calming, like waves on a beach. She lets her hand descend to his neck and circles one of his curls with her index finger. She's grateful that they don't love each other. Instead, they have a kind of kinship. They found each other easily and will part easily, without rancor. He will think better of the minds of women because of her.

But it's not enough. She rises from the bed, where Brant has made happy shallow love to her, and she gets dressed quickly. She drives

back to Carlo Pavorese's house and lets herself in with the circular
key. The black Labradors jump all over her.

For the remaining five days she does not go back to her apartment,
but instead moves from room to room in Carlo Pavorese's house,
soaking up what she thinks of as the atmosphere. Even on the
bookshelves there is a sense of incompatibles being thrown together
to see what kinds of explosions can be created. Dante, for example,
is placed next to Nietzsche. In Carlo Pavorese's shelving system, St.
John of the Cross is next to Baudelaire, Walt Whitman next to
E. M. Cioran, and Karl Marx is mated with Emily Dickinson.
Boethius and Wittgenstein, Pirandello and Sophocles, Kant and the
autobiography of Doris Day.

Wherever she goes, the dogs follow her, and as they lick her, and
bark, and pull her outside, she thinks of her own life, her parents'
careful preparations for her, her brother's pride in her efficient mind,
having brought her to this darkened house, where the twentieth
century lives in the form of a large gargoyle man who, sooner or
later, is going to make love to her, because she wants him to. As
soon as he is back, he bends down hugely and gives her a kiss on
the cheek. The dogs jump up and put their front paws on his chest,
and he hugs them. He is dressed like a dignified but seedy haber-
dasher in a small town where no one is really interested in clothes:
the pants and coat don't match in either pattern or fabric. They are
the clothes of a man who doesn't look in the mirror often enough.
"Good to see you," he says. "I'll cook dinner."

He prepares lamb in a sweetish sauce. At the table he begins to
talk, and the talk turns into a monologue that Dorsey finds herself
unable to interrupt.

"I've just heard a lot of papers," he says. "I go to these conferences, you know, as a *spy*. They think I'm a physicist, just like them,
but instead I'm listening in on what recipes they're brewing in their
witches' pots up there on Parnassus. Experimental results. I hate
experiments. I always have. And, of course, the lovely theories. The
creation and destruction of matter. Our field, Miss Welch, has
become positively biblical. First and last things. Now that we have
found a way to destroy the Earth fully and sufficiently, we are
prowling around in the origins of the universe. These men would

build black holes, if they could figure out how. After all, if you become a god, you have to create something, don't you? And there, unfortunately, is the joke on us. We have studied matter, but all we can actually do is destroy it. And the angel of death descends with his baskets of cash. Isn't that funny?"

"Carlo," she says, "why don't you—"

"God plays a trick on smart people: he lets them discover secrets that will kill them. And He doesn't make them smart enough to know how to forget what they've discovered. It's terrible and I love it. It's my life."

She leans back, alarmed by the fatigued irony in his voice, and pours herself a glass of burgundy. He holds out his own glass, and in silence she fills it, noting without meaning to that his hand is shaking. The mantel clock fills the silence with its woody hollow tick. "Lighten up," she says, in an ineffectively cheerful tone. But it's not as though he's a good listener, or pays attention to any advice or instruction she gives him. He is always half-absented from whatever room he inhabits; he is here, but he is also out there, where the neurons spin and snap.

"You know I was in Los Alamos."

"Of course. Everyone knows that."

"I did some of the calculations. A group of us, under Feynman. I was very very young. They wanted that: quick minds."

"It's not so unusual," she says, wanting to head off this topic. "There were a lot of people who—"

"—Up there on the high elevations," he says, having tuned her out, "in that military monastery, what devotion we had! And Oppenheimer—he was effective in bringing people together to work out solutions. He was like Jay Gatsby: he saw the possibilities. He even acted like Gatsby. Polite. Courtly. Self-obsessed. And of course we all thought we were doing this service, this patriotic calling. Because everyone thought the Germans were building a fission bomb, too. But the problem was, you know, it was often fun working out the complexities of the thing. You do get to love your own mind after a while."

"—I know all this, Carlo. Everyone knows that—"

"—You don't know. Listen to me. It was like building a huge, complicated toy," he says, gazing down into his wine and taking

two deep breaths. "It was as though all of us had been brought there
to have this toy built, and it wasn't until the thing had actually
exploded that grown men saw that it wasn't a toy and started to
vomit into the bushes. Well, they'd been drinking, of course. The
celebrations. The . . . unpalatable celebrations. We had made this
wonderful thing, this sexy contrivance, all for the sake of Death.
It was *him* we served."

She looks out past the dining room into the living room, dusty
and neglected, without any primary colors except for the pictures
on the walls. The two dogs thump their sleek tails underneath the
table, and when she drops her hand to her side she feels a long wet
tongue licking it.

"It's all done," she says. "It's history now."

"Well, it isn't history, is it, if it lives with you. Those things live
with everybody. They force you to think about them, those bombs.
You live in their shadow and they steal your soul, just suck it up,
like that." He snaps his fingers. "They make everybody feel crazy.
They replicate themselves. The big babies. They have their own
baby boom."

She thinks: what's the use even talking to him?

"Someone has to have a bad conscience," Carlo Pavorese says,
standing up, bread crumbs falling from his shirt onto the floor,
where Trayf and Tummler lick them up with loud slurps. "That was
the job the gods gave me. Come back in a few days. I'll be cheerier."
He walks into his study. After a minute, Dorsey hears one of the
Joe Venuti records being played softly on Carlo's phonograph. She
decides to leave him alone in there, and she walks to the door,
accompanied by Trayf, who puts Dorsey's hand in her mouth,
playing with it.

It happens now that at certain times of day she cannot remember
where she is. Working to finish her dissertation, she must stop and
think about where she is located: I'm in the science library, I'm in
Kearsley Hall, I'm at home. When she is at home, in the apartment,
she works. She calls friends. She receives phone calls. She is encour-
aged: her work is going well, and she is almost finished. But what
is this, happening to time? Some days, completing the thesis, she
works for so long that when she looks up at the window, it is not

noon, as she thought, but night, and she has passed through the day without knowing, exactly, that it had been there. Sometimes it's supposed to be night, but it's early morning instead. She forgets to eat. It's a rare pleasure to forget to eat, to go without food and not to miss it. This is the pleasure of monks and contemplatives. She sees with delight that she is losing weight, and, after being invited again, she shows up at Carlo Pavorese's house, in her new, more slender self.

As unobservant as he is, he notices that she is thinner and feeds her T-bone steak. "Oppenheimer, you know, lost so much weight at Los Alamos that by the time we tested the bomb he was down to 115 pounds. He had what I think you would call an hysterical personality, and his wife didn't help matters much. And of course he smoked constantly. He treated his body as if it were an appendage to his mind, a stalk. I heard people there say that he looked like a faun: you know, the delicate features, the long ears, the liquid lantern blue eyes. Some said bird, but no, it was not that either. I heard someone else say that he was cultivating the look of what the Jews call a *tzaddik,* a holy man. He had a great yearning for God, Oppenheimer did. And after all, he called the first bomb test Trinity, didn't he? So here's a man who yearns for God and manages to get the first A-bomb built. This is a joke, of course, a cosmic joke, but no one is laughing, at least not yet."

"Carlo, can we talk about something else?"

"Sure," he says. "What do you want to talk about?"

"What about the trees in your backyard?"

"What trees?" he asks. "I never noticed any."

The telephone rings, and though she's not sure what time it is, she is certain that it's night, because it's dark.

The voice is slurred and uninflected. "What's the matter with you?"

When she hears her brother's voice, she is instantly awake. "Hugh! My God, how are you?"

"I'm drunk," he says. "I snuck in this bottle of Jim Beam and I'm sitting down here in the basement at my workbench, and Laurie doesn't know that I'm here, because, you know, she went to bed. I guess she was tired or something. Maybe she was bored. Maybe she was tired of being bored. People go to bed when they're bored. Are you ever bored?"

"I'm almost never bored," Dorsey says. Though her brother's tone is woozy and alcoholic, it's friendly. "So how *is* Laurie?" she asks.

"Ever the same," Hugh says. "We make love but she won't kiss me. Why is that? Are you sure you aren't ever bored? I get bored."

"I'm too busy to be bored. Hugh, what did you mean when you asked me what the matter was?"

There is a long pause at his end of the line, and she can hear him making oral sounds, like lip-smacking. "What?"

"You said, 'What's the matter with you?' You didn't even say hello."

"Sorry sorry sorry. Very rude of me. I will remember from now on always to say hello."

"Hugh."

"What?"

"You said, 'What's the matter?' "

"Well, what is?"

"Nothing's the matter."

"Oh, no. You can't pull that stuff on me. You can pretend to your smart brainy friends that you're all right, but seeing as how I am your brother, you cannot fool me, for I see through your little stratagems." Dorsey realizes, as she has before, that when her brother is intoxicated he has considerable powers of eloquence, and the thought comes to her that perhaps he isn't as unintelligent as he sometimes makes himself out to be. Maybe his lack of intelligence is a hoax. Maybe he's only pretending to be average. "I see through your stratagems," he repeats. "I know your mind. I have this feel—" he laughs softly, a broken and compressed laugh—"this *feel* for what's going on inside it. So what's going on?"

"Nothing's going on. I've just pretty much finished my dissertation, and I think I'll probably take next year off before I start to teach. There are various little jobs, informal post-docs that I can pick up, and—"

"No no no no no nope," he says. "Not what I meant."

"Huh?"

"Who's the person?"

"What person?"

"Must I reveal what I know?" he asks. "Very well. I will reveal what I know. I see this person. I look out of the corner of my eye and there he is. Tall dark and handsome. Or ugly. Who knows. Anyway I had this, I guess you could call it a dream, and there you were, all swelled out in your California clothes, and there was this guy with you. It was like one of those dreams that comes on and announces itself, and I thought, well, what the hell, call her up, let's find out who this fellow is that's going out with my sister."

"What did he look like?"

"Look like? I don't remember what he looked like. I hadn't ever seen him before. I don't have a good memory for people I meet in dreams. I forget them right away. Am I way off base here? Am I losing my mind? So who's this tall person you've been seeing?"

"How should I know? He's in *your* dream."

"Maybe he's a big tall ugly guy," Hugh laughs. "Maybe he has bad teeth."

"This is all news to me," Dorsey says.

"Well, I thought I'd check. Of course it's none of my business, who you hang out with, who you see. Don't think that I'm *scouting* here, or checking on you in any way at all. If you thought that, you would be wrong. All I want to do here," he says, and his voice seems to fade out for a moment. ". . . not checking on you, just sort of concerned," he says.

Dorsey, in bed, tries to relax herself.

"Who d'you have to look out for you?" her brother's voice says. "Who's around to check?"

"I can take care of myself," Dorsey tells him, falling back in the bed, so that her head is on the pillow and her eyes are closed. It strikes her that none of this may be as sinister as it seems.

"The man in my dream did not actually like you," Hugh says. "It was more intense than that."

"You're imagining things," Dorsey tells her brother. "How's the weather in Michigan?"

"Snowing here," he tells her. "It comes down by the yard. By the bolt. Three feet in one hour, one full yard of snow."

"No snow here. I miss it. We do get a few clouds now and then." She chuckles, with effort.

"It must be nice having all that sun."

"No, actually, it isn't." She waits. "In fact I don't like it at all. I'm almost sick of it. Have you ever heard of anyone getting sick of the sun? It seems almost molelike, doesn't it?"

"I don't think so," Hugh says. "I've gotten sick of the sun many times. There have been many days in my life when I could not look at the sun for one more minute, that's how tired I was of it. You certainly have to endure a lot of light to get through a lifetime," he says disconnectedly. "Well, kiddo, I miss you."

"I miss you, too."

"Call me," he says. "Call me the minute you need any help. I *think* that's what I'm here for."

Long after he has hung up, she continues to hold the telephone in her hand. A lucky guess, she thinks. He made one lucky guess.

In a mood of exasperated pastoralism she drives Carlo Pavorese all the way over to Mount Tamalpais. During the drive up he squints at the sunlight and studies the trees—pine and fouquat and poplars—with an expression of skepticism that could easily be taken for disbelief. Dorsey glances at him long enough to make herself sure that she has actually spied this look of rationalist withdrawal on his face. There's no mistaking it: the entire landscape has become a baroque configuration of shadows, of atoms and molecules that have achieved a certain form and are arrayed in distinct colors but are not, for that reason, worth thinking about or even worth looking at. The sky is an unsubtle primary blue, as if colored with school paint and lit with a six-hundred-watt bulb. Dorsey sees a beautiful downward sloping meadow facing the Pacific, the meadow's upper ridge clustered with live oak, and for a moment she sees this scene as he does: the blues and the greens and the other colors disappear and she gradually understands that when he gazes out at all this he sees a generalization of matter. He sees nature as a field of generalizations. He sits on the passenger's side and mutters impatient sentences to himself. He means that the mountain itself is just a junkpile of soil and rock. And she sees that particularity—two hikers, a man and a woman both with blue backpacks, and hiking boots and cut-offs, walking past the blue spruce and jack pines, the various flowers and grasses—all this particularity bores Carlo Pavorese to death. They are specific examples of already established principles. The world is a construct of meaningless variables. When she stops at a parking space, he will not get out. He regrets being in the car; he regrets having been persuaded to come. Mount Tamalpais is an intellectual failure, a chic hangout for nature admirers; it cannot satisfy his thirst for the absolute.

As she prepares for her dissertation defense, Dorsey can feel the world losing its grip on her. Something eerie and unmeasurable is beginning to happen to her sense of sequences. They're somehow experiencing—or *she's* experiencing—time lapses, a shuffling of space into time, and when she tries to take inventory she finds she's missing whole days, shoplifted from her memory. For no particular reason that she can see, the transitions are being left out between the days and the weeks. Brant Wachtel has been her boyfriend; now he is gone; now she sleeps in the apartment on Revere Street alone. But no: she awakens, and Brant is still here, sleeping beside her, stretched out naked—this is California and he shuns pajamas—breathing wetly, his curls tumbling down the back of his neck as they always have. She met Brant in a record store, over the bin for cut-outs, and she returned his first glance because of those curls. But when she wakes up again Brant isn't there. Could he have come in for a few hours, and left? Is he here, or not? And then, it seems, almost at once, she herself is not in the apartment but is back on Mount Tamalpais, outside the car, holding, of all things, a dandelion: wet stalk, yellow flower, jagged green leaves, clumped root system. She is trying to sell the dandelion to Carlo Pavorese, sell him on the *idea* of the dandelion. It's free, but he still refuses to buy it. I won't buy it at any price, he says; I won't buy it if you give it to me. But look at how beautiful it is, she tells him. Look at the systematic logic contained in the structure of this plant. You look, he says. You're the aesthete. I have better things to think about than dandelions.

After her successful dissertation defense in a room filled with the best scientific minds that the famous university can keep on its payroll, she is at Carlo's, having a drink at a party in her honor. She's looking at a painting downstairs she doesn't remember having seen before. The painting shows a long hallway, hung with mirrors on both sides, leading to a door; this door is open and leads to a further, smaller hallway, hung with (in perspective, smaller) mirrors, and leading to another door, also open; through this door one can glimpse a tiny receding hallway, and at the end of this hallway is another door. But this door—almost at the vanishing point—is closed. She suspects that Carlo did this painting himself, at some early time of his life, but he's busy in the kitchen, pouring drinks for the other guests, and she's not about to ask him.

One of her friends, Danny Anderson, a fellow graduate student, comes down from the upstairs bathroom, fixing his trouser fly, and sidles up to where Dorsey is standing in the hallway, making polite talk to one of her examiners, an old gentleman who has been inquiring about her career plans. As soon as Dorsey is alone, Danny whispers, "Doesn't he ever dust in here? Somebody should buy the man a rag."

"Carlo doesn't care about dust," Dorsey says.

"I noticed you were looking at those receding doorways in that painting he has in the kitchen. He certainly has a lot of what I guess you'd call art in this place, all these various butterflies broken on sundry wheels. Did you see the Hopper reproduction he has upstairs?"

"He doesn't have any Hopper reproductions."

"Well, I don't know what it is, but I was sneaking around, and I saw *something*. Come take a look. Get your mind off your career and relativistic gravity for a minute."

She follows him upstairs. In the Pavorese room, to the side of the windows on the west wall, is a small reproduction whose colors are beginning to fade. She never noticed this picture before. It looks like a Hopper but obviously isn't; the lines are too thick. In this picture four people stand on the green front lawn of a house in early morning. They're viewed from the side: two adults, a mother and a father, and two children, a boy and a girl. They shade their eyes against the sun, but all four appear to be looking directly at it. The sun does not actually appear in the picture, but the viewer knows that the time is sunrise, because the four figures are lit in early morning pale gold. Dorsey can see part of their house behind them, a terrace and a porch. Their heads are slightly raised. The woman's 1940s-style dress is ruffled out behind her, as if an early morning breeze is blowing against it. Dorsey knows she's seen this scene before, but she can't remember where. Who *are* those people?

Danny Anderson's hand is on Dorsey's shoulder. She decides to let him leave it there.

In the picture, the father's trousers are blown backwards by the same breeze. There they are: four figures viewed laterally, in expectant American postures. Four figures looking at the rising sun, immobilized by the painter at the horizon. The family is spaced so that no one touches anyone else.

"I told you so," Danny says. "What's this thing called? *Four People Going Blind?*"

"I never saw this before," Dorsey tells him, shifting her shoulder so that Danny's hand falls off it.

"I wonder what he's working on." He picks up some of the papers on Carlo's desk and begins to examine them.

"Danny! Leave those things alone."

"I was just wondering what the old boy was up to. Let's go check out his basement."

"No. He'll catch us."

"No, he won't. He's too busy. It'll only take a minute."

"I'm supposed to be with the other guests," she says. "I should be circulating."

"One minute." He grabs her hand for a moment, and she feels the chill his drink's ice cubes have made on his skin. "Come on."

They go down the stairs, separated by twenty seconds for discretion's sake, Dorsey in the lead. When Carlo is out of the kitchen, she opens the door to the basement and fumbles along the wall until she finds the switch. When the light snaps on, she sees the steps and the handrail, and she'd like to turn around. But Danny is behind her, and she's curious. She walks down the stairs sideways, afraid she'll slip on the steep, narrow planks, and at the bottom she flicks on another wall switch.

There's the water heater. And over there is a pile of books and papers, stacked in one musty corner. And nearer the stairs is a collection of old phonograph records, next to a standing cupboard with several graying jars of preserves. There is an unclean damp smell, like a bait shop. Dorsey thinks: eels.

"Wow," Danny says behind her. "Look over there."

He points to the wall, where lined up on a group of built-in shelves are several rows of seashells, carefully positioned and labeled with index cards tacked to the front. They remind her of the roadside seashell stands her parents used to stop at when she was a child. "I bet he did that with his wife," Danny says. "Let's see: sand dollars, starfish, and those are . . . what're they called, the ones that look like—"

"—I don't know what they're called and I'm not staying down here. Come on, Danny." She hits the switch, throwing the shells into the dark, and she climbs the stairs quickly, peering through the door to make sure that Carlo isn't in the kitchen. "Come on," she says. "Move."

Without anyone noticing that they were gone, they are back in the kitchen, filling their glasses with more ice cubes.

One week later, Dorsey has invited Carlo Pavorese for lunch at an outdoor restaurant. He doesn't seem to notice the people who pass by on the sidewalk. He doesn't notice the sky. He sits hunched over, his face close to his food, his shoulders tense.

"Carlo," she says, "what is it with you and Oppenheimer? What's the deal with this biography you're writing? Why don't you just forget him?"

He hardly looks up from his shrimp salad. He glances at Dorsey quickly and lowers his eyes again. "You think it's such a blessing to be intelligent, don't you? You're an innocent. You aren't as smart as you think you are. Intelligence is bad luck. It only looks like a gift. It's not a gift; it's a debt for which you must pay and pay and pay. Oppenheimer finally—*finally!*—figured that out. Once I came on him in his office at the Institute for Advanced Study in Princeton. His secretary had announced me but he had evidently forgotten that I was coming in. It was a time of his life when he was easily preoccupied. In any case, I entered the room and waited."

He reaches for his glass of wine. He swirls the wine around in his mouth before he swallows it.

"Oppenheimer was sitting at his desk, his back turned to me, and he was staring out one of the windows. At first I thought he was bird watching, but there were no remarkable birds in those trees, and he was not the sort of man to give his attention to sparrows. To get his notice I decided to make a joke. 'Robert,' I said, 'are you thinking about physics, or your sins?' "

Carlo Pavorese leans back to study a passing car. He glances at Dorsey, then looks down again.

"You didn't joke about sin with Oppenheimer. After all, there was Jean Tatlock, his girlfriend, the one who slit her wrists, and there were the mental troubles in his youth, and of course all his flirting with Communism, to say nothing of his supervision of the building of the bomb. To say nothing of his marriage to Kitty, a Byzantine romantic relationship if there ever was one. Sin and physics. Exactly the wrong thing to ask him about. *He* knew the myth of Phaëthon, backwards and forwards."

"What did he say?" Dorsey asks, deciding that she had better pick up the check on this one.

"What did he say? Well, first he turned his face toward me. Oppenheimer's face was one of his great accomplishments. You take Einstein. Einstein's a poster saint, an icon of genius. The Santa Claus of Princeton. But Oppenheimer's face is more dainty. It's more difficult to read. The aesthete and the bureaucrat are lodged in that face, and they're struggling with each other. So he turned to me and looked. The cold sad faun's face. I was meant to see the whole of his life in an instant of time. All right. I did.

"Then he smiled. I was off his hook. 'Carlo,' he asked me, 'when did the Greeks decide that rhetorical questions were a form of untruth?' I wasn't meant to answer disputatiously. It was one of his typical sibylline epigrams. Narcissists love epigrams. You never interrupt an epigram. So we talked about the Greeks for the next few minutes. We didn't talk about physics or sin. We talked about the Sophists, how they had been unjustly attacked by Plato as mere rhetoricians. It was the sort of discussion he liked. Sin he would not at first discuss in public. He appropriated sin for himself. He thought sin was original with *him*. By and by he accused other physicists of sin. And that, young lady, is one of the reasons I think about him. He saw it all coming. He could see the whole unhappy comedy unfolding."

"What comedy?" Dorsey asks.

"You're a Ph.D. now," Carlo Pavorese tells her. "You figure it out." Finally he sits up and leans back. "Do you understand yet how a soul can be taken over? You're going to learn."

It is days later. She is back in his house, sitting in one of the living room chairs, while Trayf and Tummler lick her hands.

"Why do you listen to me?" Carlo Pavorese asks.

"You're a fine teacher. You've helped me."

"Yes. But my dear girl, *you're still here.* You come over here. You eat my food and you walk my dogs." He points into the dining room. "And you do your work at the dining room table while I pace about and act oddly. Your attraction to me is peculiar. I'm not as famous as I used to be. I'm almost a crank. Do you like to hear me talk?"

" 'Like'? No, that's probably not the word I'd use."

"What word would you use?"

"I listen to you, don't I?" She waits. "Is it love if I listen?"

She gazes at him, and he turns away.

"Yes," he says. "You listen."

At home she removes some cold potato soup in a Tupperware container from the refrigerator and warms it up on the stove. While the soup is warming, she makes herself a spinach salad. At the last minute she pulls out a frosty bag of frozen shrimp from the freezer, defrosts a few under the tap, and adds them to the salad. When the soup is ready, she sits down at the kitchen table, the evening paper to her left. She remembers some white wine in the cupboard, opens it, and pours herself a glass. She sits down again. But something is wrong. As she brings the soup to her mouth, she sees that her hand is trembling, and in the large circular soup spoon she can see the small wave motions her hand's trembling has created, a rippled surface. It's an interesting surface of ripples. She lowers the spoon and waits for the shaking to stop.

Away from physics and Carlo Pavorese, Dorsey has one friend, living across the hall from her in the building: Maude Ann Norris, a single parent who works as a buyer for a local department store, what she calls "an upstairs job," which means that she sits at a desk and does not have to stand all day, as she did once as a sore-footed clerk in the cosmetics section on the first floor. Maude Ann knocks at Dorsey's door, brings her cups of hot tea and plates of butter cookies from Denmark, complains briefly of the intransigence and disloyalty of men, and praises her son, Gerald, for his beauty and intelligence. Gerald *is* beautiful, Dorsey thinks with envy. He is Maude Ann's greatest achievement. He builds multi-storied sky-scrapers, using hundreds of differently shaped blocks. He is frisky and likes to dance on the dining room table.

Maude Ann herself has a pleasant hello-world face, which always reminds Dorsey of the yearbook photographs of the girls in Five Oaks: eighteen-year-olds who would make themselves into princesses by a sheer act of faith.

Maude Ann has heard all about Carlo Pavorese and disapproves of him. "He sounds like a creep," she says. "Okay, so he's smart. But I say a creep is a creep." Brant Wachtel may have been a minimalist when it came to character, but Maude Ann once saw him in the hallway wearing only his Jockey shorts, and the sight left an impression on her. "Where did you find him?" Maude Ann asked Dorsey. "I'd like a map to that place."

Now that Brant has left—Maude Ann thinks that his departure is bad news for Dorsey and every other woman in the building—Maude Ann complains about Dorsey's facial fatigue lines, the crazy hours she keeps, her failure to keep her kitchen well-stocked, the general disarray in the living room. Maude Ann brings sandwiches and glasses of milk in an effort to keep her friend nourished. "You're never around," she complains, "except in the middle of the night. I only see you when I can't sleep. When do *you* sleep? I never see you sleeping. You're awake all the time. That's bad. You should take better care of yourself."

When he walks around his house, followed by his dogs, the parts of his body appear to be out of synchronicity with themselves. His arms and legs are in separate time zones. Carlo Pavorese is not simultaneous with himself: no event can occur to all his body's elements at the same time. Event-waves journey through his tissues like earthquakes down fault lines. His neural paths are slow, and he is a dangerous driver, who brakes five seconds after his mind has sent his foot the instructions to hit the pedal.

His physical singularity is not a matter of taste but fact, in the same way that it is not a matter of opinion that granite is a solid rather than a liquid. His hair rises from his thin face like cold threaded flames. Dorsey finds herself ritually fascinated by the fact of Carlo Pavorese's harshness, by his blotched skin, his obsessive tormented monologues. She is fascinated by his shame. Here on the West Coast, in the country as a whole, he's almost an anomaly.

He is standing again in his living room, gesturing nervously with his right arm, his feet in the square of sunlight cast onto the floor.

"Why," he asks, "do people put up posters of Einstein on their walls? People who never read the special theory of relativity, much less understand it?"

Dorsey holds a cup of coffee in her hands, and she leans back on a dining room chair. "Because Einstein was a genius."

"No," Carlo Pavorese says. "There are other geniuses whose faces do not appear on posters. Think again."

"He had a beautiful face."

"Nonsense, and you are a sentimentalist."

"All right, Carlo. I give up. Why do people put up pictures of Einstein on their walls?"

"Because people admire power, Miss Welch, and Einstein had it. People think he invented the bomb, and that's why his picture is up on a thousand walls, in the hopes that that pseudo-kindly face will be the face of modern physics. They want our profession to be governed by Santa Claus. No one wants Oppenheimer's face on the wall. Who wants to be gazed upon by a rueful faun? A man who went around quoting Baudelaire? *'Là, tout n'est qu'ordre et beauté, / Luxe, calme et volupté.'* He used to quote those lines to me. I don't know whether he thought they referred to paradise or to physics. 'There, nothing else but grace and beauty, / Richness, quietness, and loveliness.' I wonder if that's how he felt when he discovered the theory of gravitational contraction in 1939? Not much *luxe* in a black hole."

"Carlo," she says.

"I just don't want you to be innocent," he says. "Americans eat too much candy. Their diet is very high in sugar."

Because of course she and Carlo Pavorese have slept together several times; she has let this happen, drawn to it, curiosity and the urge to clean out his shadows controlling her. It might even be love; she has no idea. The first time it happened he had made her a dinner of Sicilian fish soup, followed by a pasta in a Neapolitan sauce, and a tomato salad with basil. They sat in the dining room under the dusty wrought-iron chandelier, with the dogs at their feet slobbering quietly and waiting for handouts. Dorsey and Carlo Pavorese were discussing mythic animals. Dorsey said that her favorite was the unicorn. Carlo Pavorese waved his hand impatiently and said that women always say that. He wagged his gargoyle face. *His* favorite was the Bunyip. "It's feathered and gray and lives in the sea," he said. "It has an emu's head, which is covered with a thick pelt. Many poems and fables have been written about the Bunyip. It is said to project a waterspout behind it that distresses and over-turns fishing boats, drowning honest fishermen. The stories claim that it has a cry."

"What does it sound like?" Dorsey asked.

"Like this." He opened his mouth and made the two-note, high-low call of a foghorn. "You see?" he said. "The story is that foghorns are based on the sea cry of the Bunyip. Haven't you ever thought, when you heard foghorns, that you were hearing the cry of a large and probably extinct furred-and-feathered animal that lives in the sea?"

"I never heard foghorns until I moved out here," she said. "They don't have foghorns in Five Oaks, Michigan."

"Maybe they should. Maybe there are shipwrecks in the heart-land, too. The foghorns we have out here, those Bunyips swimming around in San Francisco Bay, I'm one of them. I have kept myself in check, Miss Welch, but you are no longer officially my student, and I must tell you that your skin and your eyes and your purity have riven my heart. Please forgive me, but I must ask you to do me the greatest favor a young woman can do for an old man."

She watched him rise from the table.

"I will walk upstairs," he said, "and you may follow me or not."

He stood, and after two minutes she mounted the stairs. She would do this for him, but she would also do it for herself, out of affection and curiosity. She waited for him to switch on the lights, but he would not, and when she edged toward a lamp, she heard him say, "Don't." He took her hand. His fingers were dry and crusty. With his right arm pressing against her back he steered her toward his bedroom: *the sleep museum,* she thought. He said he would like to undress her but was too old to understand women's clothes. Would she do it? "Carlo," she said, "I don't have my diaphragm. It's back at the apartment." She felt him nearby, standing quietly in the dark alcove. Through the curtains the streetlight gave him the barest hint of an outline, charcoal on charcoal. "What are you worried about?" he said. "I'm an old man."

She wished she had had more wine: she could not remember ever being touched by a man toward whom she felt physical curiosity rather than attraction. She had an impulse to run out of the room, down the stairs, and out through the front door, slamming it, so that its flaking blue paint would flutter down onto the welcome mat, placed there years before by Carlo Pavorese's wife and never removed by him. She followed herself, in her own mind, as she walked briskly down the sidewalk, crossing street after street, her shadow walking behind and then in front of her as she passed under the mercury streetlights, the two miles back to her apartment, coming upstairs, knocking at Maude Ann's door, to tell her what Carlo Pavorese had asked her to do.

"What!" Maude Ann would say, aghast, scandalized. He wrapped his arms around Dorsey and bent down so that his face was next to hers. He sighed. It felt like being embraced by a sheet of papyrus. "He did *what*?" Maude Ann would ask. She would go to the kitchen and make some tea, either the orange pekoe she always drank or some plain old no-name brand. She would bring out every package of cookies she owned; there would be a towering heap of cookies on a plate. His fingers were trembling. He said, "You are so beautiful," as he touched her face. Maude Ann's eyes would be as wide as headlights. She would look like Gloria Swanson. Listening to this story, to what Carlo Pavorese had proposed to do upstairs, where in fact they were now, she would be outraged. It was a relief that she could not see him, at least, that she only felt his thin knobby longing against her. The dogs were out in the hallway, panting. Carlo's voice was hoarse, like a surgeon who has spent all day in the operating room. "What beauty you have," he said, his hands touching her. What would Maude Ann be wearing? White socks (or she'd be barefoot) and her worn-out blue jeans, and her Ghirardelli Square T-shirt. She'd sit, bent over toward Dorsey, the classic pose of a woman listening to another woman, and she *would* listen, and nod.

Dorsey would drink her tea and try to explain what it was that had brought her into this old man's house in the first place. She wouldn't use the word "love"; Maude Ann wouldn't believe her. She might even say something about the call she had received from Hugh, that odd warning. She'd tell Maude Ann all about her brother, his frustrated grace and strength. Maude Ann's son, Gerald, would hear none of this; he'd be safely asleep. For a moment, lying on the bed and covered, it seemed, by Carlo Pavorese, Dorsey lost the image of Maude Ann and thought instead of the Bunyip swimming in San Francisco Bay, uttering foghorn cries. The dogs were on either side of the bed, watching. With his clothes off, Carlo Pavorese smelled of dust and glue. He said, "You are . . . a gift." Then he whispered, the only time Dorsey could remember him doing so. "I live alone . . . you shouldn't be a physicist . . . you are beautiful." She didn't want to think of what this meant and put herself back into Maude Ann's apartment, where Maude Ann was congratulating her for getting out of that old guy's place before he whispered anything else. Maude Ann would grab a chocolate layered cookie and bite it angrily and then chew with her mouth open, the way she often did. Dorsey smiled, thinking of Maude Ann's hearty eating styles. She thought of her friends; she thought of the passing gratification to women afforded by younger men, men her own age, who understood the sexual decencies. And then she thought of Hugh, her brother, and she realized that he was the only other human being on earth who probably, at this very moment, knew exactly where she was, and why she was there.

She thought: the people who come and go. She thought of a star chart, and then she pictured the stars in the southern hemisphere, the constellations, including Crux, the Southern Cross; Pavo, the Peacock; Centaurus, the Centaur; Carina, the keel of Jason's ship, the

Argo; and Hydrus, the sea serpent. Maude Ann was not interested in this and wanted more details of what Carlo Pavorese had tried to put over on her. And her brother, Hugh, was shaking his head, shaking it back and forth, leaning against one of his beloved Buicks. She could see him mouth, silently, "Don't do this." Why couldn't she hear him say that? This was not like making love with a younger man. No, not at all. There was some pleasure in it, but of an unexplainable kind: remote, unlocalized. There were the dogs gazing at her in the dark, and Carlo Pavorese needed some help, and when she finally gave it to him, she thought for a moment that it was raining and the roof was leaking, because she felt first one and then a second drop of water on her face. She held her hands up; they met Carlo Pavorese's wet cheeks.

He experienced an old man's ecstasy: unsustained, fading as soon as felt.

She didn't stay that time. When she finally did return to her apartment, Maude Ann's door was closed. Dorsey's watch said it was ten minutes past three, a time of night when the only thing worth doing was to take a shower and then try to get some sleep.

It happened three times after that. Then it was in the past, Dorsey thought: permanently in the past.

In class, Carlo Pavorese is gleeful. He is digressing about non-Abelian Yang-Mills gauge fields with smiling concentration and brilliant methodological rapidity, his chalk squeaking fiercely on the classroom's blackboard. He asks his students questions that they can't begin to answer, and he delights in their conceptual blankness, their uninformed youth. From the side of the seminar room Dorsey, who is auditing this class, despite the fact that she has been granted her degree, watches him put his old intelligence on show, not for the sake of education but to leave the young bearded blue-jeaned men in the shade, this one time. They don't know what's hitting them. He glances at Dorsey surreptitiously. Does she see the change she has wrought in him, how she has transformed him from a domesticated pedagogue to a terrifying symmetrician who scatters mathematical epigrams and one-liners? One of the students, from Taiwan, who has trouble with English, has brought in a tape recorder, and at the end of thirty minutes he frantically turns over the cassette tape to its blank side, but the machine jams—he cannot keep the RECORD button locked down—and in the middle of his performative utterances Carlo Pavorese sees the student's impotent fumbling efforts with his machine, and the professor smiles, delightedly.

They are in the Faculty Club, walled with oak, sitting across from each other at a small corner table nestled near an ivy-covered window. A cut red rose is in a glass vase off to the side. Carlo Pavorese has had a good morning, and he pours Dorsey a glass of Chablis from a carafe. She shakes her head, but he seems incapable of noticing any denials in any form from her. He is talkative today, a monologist, a soliloquician. He talks about travel, the cuisine of different countries. He compares the customs of Ireland and the Soviet Union in the manner of treating visiting dignitaries. Have you ever noticed, he asks, the temperamental similarities between the Irish and the White Russians: their passion for orthodoxy and terror, their thirst for alcohol and the whip, their habit of endless grieving, the warmth of their sentimental attachments? She's not listening closely to this; she knows that he hasn't noticed the failure of her attention. Dorsey is looking at the window, at the chandelier, and at the floor.

"I brought you a poem," Carlo Pavorese says abruptly, reaching into his sportcoat pocket. "I want to show you this poem." He hands it to her, just at the moment that the waiter brings her the dish she ordered, broiled sea bass. The poem has been typed out—she can recognize the type style from Carlo's upstairs Underwood—but there is no name attached to it.

"I don't want to read a poem now," she says.

"All you have to do is glance at it," he tells her. "Maybe you could just skim it."

"I've just been served my lunch," she says. "Let's save it for after the meal."

His hand does not withdraw. "A poem," he says. "How often do I give you a poem?"

"How often do you write them?" She is trying to eat her lunch.

"You can eat and read this poem." It is still being waved in her face like a flag. "It's a short poem."

"All right, all right."

She unfolds it and puts it down on the table to her left, where the salad bowl had been until the waiter took it away.

CROSSING

It was evening when we came to the river
with a low moon over the desert
that we had lost in the mountains, forgotten,
what with the cold and the sweating
and the ranges barring the sky.
And when we found it again,
in the dry hills down by the river,
half withered, we had
the hot winds against us.

There were two palms by the landing;
the yuccas were flowering; there was
a light on the far shore, and tamarisks.
We waited a long time, in silence.
Then we heard the oars creaking
and afterwards, I remember,
the boatman called to us.
We did not look back at the mountains.

At first she doesn't know what she thinks of it. But the poem does not seem to be a gift. The use of "we" in the poem makes her uncomfortable. And because she is carrying around Carlo's shadow with her, she no longer has to be polite to him about everything he does.

"Did you write this?" she asks.

"Why?"

"Curiosity."

"All right. Let's say 'a friend wrote it.' Let's say that. What do you think of it?"

Dorsey lifts her wine glass, sips from it, puts the glass down and leans back to gaze steadily at Carlo. "A friend wrote it? In that case, I don't like it," she says quietly. "It's not a good poem."

His face is rigid. "How would you know?" Now his expression flickers in and out of its gargoyle mode.

"Because"—Dorsey stares at him now—"I'm an intelligent woman, and I can read. All right. Let's say your friend wrote this. Who is this 'we' in the poem? And look at how inept this third line is, with the clause introduced by 'that.' It's misplaced, isn't it? It seems to modify 'desert' but it really modifies 'moon.' And ranges don't 'bar' a sky. It's the wrong verb for that context."

Carlo Pavorese watches her, his hands stilled on the table.

"All right," Dorsey continues. "This 'it' in the sixth line is what I think they call an indefinite reference. If it's the moon they found, then 'withered' is an inappropriate adjective, because the moon doesn't wither, it wanes. Something withers when it shrivels. Even for a poem, this adjective is out of place. And in this second stanza, why does the boatman call 'afterwards'? After what? All the wording here is vague." She pushes the poem away, done with it. "So maybe it is about sudden water and fertility. I suppose it's a sort of love poem. But it seems so evasive. It's been worked up. It's all about ideas instead of love. I wish I could find the world in this poem. It's so oblique. I'm sorry. Did you write this?"

The waiters pass by their table, and Carlo Pavorese glances at them as if he wants to put in another order for some other meal. His head begins to bob, and his skin appears to be reddening. He thrums his fingers on the table.

"If you had liked it, I would have written it, but since you don't like it, I didn't."

"Well," she asks, "who *did* write it?"

"Oppenheimer. It's his only published poem."

"For the love of God, Carlo!" She throws down her fork on the plate. It clatters, and some of the other people in the dining room look over at their table.

"I rather like it."

"If you wanted to write a love poem, you could have done it yourself!"

"No," Carlo Pavorese says. "I couldn't." He waits. "I tried."

"But why this? Why Oppenheimer?"

"Don't you know by now?" She shakes her head. "He invaded

me. He's invading you. You know, you remind me of Oppenheimer."

"I don't want to hear this," she says. "Stop this."

"All right. But I did admit that I didn't write it. Robert published this after he was already established as a physicist. I found it in a literary magazine called *Hound and Horn.* I typed it out and even took it to someone in our English department. I told him a friend had written it."

"And?" Dorsey is at least going to hear if her judgment was correct.

"Well, this person told me that the poem resembles in many respects T. S. Eliot's 'Journey of the Magi.' He said, 'Your friend knows the poetry of T. S. Eliot rather too well.' So there it was: Oppenheimer's unoriginality again. Such a shame."

"Carlo."

"What?"

"I don't want to hear any more about Oppenheimer. I've heard enough. Talk about yourself, if you want, but not Oppenheimer."

"It's an obsession, my dear. I can't help myself."

"Well, please try! No one is interested in Oppenheimer except you."

"Oh, no," he says. He has taken the rose out of the vase and is twirling it between his thumb and forefinger. "You're quite wrong. People *are* interested. They had better be. His was an exemplary American life. Yours will be, too, if you stay in this field. Anyway, that's why I have to write his spiritual biography, even if nobody—"

"—All right," she says, gathering her purse. "All right. One more word and I'll stand up and go. And stop twirling that rose."

"What then shall we talk about?" He drops the rose back into the glass vase and flashes her his peculiar mirthless smile.

"Nothing. We won't talk about anything."

"We'll sit here in silence?"

"Yes," she says. "That's a good idea."

He sits back and examines her face. His own face takes on an expression he seldom displays: puzzlement. For the rest of the meal, they are quiet, and gradually the men and women nearby notice the failure of conversation at the corner table for two, where the craggy professor of physics, close to retirement age, sits with the young attractive post-doctoral student, the two of them sitting there speechlessly attentive to their own failure to converse, as if neither one was able to talk, or to get up and walk away.

One week later, just before dawn, Dorsey stumbles down the dark hallway of her apartment to the bathroom, where she stands nauseated, retching. After the first wave of nausea passes, she thinks: *no, no, it's impossible, not with him, not with someone with that face.* She turns on the tap and lets the warm water flow down over her hands. After she has felt the nausea (a curdled, acidic chill) leave her body, she turns off the water, and in the dark of the bathroom she presses her hands to her stomach.

She stops going by the burglar-proofed house, believing that he doesn't want to see her. For two days she sits alone in her apartment, trying to be clear to herself about what she must do. She rises out of her chair to make toast and tea. Then she sits down again and takes her position in front of the window. At one point, late in the afternoon, she turns on the television set to the rerun station: the Lone Ranger and Tonto, Ralph and Alice, Lucy and Desi, the guileless and happy black-and-white couples of childhood.

A child is not to be blamed for its parents. It will not be the baby's fault, if Dorsey allows it to enter the world, that its father is Carlo Pavorese. Nor will it be the baby's fault if Dorsey's career goes off the main track onto a spur line where the rails are hardly visible for the multitude of weeds growing between them. What Dorsey experiences, sitting in her chair, is a war of her two futures, one with her child, the other without. Her only weapon against this child is what she can imagine of her future power and professional position. It was Hugh, she thinks, who was supposed to have the children. He was going to have the family and I was going to have the career. Her mind veers off into mathematics but comes back to the phrase, *they'll say this happened because I'm a woman.* And then she thinks, angrily and happily all at once, *all right, let them think that, the creeps.*

She stands up. She remembers the slogan her roommate in college had framed and hung on her bedroom wall, just above the dresser:

Life is what happens to you while you're planning something else. Her roommate had planned to be a television newscaster but had married a scholarly demolitions expert with thick glasses whose specialty was blowing up urban high-rises: Pruitt-Igoe had been his masterpiece. To hell with plans, Dorsey thinks; she is on her way to her kitchen to make herself dinner—she has the idea that a tuna salad and some miscellaneous citrus fruit would be nice—when she is struck, walking past the refrigerator, into near motionlessness by an image. The image is that of J. Robert Oppenheimer. She sees in her mind's eye the famous photograph of the melancholy physicist-as-a-young-man, the scientist as aesthete, his head tilted to the left, the pile of steel-wool hair, and the sad eyes like those of a child who knows he is about to be sent to his room without supper, and for once, and for the first time, Dorsey identifies herself with him, this man of high potential on whom fate played its customary tricks. Standing in the dining room, her left hand on the table, she smiles. "A withered moon," she says aloud, to no one. She likes the image. "A light on the far shore, and tamarisks." Yes. Tamarisks, of course. She turns and rushes out to the hallway to see if Maude Ann is home. She has news. The door swings open wide, Maude Ann's face. "I'm pregnant," Dorsey says, before hello. Maude Ann screams happily.

He is unavoidable in the Physics Department. She can see his teeth at the other end of the hall, and he walks toward her like a man who has been taken apart and reassembled, his arm and leg movements full of distress and waste motion. "You haven't called," she says, putting her hands in her pockets and leaning forward.

"Well, *you* haven't come around, either," he says. "I don't know where you've been. I seem to have grown used to your company. Your telephone is always busy. I came by your apartment once but you weren't there. I suppose you are angry at me. What I've done, I shouldn't have done, but I didn't think it would lead to consequences as radical as this." His breath smells of cheese, and his clothes smell of mildew.

"Carlo—" she says.

"—I just want you to know," he blurts out, "that from now on, ours will be a professional relationship."

"Carlo," she says, "I'm pregnant."

He leans back, so that he is in fact standing straight up, frail in a thick wind. His mouth closes over his front teeth.

"I'm pregnant," she repeats, "and you're the father."

"Don't say that. Not here in the hallway of the Physics Department," he whispers. He glances in both directions: no one is there, no one has heard her yet. "You're making this up. It's not possible."

"It is possible."

"I suppose you're going to sue me."

"Certainly not."

"What are you going to do?"

"I don't know," she says calmly.

"It's not mine," he says. "I know you. You've had boyfriends."

"It's yours, believe me. Remember how I said I'd left my diaphragm at home?" She enjoys his silence for a few moments, before she smiles. "Think of this as an occasion for happiness rather than panic. Carlo," she instructs him, "do the honorable thing." She cannot stop smiling; teasing demons could almost become her hobby.

"The honorable thing?" He fixes on her, indelicate with trauma, the expression on his face frozen into a disbelieving stare.

"Yes. The honorable thing. Leave me alone and don't say anything about this. Don't try to ruin my professional reputation, and I won't say anything about this affair myself. I don't know how much longer I'll be around here. I'll get a job sooner or later, I know that. Put a glowing letter in my file—you know my work, you can glow if you put your mind to it—and we'll be square."

"Is that all?"

"That's all."

"You aren't going to get melodramatic about this?"

"Of course not. Do I look melodramatic?"

"No," he says. "Actually, you don't."

She stands in the hallway, studying him on her own time. "You know, Carlo, sometimes I do love you. But we don't fit, the two of us. You're probably not as bad as you think you are. You're dazzling but you're not permanently blinding. Your suffering doesn't mean you've been really wicked, you know. Maybe it's just a hobby, something to fill the hours, like ballroom dancing."

He looks at her, and she breathes in deeply, the processed cement-

and-glass air of the Physics Building. Two members of the department, Ti-Hua Lee and Maurice Ableuhkov, have just turned the
corner at the other end of the hall and are approaching them. Dorsey
quickly puts her hand on Carlo Pavorese's shoulder, leans forward,
and gives him a brushing, almost-social kiss on his cheek. She has
to stand on tiptoe to reach his shabby face. When she pivots and
begins to walk down the hallway away from him, she sees that both
professors, Carlo Pavorese's colleagues, have seen what she has just
done and are now visibly struggling to pretend that they have not
seen it. But it has happened in exactly the manner Dorsey wanted
it to: the kiss was a public gesture, an acknowledgment of affection
that cannot be rescinded, given and witnessed on the second floor,
the east wing, to the accompaniment of the secretaries' typewriters
clacking away in the main office.

She wakes up at night and stares at the window. He hates thoughts,
she says to herself. He hates having them. But once he has them he
makes the mistake of believing that they all originate from him. But
ideas don't originate anywhere, just as water doesn't originate in
clouds. Ideas are there, waiting, for someone to seize them. Carlo
wants to have the guilt that the gods feel, when in fact he's only
entitled to guilt at the human level. His egomaniacal guilt is an
intellectual mistake. She leans back on the pillow and falls asleep
easily.

In two weeks she develops a light fever. She has been staying at
home, concentrating on her own work, and after a few days the
fever passes, and she forgets all about it. Now that she's pregnant,
he has stopped trying to call. The days are getting longer. It's spring.
She's made some calculations: at this rate, and even with some help
from Hugh, she'll run out of money in six months.

There is this man she keeps running into at the Safeway, especially
in produce. He's always pushing a cart in front of the vegetables,
never hesitating to squeeze heads of lettuce or eggplants or tomatoes
or anything else that's round, and the manner in which he grasps
the merchandise is innocently sexual, an open pleasure in clutching
resiliant circular objects. When Dorsey again catches a glimpse of

this man, whose face is neither handsome nor ugly but is instead stripped-down to its unidentifiable essentials, he beams at her. The second time he sees her looking at him, he says, "Don't you love vegetables?" The voice is smoothed out, like something from a radio. She's trying to think of where she's seen him before; there's something about his face that she associates with the kitchen. "This is typical. You're wondering where you've seen me," he says, pushing his shopping cart around so that it blocks hers. "Commercials," he says. "I'm the teller in the Pacific Savings and Loan ad, the one who says, 'Why yes, Mrs. Robinson, we're here—' "

"—Now I remember," Dorsey tells him. "But your hair is combed in the commercial. And you're wearing glasses."

"Horn-rimmed. I told them that bank tellers don't wear glasses like that, they're all very vain people, bank tellers, being in public, they all wear contacts, but . . ." He reaches for some green onions. "Sorry." He catches himself. "I didn't mean to be rude." He holds out his hand. "My name's Simon."

"Dorsey." His hand is small, almost the same size as hers.

"Dorsey. What a funny name." He gazes in distaste at the parsnips.

"I was named for an aunt," she tells him.

"Well, I was named for an apostle. My parents were Catholics. They named the boys for apostles and the girls for stigmatized saints. So tell me, Dorsey, what do you do?"

"Me?" She smiles. "I'm a pregnant astrophysicist."

"That's quite a job, Dorsey." He doesn't wait. "I notice you're not wearing a wedding ring. Is this pregnancy the result of scandal?"

She nods, smiling. "Yes, it is."

"Good." Simon is beaming at her. "Want to come over to my place for dinner?"

"No, Simon, I don't think so."

"Ah," he says, "you still have some shreds of honor left. So who's the lucky man, Dorsey?"

"This old guy."

"Ah. One of them." He scratches his cheek, as if he were trying to think about old people. "You haven't put anything into your shopping cart." He points down at it.

"You're blocking my way."

"Yes, I am." He moves so that she can pass. "Just a minute." He writes his name, address, and telephone number on a worn yellow piece of paper he has fished out of his pocket, and he hands it to her. "Just in case," he says.

"Just in case of what?"

He shrugs. "You're a pregnant astrophysicist. Maybe you're going to need some help from strangers who will come when you call." He looks suddenly serious, all the facial lines of joking gone. "I'm one of those people who offers to help, and the thing is, I actually mean it. You should believe me. I'll actually help you, if you want it."

"What's the catch?"

"I'm unusual," Simon tells her.

"Everyone's unusual."

He shakes his head. "No, no, they aren't. People are *not* unusual, Dorsey, believe me. They say they are, but they're just like everyone else. But you take me: I'm really odd. For one thing, I'm not the same person from day to day. And I'm so interested in people, I can't stop myself." Dorsey looks puzzled, but he will not explain the sentence.

"I don't think I understand."

"Well, come over and find out," he says, and smiles. This smile is a promise, a bonded guarantee of surprises and disillusion. Even after Simon is gone, his smile somehow remains, drifting unattached in the fluorescent lighting above the produce, the lettuce and zucchini, a spirit of benign interest in Dorsey and her situation. As she drops a bag of grapefruit into the cart, following behind Mr. Bryant, the store's manager, Dorsey tries to think of the last time anyone was playful with her. But no: she has been surrounded by ambassadors from the serious world, grim-faced men sworn to carrying around their terrible dignified weights. Now, turning the corner in the produce aisle, she sees this same guy, Simon, stopped in front of the dairy case, bent over, closely talking to a somewhat pudgy woman wearing curlers under a pink scarf. The woman says something and Simon leans back and laughs. His laughter carries down the length of the supermarket, the last row of the balcony. It's impossible, Dorsey thinks. He can't be interested in everybody.

·   ·   ·

A month goes by. She has felt the chemistry of her body changing, sending up a kind of repetitive chemical chant, above and below the audible frequencies. It is a song without demands. It is just there, going on, as if she knew how to sing back to it without anyone for once teaching her how.

She has seen Carlo Pavorese twice in the Physics Department. Both times he pretended not to notice her, though he has put a letter in her placement file that carefully and containedly glows. On one occasion he has walked down the corridor, speaking to a colleague, and he neither nodded to her nor waved. The gargoyle face passed, talking, floating above its body. Then, a week later, she sees him standing in the hallway under the red EXIT sign, speaking to a student. He glances at Dorsey, then looks away. He is back to business as usual.

Then she receives a letter from him.

Dear Dorsey Welch,

I do not feel the need for justification, but I do want to say something true, something that is not a lie. This is not as simple as it sounds, especially in a letter. I have, in this house, cartons full of odious letters, filled with lies: the lies of business, the lies of love, the lies of promises not kept and futures that did not come to pass. I don't want to add to the current oversupply of lies.

So I will say nothing that is not true. Here is something that is true: in New Mexico, when the sun rises, the air is so clear that you feel that you are seeing light in its purest form. It is the most beautiful place in which I have ever lived. I notice beauty, despite what you may think. In the Southwest the sun's light reaches your eyes in some sort of unmediated radiance. Down there, light arrives raw.

You have read about the Trinity test, I am sure. I have only one thing to add about it. It happened before sunrise, as you know. I was out there. I had dark glasses on, but I saw it. And I will tell you something about the light of the bomb, the first light like a momentary morning star, and how it changed my life.

Remind yourself of one thing. We all begin as children, gazing at the stars. We want the stars to come down to us. We want to have a star right here, on Earth. We want to have a star we ourselves have made. And that's what it was, that morning. It was the first star that men had made, it was pure light, the sun's rival, brilliant and unmediated and beautiful. I will not say that it was God. But I will say that if there is a God, then we had stolen one of His largest wonders. And we are still looking around to see who will volunteer as Prometheus, to have his body made as a payment in return for this perfect fire. Who knows? Perhaps we will all have to be Prometheus.

I said I would say no lies. So I will not say that I loved you. But I loved the light you gave off. To this day I do not know why you spent so many hours listening to me. I think you were dazzled. I think you love light, as odd as that sounds. And you were not an innocent. It's complicated, isn't it, having the brains and the bad conscience, both at the same time?

Perhaps, as the poet Cavafy writes, the light will prove another tyranny.

In America we are too innocent about the prices for things. But you are not. Oppenheimer was not. Whenever the bill came, he paid it. He paid and paid. When he died, his pockets were empty. You cannot have so much light without paying off the gods with sacrifices, with deaths. Light is everything, I swear it. The bills are coming. Someone must pay them.

Whatever you ask me to do, I will do.

Yours,
Carlo

On weekends she and Maude Ann read the want-ads searching for good deals on cribs and baby toys, but this process is a joke, since Maude Ann has already agreed to sell Dorsey Gerald's crib for fifty dollars, a steal, once the baby arrives. Late on Saturday mornings Dorsey sits in her favorite chair, one Caesar salad after another on the table to her left, lined up, and as she eats, she reads through the books, becoming an expert on babies and infant development and birth. She reads Spock and T. Berry Brazelton and Selma Fraiberg and the publications sent to her from the Lamaze Institute, and soon she is hinting to Maude Ann that there are certain . . . *things* she might try with Gerald, especially when the boy starts to dance on the dining room table after dinner, antagonizing his mother, in reaction to her refusal to take him outside to show him the moon. Gerald is a moon freak. Dorsey is deeply sympathetic to the boy's curiosity in this matter. Maude Ann is not, and when she begins to catch Dorsey's tone of smug maternal knowingness embedded in sentences of disguised advice, she says, "You just wait. It's not as smooth as the books say it is. Keep on reading, and see how much good it does you." But then she softens. "Don't get me wrong," she says, when she sees Dorsey's worried look in reaction to either her remarks or Gerald's dancing on the edge of the dining room table. "I never said the books wouldn't help a little."

She is being talked about, she knows, in the halls of the Physics Building. Feeling that she wouldn't be able to disguise her pregnancy forever, she has told one of the secretaries, and now the news is everywhere. She has excited a microswirl of gossip and speculation and final judgments, and she has discovered this from Danny Anderson, whose bland face gives him unlimited licence to gossip. Standing near the coffee machine, pretending to bend over slightly, conspiratorial, Danny tells Dorsey in a low this-is-the-truth mutter that "people" are "saying" that Dorsey got herself pregnant because she didn't want to get a job because her new work wasn't panning out. This pregnancy—no one seemed to be interested in who the father was, fathers could be found anywhere—was going to be Dorsey's means of self-justification for her failure to publish new work. "Of course *I* don't think so," Danny says, "but I thought you should know what people are saying in the halls."

"Thanks, Danny," Dorsey says, smiling. "That means a lot to me."

In her fourth month she invites herself over to Simon O'Rourke's for dinner. He lives in an old house, painted green, with a broken swing on the front porch. Before dinner they sit together in the backyard, and Simon points with a graceful gesture at the small bells he has attached to the branches of the eucalyptus. "No particular reason for it," Simon tells her. "I thought it'd be nice."

Simon doesn't have many reasons for much of anything. In this respect, he reminds her of her brother, Hugh, as a very young man. Simon doesn't think about things. He puts pictures up on the wall —magazine illustrations, reproductions of famous works, and his own pencil sketches—but he says he doesn't know why he likes what he likes, and he doesn't care. "I like you," he says, looking over toward Dorsey, and then glancing back at the kitchen to make sure that his main course, a stuffed fish, isn't burning. "I like a lot of people." And in fact the phone rings often. This particular evening his standard answer is that he can't, tonight, but try him tomorrow.

"You do have a great number of friends," Dorsey says, sitting in the rusty lawn chair, clicking the ice cubes in her lemonade against the sides of the glass, as she looks at the California sky darkening toward evening.

"I'm promiscuous," Simon tells her. "It's a fact."

Well, who else, she thinks, would try to pick up a pregnant astrophysicist in a supermarket? Someone has to try. She sits back, contented, gazing over toward Simon's tiny two-row vegetable garden, at his sagging clothes lines, at the back fence, in need of a paint job. Simon, a compulsive talker, is rattling on about working in television commercials and local theaters, the people he meets, and the sexual characteristics (rabbit-like, undiscriminating) of actors. Dorsey detects a slur against her own attractiveness and ignores it.

In a few minutes he calls her inside, and they sit together at the wobbling dining room table, crested with permanent yellow and gold stains. "I got this at the Salvation Army furniture store," Simon explains. "It probably belonged to a maniac. Look at these stains. They're painted on. I can't get them out." He serves her the fish and rice, and a Caesar salad by request on the side. He pours her a glass of wine, and she even drinks a little. He does not turn on any lights, and the dining room gradually darkens until they can hardly see each other.

"I could turn on the lights," he says.

"No, don't. I like this."

"Me, too."

They lean back together, in their respective chairs. Outside, cars pass on the street, and from the back comes the evening song of a bird Dorsey can't recognize. Then, this time from the front, she hears the sound of one of Simon's neighbors turning on a hose, and then the sound of a spray, as he waters his lawn. The neighborhood settles in toward night.

"Simon," she says, "you might actually have a talent for marriage."

"When?"

"After this baby is born."

"Hmmm."

"You'll think about it?"

"Certainly. It's not a bad idea. I'd like to be married."

"You must have had some proposals."

"I've had some," he says.

"What do you usually say?"

"No. That's what I say. Or I say I'll think about it, which is the same thing."

"Have you ever proposed to anyone?"

"Not that I remember. Maybe once. I have a terrible memory for things like that."

"You'd be an odd husband, but a person could do worse."

"You'd be an odd wife," he says. "But you're real pretty and I like it that you're smart."

"I didn't think you'd mind if I mentioned it."

"I don't."

"I was just feeling so calm here," she says. "Peaceful. And then when I heard your neighbor—"

"—Mr. Chesterton."

"—When I heard your neighbor, Mr. Chesterton, turn on his hose to spray his lawn, I felt so glad to be here, and I thought, well, what kind of husband would you be?"

"You hardly know me."

"I hardly know anyone." She waits. "You don't get to know people better by knowing them longer."

"Yes."

'If you'd turned the light on, I wouldn't have said this."

"I know."

"Is there anything fundamentally wrong with you that I should know about?"

"I sleep around."

"I can manage that," Dorsey says. "So can I talk to you again after the baby is born?"

"Sure."

She sits in the dark and hears his plate and wine glass being moved out of the way. Then she feels a hand in the dark taking her hand and holding on to it. His fingers are warm. She almost says so but decides to wait to let him speak the next sentence. She waits a long time. Later that night, he makes love to her quietly.

With Maude Ann as her coach, she practices the Lamaze breathing exercises, the timed and rhythmic inhales and exhales. The Lamaze class is held in a local elementary school library. On all four walls are bulletin boards with displays that sermonize about the value of reading and books. The couples sit on the carpeted floor while the Lamaze instructor, who is physically and spiritually incapable of using the word "pain" and says "discomfort" or "unanticipated reflex" instead, gives them the breathing exercises and back massages in a brisk, forthright manner. She has had three children herself, she tells the class, and amused herself before the birth of her third by writing the baby's name in the air with her foot. This lightheartedness strikes Dorsey as much too West Coast for her taste. There is going to be pain, she says to herself, and lots of it. Whatever happens, she isn't going to be able to write the baby's name in the air with her foot. She doesn't know what the baby's name will be. She refuses to think about names. When the baby is born, then she knows she'll know.

Dorsey, who now has no medical insurance, has visited an obstetrician twice and paid in cash. Her doctor, Gerda Hoffmann, has a mild German accent, curly gray hair, and large reserves of optimism. Both times Dorsey has been examined, Dr. Hoffmann has said that everything seems to be going well. "Extremely vell," she has said, smiling at Dorsey. "And you look vonderful, radiant."

· · ·

"What's going on?" It is Hugh, calling, checking things out. Dorsey has been at home, working. Her desk is covered with her work sheets, and she meant to turn the telephone's ringer off but forgot. The ringing of the telephone is like a brick thrown through the front window of her concentration.

"I was just working here," she tells him. Her secret from him has started to kick her.

"No more crank calls?"

"No more," she says. "How're you? How's business?"

"There's a recession on," Hugh tells her. "Business is terrible. I can't remember when it was worse. Showroom traffic is way down and people aren't even thinking about anything on wheels. I couldn't sell a bicycle these days. I think about doing something else. I'd like to be a carpenter. I'd like to make toys by hand. At least it'd fill the time. You can't imagine how slow a day is in an automobile showroom when no one comes in. You can tell what time it is just by the angle of the sunlight and where it's moved on the showroom floor."

"You'll be all right again," she says. "Ignore the light."

"I can't get over this feeling that you're keeping some big secret from me," Hugh tells her. "What is it? Have you discovered a new planet?"

"Not yet," she tells him. My brother, my only family, I should tell him I'm pregnant and I'm going to have a baby in two months or less. "I've made a new friend," she says. "A man who makes commercials."

"Good," Hugh says. "Well, listen. Take care of yourself, and let me know when you discover that planet. You should name it after me. Uranus, Neptune, Pluto, Hugh. Keep me informed."

"I will."

She hangs up in a state of pure harmonic relief. Without knowing why it is necessary that Hugh not be told about this child, she thinks: well, from now on he'll leave my mind alone.

Late in her eighth month, when Dorsey wakes up with another fever, she spends all day lying in bed, sipping water and listening to a classical music station. It is Dvořák's birthday, so she hears the "New World" Symphony twice, once in the morning and again just before dinnertime. The music makes her homesick for Five Oaks. The next day the fever has not gone down. When Maude Ann comes in at eight o'clock, she aggressively projects a worried look and begs Dorsey to eat an egg, and Dorsey agrees, but when the cup is actually placed in front of her with its gloppy white and semi-liquid yellow, she can't stand to smell it, much less eat it. Maude Ann threatens to call a doctor in the evening, to drag Dorsey to the emergency room of the hospital, to bathe her forehead with cool wet washcloths. Dorsey says she's all right. Her body feels violated, but it's not a feeling she knows how to get rid of.

On the third day of her fever, Dorsey is lying back on the pillows, too hot to stay under even one sheet. The baby is nudging her with soft kicks. She is dozing her way through a thin, superficial dream state that is remarkable at first only for the clarity of its details. She sees a color television bolted to a table and wallpaper with a Venetian canal motif: it's motel wallpaper, naturally, and in turning around, she sees her brother in the motel room's bed dozing next to a woman with short brown hair, and, in repose, a kind face: a Girl Scout leader's face. The woman is not Hugh's wife. Dorsey is pleased by this sight, by the possibility that her brother is in love with someone other than Laurie, a timid and unaffectionate woman, in Dorsey's opinion. Well, good for you, Dorsey thinks, watching her brother breathe lightly. The woman next to him shifts her weight in the bed so that her breasts are pressed against him, and Dorsey feels a shiver of pleasure on her brother's behalf that he has found a lover who, with graceful physical ease, has turned the warmth of herself in his direction.

The contractions start two weeks later in the afternoon during a ten-minute break she has taken from her work to watch a Laurel and Hardy movie, *Saps at Sea*. She is sitting in the living room in the rattan chair, her favorite for warm weather, and she is laughing quietly when she feels a pair of hands at once take her around the hips and begin to squeeze, gently at first but with conviction. Instantly she looks at her watch—it is twelve minutes past four—and gets out of the chair, pushing herself up with her arms, and wobbles out to the hallway to knock on Maude Ann's door. She doesn't answer. Dorsey comes back to her own apartment and sits down on the sofa, next to the telephone. But without Maude Ann, there is no one whom she wants to call except Dr. Hoffmann, whose answering service assures Dorsey that the doctor will call her back very soon.

Every half-hour she checks to see if her friend has returned home, with no luck. When the contractions come in five-minute intervals, she calls the cab company to take her to Findley-Blair County Hospital, where Dr. Hoffmann has told her to go. She tells the cabbie not to speed, that she has plenty of time, but upon seeing her, his eyes widen with panic and the dread of responsibility. In respect, he takes off his cap to show her his bald head. Once en route, he cannot resist hysterical braking stops and prolonged honking at intersections. His hacker's licence says that he is Alan Chakmadjian. Dorsey looks at his sweating bald head, at the thick hair growing out of his ears. "Mr. Chakmadjian," she says, "it's all right. We have plenty of time. I'm not going to have a baby in the back of your taxi."

The wrong thing to say. He speeds up, brakes harder, swears and mutters. At a suddenly stopped intersection, the small suitcase Dorsey has packed slides off the seat and falls to the floor. She resolves to calm herself and looks out the window, inwardly attentive to her contractions and the slow waves descending from the walls of her uterus to her cervix. Mr. Chakmadjian has chosen a route to the hospital that takes them through franchise alley, past a Hungry Penguin, a United Coney Island, a Midas Muffler and a One-Hour Martinizing, a Burger King and a Heap Big Hamburger. A few trees would have been nice, Dorsey thinks, closing her eyes and imagining a California redwood from north of here and a few elms and maples from the Midwest. Another contraction grips her, and she leans over, remembering to breathe steadily, imagining the maple tree in her parents' backyard that she and Hugh used to climb. Reflected light from its leaves in the fall would turn the east-facing walls in the kitchen and dining room rust red for two hours in the afternoon. Opening her eyes, seeing an Arthur Treacher's Fish and Chips, she thinks: we never tapped that tree in the spring, though its bark was sticky with sap; we never did that. Above the fast-food restaurants she tries to find a stretch of sky, but with all the artificial light, no trace of a star is visible, nor is there any sign of the moon, her familiar. At last, beyond some gold arches, she sees the lighted upper floors of the hospital in the distance.

She gives Alan Chakmadjian a generous tip for his passionate driving, and she carries her suitcase through the automatic front doors and into the white-walled and blue-carpeted lobby. Under the badly adjusted color television set, showing cartoons, the men and women waiting in the lobby look at Dorsey, standing alone, and smile before whispering to one another. The children ignore her. Two weeks ago she pre-registered at this desk, so now she simply signs in and is taken after a ten-minute wait to an examining room. No, she says, this birth will not be assisted by the father. She is dilated to three centimeters, a third of the way. A young O.B. nurse, who says her name is Miss Lovingood, wheels her upstairs to the labor room. The hallways fan past her in a hurried, blurred rush of earth-tone paint and glass paneling and doors labeled NO ENTRY through which, she notices vaguely, men who look like doctors, but who may be impersonators, disappear. Each one of the wings is color-coded; they wheel their way through yellow and green before arriving at blue.

Alone, she lies on a white cloth-covered gurney in a vengefully well-lit chrome and tiled-block prenatal room. She's wearing a hospital gown but doesn't remember how she got it on. The point is, she thinks, I am doing this by myself. Look: there's no one here. No man, and no woman. She tries, by herself, to remember the patterns of breathing, the cleansing breath followed by the shorter pants over the wave of the contraction. With her eyes shut and her mouth open, drying out, she tries to tell herself a story about the pain, until the pain magnifies and glistens and lets itself be known as what it is, pain, and not a character in a narrative. Her water breaks after she has made her bent way to the bathroom. In the periods between the contractions she thinks of the astonishing purity of pain, how it will not be mixed with any other sensation. She opens her eyes and stares at a chrome-plated wall switch. An unknown period goes by until a peristaltic wave of pain travels through her lower back and stays there, and she concentrates on the switch, its two screws and beveled edges.

She uses one of the screws as a focus point as she breathes. It's a dull screw, an ungrateful sight, so she looks above the switch plate at the notice in red letters glued to the wall.

PLEASE TURN OFF LIGHTS
WHEN YOU LEAVE THE ROOM.
SAVE ENERGY!

For the next contraction she focuses on the two Fs in "off." Then she looks up at the speckled rash on the wall tile, small impurities in the building material or spots where it's been soaped and not rinsed, and she sees a pattern of five stars like Canis Major, with a large speck on the wall right where Sirius should be, and she imagines the constellation moving out of the sky onto the wall near her gurney for her benefit. Since she can see Canis Major on the wall above the switch, a side view, she focuses on that, and for the next contraction she moves her gaze up the wall to find Canis Minor, the little dog, only two specks. Then, contraction by contraction, by herself, alone in this room (where are the nurses? she wonders; they've forgotten about me) she sees on this wall the constellations that are easiest to imagine: Cassiopeia—herself—and the great bear, Draco and King Cepheus.

She tries effleurage on her belly to no effect, and finally Miss Lovingood returns and says Dorsey's room is ready, but Dr. Hoffmann hasn't answered the calls, so the delivery will probably be done by Dr. Keenan, a resident. Dorsey is moved onto the bed in her room, and at last she sees a clock. It's three-thirty in the morning, when every party is over and everyone's gone home. The contractions are now beginning at her back, achieving full expressionist intensity below her navel, and then waving out in both directions toward her hips. The stars move backwards for a millisecond, and then move forward. Dorsey is full of time. Squeezed into the next contraction, she becomes a narrowing gate where the past and future are meeting. Time is flowing down the walls of the universe into her and then flowing out of her back through her vagina before it streams into the void. For another two hours she is a sentence searching around for its period. The Mississippi River flows backwards, the sun rises—already sick of itself—in the west, and Dr.

Keenan says, "Give us a push, Miss Welch." She can see the period, a dot, to end the sentence, and she tries again. It's not so tiring as dying, but she couldn't do this forever. Her feet are freezing. She is cutting her way through thick ropy undergrowth on her way to a clearing. Light is splashing all over her, the light of stars wheeling above her, and then, in great heat, pushing out from under her. She is about to give birth to a ball of light. "Push," the doctor says. There is a one. Then there is a two. Then there is a three. At last there is a four.

The baby cries, and everyone in the delivery room laughs and congratulates her. They drop the silver nitrate into his eyes, test him and give him an Apgar of seven, and in half an hour Dorsey is back in her room, in the bed, not by herself this time, but with the baby, and a nurse standing in the doorway, watching over them with a smile. It turns out, Dorsey thinks, it turns out that people are acceptable after all. She holds on to the baby. Soon it will have to go back to the nursery. This infant has, is, a tiny replica of her own father's face. At first she can't quite believe it, this baby, looking like her father, but there he is, sheared out of time.

"Noah," she says, unprompted, without thinking.

The next day she calls Hugh first, then Simon.

Dorsey is holding the baby in her arms when Hugh appears, looking exactly like himself, except that he's carrying some cut flowers, carnations and baby's breath, probably from the downstairs gift shop. Everything about his face is tentative. How much older he looks! Dorsey thinks. Of course he's not handsome anymore—he hasn't really taken care of himself—but at least he still carries around his own personal cloud of friendliness. As he comes closer to her bed, he smiles pleasingly, but he says nothing, as if he needs a prompt. He's shy! He doesn't know what to say. So Dorsey speaks up. "I suppose this needs some explanation."

In his characteristic way, he shakes his head and moves his arms in a don't-bother gesture. "I'm not clever," he says, his usual disclaimer. "You know I'm not. You don't have to explain things to me." He disposes of the flowers on the windowsill and comes toward the bed to kiss Dorsey on the forehead. His lips leave behind a sensation of tickling pressure after he's straightened up again. "Your baby is beautiful," he says, his calmest tone. "He looks a lot like Daddy."

"I know." She waits. "You like the name?"

"Noah." He nods. "Yes, I do. It's a beautiful name."

She is suddenly warmed by the presence in this room of her brother and her new baby. "Oh, love," she says, "thank you for coming." She feels tears threatening, and with her free hand she reaches out and squeezes him on the wrist. "I mean," she falters, "with no grandparents, or parents, or cousins, you're the only . . . the only . . ."

"The word is 'family.' "

"Is it? Well, thank you anyway."

"You're welcome." She slips her hand into his, feeling the old thickness of his fingers, their dull strength. "I can't stay for more than a couple of days, just long enough to get you back to your place and set up."

"That's fine," she says, not really wanting to ask him to do more than be around for a day or so. "The baby's healthy. We'll be going home today."

"There's something I want to ask you," Hugh says, his face taking on its Serious Look, its investigator's peer. "I'll just ask you once, and you don't have to tell me, but I want to do this, and then I won't bother you again." She sees him touch the baby's forehead; everything he does is so tentative! "Will you tell me who the father is?"

Dorsey gazes at the sunlight, thinking of her baby and Carlo Pavorese. "Do you remember calling me and asking me who I was seeing? You said I was seeing this person, somehow."

Hugh shakes his head.

"You said," Dorsey continues, "that I was seeing somebody who had bad teeth and was maybe tall. I swear I don't know how you knew."

"I don't remember any of this."

"You don't have to. You won't ever meet him. I won't let you. He's a strange, wonderful, terrible man. I'll say his name and then I won't ever say it again. All right?"

He nods.

She speaks his name, then closes her eyes. She can see the old man in front of a classroom, robed in the light he himself has generated out of the power of his mind, and then the image of the fond old man is absorbed, slowly and then with increasing speed, by fire, until there is nothing left of him in her mind but ash.

IV

10

Hugh sits with his mother and father on metal folding chairs near the front of the Five Oaks High School gymnasium. The school has no auditorium, so graduation ceremonies are always held here in early June, the Five Oaks rainy season. Everyone in town connects graduation with the smell of varnish and the sound of the graduating girls' high heels clacking on the slatted wood floors. Looking at his watch, Hugh wonders if the school superintendent, Mr. Vermilya, will misplace his reading glasses again, as he did at Hugh's own graduation five years ago. His watch bores him, so he glances up at the basketball hoops that have been lifted on cable pulleys so that the backboards face the ceiling. The scoreboard is in its usual place, attached to the wall above and behind the stage.

VISITORS	HOME
00	00

Hugh's father clears his throat nervously. Dorsey is the class valedictorian and will be giving a speech.

"Come on, Dad," Hugh says, turning to give his father moral support and a grown-up pantomime punch on the arm. "She'll do a terrific job. It's a good speech."

Hugh's father turns his hands over; the palms are damp, little rivers of sweat in the lifelines. "Of course it's a good speech," Hugh's father says. "It better be. I helped her write it."

The band strikes up "Pomp and Circumstance" at five minutes past one o'clock, and the graduating class marches in, the boys in black robes and the girls in white. Dorsey, wearing a small flower at the front of her robe—Hugh can't tell what it is—walks in near the head of the line, carrying her speech and displaying her brave smile. She sits at the aisle side of the front row, for easy access to the stage. Hugh's mother scrabbles in her purse for a piece of Kleenex; then, with furious gestures, she begins to clean the lenses of her glasses. "Urk," she says, for no particular reason that Hugh knows of. She repeats the sound, as if she had been right the first time. "Urk."

"Whattarya doin', Mom?" Hugh whispers.

From the side of his mouth, Hugh's father, arms now crossed, says, "Your mother is making a peculiar sound. This is a sentimental moment for her, and she has the right to make such sounds. I think you should leave her alone."

"I'm *just cleaning my glasses,*" Mrs. Welch whispers vehemently. She puts them back on and gives Hugh a sharp unmotherly look before checking the stage and the front row of seniors, Dorsey's row. She gives the impression that her head is being buzzed by a mosquito. "Goodness," she says. "What a large pile of diplomas."

"It's a big town. They have one for everybody who graduates," Mr. Welch mutters.

"I *know* that!" she says, batting his arm with the program. "Shh!"

The audience rises while the Reverend Ewald Valentine reads the invocation. Hugh's father and mother do not look down at their shoes as do most of the members of the audience. They watch Mr. Valentine with skeptical expressions, as if he were doing something silly, and in public. The minister is asking God to look down upon these children who will go forth from this room as men and women, no longer children except to God Himself. "What's the matter with him?" Mrs. Welch whispers. "Doesn't he read the newspapers?"

Hugh has tuned out of both the invocation and his mother's quips and is instead paying close attention to a girl sitting on the outside row of the clarinet section in the band: she has dirty blond hair and a free-thinking smirk. Hugh looks at her, and after a few seconds she looks back at him. It's easy for Hugh to get girls to look at him. He flashes the dirty blonde his killer smile, then waits for her to grin. Right on cue, she almost does. Goddamn jail bait, he thinks. I wonder what her name is.

"Amen," the Reverend Valentine says, and everyone sits down. Mr. Vermilya rises and does what Mrs. Welch calls "a brief blah blah blah" about this school year in Five Oaks and the little crises and triumphs that any school . . .

Time to tune out again. The blonde is examining her fingernails in a flirty way. Hugh tips his head back and stares at the ceiling. He was never much for school and it's no special pleasure to be back here and to have his teachers ask him how Holbein College was, when in fact they all know he dropped out of Holbein years ago and is working on a commission basis at Bay City Buick, thirty minutes south of here. Hockey scholarship, business school, all down the drain . . . The ceiling, Hugh suddenly notices, is stained, as if someone had thrown several pots of coffee at it. The roof's leaking again, he thinks, counting up the stains. Five. Contractors always take advantage of school boards, shortchanging them on building materials, playing them for goddamn dorks.

Somebody else speaks, and then somebody else, fat Mrs. Scherer, a retiring art teacher, gets a plaque. The gymnasium warms up with the body heat of nervous families afraid that their children will fall on the steps up to the stage. Hugh loosens his collar. He catches the dirty blonde grinning at him. He's got a date for tonight, if he wants it. He'll have to do a bit of shuffling, rearrange some other women —grown-ups—for some other nights, but this is an opportunity he can't miss. He falls into a reverie about fast girls in high school in late spring, the backseats of cars, long drives, beer and the sound of crickets in the long grass . . .

There she is, there's Dorsey. She stands in front of the Five Oaks audience to loud applause, acknowledging the fact that she's the class valedictorian, the only member of the class to be a National Merit Scholar, the first Five Oaker to have that distinction in six years, and the first Five Oaker, ever, to go off to Cornell University in New York State, where she will major in physics, on a full scholarship. The whole town is so proud of her they'd have a parade for her, if she asked them to. Last week she had almost the entire page of the *Five Oaks Gazette* to herself, complete with picture.

She unfolds her speech and gazes out at the audience with a falsely modest expression. Hugh checks her out and thinks, yeah, she looks all right. For a bookworm, she's actually cute, though her short hair (heavily sprayed) gives her a helmeted look. Her hair's always been short. She's never had the impulse to let it fall. She's presentable, Hugh thinks, but she doesn't have the cheap sleazy allure that he himself is partial to.

Hugh's father makes a faint, dry, back-of-the-throat noise, and momentarily puts his hand to his chest. Then Mrs. Welch grabs her husband's hand and holds on to it tightly.

The applause quiets and Dorsey smiles one last time before beginning her speech. "Today," she says, raising her hand quickly to her forehead, "we, this year's graduating class of Five Oaks, will receive our diplomas and go our separate ways. Some of us will become carpenters and plumbers, others will become engineers and scientists and housewives. From being a close-knit class, we will go on to reflect the diversity of the world. The writer Albert Camus has written, 'We must be content to live only for the day.' " Hugh hears some people stirring behind him. They don't like the quote. "And so it is with all of us. From day to day we each will be content with the gifts we have been given by nature, our families, and our teachers."

Hugh shifts in the metal chair, as Dorsey pauses. *For Chrissake keep going,* he thinks. *Salesmen don't stop.*

"What kind of a world is it that we go out to? For all of us, it will be a future of opportunities and challenges. Like every other graduating class, we will meet up with successes and failures. Some of us will find ourselves in fancy restaurants eating omelettes, while the rest of us eat our egg salad sandwiches from lunchboxes."

"My sentence," Hugh's father says out of the side of his mouth.

"Don't gloat," his wife whispers. "It's not becoming."

"But in one respect," Dorsey says, peering down at the podium, "our class, and the classes of the last twenty years, are different from the ones that our grandparents were part of. What is the nature of this difference? We can sum it up in one word: science. The young people of this country are aware, as their grandparents were not, of both the terrible destructive power of science, as well as its tremendous power for good, in the search for truth. As a woman who plans a career in science, I—"

She stops.

Hugh fixes on his sister. Dorsey's hands are on both sides of the podium as if she's braced there against invisible gale-force winds.

"Oh, God," Hugh's father says. "She's going to faint."

"No. She just lost her place," Hugh says.

The entire gymnasium falls silent. All coughing ceases. Some sort of event is occurring, winning Dorsey a moment of complete attention.

Hugh closes his eyes. He knows what the next sentence should be because Dorsey has read him the speech three times, sitting cross-legged in her faded jeans and T-shirt on her rumpled blue bedspread. "As a woman who plans a career in science," Hugh says to himself, "I know that the world's future is in danger." Dorsey repeats the phrase, after him. "But only through the exercise of intelligence and love of truth will all mankind be able to cope with those dangers and overcome them." Sentence by sentence, Hugh leads his sister through the rest of the speech to its final phrase, " . . . that we *have* been some use to the world." Dorsey looks up, smiles, and folds her speech. A noisy admiring roar of applause breaks open into the air and echoes off the cement walls and wood slats.

After the ceremonies, Hugh and his parents find Dorsey outside on the high school's wide front lawn, where other parents are taking snapshots of their children, flashbulbs popping in the f/16 sunlight. Dorsey is smiling, holding hands with friends, being kissed on the cheek. Her father and mother and brother surround her on all sides and lead her away to an unused portion of grass.

"You were wonderful," her father says. "Congratulations, kid."

"Thank you."

"And you looked so beautiful," her mother says, leaning forward to kiss her. "We were all so very proud of you."

"Really?" Dorsey asks, touching her hair with the diploma cover. "Was I all right?"

"Yeah," Hugh tells her. "You were sensational. Only—"

"—Only what?"

"Only how come you stopped in the middle of your speech?"

"I've been telling people I lost my place," Dorsey says, poking into the grass with the toe of her shoe, and smiling.

"Don't do that, honey," her mother says. "It'll ruin the leather."

"Well?" Hugh asks. "Is that it? Did you lose your place, or what?"

"No," she says. "Of course I didn't lose my place."

"Well?"

"People weren't listening carefully enough. They were starting to cough and shuffle," Dorsey says.

"They always cough and shuffle," her mother says. "People in this town don't know how to behave in a group environment."

"Anyhow," Dorsey says, "that's why I stopped. So they'd pay attention."

"I thought you were going to faint, Princess," Mr. Welch says, reaching for her mortarboard and fingering it. "You had us all worried. You mean it was all a trick? Where'd you learn it?"

"*I* wasn't worried," her mother says.

"In Mr. Wigginton's speech class," Dorsey says, "we learned that if you lose their attention, you just stop. They'll start to wonder what's going on, and you'll get them back. Daddy, what are you doing with my mortarboard?"

"Feeling it," he says. "It brings back memories." He returns it to her, takes a picture of her with her mother and brother, and then Mr. and Mrs. Welch begin to stroll around on the grass where the other parents and students are standing. Circulating, they collect praise for their daughter and give praise in return. Hugh doesn't move.

"You liar," he says. "You know, I thought Pop was gonna just keel right over. You scared him so much he turned this sort of shade of ghost white. He was clutching at himself. So what's all this bullshit about getting everybody's attention?"

"I had to tell them something."

"I guess so." Hugh waits. She won't tell him; he'll have to ask. "So what happened? Come on, Cass. Spill it."

"It wasn't making any sense."

"Huh?"

"I was looking down at the words, and they weren't making any sense. None of it was. The gym wasn't, the speech wasn't, nothing there was making any sense. I was feeling sort of dizzy, actually, and then, I don't know, I sort of started up again like it was a job I had to do, and I got through it all right. I never did like public speaking."

"Well, you did a real good job," he says. He lets her go off with her friends, who are standing a few yards back waiting for him to finish talking to her, and once she joins them the girls laugh happily, reaching for her hand, and the boys pat her on the back as if she were one of them, experienced, cynical, and tough. It's just like Dorsey to give four different explanations for what happened, and Hugh is sure each one of them is partly true.

Taking off his tie and stuffing it into his jacket pocket, he heads off to the west doorway that leads into the band room in search of the clarinet-playing blonde. He'll offer to give her a ride home. He'll tell her he once played the clarinet himself. He'll tell her how she kept distracting him all the way through the graduation, the way she was licking her reed like that. Then he'll start in on the compliments. For openers, he'll tell her she's beautiful. He'll say it again and again. Hugh is generous with compliments because they make people happy and always get pleasing results. He has discovered that no one argues with him when he starts in on the praise. It works with girls; it works with customers. Hugh can't imagine a situation he couldn't get out of by just heaping on the praise in a slow, sincere voice, looking the gratified victim right in the eye.

11

During Dorsey's senior year, she hasn't been invited out often on dates. The boys in her class seem to be scared of her—she has a cool ironic streak she picked up from her mother—and the only steady attention she's received has been from Donald Enderfurth, who is vice president of the Physics Club and with whom Dorsey organized a field trip to an experimental nuclear reactor outside Detroit. Donald has said that he admires Dorsey's mind, and he's taken her to several movies at the Wolverine Arts Theater, followed by burgers at the Golden Oaks Grille. To Dorsey's disappointment, he hasn't tried anything with her. Boys who try things don't go out with Dorsey. Donald and Dorsey's evenings have always ended unsoulfully with a good-night kiss at Dorsey's door. On their last date, Donald announced, right after the ritual kiss, that he really enjoyed *talking* to her. "You're deep," he said, holding her hand but moving back. "You've got so many ideas." He said good night and turned to go.

She went inside, appalled, and stood in the dark kitchen by herself, drinking a glass of tap water. As Donald drove away, she imagined herself as an old maid wearing a white frock coat in a laboratory, carrying a clipboard, and surrounded by test tubes filled with caustic yellow and pink industrial fluids.

There might be something she could do about her appearance, she doesn't know what, but there is nothing she can do about her ideas. At certain times, she's tried to act stupid, but it hasn't helped. She didn't win any friends. No one believed she was stupid, not for a minute.

She wasn't invited to the prom last year, but this year she thinks maybe Donald Enderfurth will call, or, if not Donald, Gary Burgess. Gary is not much to look at because of his facial scars from a childhood boating accident, but whenever they run into each other, he always asks Dorsey for the time, and she thinks these swallowed nervous overtures may eventually lead to something. The prom will be in the gymnasium, as usual, and the prom committee has booked a band called Hot Wax, from Mt. Pleasant. The gym, she has heard, will be decorated with last year's orange crepe paper and blue spotlights, and, on the walls, posters borrowed from the foreign language teachers, showing the Eiffel Tower, the Arc de Triomphe, and corks popping out of champagne bottles.

The senior girls outnumber the boys by seven, so not everyone is going to get lucky. Besides, Dorsey has other matters to think about, such as which university she's going to attend in the fall. All the same, she'd like to dress in a formal gown; for one night she'd like to stop being smart, and wear gold earrings and show off the white of her shoulders. She'd like for once to look like a woman, and make some man sleepless, tossing and turning, thinking about her. Her own preoccupation with love strikes her at times as faintly contemptible.

By late spring she has taken to doing her homework in the back study, where she can gaze out through the large windows down to the Five Oaks River and The Lake, as it is called, though this lake is only a broadening of the river behind an old hydroelectric dam. Here, in the study, she works on advanced calculus, memorizes vocabulary words for her German class, where they're reading *Steppenwolf,* and is within arm's reach of the telephone in case Donald Enderfurth or anyone else should call her with a last-minute invitation.

One evening her father comes in after work and sees her in his

leather chair, her knees drawn up close to her chest, a compact
circular mass. She has a copy of *As You Like It* open, but she doesn't
seem to be reading it. She's wearing a vague, puzzled expression.
Dorsey's father rolls up his newspaper and taps her on the head
with it.

"Wake up, wake up, wherever you are," he says. She looks at
him but does not smile. He turns away, fishes a cigarette out of his
shirt pocket, and lights up. "You have your own phone in your
room," he says, exhaling smoke. "How come you're down here,
sitting in *my* chair?"

"The view is better," she says.

He opens the newspaper and pretends to read it. "He didn't call?"
She shakes her head. He glances at his daughter and starts to sing.

> " 'All alone, by the telephone,
> Waiting for a ring, . . .' "

"Stop it, Daddy." She covers her eyes with her hand.

"I'm sorry. I was only trying to be funny."

"I know. But it isn't funny."

"All right." He nods, then lets himself down onto the sofa,
accidentally sitting on top of a month-old issue of *Newsweek*. He
pulls it out from under his seat, stares at the cover, then tosses it to
the side. "I agree. It wasn't funny. It used to be funny but it isn't
anymore."

They sit together in the room, neither of them actually reading,
though Dorsey's father occasionally glances down at the front page
of his newspaper. Outside, the late afternoon darkens into a luminous spring dusk. They both hear Mrs. Welch clattering pans in the
kitchen as she prepares their dinner, and from the front of the house,
across the street, comes the sound of their neighbor, Burt Atwood,
mowing his lawn.

"You know, I was smart, too," Dorsey's father says quietly. "It's
not enough to be smart. You have to be tough. An upstart. You
have to learn how to wait. Sooner or later in the Big Casino the
odds change so that they're in your favor. There's always good news

somewhere, and the good news is that the rest of your life isn't going to be like high school."

She thinks it's sweet for him to say what he's said, but she doesn't believe it. She thinks the rest of her life is going to be just like high school. It's going to be like high school until you die.

12

In early April, Hugh gets a call during the day at Bay City Buick, and the call is from his mother. "I don't think Dorsey is going to be invited to the prom," Hugh's mother says, as soon as she has her son on the line. "I don't think it's important, except that I've noticed that she's getting moody, which, for her, is *quite* moody. She's beginning to have doubts about people. Not some people: *all* of them. Do you still know anyone, some nice boy, in the senior class who could . . . ?"

Hugh leans back in his office chair, behind his desk, his ink blotter, and his nameplate (his first). He checks the showroom to see if anyone could possibly be monitoring this conversation.

"Ma," he says, "you shouldn't call me here with questions like this." He waits for her to respond, but instead she gives him for free that maddening silence of hers. Looking down, he checks the polish of his cordovan shoes. "No, I don't know anyone in the senior class. I'm five years older than they are. They were seventh graders when I was graduating. They were just little twerps."

"I thought maybe you could help," Mrs. Welch says. "I thought you knew everybody. You *do* know everybody." She waits again;

it's one of her ironic silences. "For example, do you know Donald Enderfurth? He's a timid, unattractive boy who's taken Dorsey out a few times, but at this point he's the only person standing between her and her usual angry solitude. I don't want her to hate men all her life, if I can avoid it. Anyway, I thought that maybe if you knew him, you could pressure him somehow. You know how to pressure people."

"Pressure him. How would I pressure him?"

"I don't know. Threats. Bribes. Tell him you're a lawyer and you'll sue him unless he invites your sister out."

"Now you're not being serious."

"It was just a thought," she says. She luxuriates in another long pause.

"What is it, Ma?" he asks, knowing she has something else on her mind.

"I'm worried about your father. He's been complaining about chest pains. He's low on energy, and he's looking old fast. His hands are always damp; I don't like that. I keep telling him to get to a doctor, but you know how he says that they're all quacks."

"He's right."

"Oh, Hugh, would you talk to him? The men in his family, and this will include you, have . . . well, his father, your grandfather, had a bad heart, and your father once said he thought he'd inherited a bad one, too, but I don't believe him. Anyhow, I won't nag."

"All right, all right," Hugh says. "I'll give him a call."

"Thank you." She makes an odd noise; it sounds as though she's chewing gum. "How are you, dear? When are you going to invite me down to your apartment?"

Never. "Soon," he says. "I just need a little more furniture. That's all. A few more tables and chairs, to give it some respectability."

"Well, that would be very nice. I know you have certain gutter tendencies and I just thought it would be bracing to your moral character if your mother threatened to visit."

"Right, right." A customer walks in through the side glass door. "Listen, Ma. I have to go to work. Are you okay?"

"I'm okay as long as your father is okay. Remember to call him. *You* do the nagging. You know how."

"I will. Talk to you soon."

"Good-bye, Hugh. Take care of yourself."

He checks out the customer: four-door LeSabre material. Hugh gets up and goes out to make the match. In ten minutes he's completely forgotten about his mother's phone call, and he won't remember it until six months after Dorsey's graduation, when his mother calls him again, but from the emergency room of the county hospital this time, after his father's first heart attack. There's a tone in her voice he's never heard before: it's high and trumpetlike. "He'll be all right," she says, but the trumpet tone in her voice says he won't be. The trumpet announces that the end is coming, for both his father and for her. The tone of her voice is full of conclusions, and when it comes, Hugh sits back in his cubicle, and he sees himself alone in the world with his sister, just the two of them.

13

For her senior science project, Dorsey makes a four-inch reflecting telescope by herself, having ordered the parts from an Edmund Scientific catalogue. When the telescope is finished, she takes photographs of the moon's surface with her father's Nikon. She develops the photographs in the high school darkroom and makes the enlargements herself. Her most striking photograph is of the Mare Imbrium, the Sea of Rains, a dark section of the upper left quadrant of the lunar surface. This photograph, along with six others, and her telescope win her first prize in the Bay County Science Fair.

She thinks about her telescope during her boring classes, such as English. Her English instructor is Mrs. Iglehart. The class is supposed to be enriched—all the students in it are planning to go to either college or junior college—but in Dorsey's opinion Mrs. Iglehart makes nothing out of the books she assigns. She has the soul of ignorance: she doesn't seem to know why anyone should read, and her idea of a good class discussion is one in which the plot of the text in question is thoroughly and exhaustively summarized. Starting in February, and going on interminably through March, they are studying *Hamlet.* With false enthusiasm, Mrs. Iglehart has repeatedly called it Shakespeare's greatest, most wonderful play, a true monument of Western literature.

During most of the discussions, Dorsey has kept her mouth shut, but one day near the end of March Mrs. Iglehart comes into class looking strangely manic and, speaking very quickly, tries to start off a discussion on the reasons for what she calls the play's "special greatness."

Dorsey looks at her and thinks of the little old lady from Pasadena. "Why," Mrs. Iglehart asks, her voice dry and hollow, "do so many people, the world over, identify with Prince Hamlet?" She makes an up-and-down motion with her index finger: does the motion suggest the world, or the Prince? Dorsey isn't sure.

The students look down at their desks or the floor or their fingernails. It's a Five Oaks spring, and the sun hasn't been out for weeks, and there's mud everywhere. On some days it snows, and on other days it rains. Outside, the grass is steel gray and the trees are still skeletal and barren. The air smells of aluminum and old mattresses. No one in the class is going steady with anyone else in the class, so that productive tension is absent, and it's too much trouble to write notes or even to be interested in life on days like this. High schools in the Midwest, Dorsey thinks, are cocoons within cocoons within cocoons.

John Raftery, an acned pole-vaulter, says, "Is it because he has so much trouble making up his mind?"

If Five Oaks is a cocoon, Dorsey wonders, then where is the damn butterfly? "Perhaps," Mrs. Iglehart responds, her head shaking with pseudo-Parkinson's disease, "but why do so many people identify with indecisiveness?"

Dorsey looks at John Raftery's ankles. He's not handsome, but she's noticed his long hands, and she likes the easy width of his shoulders. "Because lots of people are indecisive, that's why," Dorsey says, not bothering to raise her hand or to look at Mrs. Iglehart.

"What? Excuse me? Dorsey, what did you say?"

She imagines herself on a cruise, on a huge ocean liner, to ... Nassau. The sun burns off bright surfaces there, and the air smells of palm oil and sand. "I was saying," Dorsey says, "that a lot of people identify with Hamlet's indecisiveness because a lot of people are indecisive."

"That's circular," Mrs. Iglehart tells her. "Perhaps people see reasons why they are indecisive in Hamlet's actions."

She is with someone out in the open air, and this person's breath smells of mint. She tries to quell her daydreams, but they steam up angrily from her subconscious like vapor from a teakettle. She raises her hand. "Actually," she says, "I don't understand why all these people *do* identify with Hamlet. Indecisiveness is only one of his problems. I think Hamlet is repellent. He kills people like Polonius without ever feeling sorry, but he won't do what he's supposed to do, which is kill Claudius, until it's too late, and then he's basically killing Claudius because Claudius has already killed him. Hamlet's a sort of egomaniac. I suppose people think he's lovable, but *I* don't think so."

The sea breeze blows over her. Someone is with her. She lowers a grape into her own mouth and squeezes it slowly between her front teeth. She looks over at John Raftery, now, and sees that his eyes are blue. It's the only primary color in the entire classroom. She's never noticed before. Mrs. Iglehart has a pencil in her hand, and when she raises her hand to her forehead, a gesture that means she is thinking, the pencil leaves a faint trace on her skin. Dorsey throws an idea projectile out of her head toward John Raftery. Look at me, she commands. "Why do you call him an egomaniac?" Mrs. Iglehart asks Dorsey.

John looks at her. They are in London, in the Savoy, ordering from room service. "Because he's always thinking of himself, of how everything he does will appear to others. Hamlet wants to be popular. He wants to be popular more than he wants to be right. He wants everything to *look* right. It's a mystery to me why people like him. *I* don't ever want to meet anybody like that. I mean, I *have* met people like that, lots of times. He's the sort of guy who's always combing his hair and asking you, 'How did I look? Did I look okay?' "

John laughs, but he seems uncomfortable. There are other boys in the class she likes better, more interesting and thoughtful. She actually sympathizes with Hamlet, a man paralytically bewildered by the wars of love. Love must be powerful if it brings such scarifying people as those who live in Five Oaks together. She looks over at Tricia Blakely, who's in the next row, not paying attention, giving off her usual icy sexual heat. Mrs. Iglehart walks closer to Dorsey's desk, and Dorsey sees fatigue lines on her face and liver spots on her hands. "Well," Mrs. Iglehart asks, "if you find Hamlet such a repellent character, what do you think he *should* have been like?"

"What?"

"How should he have behaved?" Mrs. Iglehart tilts herself backwards, and she scratches one hand with the other. Whoever married Mrs. Iglehart, Dorsey thinks, was a hero of love, and deserves a chest of medals. I'm going to be a virgin all my life, she thinks furiously. People will point and laugh. The air smells of chalk dust, a mortuary smell, and Mrs. Iglehart's eyes are squinting with a mild, itchy anger. "If Hamlet shouldn't have acted like Hamlet, who should he have been like?"

Whom. Whom should he have been like. Dorsey thinks for a moment, then says, "Antigone."

There is another long, dead pause in the classroom. Somebody (but not John Raftery) with blue eyes and sensitive hands is pouring wine in Dorsey's hair. Mrs. Iglehart's eyes unsquint. She looks quickly out the window at the dull thick horribly impossible gray sickening blank of Five Oaks in March. Then she looks back at Dorsey. "Antigone? We haven't read *Antigone* in class this year."

"That's all right," Dorsey says. "*I've* read it." They are making love on the carpeted floor; they are going out for dinner in evening clothes; they are seeing the lights of the city. So-and-so, intelligent cosmopolitan, takes her to the theater and kisses her on the cheek when the lights dim.

"Well, then," Mrs. Iglehart says, "perhaps you'd like to tell us about it."

All right. Once again I have to make a spectacle of myself, she thinks, before speaking. She tells the class about Antigone and her brother Polynices, how Antigone knows what she must do and then does it, despite the authorities, personified by King Creon. Antigone, Dorsey says, doesn't have to moralize in order to justify her actions, because she knows what kinds of obligations she owes to her brother, even in death. "Antigone doesn't try to be nice or clever or charming," Dorsey says, throwing the sentence at Tricia Blakely, John Raftery, Carol Sue Trenbeth, and Bill Fitzgerald, who are insanely popular. "She just tries to do what she thinks is right. There's a difference."

"Yes," Mrs. Iglehart says.

They're going to put me in the Ripley's Believe-It-or-Not Museum, Dorsey thinks. Nearly everyone in the class stares at the floor. A few people are listening to her, but most of them look bored or as blank as the faces in police sketches of criminal suspects. "Well," Dorsey says, "you asked me who Hamlet should have been like. I thought he should have been more like her."

"Whose class did you read that play in?" Mrs. Iglehart asks.

"I didn't read it in anybody's class," Dorsey says, sorry and humiliated that she ever spoke up. Good-bye to Nassau, good-bye to grapes and hammocks. "I read it at home."

Muffled sinus laughter cuts through the room as the intensity of the whispering increases. If Dorsey were to look up, which she is careful not to do, she believes she might see faces opening with staring contempt and lightened with sneers.

"You must have quite a library at home," Mrs. Iglehart says in an odd tone. This tone seems to Dorsey to be close to the opposite of praise, whatever that is, without quite hitting it. More choked laughter is seeded, blooms, and wilts behind Dorsey's desk. Mrs. Iglehart moves in her peculiar sideways walk toward the blackboard. "How nice that someone reads at home," she says distantly.

Dorsey wants to say that the point is not that she reads at home, the point has to do with Antigone's honorable behavior in contrast to Hamlet's self-centered brooding. But from now on, there really is no point to the rest of the day except to get safely out of the classroom and down the hallways without being singled out as an intellectual sideshow any more than she has been already. The world of human beings is insufferable, not to be tolerated. She has never been laughed at by the periodic table or a theorem or an equation. To hell with all these people, she thinks; damn them all.

14

Hugh's apartment in Bay City is a one-bedroom unit in the Evergreen Court complex, four blocks down Bay Road from a K mart and a McDonald's, and only five minutes' drive from Bay City Buick. He has furnished the apartment with a dining room table and chairs, a black vinyl sofa, a rocker, a side table with a decorative lava lamp, shelves for the stereo and records, a bed, and a dresser. The television set is on a rolling stand in the living room corner, and for color and variety he has hung a spider plant from a hook on the living room ceiling. The plant takes frequent watering, and Hugh isn't always sure that it's worth the trouble.

But the women who come into Hugh's apartment notice the plant right away; it seems to signal to them that Hugh can take care of living things. They sit down on his vinyl sofa and he brings them a beer or rolls them a joint, and they talk about their own plants —philodendrons and wandering Jews and African violets—and their jobs, and their cats. There are always stories about cats, when you deal with single women. Hugh makes the acquaintance of these women in the dealership and in the Romper Room Bar on Bay

Road, and he still has a small inventory of girlfriends left over from high school who continue to live, in one capacity or another, in Five Oaks, thirty minutes north. All day he thinks about selling cars and making money, and all evening he thinks about women, whether they are in his apartment, talking about their cats, or not.

He has lost interest in hockey and politics. After he could no longer skate competitively, he didn't care about the sport enough to read the scores of the local or national teams in the evening paper. And as for politics, once he had flunked his army physical at Ft. Wayne in Detroit (some hearing loss in his left ear—he'd never known he had it), and once he knew he wouldn't be going overseas where some of his classmates and friends seemed to have disappeared, he became himself. The war is on television every night, less and less of the war as the years pass, and that's where the war stays. Hugh figures that he himself is now living the life every young man wants to live: good job, a good variety of women, weeks and maybe years of fine times before settling down.

In his free moments he thinks about the clothes women wear, the gut-clutching curves of their thighs and calves, their blue and brown and green eyes and gold earrings and the perfumes they put on themselves, all over, everywhere; he thinks about the way they laugh and whisper his name when they're close to him. He thinks about the way they sing. Most of his records are of women singers and Motown girl groups, the Marvelettes, the Supremes, and Martha and the Vendellas. Sometimes it seems to him that nature is playing a joke on him at his expense: it has taken away his free will, taken away his conscious mind, and has put instead the image of a singing woman in front of him, endlessly receding as he races toward it, like a dog chasing a mechanical rabbit. This is great, he thinks. This is just great.

He's had one-night stands with four of his customers, two of them married. After seven months he knows a good percentage of the eligible women in Bay City. His favorite, his semi-regular, is Mikki Mead, who is nineteen years old to Hugh's twenty-two, and who works in the baby clothes section of Montgomery Ward. To exactly the degree he likes it, Mikki lacks refinement. If anybody asked him to describe her, and no one has, he'd say: she's cigarettes, beer, one joint before making love, tight blue jeans over a sweet little ass, blond hair out of a bottle, pointy apple-sized breasts, and Sunday afternoons at the bowling alley. What he likes best about her is that when she comes, she laughs out loud. She doesn't seem to be interested in much except satisfying her various appetites. That suits Hugh.

He can't believe his good luck. With all this war going on on television, here at home there are still plenty of women like Mikki who will actually take off their clothes and get into bed with him. To think that all through childhood, sex was being kept a secret! This free-for-all, this opening of mouths and the sweat and cries and the spilling—it was all a locked book, sealed shut. Why not tell children? Because they would be more angry at adults than they already are. They'd be disgusted.

The idea of children appeals to Hugh slightly. He wants to be the first parent in the history of the world who tells his children the whole truth about life. But he doesn't plan to start this project until he has sampled and tasted more of Bay City's women, an intention that may take years to satisfy. Sometimes, toward the end of the month, a time when his energy level tends to be low, he slows down, does some accounting, and balances the psychic books. When that happens, he calls up Laurie Boyd and takes her out to dinner.

Laurie, unlike Mikki, reads menus. She looks off into the middle distance, having thoughts. The only occasions when she smiles are those rare moments when she has a reason to smile; she doesn't have Mikki Mead's for-no-reason Disneyland grin. She doesn't ask Hugh questions, but when he talks she bends forward, listening intently. She works as a secretary part-time and goes to school at Saginaw Valley, majoring in library science. Except for her hair, which has a light brown sheen, he always has trouble remembering the specifics of her appearance. Her personal gravity prevents her from having all the available fun there is, and something about this deficiency interests Hugh. That, and her habit every time she sees Hugh of taking him seriously. When he gazes at her across the table as she nibbles at her salad, he thinks: I've taken her home and shown her to the folks and Dorsey, and here I am with her again, and we're still talking. He has no idea at all why he likes her.

She's the sort of woman that other guys say is no prize. She has an alcoholic father. And Hugh's interest in her has little to do with

Laurie's talents as a lover. Often she has back pains, the result of an automobile accident in high school. No matter how he turns up the romantic atmosphere with candles and music and wine, no matter what he says to her, her kisses have an absentminded unresponsiveness. To Hugh this is a challenge, as if she couldn't be had. They've been to bed together several times, and it's been all right, but she doesn't groan or laugh or pant. With Laurie the air in the room turns serious, but it also turns calm, as if ordinary things, too, had a right to be there.

He likes to shuffle the pack, mix Mikki and Sharon and Rita in there with Laurie, but he puzzles himself sometimes, coming back to this woman who seems to offer him nothing but a long haul over bad roads in high, unforgiving country.

15

Hugh brings Laurie home for the first time in the fall of Dorsey's senior year, when Dorsey's upstairs room is cluttered with piles of application forms to colleges and universities, the booklets and letters and catalogues lined up along the wall from the typewriter to the bed and from there to the door. She'd like to show these forms to her brother, but she doesn't see him often, and she doesn't think he'd enjoy looking at them anyway, after what happened to him at Holbein College. Usually Hugh comes home for Sunday night dinner by himself, but this time in October he has called ahead on Thursday and warned his mother that he'll be bringing a girl on Saturday. Dorsey's mother takes this news circumspectly and prepares one of her usual roasts. "I don't see the point," she tells Dorsey, "in getting all gussied up for one of Hugh's little sweethearts. That boy isn't going to get married for another seven years, I'll take book on it. This isn't serious. Young men aren't serious, and *Hugh* isn't serious. You just watch."

"Six years." Dorsey is in the kitchen, writing her autobiography for the University of Pennsylvania entrance form on the dinette table and occasionally looking up to watch her mother organize the meal. Her father is sitting outside on the front stoop by himself, wearing his maize-and-blue University of Michigan cap, smoking one of his Saturday cigars, and listening to the end of the football game on the radio.

"Take your pick," Dorsey's mother says. "I know that kid. He's in no hurry. Why should he be?" She allows herself a smile. "The boy is too handsome. He's wasting the gifts your father and I gave him if he doesn't play the cock of the walk."

They hear Hugh's Buick pull into the driveway exactly at six o'clock. Dorsey and her parents gather at the doorway to welcome Hugh and his girlfriend in, and in the general commotion of greetings and handshakes and the removing of coats, Dorsey sees a startled and almost frightened look on her mother's face just beneath the visible line of sociability. Something's wrong, and what's wrong is the girl, and the careful way Hugh is treating her. He's watching out for her, husbanding her. It's odd, because she's not pretty in the cheap and flashy style Hugh likes best. It's as if he's trying to prove that he's a serious person by taking out a plain woman who can appeal only to a man who thinks. Dorsey sees her mother exchange a glance with her father: *watch yourself. This is serious.*

Before dinner, Mr. Welch offers Laurie a beer. She says that ice water is fine. He shrugs and gets her what she wants. At the dinner table Hugh and Laurie sit across from Dorsey, not saying much. Dorsey talks instead about the mechanics of grinding mirrors for telescopes, and as she does, she tries to imagine whom Laurie reminds her of. Some actress. Somebody like Paula Prentiss. Not with the smile, but similar. The comparison makes her nervous, and she hears herself chattering about colleges, the trip the Physics Club is going to take to a nuclear reactor, and she's just started to talk about atomic fission when her father interrupts her.

"Dorsey, you're hogging the show. Our poor guest hasn't been able to get a word in any which old way. Miss Boyd, tell us a little about yourself."

"Laurie."

"Laurie. Tell us a little about yourself, before my wife here gets into the act and does it herself."

Laurie looks at Mrs. Welch. "Excuse me?"

"My wife," Mr. Welch says, "engages in what she calls 'human speculation.' It's just a parlor trick in poor taste and of course I do my best to discourage it, but sometimes, when conversation flags, I can't stop her from launching into her show. So you should jump in here and tell us all about the Boyds."

"I still don't understand," Laurie says. Dorsey is gazing at her face. It's not Paula Prentiss. It's somebody else.

"My husband," Mrs. Welch says, "likes to let very black cats out of very dirty bags. As he says, it's a parlor trick, a little game we sometimes play in private." She throws her husband a mock frown. "I keep telling him not to bring it up in front of guests, but, as you will discover once you are married, no wife can successfully muzzle her husband entirely, and it's not always wise to try."

"What do you mean? What do you do?"

Mrs. Welch smiles. "I . . . guess about people," she says.

"It's like a carnival midway," Mr. Welch says. "You give her a dollar, and if she can't guess your weight, you win a free dinner."

"You guess about people," Laurie says, the statement almost sounding like a question.

"Come on, Ma," Hugh says. "Don't."

"Oh, just small things."

"Don't."

"What small things." Laurie's questions leave off the rising final inflection.

"Histories. Parents. Origins. That sort of thing. Nothing special. Nothing anyone couldn't do. Everyone does it."

"Oh, I don't think so," Laurie says, raising her napkin delicately to her chin.

"Well, I do. We *all* interpret, Laurie. And this has been a little hobby of mine for quite a spell of time, but I don't do it unless someone asks me."

Dorsey, Hugh, and Mr. Welch all speak at the same time, interrupting, changing the subject, making a familial commotion. Mrs. Welch holds up her hand and says, "You see how nervous I make these people? Isn't it awful? Here I am, the hostess, wife, and mother, and no one trusts me. It's quite deplorable."

"With strangers," Mr. Welch says. "We don't trust you with strangers, sweetie."

"Do you think I am about to terrorize this poor young woman, our guest? You know I don't do that. I don't terrorize."

"Go ahead," Laurie says, putting down her fork and reaching for her glass of water. She looks at Hugh's mother, her face set. "Tell me something about myself. I'm not terrorizable."

Hugh tries to protest but Laurie shushes him, something Dorsey has never seen any woman his age do to Hugh. Meanwhile, Mrs. Welch has started to stare at her son's girlfriend, and after a few moments she says, "You're a practical woman. You can fix things. You're good at sorting—"

"—She's going to be a librarian, Ma," Hugh says. "She—"

"—Let me finish!" Mrs. Welch resumes her smile. "You're good at sorting and gardening. You're very good at drawing, but you don't like to cook very much. Your greatest emotional talent is for tenderness."

"What about my parents," Laurie says.

"I don't do parents," Mrs. Welch says.

"You said you do parents."

"Did I? What a good listener you are. I don't do parents on the first time out. I don't do parents at the dinner table. That would be improper." She waits. "Well, did I get anything right?"

Laurie smiles back, when she sees that Mrs. Welch is finished with her. "No, I'm afraid not. You're not right. I'm not very practical. I can't fix things. So far, I haven't been much of a gardener, and I'm afraid I can't draw anything more complicated than a dog. What was the other thing? Cooking. Yes, that's true, that I don't like to cook very much."

Dorsey is about to ask Laurie if she is tender—just for laughs, just as a joke—but one glance from her father silences her.

"Too bad," Mrs. Welch says, laughing like someone in an opera. "My little parlor trick has failed me again."

"Now we'll have to shut down the cabaret," her husband says. "Dismantle the stage and send the musicians home."

"Anyone for dessert?" Mrs. Welch asks, eyebrows raised, looking around quickly. "Banana cake, baked entirely by myself, though not from scratch, thank goodness. Dorsey, would you help us clear? Laurie, you and Hugh sit there and luxuriate in the service. Hugh doesn't get this kind of attention very often, do you, kiddo?"

She doesn't wait for him to answer; she picks up her plate and two of the serving dishes and carries them out to the kitchen. After taking Laurie's and her brother's plates—Hugh winks at her as she does—Dorsey follows her mother out to the kitchen, where her father is muttering in an agitated manner to himself, while Mrs. Welch scrubs dishes in the sink, creating a violent circular spray of soapy water. "Dorsey," she says, "would you get the cake out? It's over there, by the refrigerator, under the tin foil."

"You were sure wrong about Hugh's girlfriend, Mom," Dorsey tells her, taking the plates over to the sink.

"I wasn't wrong."

"She said you were. She said you—"

"—Your mother was misrepresenting. Weren't you, dear?" Dorsey's father still has not looked up.

"Yes. That's a good word. That's exactly what I was doing." She turns around, her hands dripping soap onto the kitchen floor, and looks at her husband. "I certainly hope that girl learns tenderness," she says in a dispirited monotone. "It does no harm to make her think she might have a talent for it."

"Why?" Dorsey asks. "What's the big deal about tenderness?"

"You explain," her father says, going back into the dining room.

"Well, I think we're going to see more of her." Mrs. Welch dries her hands on a dish towel and starts to cut up the banana cake, passing the knife through it carefully in long parallel lines. "That woman is very serious about Hughie. I just want her to be nice to him. Here, take this out to her." She hands Dorsey a plate, a huge slice of cake, which Dorsey takes in to Laurie.

As soon as Dorsey has served the cake, she excuses herself to go to the bathroom. Standing in front of the sink to wash her hands, she gazes into the mirror to check her hair and face. She feels a low chemical itch of recognition that alters itself quickly and subtly into a wave of discomfort. The soap falls out of her hands and slides down toward the drain plug. It isn't Paula Prentiss, she thinks; it's me. We could be sisters. She feels like family to him. He'll keep coming back. It can't be me he wants, she thinks. That's impossible. She dries her hands and goes back out to the dining room, remembering to smile, to make a social effort.

16

On Sundays Hugh drives out to the house in the early afternoon to visit his sister and his parents, but after Dorsey's senior year has started, she's so often hidden away upstairs studying that Hugh feels like a boor interrupting her, so he hangs around his father for company instead. His mother does not socialize on Sunday morning or early in the afternoon. She reads the Sunday papers, the Detroit *Free-Press* and the *Detroit News,* with scholarly concentrated attention, satisfying her scandalized curiosity about the world, a pair of scissors and an X-acto knife close by in case she has the urge to clip anything out. She puts the clippings into a box, and then the box is carried down to the basement and filed with the other boxes of clippings stacked against the south wall.

Throughout the summer Hugh has asked his father if he'd like to go fishing, and each time the old man has said no, not this time. This continual lack of interest is new and disturbing. In the third week of September Hugh asks him if he'd like just to go out onto the lake and sit there in the rowboat while Hugh pulls the oars for a spell, and this time his father says yes.

It's a cool Sunday, the leaves just starting to turn, the sky a luminous, silvery blue. Riding in the car down to the Hasselbachers' dock, where Mr. Welch's rowboat is tied up, Hugh's father smokes quietly and makes small throat-clearing sounds of pleasure whenever he sees a color he likes on a sumac bush or a sugar maple. They park their car on County Road E and walk down the Hasselbachers' driveway to the dock, Hugh slowing his pace so as not to draw too far ahead of his father, who is walking with short steps. He bends down and picks up a rock. "Jasper," he says, throwing it off into the woods. He is still looking down. He points at the undergrowth. "Do you know what that is?" he asks. Hugh shakes his head. "Walking fern," he says. "The tips of the leaves touch ground, root themselves, and then sprout new plants. It's very rare." Hugh nods. His father has bored him for years lecturing him about ferns and other stupefying forms of plant life.

A few minutes later the old man—*old!* Hugh thinks, he's only fifty-four—eases himself down into the rowboat, and Hugh pulls them out into the lake. In the bay the tentative waves, three fingers high, slap against the boat. Hugh faces his father and rows with short forward arcs. Mr. Welch settles himself, a cushion at his back, and lights up a cigarette. He gazes north toward town, at the dilapidated Five Oaks Amusement Park, the town's only claim for tourist dollars, and then he looks down again at the lake. He lowers his hands to the water, and a wave splashes into his hand and douses his cigarette.

"What the hell. I didn't want it anyway," he says, flinging it with a wrist flick into the water. He leans back and smiles at Hugh. "So, kiddo. How's business in the dealership?"

"It's okay. I like sales. How're things at the agency?"

"Fine," Mr. Welch says. "Mrs. Wieland had a fire in her kitchen last week, six hundred dollars at least of smoke damage. The damn fool was pouring brandy all over the main course, she'd been reading Julia Child or some other arsonist, and the curtains caught. It's lucky she didn't burn down the house. And Mr. Forster, you remember him—"

"—The manager at the I.G.A."

"That's the one. He got himself into another auto wreck. This earth has not seen in its history a worse driver than Harold Forster. He makes Ben-Hur look like a Sunday driver. He drove into the ditch and united his car with a tree. Walked away from it, as usual. God loves that man and will protect him in perpetuity, I have no doubt. How I'd love to cancel him, and that pyromaniac Mrs. LaMonte, out there every summer with her shed full of illegal class-B fireworks. She burned the roof off her shed last year and of course won't tell me how." He looks again toward the town, getting smaller as Hugh continues to row. "Well, they're all good people," Mr. Welch says, shrugging.

"No, they're not."

"Maybe not. It's true: I know personally a dozen couples having affairs, several men who beat their wives, and one woman who beats her children black and blue where it won't show, and I know a man, actually a friend, who is altering the books on his business with ghost payrolling and plans to leave town with the money he's gouged from the company. I know quite a number of fools and stuffed shirts and would-be members of the criminal class, and I talk to these people every day. This town is full of villains. I should know. I deal hourly with Elks and Moose, warlike men, who think that Richard M. Nixon is a fine upstanding fellow and who supported the late calamity in Vietnam with every cell in their bodies. I have the requisite shame all Americans should feel. My own father worked the land, broke his health doing it to get me an education, and here I am wearing white shirts at a desk, selling policies for fire. But I don't change people, Hugh. I insure them. I send them checks when fate plays them dirty tricks. Financially, I am God's apologist."

Hugh nods, still rowing.

"Aren't you going to argue with me? Aren't you going to tell me I should revise people in this town, make alterations in them?" His son shakes his head. "Too bad," his father says. "I could have used a lecture. My moral standards need elevating. You were never much of a moralist, were you?"

"Too interested in cars and girls," Hugh says. "I love sex."

His father's face turns red quickly. "Don't talk like that in front of me. I can't stand to hear it. I'm not one of your friends; I'm your father." Mr. Welch frowns at his son's hands.

"All right, all right."

"Think you'll ever go back to college?"

"Not a chance," Hugh says. "I don't have the brains for it. Dorsey got all those."

"You got them. You just don't believe you got them. At least you didn't come out ugly," Mr. Welch says. "You just remember what I've always told you. You watch out for Dorsey."

"She won't need watching out for. She's too smart."

"Everyone needs watching out for," Mr. Welch says. "And that includes your sister. She's got a sweet streak. People are going to take advantage of her, this is America, after all. Stop rowing. We're in the middle of the lake."

Hugh brings the oars into the rowboat. The two of them sit quietly for a few minutes, drifting toward the east side of the bay. The breeze from the west ruffles Hugh's hair; he can feel the sun's light on his face, but it is without warmth, a cold light. Looking toward the small white wooden struts and beams of the Five Oaks Amusement Park roller coaster, he asks, "How come you didn't want to go fishing? I saw all your rods and reels cleaned in the basement."

"Too much trouble," his father says. "Tires me out to fish when there aren't any fish. Besides, this river has started to fill up with chemical whoopee. It even has a touch of radioactivity in it. People've been catching fish with weird growths. Harry Gertler caught a bass last week with a tumor in its side that looked like a fireplug. It's the power plant upstream, but they deny it, of course. Where the radioactivity comes from is anybody's guess."

They drift for another fifteen minutes. Every so often Hugh's father grunts with pleasure. Occasionally he shuts his eyes and breathes in the lake air, a heavy water and weed scent. Hugh looks at the lines on his father's face and watches him breathing in and out, and for a moment he has a sudden fear: that his father is going to wave good-bye, first to Five Oaks, and then to him. He stares at his father's right hand, afraid that it is going to elevate itself into the air and start waving back and forth, and the only preventive measure Hugh can think of to keep that hand from waving is to tell his father how much he loves him. If his father starts to raise his hand, Hugh has already decided, he'll blurt it out. He'll say, "I love you, Pop," and the hand will go down again, he's sure. But in fact Mr. Welch doesn't wave to anyone. He lets the sun shine its chilly September light on his face, and when he opens his eyes, he gazes at Hugh and says, "What're you looking at? When did I become so interesting?" The old man laughs. "I never could manage heart-to-heart talks, could I? Come on, let's go back."

Hugh turns around, so that his back is to his father, and he rows toward the Hasselbachers' dock, hearing, from time to time, his father's words of thanks and encouragement. The words push themselves into Hugh's body, giving him strength, so that by the time they reach the dock, he feels capable of rowing his father across any river, anywhere.

17

In the summer between her sophomore and junior years, Dorsey finds it difficult to get her mother's attention. When she isn't reading in the cane chair out on the porch, Mrs. Welch stands at the kitchen counter in front of the south window with her FM radio tuned to the classical music station in Saginaw. She cuts and peels and seasons the ingredients for the evening's meal while she hums along with the music, whether she knows the piece or not. She can hum along to anything, even Webern: quiet little twelve-tone squeaks. If she's not in the kitchen, she's outdoors pottering around in the vegetable garden, and if she's not on the porch, or in the kitchen, or out in the garden, she's working as a clerk at the Five Oaks City Hall. "If I were to come down here for breakfast with my blouse on backwards," Dorsey tells her, "you wouldn't notice."

"Your father would notice," her mother says, gazing out the south window as she washes her hands.

"That's what I mean. *You* wouldn't."

"Why should I, when he would?" Mrs. Welch asks, and Dorsey is for a moment stumped and syllogized. She hands the breakfast dishes to her mother, who rinses them dreamily. Whenever Dorsey's mother has her hands in running water, she is deaf to most human concerns.

"Mother, listen. I want a telephone in my room."

"You'll get over it."

"I don't want to get over it. I want to make my own calls. In private."

"In private? There's no privacy here. This is a family. We all snoop. Besides, you don't have that many friends, and the friends you do have are all decent people. I don't see the point."

"I'm going to be a junior," Dorsey says. "I've got my own social life. People are going to call, and I don't want all of you keeping track of me." She has her right hand in a fist on her hip, and her left arm crosses her waist so that she stands in a combative position, although her mother doesn't appear to notice.

"We can't afford it," Mrs. Welch says.

"What if I wired it myself?"

"Cass, that's illegal."

"There's that old junk telephone in the basement that's not connected up. How about if I tap into the telephone lines in the house and wire that telephone into my room?"

"They'll charge us for it," Mrs. Welch says, scrubbing a plate. "They have machines to check."

"Not if I wire it," Dorsey says, already out of the room.

First she bicycles down to Our Own Hardware for the wires. Her next stop is Knapp Radio and TV, where she buys a high impedance resistor. Back at home, she removes the plate from her parents' bedroom wall, taps into the wires, and runs her extension line along the floorboards, down the hallway and into her room. Before she connects the telephone she's brought up from the basement, she puts the resistor on the line and then connects the wires to a trip relay and a battery-powered buzzer in a box, so that her phone will buzz, not ring, on incoming calls. With the resistor on the line preventing a voltage drop, the sleuths at the telephone company will never know that there's an additional phone hooked up in the house. She feels quite pleased with herself, sitting there in her room, her new junk telephone on her desk, and she decides to make her first call.

"The time," the recording says, "is eight twenty-three, and twenty seconds."

She hangs up and calls her brother at his apartment. "Halloo," he says.

"Guess who?"

"Hi, kid. How the hell are you doin'? What's up?"

"My new telephone, that's what."

"What telephone? They didn't get you a phone, did they? Jeez, Cass, you get everything. They never got *me* a telephone."

"No. I took that old phone from the basement and wired it myself, and this is my first call to someone who isn't a recording. Can you hear me all right?"

"You sound as if you're next door. You sound . . ." She waits while her brother searches for the word. "You sound intimate. No, that's not what I mean. I mean you sound close. Kid, you are a goddamn genius, pardon my language. Listen, I'll be seeing you in a few days. I've got a friend here right now, a lady friend, so I've gotta go. You take care of yourself, okay? And congratulations on your new phone. Don't spend all your time on it, okay?"

"Okay. Thanks. 'Bye. See you later." Dorsey always has trouble ending telephone conversations; often she must say "good-bye" in four different ways before she feels that the conversation has been properly concluded.

She hangs up, pleased with herself, and looks at the poster over her desk of Bob Dylan, the side-view Milton Glaser graphic, the singer's hair sprouting flowers. At this moment she feels a sense of intimate . . . yes, that's the word, she thinks, intimate communion with Bob Dylan, a man who has beaten the system in his own way, using creativity and mother-wit.

If Dorsey's parents notice the wires tucked along the edge of the hallway, they don't mention it, and when Mr. Welch one Saturday morning comes in to find Dorsey talking on her telephone, his reaction is so blatantly calm that she thinks he must have believed that the telephone had always been there. After she's finished, he says, "When I saw you talking on the phone just now, you reminded me of my mother." Then he turns to walk down the hallway.

With the telephone on her desk, Dorsey expects things to change:

more calls, more invitations. But usually when her phone buzzes, it's for her mother or father. When it's for Dorsey, it's nearly always from someone who needs help on a math problem. As the months pass during her junior year, the books and papers and catalogues from colleges pile up on her desk around the telephone, so that by January she can hardly see it, sometimes just the black curve of the receiver edged above a pile of papers, and often for days at a time she forgets that it's there.

18

During his second year at Hol-
bein College, when he knows with a sickening certainty that
he is flunking out, Hugh shares an apartment with another hockey player, Billy LaMarque, who hardly studies at all, but who
waves his B— and C+ papers and tests in front of Hugh to
demonstrate that this is not a serious place, anyone can do all right
here. "This stuff is one hundred percent bullshit, man," Billy says,
referring to his English and history papers, and to the chem and
econ exams that the oddball professors force their students to
take.

Billy sits in front of the television set, a big bowl of popcorn to
his right, his textbooks opened up and piled on the floor to his left.
He leafs lackadaisically through the required reading as if he were
shopping in sporting goods catalogues. Sometimes his girlfriend
Linda comes over, and they party in Billy's bedroom. He goes off
to tests in the morning hung over, unshaven, unrested, smelling of
Linda. Whatever tests he takes, he always passes. "Absolutely nothing fucking to it," he says, tossing a biology exam (B+) onto

Hugh's desk as proof. "I'm a fucking moron, and if I can do this, so can you."

Hugh can't. The world has opened up its small details to Hugh in these courses, presenting him with a night parade of details and facts that march by on the page and then vanish, unretrievable, into his brain, and no matter what Hugh does, he can't remember the material. He believes that it is his role—his job—to flunk out, just as it is always Dorsey's role in life to succeed. When he can remember the assigned material, he can't make sense of it. He is immersed, he thinks, in the thick helpless experience of being stupid. The aptitude tests that showed him to be above average were cruel hoaxes, he thinks. His mind feels like a kitchen sieve. As a favor to his kid sister, he takes a course in astronomy, but he falls asleep during the 8:30 A.M. planetarium lectures, and he can't remember the plane of the ecliptic or what parsecs are or the classification system of stars or the difference between the temperature of the nucleus of a planetary nebula and the temperature of the exciting star of a diffuse nebula. In his European history class he can't remember Chartism well enough to "define it, using specific examples"; he can't remember how Louis Napoleon became president of the republic, or why; he can't remember why Metternich resigned and fled to England.

Hugh sits at his desk in the apartment day after day, positioned in front of the window, looking straight out at the residential street, waiting for a car to go by so he can check its licence plate and take his mind off his own mind. He's been slapped with academic probation. One more semester of serious screwing up and he's out of here. His pride has kept him away from physical education courses and speech classes and other dumb-jock specialties. He has a right, he thinks, to learn something about the world, the way it really is and has been. He has a right to know why the Frankfurt Assembly met from 1848 to 1849 to bring a unified Germany into being, even if he can't remember the reasons, after being told.

The facts from French, calculus, English, chemistry, and all the other classes Hugh has taken and mostly failed rise up to the surface of his mind for a few moments, like drowning swimmers, and then disappear again. Wordsworth was born in 1770 and saw the French Revolution . . . *La neige qui n'a pas cessé de tomber depuis trois jours, bloque les routes* . . . Prove Cauchy's inequality:

$$\left(\sum_{i=1}^{n} u_i v_i \right)^2 \leqq \sum_{i=1}^{n} u_i^2 \sum_{i=1}^{n} v_i^2.$$

[Hint: use Theorem 2] . . . the battle of Caporetto resulted in the defeat of the Italian forces in Venetia during World War I . . . a magnesium salt of acetic acid is CH_3CO_2MgBr . . . "A grief without a pang, void, dark, and drear,/A stifled, drowsy, unimpassioned grief" . . . the red shift indicates that a stellar entity is speeding away at such-and-such a speed . . . the Peace of Westphalia was . . . the golden crescent of Islam means *hheshoom* . . . ammo aldehydes . . .

His girlfriend of three weeks, Tracey Donaldson, calls and in a light tone of pure seduction asks him out to lunch. "We'll pretend it's Sadie Hawkins day," she says, and when Hugh turns her down, her voice drops half an octave in anger. He offers to take her out to a movie on Sunday night, the night before a big test in English. What the fuck. At the kitchen table, in the light of day, he plays solitaire, then opens a can of tuna and eats the whole thing, twenty-four grams of protein. He returns to his bedroom, rolling up his sleeves, to the desk in front of the window, to the books full of their teasing facts and opinions, a mess of weighty unabsorbable information. He holds his inadequate head in his hands. When he first looks at his watch the time is five minutes past twelve o'clock; then it's two. He reads assignments, returns to them the next day, and remembers nothing at all, not a word. Inside his gut is a glowing ball of tension. He's never had to consider before the power of any one mind to think, to combine a set of ideas into a new idea, and he feels at these moments when he lies on the bed staring at an oblong crack in the ceiling that he doesn't belong here because he's been cheated out of having a mind because Dorsey got it all, because that was how it was arranged; that was the plan.

Hockey practice is from three until five. Hugh is a defenseman, and the worse his studies are, the more he enjoys breaking plays, checking, and working up a sweat. He outplays his own teammates so hard that the coach chews him out for being a solo artist. "This is a team sport, Welch," the coach yells. "I'd like to see an occasional pass." Afterwards, in the locker room, Hugh congratulates himself for not having been faked, deked, or tripped. He's blocked more shots than he could count. He's had the right spirit and has tried to charge up the other guys. With the hot water in the shower scalding over him, Hugh closes his eyes and for once knows that he belongs here. He's one of these guys. They need him. He can skate into a shitstorm and come out owning both sides of the puck.

But after dinner he's back at his desk in front of the window, studying Riemann sums, working on problems, getting nowhere. The telephone rings and it's his mother, telling him again of how proud they all were to see him in the game two weeks ago, how excited Dorsey was to see him in action. While he's talking on the phone, Billy and Linda come into the room, six-packs of beer weighing down a brown paper bag that Billy's carrying, and, yes, some girl trailing behind the two of them, giving Hugh the once-over. Hugh's trying to tell his mother why he's having so much trouble with school, but the strange girl is sitting down with Billy and Linda and they're popping tops, flipping on the stereo, so Hugh has to get off the phone.

The girl's name is Christy or Chrissie, Hugh doesn't quite catch it, and she's Linda's friend, and she, too, has seen Hugh in action. In fact they've met at a couple of parties. In the kitchen, out of earshot of Chrissie and Linda, Hugh tells Billy that he's got to study, but Billy says Hugh should thank him. Almost three six-packs later, the apartment's in a gray-out from the cigarettes the girls have smoked, and Chrissie closes the door to Hugh's bedroom with Hugh in it, and she woozily takes off her sweater and jeans and puts them on Hugh's desk, over the pages of calculus, over the *Norton Anthology,* the dittoed syllabus from chemistry class, the blue book with the flailing answers on European history. The skin all over her body is pale and smooth and she says she never wears a bra. "Oh, yeah," she says, looking down at a green book on the floor near the dresser. "Calculus. I took that. It was neat." He would like to get her to leave, but he has an instant thick hard-on and the day hasn't gone well. He takes his clothes off with the giddy excitement of a drunken nonswimmer standing on the edge of a diving board. She traces her fingernails over the scars on his forehead where hockey pucks have hit him, and she lowers her other hand to his cock, and after she says his name it's hopeless, he plants his mouth on hers and they move together immediately, experts in this. Deep in bed, later, while Chrissie or Christy is sleeping, Hugh thinks: I'm going to flunk out of here. All these women are going to go away, and I am going back to Five Oaks, and that's where I'll have to live my life, always, until the day I die. She shifts in the bed so that she's comfortably against him, and he puts his arm around her, this woman whose name he's not even sure of; as she wakes, wanting him again, her hair crosses his chest like a broom of silk, brushing him softly out of school, expelled.

19

Dorsey's parents keep their voices down so much that she doesn't know if they're capable of shouting. Their quietness annoys her. Other kids get yelled at. Their family lives are noisy and dramatic and violent, busy with slaps. She's heard about parents who break dishes and tear up lampshades and threaten their children with belts. But her own parents keep their silences to themselves.

She sits in the back seat of the car on a Friday night on the way to the hockey game between Holbein College and its opponent for this week, North Central State College, and as she watches her father smoke and her mother twiddle the radio dial, she wonders how they're going to manage some enthusiasm for the Holbein team once the game starts. Her father has an alert, tense look, and his face is tinted a light green from the dashboard lights. He and Dorsey's mother speak to each other quietly, but Dorsey can't quite make out what they're saying. The subject is Hugh's bad grades, academic probation, and Dorsey doesn't want to hear about it. She settles down into the seat. She thinks there's something too genteel about her parents, something that's been held in the familial cage for too long.

At the ice arena, they sit down on the third row on the Holbein side in the middle of a clutch of students. The Holbein hockey team has three cheerleaders in red H letter sweaters and short red skirts, who are trying to rouse the crowd into some kind of enthusiasm. They aren't getting any out of Mr. and Mrs. Welch. Dorsey's mother is knitting. It's some kind of baby sweater for some kind of baby, Dorsey doesn't know who. And her father is still wearing his hat and coat; he looks . . . Dorsey can't think of the word, and then she can: *wry.* Her father looks drily humorous as he gazes up at the scoreboard to check out the amount of time left before the first period begins.

From the entryway to her left, the Holbein team takes the ice, warming up by skating in a fast counterclockwise circle, while the North Central team skates clockwise down at the other end of the rink. Dorsey's mother looks up from her knitting to see Hugh, number twenty, flashing by quickly, a red blur, quick ice-metal strokes. She looks down again. On one of his passes along the Holbein side, Hugh sees Dorsey and winks. He's padded all over except for his face, which looks hard and aggressive. Dorsey's father has started to hum what sounds like "Blue Moon." He makes occasional nervous throat clearings, and Dorsey offers him a Smith Brothers cough drop, which he chews instead of sucks.

They're so close that once the game starts Dorsey experiences it as a blur of young men in different colored uniforms ramming into one another, shouting and grunting and calling out encouragement and advice—the Holbein bench is only fifteen feet to Dorsey's left —and the noise and animal energy excite her. In the noise of the shouting she can still hear the flat smack of the puck as it hits the boards, almost a gunshot. In the first period Dorsey yells so loudly she can feel her throat growing hoarse. Hugh is checking and blocking shots, dropping to his knee and sometimes sliding into the shot, a rush of energy. She cheers for him whenever he's anywhere near the puck, and when one of the North Central men manages to get by him and score a goal, she feels humiliated and sick.

By the second period, when Holbein has tied the game, she has calmed down and isn't taking things personally. Still trying to scream, and losing what's left of her voice, she notices how intuitive Hugh is on the ice, how he anticipates moves by the forwards and defends against them before those moves have actually been made. On the ice, Hugh maintains his balance, the peculiar physical equilibrium of his body's force, no matter at what angle he hits or is hit by the other men. When Hugh is checked by another accelerated body using him as its unmoving object into which all its forward energy is thrown and absorbed, he doesn't even wait for the shock to dispel; he lets the shock inhabit him. He expects to be hit. He expects to hit back. His body thrives on these impacts.

Having lost her voice, Dorsey during the third period lets her eyes go out of focus, so that she watches the game as an abstract spectacle of objects moving across a field of low friction. She sees the men abstractly, almost as if they were Isaac Newton's billiard balls set in motion on a green pool table and bouncing off the cushions in absolutely predetermined and predictable angles. She still watches Hugh, but now that Holbein has scored two more goals, she's sure his team will win, and it's no longer a human drama; it's physics. It's Newton's laws of motion enacted upon the puck, crossing the blue line; the young men, pushing backwards against the ice with their blades to throw themselves forward toward the puck and each other and the goalie; and the goalie himself, masked and faceless unlike the other players, the resistor to whatever charge of opposing energy comes hurtling his way. The goalie is Maxwell's Demon, whose job is to sort, to say yes or no, to keep certain objects from entering the wrong space.

The goalie always says no to the puck. The puck, a forward moving projectile, must not occupy the space protected by the masked demon; if it does, a light goes on and half the men raise their arms and their sticks into the air in celebration. Sitting back, very quiet now, Dorsey sees the action on the ice as the drama of physics and—she does not want this to be true, she doesn't want life to operate this way—sex: forward projectiles, protected areas, raised arms. The men want to throw this thing into an area that is guarded, shielded; if they overcome resistance, if they get this part of themselves into it, and do it often enough, they win. If there's no resistance, there's no game. Dorsey looks at the webbing around the goal box and then down at her mother's hands, knitting a web of cloth for a baby.

What is the connection between physics and sex, she says to herself, and who will ever explain it to me?

Women resist; men overcome their resistance. Is that it? That's too simple. It can't be right. The puck slides along the boards, and a horn sounds. The game's over. Dorsey's father has been very quiet, and hasn't shouted once. She's annoyed with him, and she runs down to the side of the rink. Hugh skates over to her and drapes her with one of his big sweaty arms and ruffles her hair with the hard leather of his glove, which he took off once tonight, for a fistfight. His face is reddish white with exhaustion, and his body smells of an odor that Dorsey has just now started to associate with adult men after periods of physical work. She doesn't mind the smell; it's different from hers.

"You looked great," she says to Hugh. "You looked . . ." She can't think of an adjective. "Sensational!" Right away she knows the adjective is wrong, too girlish, for a girl who has started high school. Her brother laughs. He knows it's the wrong adjective, too; his face shows it, but he likes her pleasure in his honor as a winner, a warrior.

"Talk to you later," he says. He clumps off down the tunnel behind the Holbein goalie, and at once, off the ice and on solid planked wood ground, the truer surface of the earth, Hugh looks as awkward as a seal or some other animal forced to move in a medium unsuited for it. He wobbles and tilts. She's never seen his power turn so quickly into precariousness: one hundred sixty-eight pounds balanced on two thin blades.

In the car Dorsey sits up in the front seat with her father. She resists the impulse to put her booted feet up on the dashboard. "You didn't cheer," she says, staring out at the two cones of their headlights on the highway. "You didn't cheer Hugh once. He needs cheering."

"I was watching him," her father says.

"You didn't cheer. It's not just anybody. It's Hugh."

"I was watching him."

"It'd mean a lot to him if you cheered."

"He doesn't expect me to. I'm not that kind of father."

"You should surprise him. Get excited about what he's doing."

"He wouldn't notice."

"Yes, he would. He would too notice. It'd make him happy."

"Well, he knew we were there. We were doing something for him."

"What? What were you doing for him?"

Her father waits. "We were there."

Dorsey slumps down in the front seat. Their car passes a farm with a long white fence for sheep, and in her anger the fence blurs so that it appears to be a series of boards and sticks zooming past the car, thrown by some furious nocturnal giant.

20

A big date. It's mid-June, the summer after Hugh's senior year of high school, Saturday afternoon, and he's in the driveway, soaping down the heavy Chevy with Ivory flakes dissolved in warm water. Detergents and hot water damage the paint, his dad has told him; you have to use something milder. Tonight he's taking out Evelyn D'Agostino, who has, Hugh thinks, been panting after him for weeks now, though she has the reputation of being a nice girl, not a slut. They're going to go to Dellum's Restaurant and then to the King Drive-In theater to see *Bunny Lake Is Missing,* and then . . . what they'll do all depends on Evelyn's attitude, as demonstrated by her clothes, her perfume, and what she does in the dark of the front seat.

He has soaped off the roof and the hood. Now with the rags from his mother's collection in the basement he's soaping down the doors and fenders and the grill. After rinsing them off with the hose, Hugh looks at his car's chrome and red paint, and he breathes steadily, proud of himself and the car. The car was a bargain at seven hundred dollars, and it's got guts and pride, a can-do car. This car says, Why the hell not?

Hugh's mother leans out of the kitchen window, almost losing her glasses, and asks him to please turn down the radio, it's distracting her. So he turns down WFOM so it's loud instead of super-loud but still loud enough to make the dashboard rattle when the Beatles or the Kinks come on. After shutting the door, he almost steps into a puddle he's made in the driveway, ringed with soapsuds. He looks at it. He's barefoot. He steps in it. It feels great.

His mother calls down from the window again. Someone's called, wants him on the phone. He reads his mother's lips: it's Turtle Findley. "Tell him I'll call back," he shouts. Turtle Findley is not an important person. Not sharp, not a good athlete, not funny, not a make-out artist, just a general slob Hugh has allowed to talk to him. Today he can't be bothered. Too bad about Turtle, and guys like him, the ones who didn't get the looks when they were being passed out, and who ended up with faces like rodents and reptiles.

Well, look who's here. It's the Shrimpo, carrying her new camera. She's been all over the house, taking pictures of everything, including the front door, their mom and dad, the upstairs windows, the elm tree in the front yard. If she can get it into the viewfinder, she'll take a picture of it, and then she'll develop it herself. Hugh's soaping the door on the driver's side, humming along to "Please Please Me," and Dorsey's asking if she can snap his picture.

"Relax," Hugh says. Dorsey sits down in the shade of the hill that slopes to the driveway, and she watches him do the car. She tilts her head, steadily gazing at him. Hugh loves being idolized. The Shrimpo can't take her eyes off him, and he knows it. He grins at his little sister, Miss Brain Cell, and he wishes she were a little cuter, more of a knock-out, though she looks okay when she tries. He wishes she weren't so serious. She doesn't enjoy anything except her own ideas. Of course, she's in junior high, the armpit of life. She doesn't have many friends, though, and no one ever seems to call her.

He rinses, leaves the hose running in the driveway, and runs over to his sister, and pulls her by her hand to her feet. She asks him what he's doing and he tells her to put the camera down, and she does. "Let's dance," Hugh says, and she blushes and tries to get away and sit down again, but he won't let go of her hand. "Look how easy it is to dance to," he says, whistling out the tune—"Where Did Our

Love Go?"—and he feels how small her hand is. Because his hands are soapy, she wriggles away from him. "Suit yourself, Shrimpo," he laughs. "Come back when you want to learn a few steps."

"Yeah," she says, picking up her camera. She puts it at eye-level and takes a picture of Hugh, and he stands still for a minute, but then there's a horsefly buzzing around his head, and he has to move, so he lunges forward, trying to stomp Dorsey's foot. She squeals and leaps backward, and he runs over to the other side of the car to get the hose. It's a fact: sisters should be doused. He's got the hose and has lowered his thumb over the nozzle to make it squirt and he's ready to aim it right in the Shrimpo's face when the voice of The Father is heard loudly from the kitchen window.

"I wouldn't do that, if I were you."

He takes his thumb away and stands there watching his sister, Miss Brain Cell, stick her tongue out at him and then make, unusual for her, a farting sound. "But Dad," he says, "she was asking for it."

"Hugh," his father says, ending the argument.

"You're going to get it," Hugh says. The flatulent sounds continue, getting louder, more insulting. With the camera on the ground, Dorsey hauls out all her noises: squeaks, belches, farts, it's amazing what she can do. She grabs the camera and runs off. She'll be okay, Hugh thinks, rubbing the tail lights with the soapy rag to a red gleam. Anyone who can make noises like that will do just fine.

21

"Where's Hugh?" Dorsey's mother asks, glancing at the kitchen clock. Dorsey says he's left a note somewhere—the hall table, the TV set, she's sure she's seen it—telling everybody that he'd be down at the lake practicing his shots. "But it's dark," her mother says, and Dorsey with fake impatience explains to her mother what she already knows, namely that it's winter and the moon's out and there's more than enough light to skate by on the lake. "Well, it's quarter to six," her mother says, dropping some brown leftovers out of a Tupperware container into a saucepan. "Would you run down and get him?"

She sighs. "All right." It's a sixteen-minute walk but a nine-minute run to Five Oaks Lake on a path through the woods; she checks her watch to time herself.

The moon is twenty-four hours away from being full, and it gives the street a gloss like stainless steel or an old black-and-white movie. Slowed by her overshoes, Dorsey runs past the McDonalds' house, past the Fabians' and the Blairs', then cuts onto the path through the woods of Five Oaks Park. If there had been any snow this winter, she could see more clearly, but the winter's been dry so far, and in the dark the path is a forest hallway, an obscure tunnel between shrubs and thin-fingered trees. Dorsey doesn't need the light. Every step she takes is like one she's taken before on this path. She's done it blindfolded, when her brother challenged her to take the path with a scarf over her eyes, and she managed its length in eleven minutes, Hugh following her and timing her. She didn't get more than one serious scratch.

She emerges at the south end of Five Oaks Park, where the moonlit bandstand gleams in a little meadow lined with night-silver benches. Beyond it is a public-access boat dock. The town itself is half a mile up Lake Street, which she crosses now, seeing Hugh's Chevy parked behind a Ford. She peers out onto the ice and sees the makeshift rink the town council has put there, though there are no lights because Five Oaks can't afford them. The town's only lighted rink is down by the high school, a flooded surface over part of the JV football field. Hugh likes to skate in the open, the sky over his head, not under trees or roofs or lights. And he likes to skate in the dark. He says it improves his puck handling. Dorsey can see him out there, skating with someone else, probably his friend Tommy Connell. She can hear the puck slapping back and forth, the hollow sound of sticks.

The lake ice is smooth as a mirror, the result of a dry and windless December. Dorsey's never seen ice as perfectly glassed as this, and she steps out onto it gingerly so that she doesn't slip. There, at her feet, perfectly reflected, are the constellations of the winter sky, the Pleiades, Orion, Auriga, Perseus, and behind the trees shading the lake's bank, the moon, almost blotting the stars with its owlish light. As she walks across the ice, Dorsey has the sensation of being a storybook goddess, stepping across the star field of the sky. Then, looking down, she sees her own reflection, very dark and almost invisible, place a foot underneath her foot and walk upside down through the water.

A hundred feet out into the lake she turns around and sees the lights of Five Oaks, a toy train model set up on a child's board, with amusement park, working streetlights, and telephone wires, and then, behind the town and up on the hill, the lights of the houses, the McDonalds' and the Blairs', and, somewhere up there, in that necklace of lights, her own family's house, where now her father

and mother are preparing the dinner and waiting for her to return
with her brother.

She walks across more stars, the stars moving as she moves. She's
still careful not to slip on this surface until she's almost up to the
rink, when she slides for a few feet. In the dark her brother, wearing
his sweat pants and sweatshirt, is practicing blocking drills, skating
backwards in front of Tommy, protecting his zone. He sees Dorsey,
loses his concentration, and Tommy does a quick one around his left
side, catching him unprotected, and does a hard final slapshot.

"Hey, Shrimpo. What are you doing here?"

"Mom sent me down. It's dinnertime."

"Oh, yeah. I forgot." He hops over one of the boards out onto
the clear ice where Dorsey stands. "You want a ride?"

"Huh?"

"Hey, Tom!" he says. "Grab the Shrimpo's feet. We'll skate her
back."

She feels her brother lifting her up, holding her around the
shoulders, while her brother's friend takes her legs, so that she's in
a sagging horizontal as they skate back toward the lake shore, and
at first she screeches. Then she calms and, turning her face, watches
the ice speed by underneath her and listens to the blades cutting into
the ice at her head and feet, but the stars stay steady, reflected
on this unmarked surface, while the two boys, her brother and her
brother's friend, pant hard, her brother's sweat flicking into her face,
as they race toward shore, carrying their hockey sticks and this girl
between them.

22

Around the house on weekends, Hugh's father slips into a state of intelligent watchfulness, signaled by a focused-on-the-distance look that Hugh once thought indicated anger. He has seen this look outside the house, too, in rowboats; he has seen his father cast out his line and begin to reel in, nothing on the lure, and then stop, as if some sound audible only to him had begun to vibrate in the hot summer air over Five Oaks Lake. "Dad?" Hugh says, but the old man doesn't come back to the world immediately. The fingers on his right hand still hold the crank of the reel, and his left hand grasps the cork handle of the pole. He's caught something, but it's not a fish.

Doing household chores with Hugh, the old man trails off in mid-sentence and turns his head as if he were listening for something. Painting the house together, their two ladders set up close to each other, Hugh and his father discuss brands of paint, baseball, the proper technique with the brush—short unrushed strokes, his father says, the speed of a pendulum—but then the old man stops as if he'd been hypnotized. His cigarette dangles out of his mouth and the smoke curls up into his eyes, and he doesn't even blink.

But then something snaps him back, and he begins to talk. "Speaking of paint," he says, "I knew a person in town who painted his house a shade of pink, a color to wake a man up. First pink house in Five Oaks. A schoolteacher did it, of course. He lived over on Lawrence Street, next door to the undertaker. By the way, how did this town ever get an undertaker with the name of Jolley? Anyway, this man, this teacher, his name was Leo Evans, though everyone called him 'Doghouse.' Don't know why. His neighbors took the color of his house to the town council, and then . . ."

Hugh angles his brush to paint over a mothlike patch he has missed, and he waits to hear about what happened to the pink house. But his father, though still painting, has gone away.

"What happened?" Hugh asks. "Dad? The pink house?"

Hugh's father stubs out his cigarette on the side of the ladder and sails the butt down to the lawn. "The town council claimed there was no city ordinance against pink houses. And the teacher, the person everybody called Doghouse, moved away that summer."

Once, shooting baskets into the hoop installed over the garage door, Hugh sees his father, who has been watching him, suddenly turn away, as if listening to someone calling him at ultra-high frequencies. In the fall, Hugh finds his father standing in the backyard, leaning on his rake, staring fixedly at a patch of nondescript grass. He catches his father lost in thought everywhere in the house: in the kitchen, staring out the back window at the willows and blue spruce and elms on the hill; in the basement in his workroom, his tools spread out in front of him, a piece of wood clamped into the vise.

"Dad?" His father looks up from his workbench. "What're you thinking of?"

"When I was a boy," his father says, "my parents sent me off to Sunday school, where they made us memorize Bible verses. The one I remember was a wedding song. 'How sweet is your love, my bride. How much better is your love than wine, and the fragrance of your oils than any spice. Your lips distil nectar . . .' Think of asking children to memorize that." His father leans back and laughs, his hands behind his head.

"I didn't know you went to church."

"Once. Years ago. My brain is stocked with these verses we had to memorize."

Hugh decides to blurt it out. "Dad, around here you never finish your sentences. You're always daydreaming or something."

His father smiles. "No, I am not. I'm thinking about you, and Dorsey, and your mother, and I'm thinking about my own parents, and I have this feeling, kiddo, that there's an order to things, and we'll never know what it is, human beings are just not capable of it, but we get these *drifts* . . . these . . . *tunes*. The older you get, the more of them you hear."

"From where? Where do they come from?"

His father looks Hugh in the eye. He appears to be angry but at nothing in particular. "Listen to me," he says. "Everything on earth is what it is and something else. Everything gives off a signal. Most people never hear any of it. Their ears are closed. You have to listen with your whole body, everything in your soul, to even this old ugly drop-forged claw hammer"—he holds it up—"and this wood, and to everyone you know, and all objects, everywhere. You can break your soul trying to hear. But some people have a talent. Your mother does. She's better at hearing the world than I am. It's like music, but it isn't music, it's an overtone. Dorsey hears it. It's an order. Do you know what I mean?"

Hugh says he does, but he doesn't, and he's angry again because his father has included everyone in the family in this lucky group of listeners except his own son, Hugh himself, dull, reliable, strong, and deaf.

23

They do not keep any animals as pets in the house because of Mr. Welch's long-standing allergy and therefore antipathy to dog and cat hair, and because of Mrs. Welch's contempt for caged birds and bowled fish. Dorsey claims that she and Hugh are deprived children, thanks to what she calls her parents' "mindless prejudice," and she puts out saucers of milk every Sunday morning for Max, the bad-tempered neighborhood Siamese. Dorsey's real fascination, however, is with horses. She says they are the most beautiful of all animals. Along with the star chart and the large framed picture of the moon, she has tacked up on the bedroom wall a picture of a chestnut-colored American thoroughbred standing in a heroic pose in an open bluegrass field, a pillared manor house in the distance.

Hugh has stopped badgering his parents about pets, but Dorsey keeps after them. She speaks on behalf of Cairn terriers, poodles, rodents, and snakes. It's a topic that comes up every two hours with her. On a Sunday afternoon drive, sitting slouched in the backseat, Dorsey is going on about loped-eared rabbits, their loyalty and charm. She'd like Hugh to help her out here, but he's at home, listening to his records.

Her father is distracted by the weather. It's late May, a time of sudden violent thunderstorms and tornadoes in Michigan, and for the last half-hour thick clouds have been extruding from the west horizon like plastic out of a mold. The family has been driving west on unfamiliar dirt roads, playing "Spot the River" or "Spot the Lake." Dorsey has been losing the game because she's been too busy talking about the virtues of animals. She is still talking as they approach a storm cloud, over a hill two miles to the west, where for a moment a bony white farmhouse and a rusting windmill are briefly visible, before they are both obscured.

"Looks like a thunderhead," her father says.

"Actually it's a cumulonimbus capillatus," Dorsey tells them, "and you'll notice that it's got the characteristically anvil-shaped upper portion. We're really in for it now."

"In for what?"

"Rain, Mom. Bricks of it."

Already rain is sprinkling the car. Soon the downpour becomes so heavy that Dorsey's father cannot see, and he begins to mutter, changing his posture so that he's leaning forward, hunched. The windshield's interior fogs up. After pulling out a perfumed handkerchief from her purse, Mrs. Welch starts to wipe the mist away, but by now the rainfall has thickened, and Dorsey's father is complaining that he can't see anything—the road, the shoulder, the front of the car. The wiper blades push the teeming water back and forth on the glass but do not clear it. The gusts of wind rock the car and set up roaring and snuffling sounds.

"Daddy, you should stop," Dorsey says. "Look."

To the left of the car and just on the opposite side of the road, away from the direction in which the rain is falling, is a farm whose long front field is covered with grass and enclosed by a chest-high white fence. At those moments when the rain lets up, Dorsey can see four horses standing in the rain, shaking their heads as the water falls on them. One of the horses, a breed that Dorsey can't identify, startles at a thunderclap and breaks away from the group, running off into the field's middle distance, disappearing.

Dorsey's father turns the car onto the shoulder and shuts off the engine. He twists the key counterclockwise to the option slot, snaps off the wipers, and switches on the radio to see if any tornado warnings are being announced, but it's an AM radio and all he can get is thunderstorm static. Dorsey's mother, settling back, gazes calmly through the window on the passenger side, and in the storm's growing uproar she murmurs to her husband about other storms they've waited out: in New Mexico, and, before that, the one at Mitchell, South Dakota, when they were visiting the Corn Palace.

Dorsey's happy, watching the two Arabian horses and the pinto standing near the white fence, just on the other side of a huge oak. The Arabians are gray and the pinto spotted brown and white, and they seem to be enjoying the downpour, though they continue to twist their heads before lifting them up and down in a nodding gesture. After another thunderclap, the Arabians gallop off in the same direction taken by the first one.

The pinto raises its head to the rain, and, as Dorsey watches, she feels an instant of physical itching all over her body, no more than a split second, a force-field sensation inside her, working its way out, and in that instant the horse is hit by lightning.

The lightning spurts up from the horse's shoulders, and an instant later the Welches' car is enveloped in a blistering roar of thunder, and as Dorsey watches, the horse falls. It holds its head up off the ground for a moment, and its mouth opens and its lips part, so that the line of its large upper teeth and bluish-pink gums is visible. Then its legs begin a galloping sideways convulsive beating against the air.

Dorsey is quiet. She does not speak to her parents during the time that her father starts the car, and she sees, as if from the wrong end of a pair of binoculars, that he is driving up to the farmhouse and is telling the aproned woman who comes out that one of her horses has been killed and is now lying in the field, and Dorsey hears, now, her mother's interminable murmuring about accidents. Dorsey shakes her head. No, she won't listen. She reaches down and pulls off her sneakers and socks, and she sits cross-legged and puts her fingers between her toes, and when people ask her questions, she's not going to answer them.

They wait in the car until her father returns. He says they've been invited inside to wait out the storm, but, no, Dorsey will not move.

Her mother and father go inside. She waits in the back. Then the storm passes, leaving behind its sickening clarity, and the big phony rainbow.

She's home, taking down the picture of the chestnut-colored horse. She's still barefoot; the soles of her feet tingle, as if the floor is electrified. There's a knock at the door. "Dorsey?" It's Hugh's voice. "How are you doin', kid? Mom and Dad said that you—"

"—Go away." The horse is crunched up in the wastebasket.

"That's pretty wild, what you saw! Can I come in?"

"No."

"Just askin'," he says.

"Leave me alone," she says. His footsteps pad down the hallway to the stairs. She hears him descending the stairs, and then there's no more sound of her brother. She never mentions horses again to her parents, and there is no more talk about pets, and when her mother asks her, eight days later, if she's going to put out a saucer of milk for Max, Dorsey pretends not to hear.

24

"Dorsey." A winter Saturday afternoon: in her room, Dorsey is reading a junior high science book about how gases combine in deep space to make stars. She's nine years old. Hugh has sneaked up behind her in wet, snowy shoes and has put his terrible cold Egyptian mummy hand on her neck and is whispering in a new style he's picked up from the television shows he watches. He glances into the hallway, a gangster glance, also learned from television. "Come on," he whispers. "Get into your overcoat. We're going somewhere with Tommy."

Tommy is Tommy Connell. She wants to know where they're going but Hugh won't say, except that this is something he and Tommy have been planning for years. She runs into the kitchen to tell her mother that she's going out to play with Hugh and his friend. Mrs. Welch is delighted: her daughter is being included in something, for a change. Dorsey throws on her overcoat, her cap, her gloves, her scarf, and her boots, and she runs out to the front walk, where the two boys are standing together, huddled with their hands around their mouths, whispering, out here, in public. Dorsey has the sudden feeling that she shouldn't go along with them on this adventure, whatever it is. But when they see her, the boys straighten up, put on their Solid Citizen expressions, and begin to walk fast before breaking into a run.

She yells at them to slow down, and they cut off the street onto the path through Five Oaks Park, and Dorsey follows them, panting, twenty feet behind. They're easy to see because of their coats: Hugh's is red and Tommy's is blue, two primary colors rushing down the winter path through branches covered with snow. "Slow down, you guys!" she shouts. The boys laugh and keep running. Soon all she can see are the two color dots of their coats far ahead of her in a forest of pure white crisscrossed by gray twigs and branches. As she runs, she has the sensation that she isn't moving, but the forest is. She's in one place and somehow the woods and the snow and the path and the twigs are rushing toward and away from her, and since the path goes downhill, the velocity of the trees' approach in front of her and retreat behind her accelerates. She runs faster and faster past the scruffy pines and sharp hawthorns and elms and oaks and maples. She hears a squirrel chittering angrily at her, and she sees a bird, a brown female cardinal, flying in irregular swoops ahead and to the right of her, another small dot of color in this colorless forest. The bird's watching me, Dorsey thinks. It knows something about me.

At the lower end of the path, on Lake Street, near the snow-covered park benches, the boys are waiting for her, grinning. "Come on," they say, and they run up the sidewalk, Dorsey following a few paces behind, walking in their boot tracks. They run past the Municipal Liquor Store, Koehnen's Standard Oil, and the Quik-'n'-Ezy grocery. The boys stop. They're at the fence outside the Five Oaks Amusement Park, and they wait for Dorsey to catch up.

She's out of breath, panting, and she says, "Come on. What are we doing?" For an answer, Tommy points down at the cyclone fence. There's just enough room at the bottom of the fence for a kid to wriggle through. Dorsey sucks in her breath and says, no, she's not going to do it, it's illegal, they have guards, we could be arrested, and, besides, why would anybody want to go into an amusement park in the winter anyhow, *it's closed!* You can't ride anything! Stop it! But she can't stop him. Hugh is following his friend under the fence, pushing his face down into the snow and twisting his back and his butt and his legs like a snake, and now he's inside the fence, and he stands up. It's started to snow. Dorsey begins to wail. You guys! she says. I don't want to go in there! The front of Hugh's red coat is covered with snow. He looks through the fence at his sister. Don't be a big baby, Dorsey, he says. We brought you along because we thought you'd have the guts to do this. What's the matter? No guts?

I'll show you, she says. She lowers herself to her stomach, and she pulls herself under the fence, feeling it scrape and pull at her back, catching a piece of her coat, which Hugh releases. She stands up on the other side and Hugh grabs her hand, and they run toward the boarded-up house for Dodgem Cars, covered with snow. They hide momentarily behind the canvas-covered remnants of the Tilt-a-Whirl, then they run behind the Dodgem Cars toward the umbrella-shaped building that houses the merry-go-round. They rest for a minute, the boys crouching with their backs against the wall, inhaling in deep gulps of excitement. Dorsey asks Tommy Connell if he's broken into this amusement park before, and he nods and says, sure, lots of times.

It's getting darker with the snow and late afternoon coming on, and Dorsey looks toward the geometrical angles of the roller coaster's snowy white wood slats. Have you climbed up the roller coaster? she asks, but her brother and his friend have already started running toward the Fun House, and she follows them, a collaborator now. The front door of the Fun House has been boarded up, but the upper windows, protected with exterior wire mesh, have been left clear. The boys stop and stare up at the huge painted clown face on the front of the building, the mix of inappropriate colors, the painted balloons, and Hugh says that this place looks real weird in the winter. The snow is blowing in gusts over the Fun House and the semi-dismantled Scrambler behind them and the Penny Arcade locked up in the alley to their right. Tommy tells them to follow him, and he runs around to the other side of the Fun House and kicks a board that gives way immediately, and he crawls into the space the board has left, and Hugh follows him. Dorsey waits outside. She hears her brother's sucked-in muffled voice from whatever interior it is he's crawling through. Come on, he says, a distant shout. No, Dorsey shouts back, I'm not going. She hears her brother's voice, fainter now, fading away. Gutless, the voice says. Gutless.

She crawls down into the dark space. Once inside, she can't see much of anything except the black shapes of her brother's overshoes ahead of her. Dorsey realizes that she and her brother are *under* the funhouse, beneath it, in some kind of crawl space, and Dorsey wants very badly to scream. The dark scares her, and the clammy cold, and the sensation that she's going to get stuck here under a wood beam and the old funhouse is going to collapse, board by painted board, any minute right on top of her. Then, ahead and to her right, she sees a crack of light in the shape of a stalactite, and as she crawls she sees Tommy pulling himself up and squeezing his way through the crack, then her brother doing the same. There's some creature behind her making a fingernails-on-wood sound, and she thinks: big funhouse rats. And now she wants to scream the way they do in operas, a scream to put your whole life into, but instead of scream-ing she pulls herself through the dark spaces smelling of mud and the pellet dung of small animals, and she pinches her way through the stalactite-shaped opening, and she's inside.

Her brother and Tommy are standing quietly now, just gazing in the dim light, awed by themselves. They have bypassed the corridors leading into the Fun House, the ones with shifting wood floors, tilting barrels, and air jets, and they have emerged into the Fun House's central room; they have come in under the Slide-for-Life. From a few wire-meshed ceiling-level windows a cold blank light drains in, and Dorsey notices her breath in the flat air. Fun House breath. There, to the side, is the giant turning tunnel that you're supposed to walk through—when it's working—and in which everybody falls, and over on the other side of the Fun House is the whirling disk that spins and you can't stay seated because it gives you an electric shock if you do, and in front of them is another moving floor that of course isn't moving, and behind them is the high Slide-for-Life and a corridor going out, leading to the Tilted Rooms and the Hall of Mirrors.

"Yeah," Hugh says.

"Yeah is right," Tommy says, nodding.

Dorsey is scared and excited, but she's also feeling a little an-noyed. "Okay, it's neat," she says, "but what is there to *do* in here?"

"What d'you mean, what is there to do? You're here, aren't you?

How many friends have you got that've ever been in the Fun House
in the middle of winter?"

"None," she says, "but so what? There's no fun in the Fun House
if they don't have the electricity on. What can we do?"

"Well," Tommy says, a look of what-do-women-want impatience on his face, "I guess we could go down the slide."

"Where're the sacks?" she asks.

"What sacks?"

"The feed sacks," she says, "that you sit on. You've got to sit on
feed sacks on the slide 'cause otherwise you're going so fast on the
wood that you get friction on your rear end."

"They're over here," Hugh says, behind her. "In the feed-sack
box."

They each lean down to smell the thick ropy aroma of burlap,
then grab a sack and run up the stairs, Tommy in the lead, followed
by Hugh and Dorsey. At the top, there's a window that looks out
over the north end of the amusement park toward the frozen snowy
surface of Five Oaks Lake. Tommy and Hugh smooth out their
burlap and sit down next to each other, then push themselves off
and disappear down the first hump, yelling at each other. Dorsey
can hear them yelling at her to follow them. Why does she always
have to follow? She isn't sure. She lays down her sack on the middle
lane of the Slide-for-Life, and she pushes herself off, alone.

Now at last she can scream, and she does, and the scream echoes
all through the empty dim Fun House, and when she slides feet first
into the cushion at the bottom, her brother lifts his finger to his lips
and shushes her: there's a guard who goes through the amusement
park once a day, he says. Does she want to get caught? No? Well,
then. Shut up.

She slides down once more. It's okay, but sliding down into the
dark isn't her idea of fun, it's just creepy, and the Fun House has
a kind of so-what feel. So what if they're inside? Nothing works
in here, except the slide. Dorsey begins to whine in her brother's
direction. Okay, he says, we'll go into the Tilted Room.

Tommy and Hugh run, stomping, toward a doorway underneath
an unlit EXIT sign, and Dorsey follows them, finding herself in a
pitch black hallway whose floor rises so steeply that she must grab
at a handrail to keep herself upright. Tommy, ahead of her, is

laughing: a horror-movie laugh that in this narrow corridor sounds louder and weirder than any laugh she's ever had the bad luck to hear, and now her brother joins in, their humorless cackling and hawing like a duet of crazies. She pulls herself up against the hallway's incline, feeling the whisper of fabric against wood slats as her coat drags on the right wall; the corridor has started to list, so that it both rises and pitches off in the direction of the handrail. Then Dorsey sees a slit of light, a sprig of illumination that leads into the Tilted Room, which has a small and inaccessibly high window, most of whose light is blocked by two pine boards nailed across it. In the gray diluted light that does penetrate into the Tilted Room, she can observe her brother and her brother's friend imitating drunks as they stagger across the floor that angles down from the doorway where Dorsey stands with her fingers clutched around the doorframe. Tommy and Hugh ram into each other, whacking each other's arms as if they were prizefighters and the Tilted Room were some version of a ring, a room where men are supposed to fight because, after all, the floor is tilted.

Now they are gone, having quickly disappeared into another corridor on the other side of the Tilted Room. Dorsey steps at a slant across the floor, feeling a tingle of cold and nausea, tilting herself to the left to compensate for the floor's bias, and now she is in a straight, downward-sloping hallway, mostly dark but with some light seeping through the wall cracks. At the end of the hallway is a door that leads into another hall that she remembers from the last time she was in the Fun House last summer, the way out, the Hall of Mirrors. This hallway is almost completely dark, only enough light to suggest the shadows of the two boys, hooded and shapeless, ahead of her, to her right, and simultaneously to her left. In trying to catch up to her brother, Dorsey walks directly into a mirror, banging her nose and forehead against the glass, not forcefully enough to give her a bruise but enough to shock her and make her stand motionless, trying to see her brother here in the glass-framed dark. Turning to her right, where she thought she saw him, she looks down and tries to see the floor—the only way you can get out of a hall of mirrors, her father told her last summer, is to keep your eyes on the floor—and she bumps into another mirror. She's caged. And now, looking around, she can't see her brother at all or hear him. He's gone. He's escaped. "Hugh?" she says. Nothing.

She stands trembling. Now she knows. They brought her here. That was the idea: to bring her here and leave her here in the Hall of Mirrors, in the cold winter dark, trapped. She feels a wave of fear starting at her stomach and rising to her shoulders and simultaneously descending to her knees, which are shaking. Her arms are shivering and her teeth are starting to chatter. She knows it's snowing outside, getting dark, and she thinks she may die of shock and exposure right here in the Hall of Mirrors in the Five Oaks Amusement Park, and they'll find her skeleton here in the spring inside her coat and her overshoes.

She tries, one more time, to see where she is. The mirrors surround her, reflecting and breaking her image, and there she is, Dorsey, facing herself; and there she is in profile; and there she is in three-quarter profile. There are hundreds of her images here, joined together in glass. Everywhere she looks she is surrounded by herself: her face—its scared expression in front, and on both sides —and her coat (she can see the tear in the back) and all the rest of her. She is trapped by a wall of gray, cold, indistinct images of herself, fencing her in a circle. She can't see any place where she isn't. She can't see a way out, through herself. She raises her arm and a hundred Dorseys, reflected backward into darkness, raise their arms, mocking her. For a moment she has the idea, which she knows is crazy, that the hundred Dorseys are going to come out of the mirrors and kill her. "Hugh!" she says, more loudly. And then she screams. "Hugh! Come get me!"

Hugh rises from where he squats huddled with Tommy. Tommy grabs at his coat sleeve but Hugh pulls it away from him fast and reaches into his overcoat, feeling for the flashlight he has brought along, just in case. He's been in the Hall of Mirrors so many times he knows exactly how it twists and turns. She's not far away; she's standing near the entrance, shaking all over, crying in a reaching-for-breath way, and when she sees him she lets out a long stringing sob of accusations. "Come on," he says. "I was always here. We were just down the hall a little ways. And look what I brought." He flicks on the flashlight. Hugh and Dorsey, Dorsey and Hugh, and Hugh and Dorsey clutch at each other, mirrored. Eighteen, twenty-eight, a hundred mirrored flashlights shine into and away from one another. She's relieved, and she leans against him. "I want to go home," she says. He feels her arm around his waist. She can see his breath in the mirrors.

"We can't get out this way," he says. "We tried. It's boarded up. We gotta go back the way we came." Hugh sees Tommy Connell behind Dorsey, his mouth open in a metallic-breathing grin, the wires of his braces visible. "Let's go," Hugh says.

He takes Dorsey's hand, and they walk together up the sloping hallway into the Tilted Room, across its floor, and out the other side into the pitched hallway, now in the flashlight visibly painted a mad orange. Then they are back in the main section of the Fun House, and Hugh leads her toward the stalactite opening—Tommy still following them—and Hugh directs the light into the fetid opening and instructs Dorsey to follow him. He squeezes himself in by sections, lowers his head under the slide and finally gets down on all fours so that he can work his way through another squarish gap in the woodwork into the crawl space and then back out. He has the flashlight on, and its cone of light burns in a visible straight line through the dusty unused air, support beams above them, gravel below.

When they're all outside the Fun House again, the front of their overcoats marked with long straight lines of stains and gashes, they see that it's snowing harder than before, now in late afternoon's grayish-purple dusk. They run past the disassembled rides, the canvas-covered remnants piling up with snow and the spare metal parts looking like giant hibernating insects, and then they crawl under the fence and are out, silently, on the sidewalk on Lake Street. "Look at your coat," Hugh says, pointing at Dorsey's goose-down jacket, where the down is beginning to seep out of the tears. "Mom's going to murder us."

"Come on," Dorsey says. "Let's just go."

They run down Lake Street, Dorsey beginning to pant very hard as she crosses the no-U-turn corner in front of the Muni Liquor Store, and they rush through Five Oaks Park and head up the path into the woods. After five minutes of fast walking, Hugh hears his sister behind him telling him to wait. He stops and turns around, shining the flashlight on his sister's face, and what he sees gives him straight hairs on the back of his neck: Dorsey's skin looks cold-creamed, it's so white with fatigue. "I got to stop," she says, "I'm too tired." Tommy tells Hugh to leave her there, but he won't. "Go on home," Hugh says to Tommy. "You can find the way." Tommy shrugs and leaves Hugh and Dorsey together on the path; as he runs off, leaving them there, he whistles.

"I can't walk any further," Dorsey says. "I'm too pooped."

"You gotta admit it was different, what we did," Hugh says, not sure how he's going to get his sister back home and not certain that he wants to think about it. "You don't have an afternoon like this every day, right?"

"I guess not."

They walk on the path together for another few minutes, Dorsey stumbling and making crying sounds behind Hugh.

"Could you carry me a little ways?" she asks. "I'm not so big."

"I don't know," Hugh says. "I guess we could try it. Here, get up on my back."

After he squats down, she climbs on so that her legs are around his waist and her arms are over his shoulders. Hugh tests his balance and hunches forward to compensate for his sister's weight, feeling like a fireman. "You're not so—" he begins to say, and he feels Dorsey's head nod against the back of his neck. Trying to keep himself upright, he removes by mental force all the tiredness from his legs and chest as he totters and tips his way up the hill until they emerge onto Washington Street. To compensate for the burning ache in his legs, he tells himself that this is a muscle-strengthening exercise that Coach has given him for hockey practice to toughen him up, make him rocky. "You want to do this tomorrow?" Dorsey's head is on his left shoulder. Trying to lift his head, Hugh sees the snow falling in steady thickening flurries underneath the street-light.

"No," she says. "I don't want to do this tomorrow."

All the way to the front door of their house, Hugh tells himself that he's carrying this girl out of a burning building, and if he didn't transport her himself, she'd be left behind in the flames. At their stoop, he lets her down on the front mat. "Don't tell, okay?" he asks. She doesn't say anything, which is as good as an agreement, this time of day, before dinner. They open the door and walk together into

the front hallway, trying to do this in secret, hanging up their coats
so no one will notice.

"Dorsey? Hugh?"

They walk together into the furnace blast of heat and light of
the living room. Off in the corner, their father is sitting in his chair
reading a book, his cup of coffee and his pack of cigarettes to his
left; he waves to them, then goes back to his reading, as if everything
were normal and always had been and always will be; ahead and to
their right, through the dining room, they can see their mother in
the kitchen fixing dinner. She calls out, "Where'd you kids go? Did
you have a good time?"

"Fine, great," Hugh says. "The park." Hugh looks over at Dorsey
and sees that in the sudden comfort of this house she is going to cry
unless he stops her. "But we got a little cold. I think Cass wants to
take a shower," he says, pushing her toward the stairs.

"Well, be quick," Mrs. Welch says. "Supper'll be ready soon."

Hugh puts his hand on his sister's back and guides her up the stairs
to her room, where he pulls the cord switch on the light next to
her bed. "You really should take a shower," he says. "You look like
the Bride of Frankenstein." It's true: her face is pasty white and her
hair is sticking up at weird angles. She's snow- and mirror-shocked.
Hugh backs out of her room and closes the door softly behind him.
After walking into his own room across the hallway from Dorsey's,
he shuts the door but leaves the light off. He sits down on his bed.
He does not snap the light on or stop whispering the foulest words
against himself that he knows until he hears his sister pad into the
bathroom and turn on the hot water.

25

Hugh stands in his sister's doorway. He has helped Dorsey bring a stepladder up to her bedroom and now watches her as she perches near the ladder's top, attaching black construction paper to the ceiling with transparent tape. She is careful to make the edges of the paper overlap, so that the off-white paint of her ceiling doesn't show through. As soon as she has successfully taped up another sheet of paper, blacking out another rectangular area, she lowers herself to the floor. Then, after some calculations punctuated by sighs and quiet groans, she moves the ladder. In this way she has so far covered over three-quarters of the blank white space over her head.

Dorsey's mother walks by in the upstairs hall, looks in, and with a tone of pleased unsurprise says, "Look who we've got here. Miss Michelangelo. Or just plain old Cassiopeia in her famous chair." She disappears downstairs with a load of dirty laundry.

"Come on, Dorsey," Hugh says. "What's the big secret? Tell me what you're doing. I helped you bring the ladder up here. Gimme a break."

"No secret," she says. "I'm just making my ceiling dark. That's all."

Something else is definitely going on here, but Dorsey won't tell Hugh what it is until it's either finished or dismantled. Whenever she has a project, she won't tell him or anyone else what its purpose is until the project is ready to be shown. If it meets with failure, as was the case with what seemed to be an alarm system in her closet a few weeks ago, she won't explain what she had in mind. She trusts no one.

Hugh walks back into his own room to listen to the Top-Forty countdown and to work on a model airplane, a Messerschmitt, which he is making with balsa-wood sticks and tissue paper. Every few minutes he hears his sister groan, girlish groans he would do anything to stop.

In another ten minutes he has part of the left wing set in a clamp, and he stretches his legs by standing in his sister's doorway. She has finished covering over the ceiling with black paper and is looking up proudly at what she has accomplished. In her right hand is a white crayon.

"What're you going to do now?" Hugh asks.

"Just watch."

She tugs and pulls at the ladder so that it stands in the center of the room, and once again she climbs up. She raises the crayon and quickly puts on the black paper a pattern of dots.

"Stars," Hugh says. "Whyn't you put them on the papers before you put the papers up?"

"Because," Dorsey tells him.

Hugh returns to his room and the model plane. The plane, at least, is real: it looks like something, and has wings and a fuselage and a stabilizer, things you can touch and repair. The radio's DJ, Sandy Beach, shouts out two commercials and then plays three in a row, the Coasters and Buddy Knox and the Everly Brothers. Minutes pass in the pleasingly empty way time has of flowing past whenever he's in his room with the radio on, and when Hugh accidentally squeezes out a thin line of airplane glue on his finger, he wipes his hand on the rag he swiped from his mother and decides to see how far his sister has gotten in her sky project.

From the doorway, he can see a spattering of newly applied white dots in no pattern all over her freshly taped up black-paper ceiling, and she is still adding new dots in the northwest corner.

"Looks like a snowstorm," Hugh tells her.

She doesn't turn around. She has the air of a dedicated engineer who knows she is working on a project that will someday aid humankind. "Well, it isn't."

"It's a made-up sky, right?" he asks. "You're making up all these stars and you're putting them on the ceiling. Pretty smart. Dorsey's new constellations. Wait till I tell Mom."

"You're so dumb, Hugh. So ignorant. You don't know anything."

"Smile when you say that," he says, a very popular line among his friends at school. "Okay, Doctor IQ, if this sky isn't all made up, what is it? I don't see the Big Dipper anywhere, and I've been looking."

"Think," she says.

"Think?"

"Yeah, think."

"I give up," he says.

"They're the stars of the Southern Hemisphere, stupid. Look straight up. All right, that triangle there? It's Octans. And over there? That's Tucana, which is a Toucan, which is a bird, for your information. And below that? Those stars there? That's Hydrus, which is a sea serpent. And over here, right above me, is the Southern Cross. Maybe you've heard of that. Or you would have, if you read anything except those dumb comic books."

"How would you know how dumb they are? You've never read one."

"I don't have to." She taps out a few more stars, then looks down at her brother. "See how high I am?" she asks. "I'm way up here, looking down at you, and you're way down there."

Hugh understands that he is being insulted. Where did she learn how to do that?

"These aren't real stars," he says. "They're all made up."

"Well, some of them are real," she says, in a child's tone of stubbornness. "I put up a few on my own, by myself. But that's what I wanted to see, the stars in the Southern Hemisphere."

"How come you wanted that?"

"Because anyone can go outside and see the stars that you *can* see. I wanted the ones you can't see. The stars you can't see are the ones you've got to draw for yourself," she says, in her most maddening Little Miss Perfect voice.

It makes Hugh cringe, this snotty superior tone his sister sometimes takes on, and he leaves her up there, installed on her ladder like a tinsel princess with her brand-new sky taped to her bedroom ceiling, and he slams the door to his own room, just so she gets the point of how angry he is about her Queen-of-the-World problem attitude.

The transparent tape holds for almost three weeks. Then, corner by corner, the black sections of the Southern Hemisphere's night sky begin to loosen, and during the day, while Dorsey is at school, they flutter down to the floor, so that when she gets home and drops her books in her room, she finds pieces of the sky not over her head, but on the rug, on top of her bedspread, over the dirty clothes, scattered everywhere at her feet. And at night, a week before she finally removes the paper sky she has made herself, she can sometimes hear the hushed floating fall of paper as the stars give way to gravity and come easing down.

26

Morning—summer—and Dorsey
has twisted the shutoff valve on the toilet tank, so no water can flow
in, flushed the standing water out, and is now taking the tank
assembly apart, piece by piece, setting the pieces out on the bathroom floor. There on the floor, near her left knee, is the floater; and
just above it, underneath the bathroom window, is the connecting
rod; and over here, by her mother's laundry hamper, is the (slightly
rusty) intake valve; and close by her right knee, dripping on the
bathroom's yellow rug, is the trip lever, along with the lift chain
and rubber stopper plug. As she takes these pieces into her hands and
holds them up to the hard sunlight, Dorsey coos and mutters explanations to herself concerning their shape and design. With the metal
pieces standing in the light, the light itself glitters off the water that
is still dripping down into her lap and casts momentary irregular
reflections on the bathroom wall, quick jagged traces. It takes less
time to put the assembly back together, but it is a process unsweet-
ened by discovery and it leaves an ache in her legs and back. Once
she knows how the toilet works she does not sing; she's made a mess,
and now she has to clean it up.

She does not take animals apart and will not stand to see any once-living thing opened, as her father opens fish to clean them in the basement sink. He says he is "eviscerating the catch." She will not go out with her brother and aim an arrow in Five Oaks Park at a squirrel or a tree. She does not want to see the guts and brains of frogs, though she has studied them on transparent pages in a biology book she has found in the basement, the animal's pictured insides looking to her like wet gray tubing smeared with a kind of living water. The tubes make sense, but liquids that live, like blood or phlegm, make her turn away and close her eyes. "Queasy," her father says. "Squeamish."

She takes the binoculars down from the library shelf, where they are kept within reach for quick identification of backyard birds, and she unscrews the lenses one by one, examining the prisms with the frightened pleasure she feels whenever she sees some object through which light has traveled and been transformed. The binoculars are a challenge to put back together: the prisms have to be aligned perfectly, and she must spend all afternoon on the project before she has reassembled them so that a bird once again looks like itself rather than an indistinct double-imaged shifting of color disturbing the air.

In the living room on summer afternoons the sun shines through the front window and breaks apart on another prism, a piece of glass her father has given her and which she has placed on a side table directly in the sun's path. First on the wall and then on the ceiling, the light separates into household spectra, ribbons of color more beautiful to Dorsey than any man-made object in the room, any object anywhere. Her mother has told her that some people think that rainbows are a promise, the curved colors of peace. It makes sense. She sits in the living room's high-backed chair, her legs dangling down and almost reaching the floor, and she watches a strip of all the colors of light move across the ceiling, stretch, and fade. Sometimes she stands next to the prism and holds up her hand so that the colors tremble on her palm.

She holds her ear to the ground outside. She'd like to hear something from down there, but the earth has nothing to say to her, not a sound. She walks out barefoot on summer nights in her pajamas when everyone thinks she's asleep, and she stands in the still-warm grass of the front lawn, watching the stars and the moon, finding the constellations of summer. The grass feels simple and obvious against her feet, a friendly tickling pressure, and she gazes up to where her father has told her the constellation of Hercules lies, Hercules with his left arm stretched out. She likes Lyra better than Hercules, because it has Vega in it, the brightest star of summer, and because she likes to pretend that she can hear music coming from the strings of the imaginary lyre. Once she turned around to go into the house, and there, up in their bedroom window, were her parents, leaning out on the windowsill, watching her. She waved at them, and they waved back, without expressions, neither smiling nor frowning, just there, observing her, dim moonlit adults.

When she is sick—"You caught a chill watching the sky," her mother says, and it sounds like a description rather than a criticism —she lies in bed watching the afternoon sun split into colors on the prism her mother has brought in from the living room and placed on the windowsill. As Dorsey starts to feel better, she takes apart a broken wind-up alarm clock, and, unable to fix it, puts it back together, still broken.

As soon as he is home from his office, her father comes in to sit on her bed, and he asks her how she is, and Dorsey tells him, but then her father is quiet as he absentmindedly smooths her hair and holds out a glass of water for her to drink from. She's not that sick but she drinks it anyway. He smells of tobacco smoke and hair oil and shaving cream. She likes these moments when her father says nothing. Her father, she believes, is not quite like other people, but is that so because he is her father? She's not sure and doesn't know how to find out. He is never angry with her. She doesn't think he knows how to shout, and what he likes to do the most is sit with her, like this, the two of them being quiet together. It doesn't feel strange to Dorsey. It feels like medicine, a kind her brother never gives her and never seems to get himself, sitting in his own room with the radio on. He never needs medicine because he's never sick.

What she knows is that her parents watch her and let her do what she wants. Even when she's out there in the dark, by herself, they don't call her inside.

27

"Hugh. Hugh. Rise and shine."
His father bends over him and rubs his shoulders gently.

He can hardly open his eyes. "Huh?"

"It's five-thirty," his father says. "If you don't get up, you'll miss it."

In the morning dark, Hugh finds his clothes in a massed heap piled on the floor, near his tattered stuffed gorilla. It feels as if he's put his underwear on backwards and his undershirt inside out, but he doesn't care. Across the hall he can hear his sister singing as she gets dressed. He had been dreaming of summer, baseball and dogs, or dogs playing baseball—he can't remember now. The light of sunrise stands in two parallel orange lines on each side of his window shade. He clumps out into the hallway, puts his hand up on the sticky bannister, and walks downstairs, where the lights are all burning. He looks into the dining room, where the table is set with mats and silverware and glasses of orange juice but where no one is sitting, and then into the kitchen, where he smells coffee from a freshly brewed pot standing on a hand-painted porcelain trivet on the side counter. Someone has brought the bacon out. There's an opened package near the stove, and five eggs lined up next to it, and a large black frying pan on a burner, but no one is here to cook it. For a series of separated moments, Hugh can't remember why he is here, why his father shook his shoulders to wake him, why his sister has come downstairs at a run and rushed out the back hallway to the yard. Then he remembers. They're all up this early summer morning because of what's going to happen to the sun.

His mother, father, and sister are standing on the sloping green back lawn, facing east, where the sun has now risen. "Good morning, Chief," his father says, handing him a pack of several black-and-white photographic negatives. "Look through these. There may be more than you need, but just take a few away until you can see it." His father holds on to a piece of smoked glass in his right hand; his mother has a square of glass also, but his sister has another set of negatives. "It should start in about five minutes," his father says, looking at his watch. Hugh takes one of the negatives out of the pack and holds it up to the blue of the sky, and there he is, Hugh himself as a baby, held in his mother's arms underneath a whitened tree. On negatives, all trees appear as if they're covered with ghost snow, and his own face as a baby is gray, with white eyes.

On a second negative, his grandmother Welch, his father's mother, whom Hugh remembers through his sense of taste—he can remember his grandmother giving him powdered-sugar doughnuts from a white bag—stands on a sidewalk, waving. Waving goodbye. On a third negative his grandfather, whom he never knew, wears farmer overalls and sits on a tractor. Hugh has never been able to believe it: his grandfather was a farmer! He worked with his hands! He was successful so he could send his son to college to get him off the farm. And here, on another negative, he and Dorsey are holding hands; Dorsey was just two years old. In the negative his sister's white dress looks like a Halloween costume.

Another negative: the next-door neighbor's dog, Ruby, before she was hit by a reckless man, Mr. Lesh, driving his big De Soto. In the negative Ruby's mouth is open and her tongue hangs out in a friendly manner. And here's a negative of his mother's mother, Mrs. Hooker, the big granny whom Hugh never knew, also a farmer's wife, sitting on a front porch rocking chair, holding a glass of something, probably lemonade. She is laughing, her white hair black, her dark mouth white. Last: a picture of his mother, outside, facing the camera and the sun, smiling, her hand raised to shield her eyes.

Hugh looks over at his mother and sees that she is shielding her eyes now, just as she was doing in the picture. "Look," she says, and turns quickly to Hugh. "Hold them all up, Hughie. You can see now. It's starting." Hugh puts his collection of negatives together, holds it up into the air, directly in front of the sun, and looks through it.

He sees the big round image of the sun, darkened by the seven negatives through which its light has traveled, with a small bite of the sun missing on one side. This, he has been told, is the moon, which is about to block out the sun completely but temporarily. Very interesting, sort of, but Hugh is not yet convinced it was worth getting up this time of the morning for. He puts the negatives down and squints at Five Oaks Lake and the amusement park to the south mostly obscured by the trees in Five Oaks Park. "Hmmm," his mother says, but otherwise it's very quiet, so quiet, in fact, that Hugh can hear an early-morning fisherman gunning his motor out there somewhere on the lake. He looks harder at the lake and sees a dot crossing it, a dot dragging a funnel of waves.

He holds his packet of negatives up to the sun again. More of the sun has been circled out by the moon. Hugh removes one negative from the pack, the one of his mother, and the disappearing sun shines through the other six, and instead of looking at the sun, Hugh sees Ruby superimposed on his big granny, and himself as a baby over the two of them, and his grandfather on his tractor superimposed on top of himself holding hands with his sister, all of the separate images piled on top of one another, one large distinct collection of the past, and, in the middle of it, the darkening sun, now shaped like a burning three-quarter moon, shining through them.

Holding the negatives, he lowers his arm and looks at his parents. They are standing on the lawn, holding the squares of smoked glass out in front of their eyes. His father is wearing an old white shirt, a soft hat, and stained pressed trousers. In his left hand is a cigarette, burned down to within a half-inch of his father's fingers. Behind him, Hugh's mother also holds the glass in front of her eyes. The early-morning breeze blows against the front of her skirt, so that it seems almost to billow out behind her on either side of her legs. The morning breeze rustles the leaves on the old elm near them, its branches held together with support cables. Near his mother, his sister gazes through all her negatives at the sun, her face almost glazed with happiness.

"Are you bored, Hugh?" his father asks him. "Go look under the trees. Go look behind the vines."

He does as he is told. He walks over to the elm's huge trunk and looks down at the shadows its leaves are casting: half-moon shadows! Hundreds of them. He runs back to the house, where the vines are clinging to the exterior wall beside the kitchen window, and he checks the shadows: more half-moons, bits of half-moon light jumping on the house.

He returns to where his parents are standing and holds up the negatives again, but instead of watching the sun's eclipse, he gazes again at the collection of negatives: his grandmother and grandfather, his neighbor's dog, himself, his sister, and his mother, all crowdedly occupying the same space and each one distinct, and the sun being blotted out behind them.

At the moment when his father says, "Now it's almost total," Hugh looks at the world of his family's backyard: the trees, the house, his mother, father, and sister, standing in the gray stillness of the false night, no one and nothing moving, the sun blanked, shadowed. "Yes," his father says, before he drops his cigarette butt onto the gray-green of the lawn. Then Hugh notices that the birds have stopped singing, and in the bad quiet of this moment, when his parents seem unable to move and the light on the lawn makes him think of the sun sick and dying, Hugh walks backwards, away from them, and he sits on the dew-covered grass, and no one notices him there for several minutes, until the sun starts to come back, and his mother turns around and says, "Hugh, darling, what are you doing down there? Why aren't you watching?"

28

Hugh carries his sister up the stairs, down the hall, and into his room, where he has started his steam engine five minutes before. Its flywheel sets up a chattering rattle, and Dorsey looks down and says, "Machine." She holds her fingers out to the whirling wheel, the heated boiler, and the bright steel piston, and Hugh says, "No." He covers the heat source and eases Dorsey down to the floor. He intends to show her how to draw a car. She's not interested. She wants to wander around his room, take his books off the shelf and open them up. She points to a picture of a space ship and says, "What's this?" He explains to her that it's a rocket, and that someday people will go in rockets to the moon, to Mars, and maybe meet outer-spacemen. His sister gazes at him closely.

Now she has his box of crayons and is taking them out one by one, naming the colors. "Pink," she says, holding it up, then tossing it aside. "Orange. Lavender." Hugh stares at her. "Lavender?" he says. "Where'd you learn about lavender?"

She shrugs. "From Mommy." She pulls out another crayon.

"Silver," she says, holding it up to the light, then dropping it onto the floor, where it rolls underneath Hugh's dresser. "Velvet."

"Velvet isn't a color," Hugh says, picking up the crayon and reading the label. "It says here it's called 'burnt umber.' "

"It's velvet," she says, as if he hadn't spoken.

"Velvet's a cloth," he tells her, taking down a fifteen-cent glider and flying it past her face. She watches the plane make a loop up to the ceiling, then sail down and land on his bed. "Let's go outside," he says.

He bends down so that she can hop on his back. Dorsey puts her arms around his neck but keeps her head above his shoulders so that she can see where they're going. He carries her down the stairs, Dorsey making a laughing cough sound on each step, before they go out the front door and then around the front lawn to the garage, where he deposits her in his red Radio Flyer. Sitting in the back, in pink corduroy overalls, her legs stuck straight out in front of her and ending in the black-and-white formality of her saddle shoes, Dorsey stares straight up at the parallel wooden beams holding up the garage roof. Then she stares at the two huge cars, then at Ruby, the neighbor's dog, running toward them up the driveway. The lawn is patrolled by robins, and the branches are thick with buds and blooms. Hugh opens his mouth to make his police-siren howl. He pulls his sister out of the garage, stirring the robins off the lawn onto the tree branches, and, still loud with emergency injury, he pulls her down the sidewalk all the way to the curb at the first corner. Ruby follows them, halfway.

At the corner, Dorsey says, "Keep going."

"I'm not supposed to cross any streets with you."

"Turn that way." She points toward Five Oaks Park.

"That's the park. We can't go there."

"Go that way."

He pulls his sister to the end of the sidewalk, then stops at the woods.

"Turn around," she says.

He pulls the handle sharply to the side and drags the squeaking wagon back up the street. His arms ache, and his sister is singing one of her made-up songs. This one is about a pair of scissors. In the song, the scissors go swimming and meet a bad duck. Hugh thinks the song is dumb and tells Dorsey to stop it. She does, but above the squeak of the wheels he can hear the song continuing in a whisper.

Farther up the street, Mr. Forster is dropping grass seed from a brown bag on his lawn, and he waves when Dorsey and Hugh go by. Two doors down, Miss Hagburg is planting flowers in front of her porch, but she's unfriendly: she never waves. Mr. and Mrs. Polechuck, old people, are sitting on lawn chairs in front of their big, gray house, also elderly and much in need of repairs. "Hell-llooo, Hugh," they call together, raising their old withered arms, so that Hugh has no choice but to wave back. Sometimes Mrs. Polechuck bakes terrible-tasting sour fudge in her high-ceilinged kitchen with the big blue gas range that stands on four thin metal legs. She calls up Hugh's mother and invites the boy over to have some dessert, and he must sit there in Mrs. Polechuck's creepy kitchen, being polite and trying to smile as he eats her fudge that tastes like cough syrup, while she asks him, in one of the sweetest voices he's ever heard, why his parents don't go to church anymore. They once did, she says. I taught your mother Sunday school.

Beyond the Polechucks' house is Mr. LeClair's house, with its perfect lawn, and on this side of the street is Mr. and Mrs. Lesley's house, the one that always has cut flowers visible on a table just inside the large front window. Where do they get these flowers in the middle of winter? Hugh doesn't know. It is one of the biggest secrets in town. No one knows. Suddenly his sister opens her mouth and starts to scream out a song from her Burl Ives record. They've almost reached the end of the block, where the Brooks house stands. The Brookses are probably Five Oaks' richest family. Hugh doesn't want his sister disgracing herself in front of them. He spins around with his finger to his lips and says, "Shush up."

"Why?"

"Because."

"Because why?"

"Because we're in front of the Brookses."

"So?"

"They're rich."

"I don't care."

"They'll come out and hit you."

"Why?"

"Because they're rich."

"They can't hit me."

"Yes, they can."

"Why can they?"

"Rich people can hit anybody they want to," he says.

"I don't believe you," Dorsey says, sitting in the wagon, but her face tells Hugh otherwise.

"You don't ever see rich people being arrested, do you?"

"I don't know," she says.

"Well, that's why. If they don't like the way you're singing, they can come out and hit you."

"I'll still sing."

"No, you won't. You'll be bleeding."

"Where?"

"On the sidewalk."

"Where will they hit me?"

"In the nose. That's where they always hit kids."

"Hugh?"

"What?"

"I don't want them to hit me."

"Well, don't sing."

"Hugh?"

"What?"

"Are we rich?"

"I don't think so."

He turns the wagon around and starts to pull Dorsey back, passing the Lesley house again, and when he stops to catch his breath, he checks on his sister and sees that she is crying: no sobs, but wet eyes and large tears sliding down her cheeks.

"What's the matter now?"

"I want to sing."

"I guess you can't."

"It's not fair."

"What?"

"That rich people can hit."

"It's a fact."

"Who told you?"

"This kid at school."

"How did he know?"

"Some rich person hit him."

"What was he doing?"

"I don't know. Singing, I guess."

"Where did they hit him?"

"In the nose, like I told you."

"Did it hurt?"

"He said it was the worst thing ever."

"I don't believe you," she says.

All the way back to the house the wagon saws and creaks and rattles, and when Hugh pulls his sister into the driveway, she lowers herself out of the Radio Flyer and runs unsteadily toward the side door that leads to the back hallway and the kitchen. Hugh wants to hide. He parks the wagon in its proper place in the garage, then runs out to the backyard and climbs up the apple tree. Here, obscured by apple blossoms, no one can see him. It isn't until he's most of the way up that he realized that, for almost every blossom, there is a bee. He's surrounded by bees: honey bees, bumble bees, and bees with bright yellow stripes.

"Hugh?" It's his mother.

"What?"

"Where are you?"

"Back here."

Terrified by the bees, Hugh keeps himself still, like one of those wax boys he saw last summer in the wax museum in Spooner, Wisconsin. From his perch he sees his mother striding out onto the lawn, her arm on her hip, looking around for him.

"Where are you?"

"Here."

A bee is flying around his face, an inch or so from his eyes. If the bee stings him in the eye, he'll go blind, but only after his eye has swelled up to the size of a baseball and he has to go to work at the freak show in the State Fair. He squints his eyes shut.

"Hugh Bardwell Welch, come down from that tree this instant."

"I can't."

"Why not?"

"This tree is full of bees. If I come down I'll get stung."

"You should have thought of that when you climbed up. Young man, what have you been telling your sister?"

"I told her to stop singing, that's all. It sounded awful. We were at the end of the block and I thought she was going to get everybody mad at us."

"You said they were going to hit her."

"I said they *might*."

"Well, you know they wouldn't."

"I wasn't sure. Have you ever heard Dorsey sing?"

"Yes. And another thing. You were lying."

"I was not."

"You said rich people can hit anyone they want to. You know they can't. You know what you said was wrong."

"No, I don't."

"Well, you're being silly. You've never seen a rich person hit anyone."

"So? It could happen."

His mother, exasperated, tugs at her right elbow with her left hand. She has the air of a woman who hates to argue with children. "I don't want you to lie ever again to your sister. You mustn't ever do that. She's not like all your other friends."

"Yes, she is. She's just like them."

"No, she isn't. She doesn't forget."

"What?"

"Your sister doesn't forget. She doesn't forget anything. Haven't you noticed? If you tell her something, it sticks to her. It always will. So when you talk to her, tell her the truth. Promise me."

He mutters something, and his mother turns and walks away. It seems that she will not punish him after all. At once the air is filled with the smell of apple blossoms. He got away with it. The pounding of his heart subsides. He lowers himself toward the ground, and as he is placing his foot on the grass he feels an icepick's point thrust into his hand. Scared and horrified by the pain, he yanks his hand away from the branch and sees a bee slowly but urgently detaching itself from its stinger and then flying unsteadily away. Yelling, Hugh runs into the house, screaming now, shouting. Between shouts he tells his mother and father that he's been stung, and he holds out his pinked hand for evidence. His father rushes out to the backyard and returns to the kitchen with a handful of mud. Meanwhile, Hugh's mother has rolled up some ice cubes into a dishcloth and is trying to apply it to Hugh's hand, but it's difficult to help him because he's screaming so much and clutching his hand as it swells. He runs around the kitchen in a frantic circle. In the center of his pain, in the middle of this unjust punishment for something he never meant to do while he was trying to give her a ride as a simple favor after showing her his steam machine, he sees his sister, Dorsey, standing in the kitchen doorway, scared too by all his human noise, all his yelling. His eyes wet with his tears, Hugh sees something unbelievable, his sister sticking her tongue out. She turns her back on him and walks into the living room, and the pain is a lens for a split second and focuses a thought: I won't forget this either; I will remember, too.

29

She toddles into his room and turns his Wood River gas station upside down, breaking off one of the crowns on top of the pumps. She puts his soldiers into her mouth and then dumps them back on the floor, covered with girl slime. While he's watching "Kukla, Fran and Ollie" on their new Bendix TV set, she appears out of nowhere, reaches up to the channel changer, and, before he can stop her, switches the set to "The Stu Erwin Show"; then she toddles out of the room, a deep smile on her face. She steps on his flashlight and opens it up and throws the batteries out of the window.

But so far they haven't bought her a bed, because she can't figure out how to climb out of her crib, and this is why, when she's supposed to be taking a nap, Hugh comes into her room with a thick tablet of his mother's typing paper. He sits himself down on the floor, heavy with purpose, and rips off the first sheet, crumpling it up. He tosses it like a basketball into her crib. The projectile startles her. She looks up at the ceiling, as if it had started to rain paper balls, and when Hugh's second one comes sailing into the crib and hits her on the arm, she sees her brother and laughs.

She loves games. She picks up one of the balls and shoves it out through the slats in the side. This is not what Hugh had in mind. What he had in mind was to turn his sister's crib, with his sister in it, into a wastebasket. So he crumples up paper again, more paper, more balls, and throws them in faster and faster, and as fast as he throws them in, Dorsey shoves them out again, so that they form a small waterfall of paper dropping over the side of the crib onto the floor.

With the persistence of desperation, Hugh continues crumpling the paper and throwing it into the crib, until the result he has been hoping for is partly achieved. There is now a one-inch layer of paper, like the first snow of winter, covering the blankets and pillows and stuffed animals in Dorsey's crib. Her music bear is completely out of sight. Having thrown in all this paper, Hugh expects Dorsey to yell at him, to be unhappy, but she won't be unhappy. She laughs and smiles and throws the paper balls up into the air over her head. Looking at him through the bars, she has the grateful expression of a prisoner or an animal at the zoo who is being entertained. She makes a happy gurgle deep in her throat and lets herself fall over sideways into the snow sea of paper.

But Hugh won't quit, despite the failure of his plan, his creation of joy in his sister instead of pain. He runs into his mother's upstairs room, takes another tablet of typing paper, and returns to Dorsey's floor, crumpling up more, trying to raise the level of trash higher, so that, maybe, Dorsey herself will disappear in all the paper, and they'll take it out, and she won't be there, and they'll throw it all away . . .

"Hugh."

He turns. It's his mother, standing, arms crossed, in the suddenly very large doorway.

"I would like to know what you are doing."

"Nothing."

Her voice is calm. It's always calm. "It doesn't look like nothing. It looks like something. It looks like you are filling up your sister's crib with paper."

"I guess so."

"And why are you doing that?"

The months of resentment blow out of him like a door opened

suddenly into his heart. "She gets everything," he says, "and you and Daddy are always looking at her and playing with her, and she breaks my stuff and puts it into her mouth, and she smells funny, and you're always fussing over her, and she cries a lot, and you don't care about me anymore, and when you do, it's only to tell me off about stuff."

"Hugh, first we're going to empty Dorsey's crib. Then we'll talk. Bring in the wastebaskets from your room and from our bedroom, and we'll clean this up."

As soon as they have emptied all the papers, she takes him by the hand and leads him into his room. She shuts the door. Hugh stares at the lock. His mother kneels down and puts her hands on his shoulders. She looks directly into his eyes. After so many weeks of inattentiveness, this intensity from his mother makes Hugh's knees quake. She's going to tell him something terrible, he knows. He's going to be sent away. They're going to sell him for fifty dollars to his Aunt Marjorie.

"Now listen to me," she says. "This is important. Are you listening to me?" He nods, able at least to move his head. "Your sister is younger than you are. She is always going to be younger than you are. She will never be older. That means something. What it means is that you may have to take care of her. Your father and I may not always be around. You are Dorsey's older brother. That is a responsibility. Are you listening to me?"

Hugh nods, hopelessly.

"I want you to make me a promise," she says. "I want you to promise that you will be a brother to Dorsey, and look after her, and watch out for her, always and forever."

She stares at him, pounding her gaze into his heart.

"Do you promise? Raise your right hand and promise."

The hand goes up. He nods, says "I promise," and begins to cry.

"Good," she says, rising. "Very good. I'm so glad that you promised. It's very important." Hugh's mother is standing now, gazing down at him with a warm smile. It's so clear: there's nothing he can do except what she wants. Whatever he thinks, she already knows it, all the big and little thoughts that he's had and is going to have. Quickly turning, she disappears from the room, leaving Hugh alone with himself, surrounded by his picture books, his stuffed animals, the toys broken by his sister. He clenches his hands into fists, then closes his eyes. He begins to jump. For as long as he can manage to do it, he throws his weight into the air and then with both heels against the floor, rising and falling.

30

Because the grandmother—the one who gives away doughnuts—had asked for a baptism, Hugh's father and mother bring Dorsey down to St. Stephen's Episcopal Church eight weeks after the child is born. They also take Hugh along, to watch. He sits in the back of his father's gray Nash with his grandmother, who tests him on trees all the way to the church. Her long curved finger smelling of Florida Water points past him, beyond the car, out through the window to where some tree stands, and Hugh says, "Oak," and the doughnut grandmother says, "No, dear, that one is an elm." So on the next guess Hugh says, "Elm," and his grandmother says, "That was a very good guess, Hugh, darling, but, no, that tree is an ash." Each time he makes a wrong guess—and they are all wrong, every one of them—his grandmother raises her right eyebrow and smiles, and Hugh thinks that it must be that she really likes him to be wrong. It's why she's there and is so old: so she can test him, and he can be wrong.

She has a voice crackly with age like someone on short-wave radio, and when she walks, her joints creak. She wears museum clothes. She takes Hugh's hand and walks him into the church. His mother and father disappear with Dorsey into the back, and then they reappear with Mrs. Lesley and Mrs. Forster, who will be Dorsey's godmothers, and Mr. Lesley, who will be the godfather. Hugh looks up at the ceiling throughout much of the service, at the thick crossbeams holding the church's slant roof in place, so it doesn't fall down and crash on everybody's head and leave them crushed and screaming in a human heap. He squints to look at the stained-glass windows through his eyelashes. The colored pictures lose their outlines, but the colors, especially the reds and blues, come to life. He doesn't think he's ever seen any red as red as this glass, not even his own blood from his finger on the glass slide at the doctor's office.

There is much standing up and sitting down and kneeling. Hugh starts to twiddle his thumbs. His grandmother brings down her hand, now wearing a white glove, over his two hands. "Watch," she says quietly to him in her short-wave radio voice. Hugh wants a stick of gum, but his grandmother doesn't have any. It's hot in the church. It smells of everybody's hot clothes. He can feel the collar of his white shirt squeezing against his neck, trying to choke him, he's going to die and fall over and be buried in Five Oaks Cemetery, but all he does is cough.

The church has so many people that his cough is lost in a whole forest of coughs. Almost exactly behind him is mean Miss Hagburg, who doesn't wave, sitting next to Mr. and Mrs. Polechuck. From where he's sitting, he can also see Mr. and Mrs. Castlehoff—it's easy to see Mrs. Castlehoff with her red hair, and Mr. Castlehoff's bald head—and near Mrs. Castlehoff is Mrs. LaMonte, who sells antiques and firecrackers, and he can also see his kindergarten teacher, Mrs. Melkie, and the McConnells and the Blairs. Most of Five Oaks is here, watching, and now Hugh tries to listen to what the minister, Mr. Valentine, is saying, but the words are the biggest ones he's ever heard come out of a human being's mouth.

" 'Regard,' " he says, " 'we beseech thee, the supplications of thy congregation; sanctify this Water to the mystical washing away of sin; and grant that this child, now to be baptized therein, may receive the fulness of thy grace . . .' " Hugh doesn't understand any of it, not one word. The minister says, "Name this child."

Hugh's parents say, "Dorsey Evans Welch."

The minister repeats the name, then grabs a little pitcher of water and pours it over his sister's head. Hugh waits for her to screech, but she doesn't. He's noticed that already about his sister: she won't cry unless she has to. The minister says more prayers, makes the sign of the cross over his sister's head, and just when it seems to be over and he's going to be able to make an escape to Bacon Drug, where he's been promised an ice cream cone of any size he wants as long as he can eat it, the minister takes Dorsey back into his arms and tells the congregation that they may welcome her into the world. He walks slowly down the aisle, and the people on the aisle lean over and smile, and touch Dorsey lightly with their fingers on her forehead. Miss Hagburg bends down and kisses her. Mrs. Blair makes the sign of the cross over her. Hugh doesn't know what any of this is for. Mrs. LaMonte touches Dorsey quickly on the cheek. There she goes, Dorsey, his sister, being carried toward the doors of the church, people from all over town bending down and kissing her and touching her and waving at her, and as she goes, Hugh squints at the whole thing, and it's as though his sister is a magnet pulling at these people, so that they bend down over her and then straighten up again, bowing toward her, this baby. They're kissing her into the world. Why do they love her? Hugh wants to know. They don't even know her. He turns to his doughnut grandmother and yanks twice at her sleeve. She bends down, so that he can whisper into her ear. "Did they ever do this for me?" Hugh asks, and the old woman, smelling of doughnuts and Florida Water, says, "Yes."

31

"Hugh. Son, wake up." His father bends over him in the bed, his father unshaven, still in his blue pajamas, the morning light behind the shades in two thin strips. This is the morning, the first morning. Hugh tugs at his pillow and at the stuffed dragon he sleeps with. His father tells him to shake a leg, to shake both of his legs. His father's breath smells of the night. It smells of cigarettes and his father. He pulls the bedspread aside and places his feet on the cold wood floor. With his father's whispered help he lowers his pajamas down and raises his T-shirt up, and even in the warmth of morning, Hugh feels cold and hugs himself. After finding his son's clothes in the dresser and laying them out where Hugh can pull and tug himself into them, Hugh's father yanks at the window shade, and there, beyond the front lawn of the house, and the street outside, and even beyond Five Oaks itself, down the hill next to the lake, beyond all this of course is the sun, streaming into Hugh's east-facing window, cutting in a rectangular strip across his bed and the floor. Rubbing his eyes, the boy walks into the bathroom to pee. He holds his penis down and the water spurts into the toilet in a sort of greenish-yellow stream. When he is finished, he remembers to flush and then to wash his hands. He is careful; his mother is gone, and he wants to please his father.

Downstairs, this one morning, his father has made him scrambled eggs and bacon and toast, bacon exactly the way he likes it, fried hard so that it's stiff, so that you can hold it up, all the fat gone. Deep within the eggs is garlic powder, which his father pours over everything he cooks. Hugh smears strawberry jam on the toast, and, though he has remembered to put the napkin in his lap, he still spills a gob of jam over his shirt. His father sees it and says, "That's all right. But we'll have to find you a clean shirt. We can't have you going in, looking like that."

"Daddy?"

"What?"

"How soon will we go?"

"Right after breakfast," his father says.

With the dirty dishes left to soak in soapsuds, and Hugh sporting a clean shirt, the boy and his father leave for the hospital. Hugh sits in front for once. The dashboard is so high he has to stretch to see out into the long passageway of the streets, even to see the sun running through the leaves of the trees passing overhead as they turn and shift into a lower gear for the short blocks of the white and blue and green houses of Five Oaks. It's hard to remember ever being up this early, seeing almost no one awake, no one tending the yards or the stores, and, when they drive by the lake, no one out there fishing or water skiing, and no one swimming. He watches the telephone and electrical wires yanked up by the poles, again and again, and his father looks over at him.

"Are you excited?"

"I guess so."

"She's beautiful. You're going to love her."

"I know."

"You'll see. Don't worry. You've never been in a hospital before, have you?"

"No."

"It's not so scary. Really, it isn't. You'll get used to it right away."

"Is Mommy okay?"

"She fine. She can't wait to see you. She asked me last night to tell you how much she was looking forward to seeing you this morning."

"Is Grandma going to be there?"

"No. She's home for the day."

On Hugh's right is a front yard where a collie sits, wagging its tail and smiling at them as they drive by. And there, past the blocks where the houses stop, is the lake, so bright it hurts Hugh's eyes to see the sun reflecting off its blue surface. What will he tell his sister once she's old enough to talk? He can't think of a single thing he'll say to her. She might not like him. She might go through life ignoring him and thinking he's a creep. And here is a grove of pine trees, as they pass the outskirts of town, and an auto junkyard with broken pieces of Kaisers and Frasers and Studebakers and Hudsons and Buicks and Packards, and there is the county hospital, three floors high, white cement and glass, set back with a long sidewalk from its parking lot, where Hugh's father parks the Nash two spaces away from anybody else.

"You do this," his father tells him, "and they don't bang their doors against you when they open them." Hugh doesn't know what his father is talking about.

Hugh sees that his father's hand is trembling. He has butterflies in his own stomach. Standing in his clean shirt and pressed pants and black shoes out in the light of the parking lot, light that hurts his eyes so much he has to shade them with his hands to see his father standing there looking at him, he hears his father say, "Well, shall we go in, Chief?" Hugh has an odd spinning feeling. But it's a slow spin, a turning sensation, not enough to make you sick and not like what the kids do at birthday parties where they blindfold you and whip you around so you get dizzy and can't pin the tail on the donkey. This is more like someone rotating your whole body so slowly that you can't quite notice where you're being turned, or how. Then Hugh knows what it is. What he feels is the earth itself, turning, moving from night into day, and then from day into night. He feels it under his feet.

"Are you coming, kiddo?" his father asks, looking back at him. "Are you coming in to see her, or are you just going to stand here?" His father takes his hand. He closes his fingers around his father's hand and watches with admiration as his father pulls out a cigarette with his other hand from his jacket pocket, puts it in his mouth, and, still with one hand, removes his Zippo lighter and, quicker than it takes to hear the click of the lid being opened and the flint struck, the cigarette is lit, and puffed from, and, as soon as they are inside the front doors of the hospital, snuffed out in the big standing ashtray in the front waiting room.

With one breath, Hugh knows this is a terrible place. The hospital smells of terror and pain. It's not true that this hospital is not scary, and it's not just the disinfectant, either, which he has smelled in Dr. Greene's office. This is another smell, a basement smell, a pipes and plumbing smell, but worse, much worse than that, because it makes Hugh's hair stand up, even as he walks with his father down the yellow hallways, past the front desk and the smiling receptionist who sees his father but not him, over the linoleum that smells of being scared and lonely and being left here to die.

His father opens a door to the stairway, and Hugh goes inside. The stairs are gray; they rise until they reach the wall, and then they turn around and go in the other direction. There's a bare light bulb on the ceiling, and it makes his father's shadow stretch out as they climb the stairs to the second floor. There are big pipes in the corner, where the stairs turn, and Hugh can hear water rushing downward toward the ground.

At the second level Hugh's father holds the door open, and there they are, but when one of the nurses sees Hugh she shakes her head. "No children," she says. "No children on this floor." Then she looks over at Hugh's father and smiles. "Bill," she says, and Hugh's father calls the nurse by her first name. They talk for a moment, and the nurse disappears and then returns with a surgical mask with which she covers Hugh's nose and mouth. "So you don't spread germs," she says. "This one time." Hugh doesn't want to get dizzy, because if the dizziness overcomes him, he doesn't know what he'll do.

"What's that smell?" he asks, puffing out the mask with his voice, as they pass by flowers in a vase at the nurses' station. He raises his voice. "Daddy, what's that smell?"

"Pretty bad, isn't it?" his father says. "It's ether. They don't use it much here. They use it in the operating rooms, but not for mothers. They use it on other people."

They're passing by rooms now, rooms with their doors shut, and a few rooms with their doors open, but Hugh won't look inside past those doors and into those rooms, where terrible people are lying on their backs, gasping and holding out their hands for him to take, to pull him into their beds and make him lie down with them, breathing their terrible breath all over him, touching him with their scars. Hugh almost wants to run out, but his father still has him clutched, and where would he run to? The sun is shining through all the windows on the hallway's east side, throwing slatted light on the floor like horizontal flattened picket fences that Hugh must walk through to get to the room where his mother lies. She will be lying back in bed, he knows: her eyes closed, her face gone white, and this baby beside her that she and his father have somehow brought from somewhere into this world.

His father stops near a corner area of the hospital where they have set out hard green chairs for visitors near a window that looks out on trees and nothing. His father squats down and faces Hugh. He's going to tell Hugh how to act. What not to say. But no: in a voice dropped so low that Hugh can hardly hear it, his father tells Hugh that he loves him, he will always love him, that he is a wonderful boy and he has a sister now, and he'll have to love her and take care of her. And Hugh, behind his surgical mask, says, "Daddy, what did I do?"

"You didn't do anything," his father says. "Let's go in."

The fingers of his father's left hand curl into the palm; the hand, now a fist, knocks once, twice, on the door to the room, Number 252, and Hugh hears his mother's voice say, "Come in." The hand uncurls and pushes at the door, and from right to left his mother's room becomes visible at last.

"My two men," his mother says, smiling. She looks at Hugh. "My two *masked* men." Beyond his mother's bed is another window, like the others facing east into the sun, and though it is partially curtained, sunlight is streaming, rushing, cascading, from behind his mother into the room, lighting each one of its corners and its objects: the glass of water, the box of bedside tissues, the table-lamp-sized vase of cut flowers on the windowsill, red and white flowers whose names Hugh doesn't know. They might be roses, roses for love. "Hugh," his mother says. "Don't stand there back by the door. Come in. Come see." She smiles again, a smile as disturbing as his father's statement that he loves him, because he hasn't done anything to earn the smile, but now he walks forward into the room, the sunlight from the window hurting his eyes. Why don't they do something to keep the sun out of these rooms? His mother is wearing white hospital clothes, and something has happened to her eyes, even though she's smiling now. Her hair's combed a new and oddly different way, pulled straight back and hardly parted at all. Her skin is terribly pale.

"Mom," Hugh says, rushing forward to kiss her.

But now, at this moment frozen in sunlight, he sees her, inside his mother's right arm, asleep. Hugh stops, stilled. He sees the tufts of blond hair on his sister's head, and as his mother holds his sister up a little so that he can see her better, lifting her up into the sunlight that courses straight through her hair, he hears her say, "This is Dorsey."

"Dorsey," Hugh repeats.

"We named her last night," Hugh's father says, from behind him. "Come closer, Hugh. Come closer."

His feet take him nearer the bed. He looks up toward his mother. "Can I see her hands?" he asks.

"Of course," his mother says. With slow care, she unwraps the blanket and covering from around the baby's arms, first the right arm and then the left. His sister's skin in the morning sunlight is almost yellow, with small streaks of purple. Hugh feels himself moving toward her, and as he says her name, "Dorsey," he holds his right hand out, his index finger pointing down. His sister's skin is the quietest human thing he's ever seen: it hardly seems part of the world at all. She yawns, opening and closing her hands, tiny, the size of toy glass marbles. "Come closer," his mother says again, her voice not coming from her mouth but from the room itself, the earth, the air, and with his right hand in front of him, the index finger still pointing out and down, he reaches forward and, with unpracticed tenderness, touches his sister's hand for the first time.